THEATER
IN THE
AMERICAS

A Series from
Southern
Illinois
University
Press
ROBERT A.
SCHANKE
Series Editor

The Caffe
Cino

31 Cornelia Street
The First Caffe
Theatre in Greenwich
Village

Caffe Cino

THE BIRTHPLACE OF
OFF-OFF-BROADWAY

Wendell C. Stone

Southern Illinois University Press
Carbondale

Library of Congress Cataloging-in-Publication Data
Stone, Wendell C.
  Caffe Cino : the birthplace of off-off-Broadway /
Wendell C. Stone.
     p. cm. — (Theater in the Americas)
  Includes bibliographical references and index.
     1. Caffe Cino. 2. Off Off-Broadway theater—History—
20th century. I. Title. II. Series.
  PN2277.N5S76 2005
  792'.09747'10904—dc22   2004027788
  ISBN 0-8093-2644-2 (cloth : alk. paper)
  ISBN 0-8093-2645-0 (pbk. : alk. paper)

Printed on recycled paper. ♻

The paper used in this publication meets the minimum
requirements of American National Standard for Information
Sciences—Permanence of Paper for Printed Library Materials,
ANSI Z39.48-1992. ∞

To Doug, Julie, Jody, Rob, Milton, and Joy

Contents

Illustrations

Acknowledgments

So many people have contributed to my research on Caffe Cino that I could not possibly mention them all. While risking the ire of anyone whom I overlook, I will note some of those whose assistance was particularly important. Above all I extend my deepest admiration and appreciation to the people who created the wonderful, chaotic, exciting, mad world of Caffe Cino. They made my work not only possible but also pleasurable. In particular I thank Robert Heide, John Gilman, Robert Patrick, Robert Dahdah, and Doric Wilson for their generosity and assistance.

To Julie Harmon and Doug Wylie, Jody Nichols and Rob Reid, Joy Wang and Milton Nichols, Linda Rupp and Curtis Stone, I give my deepest love and gratitude. Their support and encouragement got me through those periods when I was sure that I could never finish. To the group (Sharon Whitaker, Carolyn Lea, Stephen Berwind, Stanley Coleman, Hamilton Armstrong, Mark Zelinsky, Christine Mather, and Don Whittaker) who kept me sane, or at least manageably mad, during my research, I also extend both my appreciation and my love. To the current and former faculty of LSU who have given me so much (Leslie Wade, Jennifer Jones, Bill Demastes, Femi Euba, Gresdna Doty, and Lesley Ferris), I offer my respect and appreciation, as I do to Gayle Austin of Georgia State University, who opened new avenues of thought for me. To Robert Schanke, Wayne Larsen, and Karl Kageff of Southern Illinois University Press, I extend my sincerest thanks for their patience and assistance. Starting this work would have been unthinkable without Bobbi, Ernie, and Jessika. Completion would have been impossible without the support of Louisiana State University, the Jerome Lawrence and Robert E. Lee Theatre Research Institute of the Ohio State University, and the Billy Rose Theatre Collection of the New York Public Library.

Finally, I am deeply indebted to Dr. Billy Harbin for his kindness, patience, and insight. Sadly, he never had the opportunity to review the final manuscript, since he passed away on June 24, 2004. An able scholar, an exceptional teacher, an effective mentor, and a delightful person, Bill set an example for me and all his students by demanding rigorous scholarship within a supportive and nurturing environment. As I mourn his loss, I value the opportunity that I had to know and study with him.

The Caffe
Cino
31 Cornelia Street
The first Caffe
Theatre in Greenwich
Village

Introduction

In December 1958 Joseph Cino opened a small coffeehouse on quiet, block-long Cornelia Street in New York's Greenwich Village. Though it closed less than ten years later, Caffe Cino became one of the most important cafe-theatres of the period. It was instrumental in launching and popularizing the off-off-Broadway theatre movement, in exploring new production styles, in fostering an emerging gay theatre, and in promoting the careers of numerous performers, playwrights, and directors. Its artistic influence extends from conventional theatre to avant-garde experimentation and from New York to cities around the world. Joe Cino's management style influenced first experimental theatres in New York and subsequently cafe and small theatre managers elsewhere.

Measuring only about eight feet by eight feet, the tiny, flexible stage at the Cino tested and trained some of the most distinguished talent of the last half of the twentieth century. It was there that Lanford Wilson staged his first plays, Sam Shepard struggled with the pressures of his early career, William M. Hoffman and Robert Patrick recognized their own interest in writing for the stage, H. M. Koutoukas exploded gender conventions in his "camps," Doric Wilson discovered his voice, Marshall Mason honed his directing skills and began a collaboration with Lanford Wilson that continues today, Andy Milligan shaped his directorial talents, Ron Link produced his first play, and a host of other significant actors, playwrights, directors, and designers worked on their first major productions or explored new directions in their careers (including Bernadette Peters, Al Pacino, Robbie McCauley, Harvey Keitel, Paxton Whitehead, Neil Flanagan, and John Guare). Writers such as Oliver Hailey, Lee Kalcheim, and Tom Eyen gained exposure before moving to influential careers in television and film. Cino productions explored new styles: pop art, camp, and the outrageous deconstruction of gender that later would be called genderfuck. Before *Rocky Horror*'s Frank-N-Furter donned his corset or *Mary Hartman, Mary Hartman*'s eponymous lead obsessed over wax buildup, playwrights at the Cino were shattering gender stereotypes and merging images from popular culture into their plays.

The location of the Cino was somewhat removed from the notorious MacDougal Street area in which masses of young adults congregated each weekend at the peak of the sixties. The crowds largely were drawn by the coffeehouses where they found poetry readings and other entertainment or chic and often politically radical conversation. For the most part, Caffe Cino fit comfortably into a quiet, residential neighborhood. It was an Italian-owned business in a predominantly Italian area; it discretely housed art events and theatrical productions without unduly impinging on the tranquility of the neighborhood.

Historically a hub of nontraditional politics, art, and thought in the United States, the Village had become one of the country's centers for the Beats by the late 1950s; in the 1960s it would be rivaled only by San Francisco's Haight-Ashbury as the center of the counterculture movement. As the influence of the counterculture grew in the Village, businesses, churches, and other organizations offered services, products, and entertainment directed at those who challenged traditional concepts of politics, art, and social relationships. In the 1950s many coffeehouses built their entertainment around readings of Beat poetry; by the early 1960s such establishments increasingly were offering revues, folksingers, happenings, play readings, and other performances to draw in the young, hip crowd. By 1960 cafe theatre had attracted the attention of the *Village Voice,* then a small neighborhood newspaper with limited circulation. Though it soon was joined by Judson Poets' Theatre, Cafe La Mama, Theatre Genesis, and others, the Cino generally is considered to have featured a regular schedule of productions of new plays before any of the others, thus earning its reputation as the first off-off-Broadway theatre.

With its cluster of coffeehouses, restaurants, and other entertainment venues, MacDougal Street was the center of the Village scene. Among the subway stations that emptied into the area, the Fourth Street–Washington Square station sits on Sixth Avenue near the old Waverly Theatre, only a short walk from MacDougal. About a half block north of the station, Fourth Street crosses Sixth Avenue, angling north as it heads west. A few blocks to the east sits Judson Church at which Al Carmines led the Judson Poets' Theatre beginning in 1961. On the west side of the intersection of Fourth Street and Sixth Avenue (and so close that it nearly forms a five-point intersection), a third, smaller road, Cornelia Street, angles off to the southwest, running to Bleecker Street. Like many streets in the Village, Cornelia has been home to the famous: James Agee's studio was there, as were W. H. Auden's home and the bookshop that published *Fuck You: A Magazine for the Arts.*

On the west side of Cornelia, just south of the intersection with Fourth Street, sits the apartment building from which dancer Freddie Herko jumped to his death in 1964 while naked, on drugs, dancing to Mozart's *Coronation Mass,* and screaming "I'm flying! I'm flying!"[1] A bit farther down on the east side, Frank Thompson operated his infamous gallery frequented by many from the Cino. Only select customers were allowed to visit the back of the gallery to view salacious artwork that featured nude boys and men. Not much farther down and also on the east side at number 28 was Mona's Royal Roost, a bar that catered largely to a gay clientele well before the Stonewall Riots of 1969. Cino sometimes dashed in for a quick drink after his evening's production had begun. Across the street from Mona's at number 31 was Caffe Cino. All these businesses operated quietly, with most attracting their customers from the immediate vicinity. In this rather insulated setting, Joe Cino presided over his tiny Caffe, hosting at first play and poetry readings and ultimately a demanding schedule of productions of works by new playwrights.

When he opened the Caffe, Joe Cino had little theatrical or management experience. A dancer whose brief career seems to have failed because of his short, heavy build, he intended a place in which friends could gather for light refreshments, conversation, art displays, and poetry readings. He modeled his enterprise after European cafes, a style that already had proved successful in the Village at the Figaro and Rienzi.

By the late fifties Village coffeehouses had attracted not only the attention of the young people who frequented them but also that of city officials who were concerned about the congestion, noise, and crowds that coffeehouses seemed to attract. This tension between the businesses and city leaders resulted in the "coffeehouse war," a long struggle in which officials used zoning, health, fire, and licensing regulations in an attempt to control coffeehouses. Officials routinely issued summonses and even closed shops, with the most intensely fought battles between the proprietors and politicians centering on the issue of licensing. Coffeehouse owners argued that the city intentionally delayed acting on their applications for licenses; city officials contended that few coffeehouses met the licensing standards mandated by regulations. Most important, officials argued that codes prohibited live performance without either a theatre or a cabaret license. Though opponents of coffeehouses cited licensing issues and the noisy, unruly crowds drawn to the area as the reasons for their actions, a less apparent but far more important cause seems to have been that the establishments attracted the "wrong" element: Beats, hippies, homosexuals, interracial couples, and persons of color.

The story of the Cino is inseparable from the story of the coffeehouse war. The cultural issues that gave rise to the coffeehouse war and the events of that struggle not only are central to the history of the Cino but also influenced productions, informed plays, and probably contributed to the death of Joe Cino as well as to the collapse of his Caffe.

Probably because of its distance from the MacDougal scene, perhaps because Cino avoided the more notorious practices of some coffeehouses, or perhaps because Joe Cino relied on his family's supposed Mafia influence, the Caffe seems to have been able to offer entertainment while suffering somewhat less official harassment than many other coffeehouses. Almost from its opening, the Cino hosted free entertainment, with lectures, art shows, and music recitals interspersed among poetry and play readings. Despite Cino's interest in the arts, much of the impetus for such activity seems to have come from patrons such as Rissa Korsun and Joseph Davies. Stagings of one-act plays or scenes from longer works quickly replaced the readings and lectures and led to staged productions in which the works were chosen almost exclusively from new plays written mostly by beginning playwrights. At the Caffe's peak, each production typically ran for one or two or sometimes even three weeks, at nine and eleven p.m. each day, with additional shows on Friday and Saturday nights at one a.m.; for particularly popular productions, an additional late-night performance sometimes was added on Sunday.

Cino's management style was, to say the least, idiosyncratic: He seldom read the scripts that inundated the Cino. He almost never produced a work on the basis of the quality of the script. He might give or deny a performance slot to a playwright solely on the basis of that person's astrological sign. He exerted no artistic control over shows. He sometimes brought back unsuccessful shows only because he had enjoyed them, not because of their artistic merit or market potential. He did not cancel shows or shorten their runs, regardless of how poorly executed or attended. He provided little or no budget for productions and never paid actors, directors, or playwrights, whose sole income from their work came from audience contributions. Given Cino's relaxed approach to management, as well as the pride many participants in off-

off-Broadway took in the amateurish nature of their work, both the quality and content of productions varied widely. During any particular week, the Cino might have presented one of the best or one of the worst productions in New York. As one critic noted in his review of the Caffe's *Alice in Wonderland,* "There is also no way to predict what will happen. 'We've had bad shows,' Mr. Cino admits. But there is always next week. If, for example, you do not like *Alice* . . . , you may like Jean Genet's *The Maids,* starting Sunday. If you do not like Genet, there is always coffee."[2]

Any limitations that arose from the lack of funding or from Cino's management style were offset by the freedom Cino offered artists and by the strength of his personality, since the Caffe became one of the most respected and influential venues of early off-off-Broadway, particularly among gay artists. It offered a safe space in which taking risk was encouraged, in which failure was acceptable though hardly encouraged, and in which friends supported each other in their challenge of social and theatrical traditions. Writers, actors, and directors learned from the success or failure of their own experiments, as well as from watching the experiments of other practitioners; they freely shared with and learned from each other. Cino supported and nurtured fledgling artists, stroked their egos, helped them through difficulties, encouraged their creativity, gave them food, and acted variously as their father figure, friend, therapist, champion, defender, critic, confessor, and guide.

Despite its accomplishments, the Cino has received relatively little scholarly attention. When Albert Poland and Bruce Mailman published the first historical study in *The Off-Off Broadway Book: The Plays, People, Theatre* (1972), they began by noting their difficulty in researching the Cino. First, they observed, *The Reader's Guide to Periodical Literature* has no listing for either Caffe Cino or Joe Cino; second, even our most important and extensive archive of theatre history, the Billy Rose Theatre Collection of the New York Public Library, contained only two items about the Cino: an obituary file and a small file of notes. This dearth of source material meant that the only way to research the Cino was to depend on the memories of those who had been there. Thus Poland and Mailman concluded, "It is as if the details were made deliberately obscure."[3]

Along with various articles in the popular press written by Cino veterans and a handful of admirers, the history of the Cino has been preserved in a few dissertations and theses and a scattering of articles in books. Unfortunately many of these accounts include inaccuracies and, taken as a whole, ignore large sections of the Caffe's history. Having had the opportunity to interview many people who are now dead, Jimmy McDonough recently added significantly to the story of the Cino in his book about director Andy Milligan, though his narrative focuses on the drug abuse, sexual escapades, and darker side of the history. The best and most comprehensive source of information about Cino productions remains the reviews and announcements in the *Village Voice,* though cumbersome to access, since it is not indexed. But even information in it must be accepted with caution, given that productions announced there sometimes were canceled just before opening or during the run, thus necessitating a replacement show. Though Cino never canceled a show because of poor attendance, he sometimes was forced to do so because the playwright had not finished the script, actors dropped out at the last minute, or similar problems arose.

Announcements in the *Village Voice* often are confusing and contradictory. Sometimes the confusion is minor: on April 4, 1963, the Cino advertised a new play by Jerry Caruana, who was, ironically enough, an inspector for the city's license department, entitled *If I Had a Heart* and scheduled to open the following week; on April 11 the Cino advertised its current production as Caruana's *Why Have a Heart?* In other instances the listing for off-off-Broadway theatres conflicts completely with the advertisement under "Cafes and Coffee Houses," making it difficult to be certain which production appeared at that time. During several long periods, the Cino neither placed advertisements nor received reviews from the *Voice,* thus leaving large gaps in its production history.

Without a license, the Cino had to be furtive in its advertisement and general public presence to avoid the attention of city officials. Furthermore many of its productions explored such issues as homosexuality and sadomasochism, topics that were discussed cautiously if at all in mainstream publications. Therefore, particularly in the Cino's early years, publicity had to be limited and had to be designed to reach only the targeted audience.

Another factor that may have contributed to the failure to preserve effectively the history of the Cino may lie in the Caffe's position outside the political debates of the period. As cultural historian Julie Stephens has noted, studies of the sixties have tended to slight the bohemian, nonpolitical counterculture in favor of the New Left and others involved in radical movements. Only a comparatively small number of Cino productions were overtly political. Generally considered the first original play performed there, James

Howard's *Flyspray* (1960) touched on such topics as class relations and pacificism; after its premier at the Cino it moved to various garages and similar venues with support from leftist sponsors. A few other productions touched on similar issues, and many of the plays that avoided political comment nevertheless centered on gender issues such as sexual orientation that would be hotly debated during the following decades.

If the Caffe can be said to have had any consistent political approach at all, it is that of questioning accepted political philosophies, social structures, and gender constructions but without offering ideologically coherent or systematically developed alternatives. The atmosphere was one more of campy frolic than of serious engagement. As Paul Cranefield emphasizes, "In some strange way the Cino was not consciously countercultural. I do not recall explicitly anti-capitalist or anti-Vietnam [War] plays there (nothing like *MacBird* at the Judson). The Cino was more its own place, like children playing dress-up, a refuge from the real, adult world rather than a protest against it."[4]

Ultimately the Cino's ideological commitment centered on its challenge of our understanding of self, particularly the gendered self. With its celebration of a fluid, unstable sexual identity, the Cino existed within that period that falls largely between the medical model of sexual identity of prior decades and the ethnic model of sexual identity that would become commonplace after the Stonewall Riots in 1969. Caffe Cino and many of the other coffeehouses were rewriting and redefining both bodies and space and thus redefined performances of the sexual, gendered self. These sites became visible evidence of the rending of the social fabric of the city and the country as the younger generation challenged authoritarian establishments.

Ultimately the story of the Cino is bound up tightly with the story of the cultural and social changes that occurred in the United States during the sixties. Caught between the various factions in the coffeehouse war, the tiny Caffe was at once very nonpolitical, only occasionally echoing the radicalism of the period, and exceptionally political, foregrounding issues of sexuality and gender that were quite radical.

1 Background and Context

few periods in the history of the United States have been as controversial, as deeply loved, or as frequently reviled as has that of the 1960s. Much energy in subsequent decades has been devoted to coming to terms with the turbulence, radical politics, sexual revolution, and drug culture associated with that period. Politicians boast proudly of their military service in Vietnam, minimize their antiwar activities, explain away their countercultural associations, or deny inhaling when they smoked marijuana; they work to dismantle, expand, or reorganize the programs of Lyndon Johnson's Great Society, to move us into the future promised by Lyndon Johnson or into a future that emulates the seemingly more innocent period of the fifties. Very much like the period itself, the Caffe Cino was complex, contradictory, and often inscrutable; certainly a product of its time, it helped to create its time. It grew out of the popularity of coffeehouses but set on a unique course that established it as one of the first off-off-Broadway theatres. It reflected the personality of Joe Cino but eventually exceeded his control, becoming larger and more successful than he ever desired.

Though we can speak of the Cino as reflecting certain traits common in the sixties, the term *sixties* is itself problematic. At its simplest, it refers to a ten-year period demarcated by the fifties on one side and the seventies on the other, though one could quibble over whether the period extends from 1960 to 1969 or from 1961 to 1970. More significant, "the sixties" is a cultural construct, a discursive strategy used by some to condemn a presumed movement to the left in American politics, by others to lament the passing of a radical (though perhaps naive) politics, and by still others to situate the origins of subsequent cultural movements, including postmodernism. Cultural historian Julie Stephens notes that the term "refers directly to a historical epoch while at the same time defying a precise correspondence to the decade itself."[1] In her summary of efforts to arrive at dates for the period, she notes that some scholars date the "sixties experience" as starting in 1964; others take the period back to 1955; one scholar, Theodore Roszak, places the sixties "within a broader setting that stretches from 1942 to 1972."[2] Regardless of the precise years included in the period, a general trend is apparent: a movement from the complacency and consumerism of the fifties to the idealism of the Kennedy era and the divisiveness of the later years.

In "The New Mood in Politics," Arthur Schlesinger Jr. captures the feeling of many as the new decade began. First published in January 1960, the essay describes the fifties as a "period of passivity and acquiescence," as an "orgy of consumer goods," as a "politics of fatigue," and as a "decade of inertia" characterized by a "policy of drift."[3] The problem, he argues, is one not of ability but of conviction: "Our trouble is not that our capabilities are inadequate. It is that our priorities—which means our *values*—are wrong."[4] The failures of the fifties had resulted in a weakened educational system, sluggish economic growth, and decline in military strength. But the new decade, Schlesinger argues, promised something different: "Somehow the wind is beginning to change."[5] In a remarkably prescient text, he predicts that "the Sixties will probably be spirited, articulate, inventive, incoherent, turbulent, with energy shooting off wildly in all directions. Above all, there will be a sense of motion, of leadership and hope."[6]

In addition to the factors discussed by Schlesinger, two events in the fifties helped to bring about the change he forecast: the arrest of Rosa Parks and the launch of Sputnik. When Parks refused to move out of the white section of a public bus on December 1, 1955, her arrest and conviction prompted a boycott of the Montgomery, Alabama, bus system. Her arrest, the effectiveness of the boycott, and subsequent events helped draw attention both to the inequitable treatment of persons of color and to the fledgling civil rights movement. Less than two years later, many in the United States were stunned when the Soviet Union launched Sputnik, the first artificial satellite, into space. Concerns over racial justice and Soviet technological superiority combined with worry over the stagnant economy and other problems to create a sense of need for urgent action.

As Schlesinger predicted, the sixties were turbulent. The FDA's approval of the birth control pill on May 9, 1960, laid the foundation for the sexual revolution. Women no longer had to depend on men for prevention of pregnancies but could take control of that aspect of their reproductive health. Much of the decade was dominated by violence or the threat of violence, as John Kennedy in 1963 and then Robert Kennedy and Martin Luther King Jr. in 1968 died at the hands of assassins. As the war in Vietnam escalated during the decade, so too did the violence associated with antiwar demonstrations. The peaceful protests of the early Civil Rights movement became increasingly violent as the riots of the middle and later part of the period were accompanied by shouts of "Burn, baby, burn." Even world conflagration threatened in 1962 during the Cuban missile crisis, when the United States learned that Soviet missiles were being moved into Cuba.

Over the course of the decade, divisions among different factions seemed to grow deeper, driven by the various crises that marked the years. The Cuban missile crisis brought home the threat of annihilation in a way that even the explosions of atomic bombs in Japan were not able to do. The danger posed by the arms race no longer seemed geographically or factually remote; now it was all too vivid, too real, and too close. As a small crowd huddled together in the Cino during those October nights of peak tension, many were convinced that missiles would start to fly at any moment, ending civilization as we had known it. The escalation of the Vietnam War in 1964 brought deep divisions over military issues. Hawks argued that the spread of communism must be stopped in southeast Asia to prevent world domination by the Marxists; doves dismissed the threat posed by the regional conflict, often arguing that the United States faced greater risks from internal dissension than from external aggression. The assassination of John Kennedy in November 1963 challenged the idealism of many—it was one of the few times that Joe Cino closed his Caffe. The inauguration of Lyndon Johnson, who hardly had the charisma of his predecessor, did little to reassure many of Kennedy's followers. Johnson's roots in the Deep South and his political background seemed to contrast with the vision inspired by Kennedy. The Cino closed permanently only weeks before two of the most traumatic events of 1968: the assassination of Martin Luther King Jr. on April 4, 1968, and the assassination of Robert Kennedy about two months later. The succession of assassinations, combined with the failure of student uprisings in France and elsewhere during 1968, helped shatter the remaining idealism of the early sixties.

The various movements of the period can be divided loosely into two groups: the first was highly political and revolutionary; the second rejected traditional terms of politics and revolution. As early as 1968 Theodore Roszak spoke of this tendency of the period's movements to coalesce around the two poles: "the hard-headed political activism of the student New Left" in contrast with "the mind-blown bohemianism of the beats and hippies."[7] Most studies of the period focus on the student radicals; as Julie Stephens argues, those who comprised the bohemian element of the counterculture largely have been slighted: "[I]t is as though, in hindsight, the real action is considered to have taken place only in the political side of the decade's experience: the free speech, civil rights, black power, and antiwar movements. By contrast, the hippies are rejected as a 'clownish sideshow.'"[8]

The countercultural group known as the Diggers exemplifies the clownish sideshow discussed by Stephens. In one of their protests, they burst into and took over a meeting of the Students for a Democratic Society, shouting in opposition to the SDS's traditional radical agenda: "America is a madhouse! They're making us all insane! Radicals are psychotic. The liberals, ha, are just neurotic. . . . Do your own thing. Whatever your thing is, do it. Do your own thing! I do what I want to do."[9] The speaker added, "If the new left took over in 15 years, it would be all the same, man, because you're not free!"[10] The Diggers, then, rebelled not just against the conservative Eisenhower era nor just against the more liberal but misguidedly militaristic Johnson administration but against all totalizing political theory. Perhaps the *Village Voice* best summarized the split between the bohemians and the New Left in its headline "The Power of Flower Vs. the Power of Politics."[11]

According to Stephens, the politics of the Diggers and other bohemians included "rejection of organization, hierarchy and leadership, the critique of intelligibility and coherence, and the call for a 'money free economy.'"[12] Whereas the radicals depended on those such as Herbert Marcuse who worked in relatively traditional political forms, the hippies and yippies were as likely to draw their beliefs from popular culture, often merging it with more traditional political philosophies. As Jerry Rubin said, "We're really brothers because we grew up listening to the same radio and T.V. programs. . . . I didn't get my ideas from Mao, Lenin or Ho Chi Minh. I got my ideas from the Lone Ranger."[13]

Though many of the artists who worked at the Cino were political activists, the Caffe more comfortably reflected traits of Stephens's antidisciplinary approach than it did that of the strident political radicals. Thus, like Cranefield, various critics have suggested that the Cino was a place to escape from the chaos and political maelstrom of the sixties. Tillie Gross, for example, says, "Although Cino and others attended demonstrations and marched for Peace, political activism was left to the Becks (Julian Beck and Judith Malina) and

The Living Theatre. For the alienated, Caffe Cino became a place to hide and to escape to, because here they were accepted."[14] Reflecting the influence of the bohemian counterculture, the Cino's production schedule had a stronger commitment to the whimsical than to the serious. When political issues emerged, the approach ranged from the rather conservative, antifeminist, antiunion *God Created the Heaven and the Earth . . . but Man Created Saturday Night* to the much more radical, antiwar *Daddy Violet.* Even the management style of Joe Cino (with his refusal to impose order and his imposition of virtually no restraints on style and subject matter) seems to have grown out of the philosophy of the counterculture.

Whereas the overall tone and style of the Cino shows the influence of the counterculture, the need for an alternative theatre grew largely out of the economic and management practices of Broadway and off Broadway. During the forties, Broadway began a stagnation that continued through the fifties and into the sixties, with the cause attributed to factors that ranged from spiraling costs to a political climate grown increasingly conservative during the McCarthy years. Unable or unwilling to take financial and political risks, Broadway, with its ever-shrinking number of productions, had increasingly turned to safe work that was dominated by stars (star writers, star performers, star directors) and by an avoidance of overt, challenging social and political commentary. By 1961 the economic situation had become so difficult that Herman Shumlin declared, "Economics is everything that is wrong with the theatre."[15] To illustrate the economic problems that faced Broadway, Stuart Little noted that *South Pacific* was produced in 1949 at a cost of $225,000 and had a top ticket price of six dollars. About eleven years later, *The Sound of Music* cost $486,000, more than a twofold increase. Top ticket prices, however, had increased by only about sixty percent. By 1961 production budgets for straight plays had risen from about $60,000 only a decade earlier to $100,000 or $125,000, with some going considerably higher. Joshua Logan argued that the economic conditions harmed not only the consumer, who was required to pay too much to attend the theatre, but also playwrights, who were forced to structure plays to meet economic demands as opposed to writing "the play they feel."[16]

As economic conditions constrained the Broadway artist, so too did political considerations. Harold Clurman noted in 1961 that with the postwar economic expansion, Americans dared not "rock the boat" or "do anything that might weaken our confidence or prestige as a world power"; with the escalating cold war, Clurman argued that playwrights dared not look critically at the United States: "If a peep of protest issued from your lips, you were thought a crank or a neurotic, if not actually subversive."[17] As a result, the politically and socially significant plays common during the twenties and thirties became far less common, disguised when they did appear through alterations in place (as in *Flight into Egypt*) or time (as in *The Crucible*). Only through such indirection could social critique safely appear on the stage. Political conditions, then, forced the playwright to avoid engagement with social, political, and economic issues in favor of a more personal, nonpolitical exploration of character psychology. Thus the outwardly directed, socially oriented plays of the twenties and thirties gave way in the forties and fifties to inwardly directed, psychological works.

Off Broadway emerged as a corrective to the conservative, money-dominated Broadway, but it soon faced many of the same problems. As production costs for off-Broadway theatres increased tenfold from an average of fifteen hundred dollars in the early fifties to fifteen thousand dollars in the early sixties, average weekly operating costs more than tripled, from one thousand dollars to thirty-two hundred dollars.[18] Off-Broadway theatres pursued, in addition to aggressive fund-raising, several ways to cut costs or make money, notably the casting of stars to attract an audience and a reduction in royalty payments by selecting older texts no longer under copyright. Since the emergence of off Broadway coincided with the entry of a new group of university-educated theatre artists, the new actors and directors tended to be more conversant with the classical texts and acting styles than were many of their predecessors.[19]

Though off Broadway developed to help correct the financial and artistic deficiencies of Broadway, it soon began to encounter many of the same problems and to enact many of the same solutions as did Broadway. Thus by 1961 the energy and creativity of early off Broadway seemed to be waning, giving way to fiscal, artistic, and political caution. Lamenting the movement's recent "reluctance to take bold chances,"[20] Robert Brustein argued that an increasing number of off-Broadway plays "look like Broadway rejects," finding their way onto the smaller stages "not because they are too good for Broadway but because they are not good enough."[21] Thus, with such notable exceptions as Julian Beck and Judith Malina's Living Theatre, off Broadway suffered from what Barbara La Fontaine called "creeping Broadwayism."[22]

A consequence of the economic and management trends on and off Broadway was the exclusion of new talent. Attracting investors and audiences so that a production could avoid becoming one of the many financial disasters (the

1959–60 season having seen about 25 percent of its shows close after five or fewer performances) often seemed to depend as much on the names on the marquee as it did on the overall quality of the production. Unknown, untried artists had few options to become known and tried.

Given the problems of Broadway and off Broadway, young artists who arrived in New York in the late fifties and early sixties had to create their own opportunities. By turning to sites such as Caffe Cino, they began a new theatre movement that was known initially as underground or cafe theatre and only later as off-off-Broadway (OOB). Centered in coffeehouses, churches, basements, and other nontraditional spaces, it surfaced in Greenwich Village and was influenced by many of the same forces as was off Broadway ten years earlier. For both movements the bohemian atmosphere of the Village was an important influence. Referring to the origins of off Broadway, Stuart Little, for example, notes the period's climate of emancipation and self-expression fostered by the popularity of Freudian psychology. New sexual and artistic freedoms were emerging and combining with a distrust of "uptowners" who lived north of the Village. These same influences intensified as the Beats gave way to the hippies.

The financial situation of the New York theatre contributed heavily to the emergence and growth of both off Broadway and OOB. But whereas off-Broadway theatres often seemed to be a less-commercialized, miniaturized version of Broadway, OOB theatres typically broke radically with the practices of prior New York theatres in their selection of physical space, operating methods, production styles, and plays. And whereas off-Broadway theatres initially averaged modest production budgets of fifteen hundred dollars or so, OOB theatres operated on minuscule budgets. Shows typically were mounted for twenty or thirty dollars or even less. Judson budgeted $37.50 per work[23]; the total expense for the Cino production of George Birimisa's *Daddy Violet* was the cost of one beer for each performance, or about fifteen cents. Even Ellen Stewart's La Mama Experimental Theatre Club (ETC), among the best-funded OOB theatres, allocated only two hundred dollars for each show in 1967, when off-Broadway production budgets were in the tens of thousands of dollars. For much of its history, Caffe Cino allocated no regular budget for productions, thus requiring playwrights and directors to pay production costs and to keep shows as cheap as possible, often by using found objects for sets and props. (One of the regular directors became so adept at finding discarded items that it has been said he could go in one side of a trash receptacle empty-handed and emerge from the other side with a complete set.) Though reduced costs allowed greater flexibility for managers, it also meant that they had to turn to inexperienced talent, since they could not attract stars even if they wanted to do so.

One of the greatest differences between off Broadway and OOB is in the focus on the playwright in the latter. One of the landmark productions of early off Broadway was the revival of *Summer and Smoke* at Circle in the Square in April 1952, which Little considers to be both the start of off Broadway "for historical purposes" and "the first major theatrical success below Forty-second Street in thirty years."[24] Though a comparable moment cannot be identified for OOB, the closest, perhaps, is the production of James Howard's *Flyspray* in the summer of 1960. Thus the start of off Broadway is associated with the revival of existing works, whereas the start of OOB is associated with the first performance of new works by beginning playwrights. Michael Feingold notes, "By and large the off-Broadway of the '50s concerned itself with the infusion of European writing (except for Circle in the Square, where the specialty was older American plays—O'Neill, early Williams—given new life by a new Studio-trained breed of young actor . . .)."[25] Off-off-Broadway, on the other hand, quickly began introducing theatre audiences to new playwrights, whose work would soon appear off and on Broadway, in movie theatres, and on television. It is no wonder then that Ellen Stewart introduced her shows at La Mama with similar words each night: "Good evening, ladies and gentlemen. Welcome to La Mama ETC, dedicated to the playwright and to all aspects of the theater."[26]

Just as the mainstream theatres of the period faced their political and economic pressures, Greenwich Village's coffeehouses faced their own political and economic pressures. Few commercial establishments became as caught up in the cultural struggles of the sixties as did the coffeehouses. Centers for those who sought to change fashions in clothing, ideas, poetry, politics, and entertainment, coffeehouses became popular symbols of the outrageousness of social rebels. Their increasingly unsavory reputation reflects a long history for such establishments in which they initially had been linked to subversive forces. When they were introduced to England during the middle of the seventeenth century, they quickly became popular and many men spent so much time in them that women circulated a petition charging, "This bitter, nasty puddle water [coffee] so attracts that we scarce have two pence to buy bread, nor can we find our husbands even to call a midwife."[27] The petition further alleged that coffee is a "depressant to masculine energies." Eventually, coffeehouses, for the most part, either disappeared or shed their disrepute, becoming quiet espresso shops.

Italian espresso shops in which men gathered for chess and conversation were a long-standing tradition in the Village by the middle of the twentieth century. Beginning in the early to mid fifties, however, a new-style shop began to appear in New York, London, and other cities, spurred in part by the patronage of celebrities: Gina Lollobrigida in London and Gloria Vanderbilt, Edward G. Robinson, and Vincent Price in New York. By 1956 when coffeehouses began drawing attention from mainstream news magazines, the sites already had developed a reputation for exoticism. In London, for example, one venue featured a ground floor called Heaven, noisily inhabited by caged birds, and a basement called Hell, where the walls were decorated with flames and devils' masks.[28] New York's coffeehouses were "similarly offbeat." According to J. R. Goddard, the Village coffeehouses were "born out of local Italian haunts and tinged by a dash of the European cabaret and the New England cracker barrel."[29] To the exotic, trendy atmosphere of the early coffeehouses would soon be added an element of danger and subversiveness as the Beats and other young intellectuals and political or cultural radicals flocked to them. Thus, by the late fifties, coffeehouses had come to represent the struggle between those who professed traditional cultural and social thought and those who challenged it. Ultimately the struggle between the city and the coffeehouses would become so intense as to merit the title "the Coffee House War."[30]

When Joe Cino arrived in New York City in 1948, the Village still was composed largely of modestly priced apartments, neighborhood shops, and enclaves of artists and bohemians in ethnic neighborhoods. Though Cino was born and raised in Buffalo, New York, very little is known about his life prior to the opening of the Caffe; even after that point, much information is missing, contradictory, or unreliable, in part because Cino himself gave conflicting biographical information, embellishing the truth or even fabricating entire stories when it suited his purpose.[31] He was born November 20, 1931. Though he sometimes claimed his birthplace as New York City's Little Italy, it seems certain that he was born in Buffalo, particularly since the city directory for 1931 contains a listing for Cino's parents, Joseph and Mary Cino, at 155 Trenton Avenue. The address is within a mile of the funeral home that would in 1967 arrange for Joe's[32] funeral, the church at which his funeral would occur, and the address to which cards were sent to Mary Cino after her son's death. Joe was the third of four boys born over a nine-year period. Gasper was about three years older than Joe, Richard about two years older, and Stephen about six years younger. At least on their father's side, the four boys belong to the first generation of the family to be born in the United States. (Joseph's father, Gasper, died in Racalmuto, Sicily, in 1945.) The family was working-class (his father's occupation having been listed as "laborer" in the city directory for 1931, though the term is so inclusive as to be useless in identifying his specific occupation). Joseph died in 1942, leaving his wife and four sons, who ranged in age from four to thirteen.

Even as a young child, Joe was passionate about opera, the musical form that he played constantly at Caffe Cino and that heavily influenced his perspective on theatre. He often went with childhood friend Angelo Lovullo to a record store to preview opera recordings, though neither child had the money to make a purchase. As much as Lovullo enjoyed the recordings, his response was far more reserved than that of Joe, who often would be in tears by the end of the recording. Though Cino and Lovullo routinely went into the shop, previewed an album, and returned it without making a purchase, the shopkeepers always allowed them to listen to the recordings that they chose, perhaps recognizing that the boys were gaining access to music in the only way open to them. Cino's love for opera remained with him for the rest of his life, with Maria Callas being one of his favorite stars. He had less appreciation for some other musical forms. According to Robert Heide, Cino never enjoyed the folk music popular in the Village and only gradually learned to appreciate the Beatles.[33] Music played at Caffe Cino most often was composed or performed by such classical figures as Rossini, Verdi, and Puccini and such contemporary figures as Kate Smith.

After their father's death, the Cino brothers seem to have drawn closer together. As attorney T. Louis Palazzo noted recently in a legal proceeding for Stephen Cino (presumably referring to Joe's brother), the boys "shared a special bond ever since their father, Joseph, died."[34] Yet a distance soon began to develop between Joe and the other three brothers, who teased him, ostensibly because of his interest in dance but more likely because of his increasingly conspicuous sexual orientation. According to Michael Feingold, "Before he got fat, he had aspired to be a dancer; that had estranged him from his family since, as one of his best friends put it, a boy from an Italian family is not supposed to be a ballerina."[35] Implicit in the friend's feminization of Cino ("ballerina") is the suggestion that the family was as concerned about Cino's sexuality as they were about his artistic impulse.

Two of Cino's friends, Lovullo and future antique dealer-artist Tony Vaccaro, decided to move to New York City in February 1948. Shortly before their bus was to leave Buffalo, Cino was speaking with the two, worrying that their departure would leave him largely isolated. Though he remained close to his mother throughout his life, tensions with his brothers and with his classmates had increased and seemed unbearable without his friends. Two hours before the bus was to leave, Lovullo finally said to Cino, "Well, maybe you should come to New York with us. . . . Do you have any money?"[36] When Cino said, "No," Lovullo suggested that he ask his mother for money under the pretext of going to Rochester to visit a family member. It seemed a solution to the problem, particularly since the proposal came from Lovullo. Lovullo was slightly older than Cino and was much respected by his younger acquaintance. Though Cino's mother either would not or could not give him money, he was able to obtain enough for the bus fare; the primary contribution from his family, he sometimes claimed, was a dime that his brother had dropped in the bedroom.

After hastily packing, Cino dashed to Lovullo's home, only to find that his friend already had left. With only minutes to spare, Cino ran from Lovullo's home, caught a man who was backing out of his driveway, and pleaded with the unknown man, "Please, mister, take me to the bus station. It's a matter of life or death." The neighbor consented, depositing Cino at the station just in time. As he ran up the hill to the terminal, the bus was pulling out for its journey. To the cheers of the other passengers, the bus driver stopped and allowed the exhausted young man aboard. When he finally caught his breath, Cino questioned his friends about what New York would be like. Would it, he wondered, be as it is in the movies?

Cino told Michael Smith that he arrived during a blizzard on Saturday, February 7: "I didn't have a dime . . . and I don't have one now."[37] Hired almost immediately on his arrival by the cafeteria of the YMCA at Penn Station, Cino was the first of the group from Buffalo to get a job. To help his impecunious friends, he encouraged them to buy milkshakes from him, to which he added three eggs so that they could get a substantial meal for the price of a milkshake. Over the next few years, he held a variety of jobs, including positions at a Howard Johnson's restaurant and at the Statler Hotel. Though he never returned to high school, he studied voice and dance in New York.

Cino had taken dance lessons in Buffalo and at the age of twelve had made his performance debut when he sang "I'm Beginning to See the Light" on *Uncle*

Ben's Liberty Shoe Hour. In New York Charles Loubier introduced Cino to the venue in which he received his professional training, the Henry Street Settlement Playhouse on Grand Street, where Loubier was also a student. Loubier describes his first meeting with Cino: "Joe was something else. I knew him from the time he was 16 years old. . . . A friend came down to see me one day to urge me to find his lover, Andrew, who was at Coney Island, swimming. I was 18 or 19. I went and met this layout of Italian boys . . . and a beautiful boy with great big black eyes and eyelashes out to there. It was Cino. I recognized the kindred spirit immediately."[38] Shortly after the meeting, while working at the Statler, Cino began his study at Henry Street under the tutelage of Alwin Nikolais. He studied there for two years, taking a variety of performance courses—acting, dancing, speech, and makeup.[39] Soon he began having some success in his dance career, first receiving a dance scholarship to Jacob's Pillow in 1953. He appeared in a selection of new works with the Mary Anthony Dance Theatre, for which he received his only mention as a dancer in the *New York Times*[40]; in March 1957 he toured with Alfred Brooks and Maxine Munt. Soon after, however, he apparently found his dance career at an end, perhaps because of his build. According to Gordy, "Photos of the young Cino reveal a round, open face, with an olive complexion, bulbous nose, wide-set dark eyes, generous, thick-lipped mouth, and a high forehead with curly dark hair; later photos show him with longer, straggly hair and a full beard. . . . [H]e felt he was overweight and too short (contemporaries estimate his adult height at 5' 9")."[41]

In 1957 Loubier got Cino a job as waiter at the Playhouse Cafe (named for its proximity to the Neighborhood Playhouse), a coffeehouse opened by Jack Pelsinger and Phyllis Bochner, Loubier's friend and future wife. Pelsinger and Bochner intended to offer entertainment (including poetry and play reading), though Loubier indicates that the plans were short-lived, since the coffeehouse was replaced by a Turkish bordello within six months. While working for the cafe, Cino hoped to have an opportunity to explore his interest in theatre. Just before he left the position with Playhouse Cafe, he had begun preparation to present a reading of *La Strada,* but it is unclear whether the reading ever took place.

Even before working as a waiter at the Playhouse Cafe, Cino had become interested in opening his own coffeehouse: "I started thinking about the cafe in 1954. It would just come and go. It would usually go when there were too many people trying to have a part in it. I would talk about it with close friends and it would just dissolve away into nothing."[42] Using savings and borrowed funds, Cino opened the Caffe in December 1958, just as the popularity of coffeehouses was escalating.

When Cino left his job at Phyllis Bochner's Playhouse Cafe to start his own coffeehouse, Bochner and Loubier also switched their focus from the Playhouse Cafe to the Cino, with Bochner acting as the Caffe's bookkeeper. In addition to their shared business and artistic interests, Cino and Loubier were close friends. When not occupied with the Caffe, the two would sometimes entertain themselves by dressing in drag and walking the streets to provoke fights with homophobic street thugs who typically ended much the worse from the engagements.[43] Soon, however, Bochner and Loubier married, moved to New Jersey, and began their family, thus decreasing the time that they spent at the Cino. After their departure, the financial records for the Cino became haphazard at best, since Cino's "system" consisted of tossing receipts and other records into a shoe box that he turned over to an accountant each year.

After a rather unpropitious start, the Cino gradually would build a base of loyal supporters and artists responsible for a brief but remarkable period in theatre history, the influence of which still can be seen in theatre today. Facing harassment from city officials, threats of financial collapse, ravages of drug abuse, ostracism from the uptown arts community, and fatigue from incredibly long work hours, Joe Cino guided his little shop until these and many other problems became so unbearable that he took his own life. The explosion of creativity at 31 Cornelia Street could not be contained within the small storefront shop but worked its way through New York, through the United States, and elsewhere. Often caught up in the cultural and political struggles going on in the Village, the Cino and other coffeehouses represented for many exactly what was wrong with their community and the nation; for others, they represented exactly what was right. Constantly jostled by—sometimes rejecting, sometimes pulled into, sometimes ignorant of—these outside forces, Joe Cino and his collection of artists would create a theatre that simultaneously rejected and co-opted the dominant world around it.

2 Finding and Forming Community

On Christmas Eve 1959, the brutal cold that had whipped into New York the prior day moderated somewhat; instead of a low of 9.5 degrees as on December 23, the lowest temperature was a comparatively mild 19. Despite enormous quantities of salt and the efforts of four thousand workers, streets remained so treacherously coated with snow, sludge, and sheets of ice that city officials planned an unusually aggressive effort to ensure that all lanes of major thoroughfares were passable. As the city battled the aftereffects of the brutal cold, aspiring actress Shirley Stoler stepped onto MacDougal Street from the San Remo, a popular cafe in Greenwich Village. Carrying more than two hundred pounds (perhaps as much as 250 pounds) on her five-foot seven-inch frame, Stoler hardly sported the physique of a leading lady, even in those days before Twiggy of the 1960s and the emaciated "cocaine look" of the 1980s and 1990s. As a successful actress years later, with starring roles in such movies as *The Honeymoon Killers* and *Seven Beauties,* Stoler took great pride in being one of the first large women to succeed in serious films. In 1959, however, she was a decade away from her first starring role in a film; she was also involved in what she later called a clichéd affair with a married man. Thus, on Christmas Eve, she and her lover had dined early so that he could spend the evening with his wife and children. After he left, Stoler stood in the middle of Bleecker Street with nowhere to go and nothing to do. Loath to spend the evening alone, she decided to visit a "funny little place" that she had noticed earlier, its twinkling lights having caught her eye. It was only a short walk from the San Remo, west on Bleecker Street, past the Little Red School House where Mary Travers and Angela Davis received their early education, across Sixth Avenue, and around the corner onto Cornelia Street. As she entered the coffeehouse, a man about her height who, like her, carried excess weight called out, "We're closed, but come on in anyway."[1] She walked into the small room with red-brick walls on which hung a variety of paintings. In all likelihood, an opera recording played, perhaps house favorite Maria Callas. Stoler worked her way through the tables and chairs and reached the group sitting in the back. Thus she paid her first visit to Caffe Cino; she returned often, sometimes as performer and sometimes as audience member. That Christmas Eve, she become part of the Cino family.

Stoler's introduction to the Caffe captures several central aspects of the Cino story: the transgressive sexuality as exemplified in her relationship with a married man; the easy openness and warmth of Joseph Cino and the group that gathered around him; the thin, perhaps nonexistent, boundary between personal and professional interests at the Caffe; and the eclectic mix of people of varying ethnicities, temperaments, and artistic tastes who considered the coffeehouse their artistic home at various points over the ten years of its existence. Precisely who was at the Cino the night of Stoler's first visit is unknown, though she does mention Phyllis Bochner, Charles Loubier, and Asterios Metakos, the Greek artist and tailor who sometimes performed at the Cino and who could make his accordion sound like an organ. Others who might have been there include Angelo Lovullo, who moved to New York with Cino; the petite, Japanese-born Taka Nakano, who was a fan and friend though not a theatre artist; the French-born Nanoosh de la Motte, who has been one of Cino's closest friends (and one of the few women to whom he was linked romantically); and actor Joseph Davies, who appeared in, designed, or directed many of the Caffe's early shows. Playwright Robert Patrick, electrician Jonathan Torrey, and others who later would be inseparably associated with the Cino had not yet arrived on the scene.

By the time Stoler walked in for the first time, the Cino had entered its thirteenth month of operation. The only detailed account that we have of the founding of the coffeehouse comes from Joe Cino. Although others have given a similar account, they may very well have gotten their information from Cino himself. Assuming the veracity of the information, the beginning of the Caffe established a pattern of reliance on happenstance and chance that would appear repeatedly throughout the coffeehouse's history. According to the story, Ed Franzen, Cino's lover and an employee of New York University, was looking for a studio in which to paint and exhibit his work at the same time that Cino was looking for a space for a coffeehouse. It seemed only logical to combine these two interests, thus creating a coffeehouse that displayed Franzen's artwork. One day in November 1958, Franzen called Cino to tell him that he had noticed a "for rent" sign hanging from a piece of manila rope in front of a storefront studio on Cornelia Street.

When I got there Ed was in conversation with Josie, the landlady, who was hanging out the upstairs window with blonde sausage curls. He said, "This is Mrs. Lemma." I said, "Oh, you're Italian." She says, "Yes, what are you?" I said, "Sicilian." So she said, " I don't even have to come down, I'll throw the keys," She threw the keys and we went in and viewed the ruins. The first thing you saw when you looked down the room was the toilet at the back. I thought, "There's a toilet, and there's a sink, and there's a fireplace. This will be a counter, a coffee machine here, a little private area."[2]

Cino and Franzen rented the space and began renovation.

Opening a coffeehouse was relatively inexpensive. Columnist Nancy Lynch quoted the cost for purchasing one already in operation in 1961 as being as little as one thousand dollars; one could be started for about four thousand dollars.[3] Given the limited size and decor of the Cino, it undoubtedly cost significantly less than the amount suggested by Lynch, particularly since Cino and his friends completed the renovation themselves. Estimates of the amount and source of funds for the Caffe vary, though Cino claimed to have started his business with change saved from his job at Playhouse Cafe: "I saved every penny I made there, I knew the next thing would be my own room. I saved all the money in a drawer, and I emptied the drawer out into a paper bag and took it to the bank, and it was $400."[4] Loubier has given the amount as two hundred of Cino's money, with additional funds from loans.[5] Franzen may have invested in the enterprise also, though his involvement was short-lived. According to Robert Patrick, a rumor around the Caffe held that Cino "had talked a lover into backing the Cino for him and then dumped the lover and taken the lease."[6] Undoubtedly the lover to whom Patrick refers is Ed Franzen, though it seems improbable that Cino cheated him out of his investment. Franzen left the Caffe and New York because of health problems, probably a brain tumor. While at the Cino, he was known as "Denta," short for "rodenta." According to actor Matt Baylor, the sobriquet may have originated with Franzen himself: "I really believe Ed coined the word. Ed felt he had rats running around in his head."[7] Franzen died shortly after leaving New York.

As December approached, Cino and his friends prepared for the shop's opening. One day, Matt Baylor, who lived just above the Caffe, stepped in to learn more about the business moving into the space. Baylor recalls Cino's facetious response: "Oh, I'm building a candy store." Shortly afterward Baylor stopped by the storefront only to find a discouraged Cino: in the first of many conflicts between Cino and city agencies, the inspector from the fire department refused to permit occupancy until the fireplace was repaired. Knowledgeable about construction trades, Baylor volunteered to do the brickwork.

With the fireplace repaired and tables in place, all seemed set for the opening: Cino had a restaurant, supplies, and a "beautiful" eagle-crested coffee machine[8]; what he did not have and had never even considered needing was a waiter to take orders or deliver the food. Even worse, Cino discovered that the coffee machine was inoperable, since it had no gaskets; so Caffe Cino was briefly a coffeehouse without the capacity for brewing or serving coffee. Fortunately, friends came to the rescue, some acting as waiters while others rushed to nearby apartments to borrow coffeepots; to maintain a more professional appearance, Cino pretended to obtain drinks from the commercial machine while actually getting them from the borrowed coffeepots. He received scant reward for all the work that led up to the opening and for weathering the various crises: Charles Loubier claimed that the revenue for the night was only two dollars. As Loubier wrote, "So was born the Caffe Cino."[9]

Since funds for staff were scarce, Cino continued to rely on the assistance of friends to volunteer for various duties, a situation that contributed to the unique atmosphere of the business. Matt Baylor had a key to the space and would open at four p.m., operating the business until Cino arrived from his regular job. Other figures periodically would provide support. Charles Loubier once recalled the night that he and Joe Cino waited on tables while both men wore German helmets with veils thrown over them. The first customers were Metakos and two of his friends: "Decked out in these helmets and veils . . . we went over to serve them. . . . I must say that Metakos didn't bat an eyelid. He simply asked for Turkish coffee, which he ended up making himself. And so it went."[10]

Descriptions of the physical layout of the Cino vary, depending in part on the period to which the descriptions refer. The space was quite small, no more than eighteen by thirty feet, with a small area cleared among the tables to serve as the stage. Later a slightly raised platform was added to become the playing area. Tillie Gross describes the inside of the Caffe:

> The Caffe Cino was a shoebox-shaped room seating about sixty people.
> A coffee mill, which originally blocked part of the entrance, was later

placed in one of the two front windows. A curtain, which could be drawn, was draped just inside the doors. It also had an iron gate that could be drawn in front of the double doors. Somewhere near the rear of the store, a counter with an expresso machine was placed at first across the room, and then moved to the left with the tiniest of areas curtained off behind it as a kitchen, which doubled as a dressing room. Just opposite the kitchen, separated by a window in the back wall, was a tiny bathroom, which also doubled as a dressing room. After a fire in 1965, the area was enlarged to allow more space for the dressing room, and space was added near the expresso machine for a compact lighting board.[11]

To Gross's description, John Costopoulos adds,

The Caffe [was decorated with] wind-chimes and Christmas lights. On the left, as one came in, was a large espresso coffee machine, usually run by Cino himself, with the wall behind it covered with photos and news-paper clippings of movie stars, opera stars, naked and near-naked youths, and glitter scattered over everything. The wall collage was counter-pointed by the collage of music on the jukebox: brief excerpts of Maria Callas singing *Tosca* alternated with Greek and Hebrew melodies, which alternated with Billie Holiday singing "God Bless the Child." Bentwood chairs around tiny tables were crowded up to the eight-foot-by-eight-foot stage, which could be elevated and shifted anywhere in the room.[12]

Estimates of seating capacity vary from seventy-five to ninety, though many more people could be squeezed in for popular shows.

For Cino and many of his associates, the space occupied by the Caffe seemed to possess mystical qualities; an air of the exotic and preternatural filled the room. Though reported six years after the event, Cino's comment to Franzen on originally seeing the space is revealing, since it suggests a particu-larly strong connection with the space itself: "This is the room, I have no idea what to do with it."[13] Lucy Silvay, the actress who originated the role of Girl in Lanford Wilson's *The Madness of Lady Bright,* recalls that the twinkling lights, the chandeliers, and the other decor gave the space a fairy-tale qual-ity.[14] According to Robert Heide, "Joe regarded the room as a magical place. . . . Things in the room as well as plays done there were somehow designated as sacred."[15] Cino emphasized the mystical nature of the space and the theat-rical event with his introduction of each performance: "Ladies and gentlemen, it's Magic Time," often followed by a dedication of the show to Jean Harlow, Maria Callas, or some other famous figure who would not, of course, be in the room; other times he dedicated the production to a lesser-known person who was in the audience. Sometimes after his announcement he would throw open a cape to reveal that he was completely naked except for army boots and a silk handkerchief.[16] Through the magic of theatre, the tiny room on Cornelia Street was converted into the deck of a ship, the interior of a sewer, a brothel, and the Garden of Eden. Walter Michael Harris, only a child at the time, recognized the magic of the space: "The Cino to a kid—maybe to an adult too—was just a magic land, like a little jewel box, a Christmas lit, wonderful, magical place where you always felt comfortable even though you were around a lot of strange people. And you always felt respected. . . ."[17] Well after the close of the Caffe, references to the space continue to emphasize its mystical qualities; thus Robert Patrick refers to his position with the coffeehouse as being that of a temple slave, the title to which he gave his fictionalized account of his Cino years (*Temple Slave*, 1994). As Heide suggests, the magic of the room could be transferred to the playwright: "'The room' was in a sense 'the mind' of Joe Cino and we brought our plays, our 'treasures,' onto the stage of the Cino for his sanction. If Joe somehow thrust his beam of light onto you— actor, director or playwright, or threw magic glitter dust onto you, you somehow had the illusion that you were divine, an apostle to the Saint."[18]

From Joe Cino's perspective, the space had its own needs and powers, with its most constant need being productions. Even if no customers came to a show, Cino demanded that performers "do it for the room."[19] Actress Helen Hanft tells of an incident in which three people (a mother, her prepubescent son, and a drunken sailor) were the only people in the audience. The sailor fell asleep at his table while the mother and son, offended by the material, soon left. Cino refused to cancel the production, demanding that the performance continue for the sleeping sailor. And for the room. Heide, Wilson, and others speak of times when no one at all showed for the performance, particularly for the late-night performance on weekends; even in those instances, Cino demanded that actors perform for the room. Often those were the performances remembered by the actors—the solitude seemed to enhance the magic they created. Actor and novelist Richard Smithies recalls performing in David Starkweather's *You May Go Home Again:*

> [W]e reached the third show on Saturday night (at one o'clock a.m.) with a house of two, the family and friends having long ago petered out.

Someone—I trust it was not me—suggested that we can the performance and go home. "No," said Cino in a tone that was soft, but admitted of absolutely no opposition, "you're going to do it, and it's going to be great." We did it, and it was. . . . The play was clean, it was crisp, it was moving in exactly the way the author had meant it to be. Those thirty-five minutes of art-for-art's sake are my most vivid memory of the Caffe Cino.[20]

If the room had its needs, it also had its power. After a particularly bad day, Helen Hanft went into the Caffe, where Cino comforted her, concluding with "[w]hile you are in here, nothing can hurt you."[21] As Hanft said on the opening night of the exhibit of Cino material at Lincoln Center, "There was magic in that room."[22] Other Cino veterans frequently echo Hanft's sentiments.

Shortly after his arrival in New York, Johnny Dodd became one of the most influential figures in the development of the Cino. According to his close friend and roommate for several years, *Voice* critic Michael Smith, Dodd was born in New Orleans in June 1941. He told Smith that when he was three or four years old, his father, a jazz trumpet player, and his mother, a stripper, separated. A child of Irish immigrants to Canada, Dodd's mother took the young boy to Canada, where she remarried. Unhappy with his stepfather's discipline, Dodd escaped by coming to the United States when he was thirteen or fourteen and spent a year in Cleveland, a year at a boarding school in Mississippi, and a year with his father and stepmother in Terre Haute, Indiana. Difficulties soon arose with his father, so that Dodd was forced to move. According to Jimmy McDonough, the father threw Dodd out of his home because of the younger man's affair with a priest.[23] The situation was, however, probably more complex, since Dodd told Smith that he had been forced out of his father's home in part because of the father's jealousy over the son's close relationship with his stepmother. After leaving his father's home, Dodd settled in Indianapolis, where he put himself through high school.

Finally in 1959 Dodd moved to New York with actor Dean Selmier. Soon afterward, walking down Cornelia Street, he met Cino. Tillie Gross has reported that, within two days of this meeting, Dodd was assisting with lights, which at that time consisted only of a rheostat to adjust the brightness.[24] It was probably not until 1961, however, that Dodd became a regular lighting designer for the Caffe. Over the years, Dodd and electrical wizard and lighting designer Jonathan Torrey added more and more equipment, often by persuading Cino to purchase a fixture or two when the funds were available; at other times fixtures would appear mysteriously, probably through less than legitimate means. By 1968 the Caffe's lighting system had become quite sophisticated, surpassing that of many other off-off-Broadway venues. Whereas the Cino had thirty lamps and eight dimmers, La Mama had only twelve and six of each and Theatre Genesis had sixteen and nine, respectively.[25] A petite, handsome man, Dodd, according to Michael Smith, was

[d]ark of hair and eyes, small, quick, vivid[;] he wove the room together as he maneuvered among the tables with his tray and his little change apron. Then he perched himself at the light board and ran the show. . . .
    It was largely Johnny's personal magnetism that kept me going back to the Cino. . . .[26]

Though he became a lighting designer of some note, forming 14th Street Stage Lighting and designing for many rock concerts and national and international stage productions, Dodd was self-taught, with the exception of a few lessons from Nikola Cernovich: "It was through Joe [Cino] that I learned about lighting, and became interested. There were no lighting designers in the fifties, except perhaps, Jean Rosenthal. But modern dance happened, and they needed lighting for their concerts. Joe knew Nick Cernowitch [*sic*], who worked with Merce Cunningham, and he sent me to Nick to take lessons. . . ."[27] Dodd quickly became one of the central figures at the Cino, though by the midsixties his attention had begun to shift to other venues as well.

Sometime after meeting Cino, Dodd introduced Cino to Kenny Burgess, who had studied art in Indianapolis. According to Jimmy McDonough, Burgess was a favorite of director Andy Milligan; the two often prowled New York City at night in pursuit of anonymous sex.[28] McDonough describes Burgess as "a kind, slightly daffy, almost ethereal soul, the sort who could remain innocent even while sucking off strangers in the crowded caboose of an abandoned truck."[29] Burgess became the dishwasher, waiter, and poster designer, sometimes working as an usher at a theatre on Fifty-seventh Street to help support himself. Because of the legal actions by the City of New York, Burgess intentionally created posters that were difficult to read so that only the in crowd could decipher the complicated designs. In creating the posters, he worked in what has since been called the hippie, or psychedelic, style. The cryptic style successfully confused policemen and other officials, thus helping protect the Cino against summonses for presenting shows without a license. Burgess told

Tillie Gross, "One day a policeman came by as I was placing a poster on the easel in the window. As he took a glance at the inside of the cafe, he commented, 'I always thought this was an art gallery.'"[30] In addition to designing many of the Cino's posters, he was an artist who worked primarily in collages. Though Burgess designed many of the posters for productions, authors frequently had to design their own. Thus, for example, Lanford Wilson created the poster for *This Is the Rill Speaking;* he signed it as Walter Tate, assuming that it would appear more professional for the advertising material to be created by an artist other than the playwright. He chose the name "Tate" because it was his mother's maiden name; he may have taken "Walter" from his stepfather's name.[31] Posters seldom gave the dates of performance, since shows often were extended. As the Cino matured, posters became easier to read, leaving behind the complex, arcane designs of Burgess; yet his collages still graced the Cino's walls.

The Caffe remained on the edge of financial collapse for most of its history, but the first months of its operation were so financially precarious that Cino had to work a day job simply to keep the business open. An exceptionally fast typist, he worked in the office of the American Laundry Machinery Company, at Forty-second Street and Second Avenue; it was a fortunate choice of employers, since American Laundry employee George Moreno introduced Cino to director Robert Dahdah. Later Cino may have worked at the Music Inn on West Fourth Street.[32] Each evening Cino rushed from his employer to Cornelia Street, often stopping at the Bleecker Street Bakery for pastries, at Murray's (across Cornelia Street) for cheese, or at another merchant for other supplies. His schedule was daunting, working days at American Laundry and evenings into the early hours of the morning at the Caffe, with only a few hours of sleep each night. Robert Dahdah recalls an instance in which the exhausted Cino fell over in his chair at American Laundry and went to sleep on the floor; the other employees and his supervisor quietly worked around him, stepping over the sleeping man when necessary but never disturbing him.

Though the Caffe became more self-sufficient in later years, Cino always had to seek ways to cut costs. Gross, for example, notes that Jonathan Torrey bypassed the electrical meter, hooking the Cino's electrical system to a streetlamp so that the Caffe's lights went on with the streetlights.[33] Different sources indicate different points to which Torrey connected the Caffe's electrical system; Delery, for example, believes that Torrey tapped into the electrical supply lines of the New York City subway.[34] As Robert Heide wryly comments,

"Con Edison never knew it was providing some of America's finest writers with free lighting."[35] When electrical meters were scheduled to be read, Charles Loubier or someone else would watch for the employee from Con Ed. As the employee approached, Cino would turn off the Caffe's lights and burn candles in an effort to hide the actual level of his shop's electrical usage.

Despite his relatively modest rent of less than one hundred dollars per month, Cino often had difficulty paying it, relying on friends such as Joseph Davies to assist.[36] According to Loubier, "He never made money. . . . [I]t was through Josie the landlady's tolerance that we were there. She'd come down at night, in her robe and curlers—'Joe, when you gonna pay the fuckin' rent?' And she'd sit down and say, 'Is the play on?'"[37]

Exactly when entertainment became a regular feature at the Caffe is uncertain, but different kinds of entertainment probably were offered almost from the beginning. Very early in the Cino's history, a fortune-teller moved from table to table, reading Tarot cards. At some point Taylor Mead, the "homosexual clown"[38] and star of various Warhol and other underground films, read poetry there, as did Butterfly McQueen, the African American actress famous for her role in *Gone with the Wind.* Some of the performances seem to have been early examples of "happenings," such as that of the professional athlete who dressed in drag and tore a telephone book in half while reciting a monologue. Other performances were improvised. Speaking at the 1985 exhibit at Lincoln Center, Shirley Stoler told of the New Year's Eve on which nothing was scheduled; she and a few other people got together and devised an evening's entertainment, the highlight of which was the auction of a slave girl. When time for the auction came, the heavily veiled slave girl walked onto the stage and was auctioned to the highest bidder in the audience. As the winner waited expectantly, the veils were removed, one by one, to reveal actor Joe Davies.

Though performances offered to the general public during operating hours often shocked audiences, the most ribald and overtly sexual performances were presented after the Caffe had closed for the day and when the only remaining patrons were close friends or select spectators or participants. Cino and others sometimes danced, gradually stripping until they were completely nude. Mona Katz of the Royal Roost occasionally brought over patrons who paid to watch the dances. One of the hotly contested rumors about the Cino concerns the extent to which the dances evolved over time into drug-hazed orgies such as those Robert Patrick describes in *Temple Slave.* Some suggest that at least late in the Cino's history, orgies were rather commonplace. Others acknowledge the open sexuality typical of the sixties but deny that orgies were an integral part of the coffeehouse's social structure; rather, they argue, such stories reflect the actions of their narrators *outside* the Cino—those who speak of the orgies have overlaid a template onto the Cino that reflects their experience in backroom bars and bathhouses rather than in the Cino. One excellent explanation for the seemingly disparate perspectives is offered by Lanford Wilson.

> There was the opera-queen crowd. They would get dressed up once a week and go to the opera. . . . There was a sex crowd that I was certainly in on, that was, you know, horny, rub-a-dub-dub and we would close down the place and be there all night. That was more or less my part of the crowd and it was very, very small. And then the realistic, poetical writer thing that Marshall (Mason), Claris (Nelson), David (Starkweather), and Sam (Shepard) were in on. . . . There was Marshall's crowd from Northwestern.[39]

Thus the group to which a person belonged helped determine his or her perspective on the Cino. Those who were not part of the orgy crowd, for example, may never have known about it.

Among the forms of entertainment offered in the early years of the Cino were art shows, with dishwasher and poster designer Kenny Burgess displaying his work several times. One of the first exhibits was of the work of Esther Travers. Travers, who lived several flights above the Cino, painted in a "musing, metaphysical manner"[40]; she also appeared in one of the few productions that Cino directed for a theatre other than his own, Tennessee Williams's *Auto da Fe,* in March 1963 at La Mama. The first mention of Caffe Cino in the *New York Times* is a listing in the art galleries section on May 24, 1959, for an exhibit of paintings by Mitchell Ehrlich; over the next year, four more announcements of exhibits at the Cino appeared in the *Times:* on June 14, 1959, for watercolors by Rex Williams; on September 20, 1959, for paintings by Walter Reinhardt; on December 6, 1959, for the paintings and drawings of Al Scarpetti; and the last on May 15, 1960, for a second exhibition of paintings by Mitchell Ehrlich. The next mention of the Cino in the *Times* occurs several years later in reference to theatre productions.

In an interview in 1965, Cino credited a group called Chamber Theatre with the first regular performances at the Caffe, though his comments are hardly a ringing endorsement of their success: "We started doing poetry readings and we had the Risa Corsin [*sic*] Chamber Theatre Group. It turned out to be a bunch of flunky poets. What a farce! They were given every second Sunday, a matinee and an evening. This went on maybe for five months."[41] So little was known about the Chamber Theatre that the 1985 exhibit of Cino memorabilia at Lincoln Center by the New York Public Library ignored them and other poetry readings. Yet it can be argued convincingly that Caffe Cino as a theatrical venue and off-off-Broadway as a movement owe more to the history of poetry readings at coffeehouses than to the traditions of Broadway, off Broadway, or the little theatre movement.

The director and organizer of Chamber Theatre was Rissa Korsun, a stocky poet and illustrator who was sometimes called the "Bearded Lady" by Cino regulars because of a physical condition that caused unusually heavy facial hair.[42] The group's name probably has a dual origin: their performances were intended for small, intimate spaces much like that for chamber music; furthermore the name echoes that of the Chamber Theatre in Israel. Their performances may have started as early as February 1959 and were certainly under way by March 1, 1959, when they presented "Stories and Tales from Jewish Life" with Korsun, Allegra Jostad, Elliott Levine, Gordon Matthiews, and Willy Switkes. An undated flyer for a reading of French surrealist poetry probably predates this performance and is the only instance in which the troupe's name is listed as Chamber Players. Performances by the Chamber Theatre consisted of readings of anthologized poems, mime performances, storytelling ("animal stories for sophisticated adults"), and similar events. Though some members of the group were poets, including Korsun, they read only published work by other authors. They performed first at four p.m. and again at eight thirty. Neither a stage nor specialized lighting was available; track lighting used to illuminate the art on the walls was refocused on readers. Despite Cino's disparaging remark about this "bunch of flunky poets," Levine argues that the group was quite popular: "We played to S.R.O. houses, with people waiting on the sidewalk for seats to become vacant. Along with laughter and applause, flashbulbs kept popping, and sales of food and drink were lively."[43]

By the end of Korsun's work at the Cino, New York had begun earnestly to control coffeehouses. Central to the dispute was whether the entertainment offered by the establishments fell under cabaret provisions. Whereas city officials argued vigorously that coffeehouses were subject to cabaret regulations, coffeehouse owners argued equally vigorously that such regulations were applicable only to establishments that sold alcoholic beverages. According to representatives of the businesses, the codes referenced by city officials had originated as part of the effort to control the sudden flood of speakeasies in the 1920s. Because coffeehouses did not serve alcoholic beverages, they were exempt from those codes.[44] Meeting the codes for cabarets would have meant increased costs for coffeehouses; it also would have meant that all their employees and entertainers would be required to submit fingerprints to and to purchase a two-dollar identification card from the police department.

At the heart of the controversy over New York's coffeehouses was the contest between factions within the Village. On one side were those groups that traditionally had made up the population of the area: various ethnic groups, especially Italian, that had settled in the neighborhood years before and older bohemians and artists who had been attracted to the area's permissive society and cheap rent. On the other side were the new groups: the Beats, the hippies, homosexuals, interracial couples, male and female prostitutes, and drug dealers. As these interlopers became increasingly conspicuous, they drew large numbers of tourists to (in the words of Cafe Bizarre's barker) "step right in and see the Bohemians in their natural habitats."[45] By the mid-1960s the influx of tourists was so great that certain areas of the Village, particularly MacDougal Street south of Washington Square, in the block between West Third and Bleecker Streets, had developed a carnivalesque atmosphere, leading many to compare the area to New York's famed Coney Island. As one of the most visible changes in the community, coffeehouses became the point on which much of the struggle over change was focused, resulting in the city's war against them.

Though most complaints about coffeehouses concerned noise and congestion, the unease that resulted from the changing social, political, and cultural climate is evident in the reaction of neighborhood residents. Because many of the new coffeehouse performers such as Bill Cosby and Dick Gregory were African American, they attracted a significant number of African American audience members. This increased number of persons of color visiting and even moving into the neighborhood concerned others in the neighborhood. Edith Evans Asbury notes that "prejudice against Negroes" is one of the factors "fanning the flames of indignation against the coffeehouses."[46] A popular folk musician in the area, Len Chandler, notes that blame for conditions in the MacDougal area was often placed on African Americans: "Of course a lot of hostility still lands on the Negro. . . . But the Negro just coming on the street— he's such an easy symbol to the neighborhood of this new wave of outsiders.

Strike at him, and you strike at a very tangible part of the crowd pressure being put on the neighborhood. Naturally. He's the easiest to pick out!"[47]

Even more distasteful to many residents than the influx of African Americans was the increase in the number of interracial couples attracted by the relaxed, open atmosphere of the coffeehouses: "The apartment-house occupants mostly of Italian origin or descent, not only resent the noise but also dislike the kinds of people they see among the crowds: teen-agers looking for trouble, soldiers and sailors on the prowl, interracial couples, panhandlers, motorcyclists, sex deviates, and exhibitionists of various kinds."[48] The reaction against interracial couples was so great that John Mitchell of the Gaslight coffeehouse claimed to have been threatened by "unspecified" police officers and ordered not to serve interracial couples.[49]

Prejudice against gay men was often as pronounced in the condemnations of the coffeehouses as was prejudice against African Americans. Homer Bigart reported that Mayor Robert Wagner ordered city officials to proceed with a drive against Village coffeehouses because of public complaints that such businesses in the MacDougal area attract "drunks, deviates and assorted strange characters in the predawn hours after bars close."[50] Bernard Weinraub noted weekend traffic in the same area: "For residents of MacDougal Street, the long night's journey into day from Saturday night to Sunday morning represents the nightmare hours—the hours when the narrow street swarms with teen-agers, tourists, tough drunks, deviates and, of course, policemen." He adds that "By 11 p.m. MacDougal is a melange of teen-agers, sailors, soldiers, motorcycles, panhandlers, students, interracial couples, homosexuals and tourists."[51]

Subtle and overt attacks against gay men and lesbians were common, working their way into advertisements and resulting in closure of businesses frequented by "deviates." The computerized dating service Click opened their advertisement with, "We'd like to say a few words about heterosexuality. It's coming back. It never left, really. It just seems that way at times. New York is a rough town for boys and girls together," thus implying that New York was an easy town for boys and boys or girls and girls together.[52] Yet establishments that catered to a predominantly gay clientele regularly were subjected to various forms of official action. A well-known gay bar frequented by Edward Albee and Cino regular Robert Heide, Lenny's Hideaway, on West Tenth Street between Seventh and Eighth Avenues, lost its license when the liquor authority increased its actions against "unsavory" businesses. According to the *Voice*, "The authority's action was based on findings that the premises had become disorderly in that homosexuals were allowed to congregate within. . . ."[53] A rather seedy establishment that affected a bohemian air, Lenny's was operated by a man whom playwright Robert Heide calls a "goon," referring to his presumed Mafia connections. The bar tended to attract patrons from the arts, as well as "neatniks": "in little sweaters with gold chains, looking like they were from the land of Peter Pan."[54]

Like Lenny's, the Fawn Restaurant had to fight for its license after it was closed because it was "frequented by homosexuals."[55] To challenge the Authority's actions against restaurants and bars, three gay men went to various bars, announced that they were homosexuals, and ordered drinks. Though serving gay men and lesbians could result in legal action against businesses, the first three bars served them; the fourth, Julius's, refused. An indication of the tone of the times is the title of the New York Times story that reported the actions of the three men: "3 Deviates Invite Exclusion by Bars."[56]

Despite the efforts of newly formed organizations such as the Mattachine Society and the Daughters of Bilitis, the situation for gay men and lesbians during the 1950s and 1960s was quite difficult. Cold war hysteria had raised concerns that "deviates" posed a security risk, so various federal agencies engaged in aggressive efforts to identify and weed out their influence. Gay men and women were routinely fired from their jobs, denied housing, and arrested for open displays of affection. Even in more progressive areas, bars that openly catered to gay crowds were routinely raided and closed. The birth of the contemporary gay rights movement is typically dated as June 1969, when just such a raid occurred at the Stonewall Inn in Greenwich Village. Thus the situation with Lenny's and the Fawn Restaurant was hardly unique. The issue was considered so sensitive that the Smothers Brothers ran afoul of the censors when they wanted to include the line "Ronald Reagan is a known heterosexual" on their television show. According to Howard Smith, "I heard that the reason the blip-masters gave for its deletion was not that it was libelous but that the average truck driver would misunderstand what it meant."[57]

Whereas prejudice against certain groups contributed significantly to the criticism of coffeehouses, many attacks against the establishments were rooted in financial issues. Some critics objected justifiably to the unscrupulous business practices of those proprietors who advertised low-cost admission but required an additional minimum purchase of overpriced food or beverages. To bars, cabarets, theatres, and other venues that paid wages to performers and met licensing standards, coffeehouses had an unfair competitive edge, since most coffeehouses neither purchased licenses nor paid performers. Furthermore, failure to pay performers gave the establishments at least the appearance of taking advantage of inexperienced and unestablished performers. Rick Allman, the owner of the Cafe Bizarre and president of the newly formed Coffee House Trade Association, a successor to an original coffeehouse trade group called the Greenwich Village Sponsors Association, argued that the controversy was fueled by vested interests in neighboring liquor and entertainment business.[58] Since bars that offered entertainment were required to purchase both an entertainment license and a liquor license, their operating overhead was significantly higher than that of coffeehouses.

In defense of coffeehouses, supporters argued that the relationship between owners and performers was mutually beneficial: proprietors depended on the entertainment to attract customers for their drinks and food, while entertainers received experience and exposure. As early as 1959, a writer for *Commonweal* recognized the symbiotic relationship between performers and proprietors, calling it "all in all, a very fine arrangement."[59] Two years later, after a few coffeehouses began to feature productions of plays, Henry Hewes defended the activity in a similar vein: "Though at first glance this might seem a commercial device that permits the owner to tack on a cover charge with no outlay of money on his part, there is some evidence that the motive is not completely mercenary. If it were, these coffeehouse theatres would quickly degenerate into the sort of tourist traps that presents [*sic*] folk singers, beatnik poets, and other eccentrics for curiosity seekers from out of town."[60] Many coffeehouses, including Caffe Cino, depended on donations from the audience after the show to pay actors; the practice was so common that off-off-Broadway was sometimes called "the pass-the-hat circuit." Most performers valued the experience and exposure far more than any income they gained (the Albee-Wilder-Barr producing team, for example, eventually taking several coffeehouse shows, including some from the Cino, to off Broadway).

Citywide financial considerations sometimes resulted in variable enforcement of regulations regarding coffeehouses. As New York prepared for the World's Fair in 1964, the number of citations seems to have increased, presumably because coffeehouses did not fit into the image that the city wished to project to tourists. Later, Mayor John Lindsay reduced actions against the sites without resolving the underlying issues because the tourists they attracted contributed to the city's income. Perhaps the city's strongest financial consideration in its actions against coffeehouses was the lost revenue from licensing. Until coffeehouses began presenting entertainment, the two primary venues for live entertainment were theatres and cabarets, the latter of which operated under regulations most applicable to the physical facilities and entertainment generally found in coffeehouses. Yet the license for a coffeehouse cost seventy-five dollars, whereas a license for a cabaret cost $150, excluding the fifteen-hundred-dollar alcohol license purchased by cabarets.[61] Furthermore regulations of cabarets involved a great deal more control by the city.

Music critic and scholar Jack Diether proposes what may be the most significant financial factor in the battle against the coffeehouses.

Seen from the real-estate developer's eyes, it [the Village] is purely and simply the most valuable piece of collective real estate in the world. Set in the heart of Manhattan Island, halfway between Wall Street and Times Square, it appears to him a still untapped gold mine, and its "cultural pretensions" simply an obstruction. . . . The coffee-house hassle is simply a small but integral part of the struggle that goes on constantly between those who would like to turn Greenwich Village into a drab but "elite" extension of Riverside Drive and those who would like to keep it an essentially Bohemian and artistic oasis.[62]

In noting that many of the complaints about the coffeehouses came from residents of nearby apartments, Edith Evans Asbury lends credence to Diether's argument, since she notes that the luxury apartment boom that started in the early 1950s had been responsible for displacing many of the artists from the Village so that wealthier tenants could move in. One of the most ambitious proposals for redeveloping the Village came from William Zeckendorf Sr., who proposed a "Disneyesque development." His goal was to lure the city's motion picture and television industry to the area.[63]

After a flurry of summonses against coffeehouse operators early in 1959, the city suffered a setback when magistrate Walter J. Bayer ruled on April 13 that the Epitome, a Bleecker Street coffeehouse, had not violated the law by holding poetry readings; other courts in other instances, however, ruled in favor of the city, thereby establishing unclear, inconsistent judicial precedents. Facing pressure from coffeehouse patrons and limited success in the courts, deputy police commissioner William Ames announced in June 1959 that the department would no longer cite coffeehouses, reading a "non-Beat" poem of his own.

Technically, a beatnik spouting poetry is an entertainer under the law,
But though in violation, to the cops he's just a bore.
He can talk throughout the night if he doesn't incite to riot,
We hope he keeps talking till his audience yells quiet.[64]

Though a coffeehouse offered to let him read his poetry in it, Ames declined:
"It was like he passed it up, man."[65]

The truce between the police department and the coffeehouses was short-lived. Police officials soon were dispensing summonses again, including one on October 4 to the Figaro, which presented classical music concerts. During a Schubert trio, two policemen entered, stopped the performance, and issued a citation. Not to be deprived of his concert, a patron invited the performers and patrons to his apartment, where they finished the concert.

It is unclear whether the Cino continued performances in 1959 after Korsun left and as the coffeehouse war was brewing. By early 1960 the Caffe had begun hosting poetry readings by figures such as George Economou, David Antin, and Robert Kelly. Economou and others of the group, including Antin, who lived across the street, were regular patrons of Caffe Cino. Several of them had been involved with the *Chelsea Review* but dissociated themselves from it because of the editors' focus on prose. Gathered at the Cino one evening, a group that included Economou (then a graduate student at Columbia) and husband-wife team Robert and Joan Kelly decided to start their own journal. In choosing a name for it, they sought to reflect their interest in the roots of the European poetry that they admired, thus choosing *Trobar,* a word from the old Provençal literally meaning "to find." The root for words such as *troubadour, trobar* became associated with poetry during the Middle Ages, perhaps because the troubadour found words to set to music. The journal was in print from 1960 through 1964, eventually expanding to include the Trobar Press, which published such significant collections of poetry as Rochelle Owens's *Not Be Essence That Cannot Be,* Paul Blackburn's *The Nets,* Jerome Rothenberg's *The Seven Hells of the Jigoku Zoshi,* and Louis Zukovsky's *I's Pronounced "Eyes."*

With Cino's support the group began a series of poetry readings sponsored by the *Trobar* and held every Tuesday at the Cino. The first of these readings to be advertised in the "What's On" section of the *Village Voice* took place on Tuesday, March 23, 1960, at nine thirty, with Economou and Armand Schwerner; the last advertised reading by the group was held on May 17, 1960, with Economou and Robert Kelly. Typically one or two poets read from her or his work each week, with poets including, in addition to those persons already mentioned as readers, Jerome Rothenberg, Paul Blackburn, Rochelle Owens, and Clayton Eshleman. The highlight of the series was an evening of medieval poetry and jazz. Blackburn read his troubadour translations, while Schwerner played the clarinet, Jimmy Weeks played the saxophone, and a now unknown person played the bass. The readings by the *Trobar* poets were short-lived because Cino's attention increasingly was focused on the dramatic performances that, by May 1960, occurred each weekend. Furthermore the poetry scene was shifting quickly from the West Village to the East Village.

Determining when performances of plays began at the Caffe is impossible, though it is clear that Cino had not intended to start a theater.

> My idea . . . was always to start with a beautiful, intimate warm, non-commercial, friendly atmosphere where people could come and not feel pressured or harassed. I also thought anything could happen. I knew a lot of painters, so my thought immediately was, I'll hang their work. I was thinking of a cafe with poetry readings, with lectures, maybe with dance concerts. The one thing I never thought of was fully staged productions of plays. I thought of doing readings, but I never thought any of the technical things would be important.[66]

In his essay on Joe Cino, Douglas Gordy perpetuates an incorrect story about the origins of the Caffe's theatrical productions. The story appeared early in the study of the Caffe and has been repeated so frequently that it has been accepted as truth: "Consensus has it that the first theatrical offerings were initiated by an acting student named Phoebe Mooney; she and other thespians would try out monologues and short scenes before performing them for their classes."[67] Mooney, however, does not accept credit for starting the dramatic performances, since her first visit to the Cino was to audition for scenes directed by Andy Milligan. With plans to tour the production, the group performed at one or two venues before appearing at the Cino.

Though Mooney may not have started theatrical productions at the Cino, she was an important early performer in the Caffe's stagings, having appeared in scenes from Shakespeare and Oscar Wilde. Her most significant work there was an adaptation of *Alice in Wonderland* in January 1962, for which she was adaptor, director, costumer, and, reluctantly, performer. The production originated from an experience with a friend of hers who was enrolled in acting classes and who encouraged Mooney to direct a play in which he could appear. She chose *Alice* because Lewis Carroll's work had just entered the public domain and thus could be used without concern about royalties or copyright infringement. Although others in the off-off-Broadway movement routinely ignored copyright laws, Mooney was concerned about the issue: "If you are a writer, you just don't want to do that to another writer."[68] After adapting *Alice*, Mooney began rehearsals with her friend and a few others; soon, however, the friend withdrew from the production, so Mooney had to find a replacement for him. Then, just days before opening, the woman playing Alice also withdrew. Having already committed to Cino to present the work, Mooney had no choice but to take over the role of Alice so that the work could open as scheduled.

In an interview with Cino in 1965 (the most extensive ever published), he set forth the steps by which the Caffe's production schedule developed. First were the performances by Korsun's group:

> What came right after that was Sunday night readings at a long pine table. The first reading we had was Jean-Paul Sartre's *No Exit*. They did it with three chairs and three scripts. The room was packed, but I didn't even think of doing it again. I thought there were people who didn't want to see this, and I didn't want to disturb the rhythm of the room. But that was a Sunday reading, and soon after that we added Monday. It was one performance a night, and before long we added Tuesday, and so on. The hardest thing was to avoid having performances on the weekend. It took almost two years to get from those Sunday readings to a full week. It was always something different every week. They went into staging right away.[69]

In this discussion Cino suggests a progressive development of the performance schedule, beginning with one performance on Sunday evening, then additional performances on subsequent days of the week, an increase in the number of performances each day to two or three, and ultimately the staggering sixteen performances per week (two every day with one more on weekend nights). In the broadest sense, the production schedule did develop in such a way, though not in quite so smooth a progression as is often implied. Comments by Cino and others point to his intent to offer a variety of different informative or entertainment events: lectures, poetry readings, play readings, and art displays, with something different every night of the week. Now we can piece together a schedule of only those events for which some record remains, probably a fairly limited list. The following outlines the development of the performance schedule:

- poetry readings, beginning probably in February 1959, at four p.m. and eight thirty, Sunday;
- play readings, possibly beginning in 1959 (by Saturday, February 7, if the dates offered by the New York Public Library are correct);
- release of the first press notice of a theatrical production of an unknown play that took place on or around February 4, 1960;
- first advertisement in the "What's On" section of the *Village Voice* on February 17 for a play reading offered on Sunday, February 21, 1960, at seven thirty, with dramatic activity becoming a fixture on Sundays (though not always, since the *Village Voice* for March 2, 1960, advertised "Poetry Reading of Light Verse" for the following Sunday);
- first review (Robert Dahdah's version of *No Exit*), December 15, 1960;
- addition of Monday to schedule for play readings (also at seven thirty) by March 21, 1960;
- series of poetry readings sponsored by *Trobar* on Tuesday at nine thirty, beginning by March 29, 1960 (anecdotal evidence suggesting that other such activity may have occurred on Thursday nights as well);
- announcement of *And the Dead Cry Lonely,* which was billed as an original play and performed on March 30, 1960, the first original play, however, typically being considered *Flyspray,* performed a few months later;
- Monday night play reading moved to nine p.m., April 25, 1960, for Edna St. Vincent Millay's *Aria di Capo;*
- last advertisement for a poetry reading, April 11, 1960 (held on April 17);
- extension of play productions to Saturday at nine thirty on June 18, 1960;
- regular schedule of performances on Saturday, Sunday, and Monday at nine thirty by July 1960;
- new "Cafe Drama" list with limited details in the *Village Voice* beginning on September 22, 1960;
- shows running Saturday to Tuesday by October 1960;
- first review of an original play (Story Talbot's *Herrengasse*), February 2, 1961;
- shows opening on Sunday and running through Saturday, by November 1961;
- shows given sixteen performances weekly by July 1962 (probably earlier), with a schedule that would remain for some time: two performances nightly at nine and eleven, with additional late-night performances Friday and Saturday (originally at twelve thirty a.m., subsequently at one a.m.).

Though the Cino initially may have offered only readings of plays, productions with blocking, costumes, and sets quickly became standard; when the transition occurred remains unclear. Matt Baylor recalls his performance with Peter Ratray in scenes from *Tea and Sympathy* in 1959 or 1960 as being the first staged production. Jeremy Johnson recalls performing in 1959 in *Separate Tables* in what he believes to be the first theatrical production at the Cino. He does not, however, recall a time in which plays were read rather than staged. Johnson performed at the Cino under the name "Larry Johnson" but began using "Jeremy Johnson" when he became a member of Actors' Equity Association, since another Larry Johnson was already a member of Equity.

As for the reading of *No Exit* that Cino describes as the first play reading, we no longer know when it took place, nor can we be sure whether any advertised production was the event to which Cino alludes. According to the announcements in the *Voice, No Exit* ran at least three times: in a reading on February 28, 1960, in a production that ran December 10–13, 1960, and in a production directed by Joe Cino that ran May 5–11, 1963. A February 2, 1961, review notes that Talbot's *Herrengasse* "marked the 50th straight week of one-act performances at the Caffe Cino," which would place the first production around February 28, 1960 (the date of the advertised reading of *No Exit*).[70] Yet readings (and perhaps productions) occurred prior to that, including scenes from Giraudoux's *The Madwoman of Chaillot* and Williams's *This Property Is Condemned,* both advertised in the *Village Voice* on February 17, 1960. The program for the New York Public Library notes the following productions before any of those listed in the *Voice:*

> Truman Capote's *A Christmas Memory,* February 7, 1959;
> Oscar Wilde's *The Importance of Being Earnest,* February 7, 1959;
> Owen G. Arno's *The Street of Good Friends,* 1959; and
> Lady Gregory's *Hyacinth Halvey,* 1959.

Poland and Mailman also list productions that occurred in 1959, though they do not give specific dates for them:

> Oscar Wilde's *The Importance of Being Earnest;*
> Owen G. Arno's *The Street of Good Friends;* and
> Lady Gregory's *Hyacinth Halvey.*

The reliability of these two sources on the dates of shows is open to question. It is particularly problematic that neither source notes the run of *Street of Good Friends* in March 1960 or of *Hyacinth Halvey* in October 1960, thus at least raising the possibility that those productions were mistakenly attributed to the earlier year.

Though several directors (Robert Dahdah, Richard Nesbitt, and Andy Milligan) worked frequently at the Cino during this period, the plays and production styles vary widely, from classics by Shakespeare (*As You Like It* in 1963) to recent Broadway hits such as Ketti Frings's 1958 Pulitzer-winning adaptation of *Look Homeward Angel* (June 1960). A great many of the productions were recent European hits, particularly those of the absurdist and other avant-garde movements: Jean-Paul Sartre's *No Exit* (February 1960), Giraudoux's *Madwoman of Chaillot* (February 1960), and Pirandello's *The Man with a Flower in His Mouth* (April 1961). Several of the European plays were written by gay men, for example, Andre Gide's *Bathsheba* (August 1961) and Jean Genet's *Deathwatch* (October 1961). Other plays were by American gay men, such as William Inge's *Bobolink for Her Spirit* (November 1960). Without a question, however, the most frequently performed playwright of the period was Tennessee Williams, whose work is represented at least ten times and appeared more frequently than can now be documented.

While the plays themselves varied widely, presentation also varied greatly, from highly experimental to quite realistic; works often foregrounded issues of difference, particularly relating to sexuality. Many of the central figures of the Caffe's history were gay, and the coffeehouse was the first venue to regularly feature work by and about gay men. Many productions foregrounded issues of sexuality even when the original work was not specifically a "gay" play. Exemplifying this style is the work of Andy Milligan, often considered one of the key directors of this period; according to Robert Patrick, Milligan's "*Deathwatch* was done near-nude, *The Maids* near-porno."[71]

Before creating such exploitation and B-grade horror movies as *The Ghastly Ones* (1968) and *The Rats Are Coming! The Werewolves Are Here!* (1972), Milligan directed frequently at both Caffe Cino and Cafe La Mama. From all accounts, his style was distinctive. Playwright Waldo Kang Pagune described a Milligan production that featured Phoebe Mooney: "I have a surrealistic memory of four characters standing against the walls, speaking loud to each other in a bare stage which was created by vacating two coffee tables. There were several young customers occupying three tables near the door and when the show was over the house was empty except for me and the cast."[72]

Not surprising, given his interest in sadomasochism, Milligan often chose works and interpretations that foregrounded a violent homoeroticism. Kenny

Burgess described him as "a fierce director" who "went for the throat"; his work would seem rather placid but would suddenly build to a startling pitch "like a cobra striking out." Burgess continues, "He knows how to direct hysteria."[73] Johnny Dodd called Milligan's version of *Deathwatch* "savage"; it was "an erotic play. E-rot-ic."[74] Though the actors were not gay, Milligan worked with them to create a strong homoerotic subtext. Dodd continues, "[Y]et the shit Andy made them *do*—actually touching each other. And violent. That, coupled with this sensual Genet language was very exciting."[75] According to Dodd, Milligan became so engrossed in the scenes of violence that he seemed to have an orgasm: "The heavy breathing, the glazed-over eyes, the mouthing of the words. It was scary."[76]

As he moved his attention from the stage to the screen, Milligan drew on the talent he had used at the Cino and La Mama. His first film of an original script, *Vapors* (1965), was set in a gay bathhouse and featured a script by Cino actress "Lady" Hope Stansbury; performers included Robert Dahdah, Haal Borske, and Matt Baylor. In subsequent films he would again use Borske, Baylor, and Stansbury, along with such Cino regulars as Kenny Burgess, Josef Bush, Maggie Rogers, Jacque Lynn Colton, John Borske, and Neil Flanagan.

The early productions at the Cino often ran afoul of publishers or agents, since Cino never obtained permission to perform works and never paid royalties. Confrontations with authors and their representatives most often were handled in a typical Cino style: by evading the issue, often by pretending ignorance. When a letter arrived from an agent or publisher, it was often "lost" until the end of the last performance on closing night, when it suddenly and mysteriously reappeared to be opened and read. The announcement was then made that the production would have to close to avoid legal action. When a threatening telephone call came from an agent, Cino used whatever evasions he could to sidestep problems; at times he would feign ignorance, perhaps by pretending to be the Caffe's dishwasher. Statements such as "How do I know anything? I'm just the little, fat Italian dishwasher" served him well in such situations.[77]

One of the best-known such events involved Harold Pinter's 1959 radio play *A Slight Ache,* which appeared at Caffe Cino in December 1962, well before its official New York debut. At the 1985 exhibit of Cino material at Lincoln Center and several times elsewhere, Robert Dahdah told the story of the interaction between Cino and Pinter's agent. When Cino received an irate call from the agent, he pleaded ignorance about everything relating to the production and the actors: "I don't know anything about it; they just showed up." The frustrated agent bellowed, "You mean to tell me that a fully rehearsed, fully costumed, fully lit Pinter production just happened to walk down Cornelia Street, just happened to turn into your Caffe, and just happened to step onto your stage and begin performing?"[78] Despite the agent's incredulity, his question is remarkably close to the truth. As Dahdah recalls, Ira Zuckerman assembled the cast and rehearsed the show without having a commitment for a performance space, making arrangements with Joe Cino for the performance very shortly before its opening. Thus the fully rehearsed, costumed, and lit show may not have just happened to walk into the Cino, but it did so on the spur of the moment and with little prior planning.

Many of the works presented during the first years were adaptations of short stories or novels (Neil Flanagan's version of Voltaire's *Candide*) or abbreviated versions of full-length plays (Robert Dahdah's adaptation of Abraham Shiffrin's *Angel in the Pawnshop*). Among the figures who presented such works was Alan Lysander James, who from 1962 to 1966 adapted and directed a series of productions based on the life and works of Oscar Wilde. James's productions were noted as much for their performers as for anything else: "A sweet older man, Allan [*sic*] James, with a cast of exquisite pretty boys, then mounted *The World of Oscar Wilde* and *Oscar Revisited,* romantic readings of the great martyr's love poems and letters."[79]

One of the major factors in the diversity of work at the Caffe was Cino's idiosyncratic method of play selection. Often, in fact, Cino scheduled a production date before a script had been completed. As the Caffe was flooded with scripts when playwrights learned of it as a venue for producing new plays, Joe Cino developed neither a system for handling the incoming scripts nor a means of selecting shows for the calendar. According to Neil Flanagan, who frequently performed at the Cino, "No judgement was made on these scripts, often a play produced was done because Joe liked the person's face. He had a way of reading people, and usually knew what you needed and wanted. It is in that way, he would agree to give you a date [for the performance of a play]."[80] Similarly, Michael Smith noted that Cino always professed to "choose the people, not the plays."[81] According to John Guare, his first production was scheduled only after Cino got the playwright's birthdate from his driver's license and consulted an astrological chart; Guare concludes, "I don't know what would have happened to me if I had been a Gemini."[82] Furthermore Cino exerted little artistic control over the productions; he provided space, lighting, sometimes free food, and that was about all. Everything else was left to each director or playwright.

As one of the first performers at Caffe Cino, Jeremy (or Larry) Johnson appeared in a variety of works, ranging from *Moon for the Misbegotten* to the Caffe's first original piece, *Flyspray.* Johnson graduated from Boston's Leland Powers School of Theatre in 1955. He worked briefly as a disk jockey in Crowley, Louisiana, and served in the military, where he participated in the Seventh U.S. Army Symphony Orchestra and Soldier Shows Company from August 1956 to August 1958. Afterward he moved to East Fourteenth Street, where he met Cino at poetry readings. Their first meeting was on the rooftop of an apartment building where a friend of his—and most likely Cino himself—lived. Johnson's first play at the Cino was *Separate Tables,* probably in 1959; he went on to appear in a variety of productions, including

- a two-man comedy show with Joe Mitchell (to give each man equal billing, the poster in one window of the Cino advertised "An Evening of Comedy with Joe Mitchell Assisted by Larry Johnson," while in the window on the other side, a poster advertised "An Evening of Comedy with Larry Johnson Assisted by Joe Mitchell");
- a production of *A Moon for the Misbegotten* with Neil Flanagan, directed by Richard Nesbitt for his thesis production in the graduate program at Hunter College; and
- two versions of Jean Anouilh's *Antigone.*

One of Johnson's most significant productions was George S. Kaufman's *If Men Played Cards as Women Do,* for which he was both the director and a performer. Other members of the cast included Vic Grecco, Fred Willard, and Dean Selmier. Willard appeared in other Cino productions, including Tennessee Williams's *Mooney's Kid Don't Cry* in 1961. Selmier established a reputation for eccentric behavior, including his assertion that he used acting as a cover for a far more dangerous career.

According to Jimmy McDonough, Selmier was an abrasive actor who often spoke of his ties to the underworld: "[H]e wrote a novel about his alleged exploits as a hit man, *Blow Away.* Recalled Dodd with a laugh, 'If you went somewhere with him you had to do these espionage things. Take a taxi up to 23rd Street, jump in another.' . . . Selmier would later legally change his name to Quasimodo due to a lifelong fascination with the hunchback."[83] Cowritten with Mark Kram, *Blow Away: A Killer's Story* (1979) is supposedly Selmier's autobiography, not a novel. He claims his disguise as an actor hid his real career as a hit man for the U.S. government. While such general information in the book as production dates of Selmier's movies matches information that can be verified, details about the murders are scanty and poorly documented. At least one reviewer accepts the truthfulness of the book, noting that the actor "gives us a self-portrait."[84] A second reviewer, Gregor A. Preston, is a bit more skeptical: "*[Blow Away]* has all the ingredients of a third-rate spy thriller. Without more verifiable details, Selmier's story cannot be taken at face value."[85]

In his work Selmier speaks of his brief period in the military during which he had been sentenced to fourteen years imprisonment for assaulting an officer. Sometime in 1960 he received a visit from a nondescript man who resembled an insurance agent: "The kind of guy who sits across the coffee table from you with the actuarial tables in his brain. . . ."[86] The man offered him a chance at freedom but a chance that entailed working for him in "whatever the assignments are,"[87] including murder. That day Selmier walked out of the military prison and boarded a Greyhound bus headed to New York, the blemishes from his military record officially having been expunged by his new employers and a new career as an actor having been constructed. *Blow Away* relates a series of murders committed by Selmier in which he used his filming or performance schedule as a cover for his movements around the world. Though *Blow Away* dates his arrival in New York during 1960, other evidence indicates that he may have been there in 1959.

Larry Johnson's most important contribution to the history of the Cino came in 1960, when he introduced Joe Cino to a young, aspiring playwright named James Howard. Howard had written a play, *Flyspray,* which he wanted to stage. Evidence suggests that the work may have been staged twice, with the first production featuring Johnson as The Naif, Howard as The Salesman, and Joe Davies as The Romantic, under the direction of Howard. When the play was first produced is unclear, though one production probably occurred sometime during the summer of 1960. The Billy Rose Theatre Collection holds a poster for *Flyspray* that lists the director as Earl Sennett and the performers as James Howard, Al Greenfield, and Joe Davies. If the work was produced twice, the poster appears to have been used for the second production. The work was part of a trilogy along with *Mound* and a now forgotten play, though it is unknown whether the other two works ever were performed. The poster suggests that they might have been; it refers to the production as "an original plays [*sic*] by James Howard," the word *an* having been blacked out.

According to Johnson, Howard satirized capitalism and military proliferation: "The play is set in a desolate bombed out area of the world; James
Howard played a man who sold fly spray after the devastation. . . . He gave a
pep talk . . . encouraging them to buy this fly spray and everything would be
all right."[88] The production ended with the detonation of an atomic bomb
so realistic that passersby sometimes would file a report of an explosion with
the police. After *Flyspray*'s run at the Cino, it played at different socialist events
and radical rallies around New York City. Despite the play's success, however,
Howard left New York to enter graduate school.

While the Cino became increasingly involved in theatrical productions, the
enforcement of ordinances against coffeehouses and unlicensed cabarets escalated. In June 1960 attempts by the fire department to close two popular
sites, the Gaslight and the Bizarre, resulted in demonstrations in favor of the
two businesses. When the fire department ordered John Mitchell to close the
Gaslight on June 10, he erected signs reading "New York Is a Summer Fire
Festival" and "Fire Department–Police State, Padlock Poetry."[89] Later in the
day, the department's chief deputy inspector, Thomas Hartnett, began tear-
ing down the signs. When Mitchell intervened, he was arrested and charged
with assault.

As the year progressed, the tempo of legal action increased; city officials
issued summonses freely to owners, to serving staff, and to cashiers. In the fall,
the Figaro was cited again for illegally presenting concerts, even though its
earlier citation had been dismissed for lack of evidence. Jack Diether describes
the outcome of the second legal action: "Judge Bayer's decision, interestingly
enough to musical people, was not based on the arguments concerning the
intent and general scope of the law, but purely on esthetic considerations.
Serious chamber music, he declared, could not be classified as 'entertainment'
under the meaning of the law. Thus, high musical art had laid steam-roller
bureaucracy low. Orpheus had tamed the furies again."[90] The Figaro, then,
was allowed to proceed with its concerts. By September city officials targeted
coffeehouses for legal action every night of the week; also in September, fourteen Village enterprises formed the Coffee House Trade Association, electing
David Gordon of Phase 2 as its president. The association sought legitimacy
and legal rights for its members, though with little success.

By the end of 1960, off-off-Broadway and cafe theatres were facing a dual
legal threat, on one side from the City of New York and on the other from
Actors' Equity Association. In a move that the *New York Times* compared to

similar legal actions in 1954 against Circle in the Square, the fire department in October again closed a popular coffeehouse, Take 3, at which *Stewed Prunes,* one of the most successful off-off-Broadway shows, had originated and was still playing. According to Michael Feingold, *Stewed Prunes* also faced action from Actors' Equity, making the three-person satirical revue one of the first off-off-Broadway productions to attract the attention of the union. When it ruled that its members could not appear in productions unless paid a minimal weekly rate of forty-five dollars, Equity posed a challenge to the besieged coffeehouse that seemed even more threatening than the legal harassment by governmental agencies. Since few of the sites actually paid a wage of any sort, actors depended on donations from the audience for the small sums they earned. Actors worked for an average of sixteen or seventeen dollars each week, less than one-half of union scale.

Coffeehouses offered a twofold argument against Equity's actions: none of the cafe theatres was sufficiently profitable to pay union scale and the establishments provided a service to their performers by giving undiscovered, inexperienced talent venues in which to gain experience and exposure. The union, however, was unrelenting, threatening to punish any union members who appeared for less than scale. Because of this pressure, actors often appeared under assumed names: Joseph Davies sometimes played at the Cino under the name J. O. Davis; during the run of Doric Wilson's *And He Made a Her,* Alan Zamp, the only Union member of the cast, had to change his name four times to evade Equity.[91]

Whether Caffe Cino was subject to the same degree of legal action that other, similar establishments suffered is unclear; Michael Feingold,[92] Douglas Gordy,[93] and others allege that Joe Cino received protection because of his family's supposed Mafia associations. Evidence does suggest that Cino's family had Mafia connections. Yet it is entirely unclear that either Joe Cino or his Caffe ever benefited from those connections. The Caffe may or may not have faced fewer legal actions than other establishments, but it was certainly not immune to such actions: its name appears occasionally in news accounts of police action, and Diether notes that "the owner has received four summonses, twice as many as the Figaro."[94] According to Johnny Dodd, legal action was not infrequent: "We got fines for not paying fines. There was once or twice when we received a deluge of summonses, but Joe, and most of the others, were not around during the day or not up early enough to go down to the department to take care of them. Everyone had been up most of the night or had day jobs. Nor was there anyone that had the personality to cope with such matters. Ellen [Stewart of Cafe La Mama] faced it. Joe couldn't."[95] Furthermore, several factors made the Cino a less conspicuous target for official action: its location in a quiet area, its avoidance of the abusive business practices of some locations, and its appeal to neighborhood residents rather than tourists. Cino took precautions to avoid policemen and inspectors by operating only after regular business hours; at its peak of success, the Caffe was open from five p.m. to five a.m. He encouraged rehearsals outside the Cino so that no one would be there during regular office hours, when city officials were most likely to be on the job. And Cino was not above a little deception to avoid legal complications.

Amidst these troubles with Equity and the city, the Cino received its first recognition in print during the winter of 1960 when Robert Dahdah's production of *No Exit* was reviewed by the *Village Voice*. Few artists are as important to the history of the Caffe or were as influential in its development as Dahdah, who acted in, directed, or wrote dozens of works there. His production of *No Exit* reflects the difficulties characteristic of working at the Caffe. On the night that reviewer Seymour Krim was in the audience, the lead actor had left so suddenly that the replacement, Bob Castagan, had not had time to learn his lines. Thus he appeared with script in hand. Krim gave the production a good review, though he was less thrilled with Sartre's work than with Dahdah's: "P.S. In all frankness, I don't think Sartre's brain can compensate for his lack of humor and juiceless tone as far as a U.S. audience goes."[96] Nor was Krim (who some months previously had written a passionate defense of homosexuality) overly put off by what later would be referred to as the "homosocial orientation" of the Caffe: "The Cafe [*sic*] Cino is a big, roomy, informal coffee house on Cornelia Street. It has a precious air—or had the night I was there—with incense burning and the faggots camping (a big boy in glasses offered his hand to be kissed by a smaller guy wearing a single earring and chewing a toothpick yet); but in spite of all the froufrou, director Robert Dahdah had staged a responsible version of Sartre's *No Exit*."[97] In a conclusion that helps distance him from the "faggots camping," Krim says of the performances of Moletta Reagan and Elizabeth Shanklin, "[T]he girls made the evening worthwhile for this bachelor."[98]

The numerous works that Dahdah directed for the Cino include most of the one-acts by Tennessee Williams and Lady Gregory, though production information for most has been lost. One of his most frequent performers was character actress Mary Boylan, his partner of many years until her death on February 21, 1984. A gifted comedic actress who bore a striking resemblance to Eleanor Roosevelt, Boylan is best known for her appearance in Tom Eyen's *Women Behind Bars* and in the film of Tennessee Williams's *The Night of the Iguana* as Miss Peebles. Born in Plattsburgh, New York, and educated at Mount Holyoke College, with theatre training at the Herbert Berghof Studio, the New School, and the American Academy of Dramatic Arts, she did so much work off-off-Broadway that she was sometimes called the "Mother Superior of the Underground."[99]

While Dahdah won the Caffe its first press attention, the first review of an original Cino play, Story Talbot's *Herrengasse,* appeared two months after that for *No Exit. Voice* critic Sandra Schmidt described the conventions Talbot used in the play: "If you are a playwright and you want to say a lot of weighty things without seeming ponderous you say them with a fairy tale. Preferably you use a couple of prostitutes and/or artists, a 'character' or so, and a convertible villain. A little one-to-one symbolism never hurts."[100] She concludes, however, that the play is not so trite as her description makes it appear. Immediately after its run at the Cino, *Herrengasse* moved to the Cinderella Club for a long run, making it one of the first Cino plays to transfer to another theatre.

By the spring of 1961, off-off-Broadway had become sufficiently established to gain the attention of a major national journal; *Theatre Arts* ran an article entitled "Fresh Grounds for Theatre," by Henry Hewes. According to Hewes, the 1960–61 season presented a third category to New York's theatre, which already included Broadway and off-Broadway venues: "It is something called coffeehouse theatre, and at the moment this theatrical brush fire is contained within a few Greenwich Village blocks. There, in way-out *esprèsso* palaces where ghoulish-looking girls serve exotically spiced coffee at exotically spiced prices, owners with nothing to lose are giving house room to productions by unproven writers and performers."[101] Hewes credits the start of the movement to David Gordon's Phase 2, a coffeehouse started for the purpose of presenting low-cost productions of dramatic and review material. Probably, however, theatrical performances at the Cino predate those offered at Phase 2; furthermore, the Cino was almost certainly the first location to offer regularly scheduled productions of new plays by unknown writers. At the time of Hewes's article, most venues offered revues or stand-up comics. Opening with a full-page photograph of Fred Willard at the Cino in *Mooney's Kid Don't Cry,* Hewes's article gave the Cino its first national exposure.

Though several playwrights had already presented original work at the Cino when Doric Wilson arrived, the young redhead from a small wheat town in Washington became the Caffe's first resident playwright. He had moved to New York in 1959 to study set and costume design, bringing with him the script of his one-act play written while he was a student at the University of Washington. A friend, Regina Oliver, took him to meet Joe Cino.

> Joe was busy behind the counter. He smiled, asked me my birth sign, again smiled (with marked patience) when I answered Pisces, made an incomprehensible comment to someone (Charles Loubier) in an impossible language (Simuloto), gave me a cup of cappuccino (my first), and a performance date, and politely refused to read my offered script.
>
> Regina moved me to a table. I asked her where the stage was, she pointed to an eight foot by eight foot space of open floor. An aria from *Tosca* ended on the juke box, a Greek song began.[102]

Charles Loubier remembers the event slightly differently:

> A well-dressed young man appeared at the front door (of the Cino one day). He walked briskly over to the table (where I was sitting). He was really quite young, very red-haired and (his eyes) literally twinkled. "Hello," he said in a clipped accent, "my name is Doric Wilson and this is what I do." He plopped a big black-covered manuscript down in front of me. "I do other things, but this is what I'd like to do here."[103]

The play was *And He Made a Her.*

As Wilson's description of his first introduction to the Cino notes, the "stage" consisted of a small area among the tables and could be moved, thus permitting the playing area to be in the round or thrust, as desired for each production. Later, Andy Milligan added the first raised stage. Descriptions of the size of the playing area vary, though twenty-seven to sixty-four square feet is a reasonable approximation. If Milligan's platform was the same used when Lanford Wilson arrived, it was made of wooden crates such as those in which soft drinks or milk were shipped. The raised stage could be placed in any part of the room, but the loose crates made for a somewhat unstable floor for the playing area until Lanford Wilson attached them to each other for one of his productions.

In the bare stage area used when Doric Wilson arrived, Paxton Whitehead directed *And He Made a Her,* which opened on March 18, 1961. Whitehead quickly cast the male roles from Cino regulars, but he had difficulty casting the role of Eve, finally settling on Jane Lowry. Lowry became one of Joe Cino's most beloved actresses. Wilson describes opening night: "Marshall Mason remembers the date of my first opening night—I don't. I remember Mona's Royal Roost. Mostly I remember Lowry's entrance as Eve—a vision sheathed in apple green, sensually, elegantly toc toc tocing [*sic*] her way (in three inch heels) from the Cino's front door, through the tables, and out into Johnny Dodd's let-there-be-light to the waiting, less-than-convinced Adam of Larry Neil Clayton."[104] An adaptation of the biblical story of Adam and Even, the production opened with Whitehead, who played the angel Silvadorf, introducing the setting as "a part of paradise commonly called the garden district. The time is after Adam's usual afternoon nap."[105] A petulant Adam complains because God has taken one of his ribs during the nap. The creation of woman produces so much unrest in the garden that the angel Disenchantralista questions God's sobriety for having made this new creature. Throughout, Adam remains both obstinately defiant and childishly peevish. He refuses to have any contact with Eve, instructing her to describe what she wants: "so that once and for all time, I can tell you that I won't let you have it."[106] Eve attempts different ways of reaching out to Adam: she appeals to him as an equal; she appeals to his intellect; she cites the Divine plan; she tries to dominate him. None of her attempts work until she begins to play the role of seductress. Only when Adam sees her as a sexual object does he begin to accept her presence. In an interview with Clayton Delery, Wilson rejected the charge that the play is sexist. Delery summarizes: "When this play was performed at the Cino some people received the impression that Wilson was saying that God intended men to relate to women primarily as sexual beings. However, that is precisely the reverse of the intention of the play. In the play it is man not God who has subjugated woman to her sexual role and man who refuses to see her in other ways. Ultimately it is a feminist message, not a chauvinistic one."[107] Originally intended to run only one week, it was extended for an additional week and brought back for a return engagement.

Three months after *And He Made a Her*, Wilson opened *Babel, Babel, Little Tower* (June 1961), the first play written specifically for the Cino. At the time, the New York Police Department not only handed out summonses to coffeehouses but also sometimes physically stopped performances. Wilson incorporated this living history into his production: after the actors in *Babel, Babel* had built a tower of the tables in the Cino, an actor dressed as a policeman entered. According to Wilson,

[A] coppish looking actor entered from Cornelia Street, ad-libbed a fracas with the waiter/doorman (Scotty), demanded the actors put the tables back where they belonged. The actors . . . refused. Authority in blue destroyed the tower. Most of the audience thought it was for real. It was very convincing. Too convincing. Opening night a front table was occupied by strippers from Third Street. They were very protective of us innocents in theatre. As the actor playing the cop approached the stage, Sunny (her specialty was tassle [*sic*] twirling) kneed him in the groin. The show did go on—limpingly. The actor has since taken up Scientology.[108]

As an unidentified reviewer noted, *Babel, Babel, Little Tower* is a "morality pastiche" that "has fun at the expense of organized religion, professional fund-raising, and the military mind."[109] As the characters look at the tower created from the tables, each interprets its significance in quite different terms; Saint Augustine sees it as a shrine to Mammon, Helen as a "cupola . . . of love,"[110] and Augustine as a "shrine of upliftance."[111] Bringing together such classical figures as Helen of Troy, Hector, and Agrippine Caesar with the medieval Christian Saint Augustine and the contemporary coffeehouse waitress Eppie, *Babel, Babel, Little Tower* reflects a form of textual and intertextual play that was to become popular at the Cino, mingling time, place, and aesthetic styles.

During the run of *Babel, Babel,* city councilman Stanley Isaacs, described by the *New Yorker* as a "seventy-eight-year-old beatnik," decided to tour the coffeehouses of Greenwich Village.[112] Isaacs opposed the city's requirement that an employee of an establishment with a cabaret license be fingerprinted and determined a "fit and proper person." He queried the reporter who accompanied him, "What's the sense? Especially since there's no good test for 'fit and proper.' It doesn't mean anything."[113] Their first stop was at 302 Bleecker Street, the Phase 2, where David Gordon greeted them. Gordon argued against the cabaret licensing requirement: "They say we're a cabaret because we serve 'beverages.' Well, coffee is a beverage, because you drink it, but it's not an alcoholic beverage. We believe that what makes a cabaret is alcohol."[114] Isaacs's next stop was at the most successful of the coffeehouses, Café Bizarre, "a converted stable hung with metal saws, chains, and anchors, plastic figures of spiders and insects, and Surrealistic combinations of oversized eyes and other anatomical parts."[115] Bernie Teichman, the host at the Bizarre, presented the argument that coffeehouses serve the community by offering a venue for aspiring artists. By the conclusion of the tour, Councilman Isaacs concluded that the "nice young people" in the coffeehouses all seemed to be "having a good time": "There's *life* down here. That's what counts, isn't it?"[116]

Wilson's third Cino production, *Now She Dances!,* brought Marshall Mason to the Caffe shortly after his arrival in New York on September 1, 1961. Mason had contacted Jane Lowry, a classmate at Northwestern University, as soon as he reached New York. She invited him to attend the play in which she was performing "down on Cornelia Street." Mason trekked down to see her in *Now She Dances!,* described in the program as a "short comedy in direct reference and indirect reply to *Salome* by Oscar Fingall [*sic*] O'Flahertie Wills Wilde."[117] Mason was enchanted by the intimate space with its twinkling lights and tiny playing area in the center of the room. He also was captivated by the waiter Johnny Dodd, "a devilish sort of person" who refused to take anything too seriously. Mason was struck by Dodd's attractive though somewhat feminine appearance; it was one of the first times he had seen long hair on a man. Mason returned to the Caffe regularly.

Doric Wilson's last play at the Cino was *Pretty People,* notable for two reasons. First, the young electrician named Jonathan Torrey, who worked on the set, was new to the Caffe and rumored to be Joe Cino's lover. Almost immediately, the story of Jonathan Torrey, Joe Cino, and the Caffe became intertwined. The second significance of the show is that an irreconcilable conflict developed between Cino and Wilson, largely as a result of an argument over Cino's desire to charge admission. Because of the complications it would cause with Equity, Wilson opposed the charge and left after a heated argument. He canceled both the remaining run of *Pretty People* and a scheduled revival of *And He Made a Her.* He would not visit the Caffe again until after Cino's death in 1967: "I stood outside of it the night of Joe's death, kicking the wall, too angry to cry, or crying too hard to harm much but my foot."[118]

Torrey is a rather shadowy figure in the history of Caffe Cino, evoking extremes of animosity and sympathy. Douglas Gordy describes him as follows: "By the time the Caffe Cino was in full operation . . . Joe had become involved in a long-term, tempestuous relationship with a young man named Johnny Torry [*sic*] (whose name has alternately been printed as Torrey, Torre, Tory, and even Torres), who worked as a professional theatrical electrician. Torry seems to have been everything Joe prized in a partner and felt lacking in himself: the proverbial tall, dark, and handsome, but also educated (Patrick recalls Torry had a Ph.D.), and strongly masculine."[119] But descriptions of Torrey vary widely, even among those who knew him well. He is typically said to have been handsome and sensual, exceptionally masculine, wearing the sort of construction-worker clothing popularized among many gay men by the Village People in the 1970s. Some people describe him as having dark hair and a somewhat olive complexion (suggestive of Mediterranean descent); others say that he had dirty blond hair that bleached very blond during the summer. Randy Gener describes him as "an Irish-German lighting designer, tall, striking, very blond, into s/m, a volatile and mean guy with whom Cino had explosive fights."[120] When Torrey became a regular at the Cino, he was a young man of twenty, born April 2, 1941, who had previously worked as an industrial electrician at Bean Fiber Glass Company in New Hampshire.

Though he worked in blue-collar occupations, Torrey was adopted into and grew up in a family of remarkable learning and distinction. His adoptive father, Norman Lewis Torrey, was appointed a professor of French at Columbia University in 1937, eventually becoming chairperson of the department. With poet T. S. Eliot, he was named an honorary doctor of letters at the University of Paris in 1951; a similar honor came from Middlebury College in 1955. Jonathan's adoptive stepmother, Elizabeth Bixler Torrey, was the dean of the Yale School of Nursing; his cousin, Jane Wheelwright Torrey, is a well-known psychologist whose work has been influential in feminist studies.

Opinions about Jonathan Torrey's personality are as sharply divergent as are descriptions of his physical appearance. Many people found him unsettling, even somewhat frightening, and attribute the primary problems in his relationship with Joe Cino to Torrey's violent temper; others believe that Torrey has been maligned, often by those who knew him the least. Drawn to sadomasochism, Torrey would, as Robert Patrick recalls, "strip, drip candle wax all over himself, turn to his target for the night, and ask them to peel him."[121] His sexual proclivities sometimes led him into situations that those around him found disturbing: Torrey once asked William M. Hoffman for advice regarding a man who wanted Torrey to murder him during their sex play.

With the exception of Andy Warhol and his Factory crowd, few figures involved in Caffe Cino have been as sharply criticized as has Torrey, perhaps, as some have suggested, because of jealousy over his close bond with Cino or perhaps because of the darker streak he brought to the Cino. Undoubtedly Torrey could become violent when angry, a fairly common occurrence in his turbulent relationship with Cino: in one rage, he splashed paint throughout the coffeehouse, destroying much of the art hanging on the walls; on another occasion he destroyed the props for a production of a Lanford Wilson play; and in yet another, he may have set fire to the Cino, though the officially determined cause was a gas leak.

A few months after Torrey's arrival, Marshall Mason went into the Caffe to propose production of a play by Claris Nelson, who was another of Mason's Northwestern colleagues. The play, *Rue Garden,* opened July 29, 1962, and starred Nelson and Linda Eskenas, a frequent Cino actress. Despite some criticism of the acting, the production received a good review: "[T]he play itself, fathered by Lewis Carroll and obviously nourished on nothing but rose petals and tears, is almost pure magic, and director Mason did an admirable job with it."[122]

Two months later a second Nelson play, *The Clown* (also directed by Mason), opened. *Voice* critic Arthur Sainer was not particular impressed with the new play: "[I]t is a failure, though her [Nelson's] faith has tempered the inadequacies."[123] Whatever the play's shortcomings, the plot as described by Sainer is interesting in the context of the Cino.

> The plot: the Prince has guests and badly needs an entertainment within the hour. The Superintendent of Theatres is too hightoned to respond, his actors perform tragedies and need months to rehearse. The Philosopher feels the problem too vulgar for his consideration. The Circus manager will bring his troupe to perform, for a fee—but the coffers are empty. Thus no one can respond properly, until the boy [a troubadour] appears and is turned into a clown for the contemptuous amusement of the guests.[124]

Whether or not the show was intended to parallel many events at Caffe Cino, it clearly does: the frequent need for last-minute replacement shows, the implicit criticism in much Cino work of the stilted and staid mainstream theatre, and the dismissal of the Cino by learned circles. Most interesting is the appearance of the outsider, the Boy, whose naïveté and innocence contrast sharply with the sophisticated world of the court. Raised in the forest where he and his father are the only inhabitants, the boy has no concept of evil or ugliness. The Superintendent of Theatre is so taken with the youth that he proclaims, "You see gentlemen? He is completely innocent! He's perfect, he's divine, he's delicious! I must have him, Your Majesty. For years I have tried to find a living example of innocence. My actors don't believe that such a thing exists, and they refuse to play anything that doesn't exist. I've found examples of witches, and ghosts, and evil incarnate, but innocence seemed impossible.

Now, at last, I have found it."[125] Persuaded to entertain at the court, the Boy can only sing the songs taught him by his father and tell stories of his bucolic world—all to the great amusement of the sophisticated members of the court.

The Boy's innocence is crushed by the laughter at his expense. He begins composing new lyrics that grow from his pain:

> Now, now,
> My heart is an old thing
> Lonely and cold thing
> Better than nothing,
> Nothing would do.
> Now, now,
> My heart is a child's toy
> Made for a small boy
> Full of a child's joy,
> Broken in two.[126]

In the person of the Boy, the outsider moves from the margins to the center but, in doing so, discovers a threatening, corrupt, overly sophisticated world that shatters his innocence. Thus the portrait of the Boy echoes the sense of alienation and otherness characteristic of many on the stage and in the audience of the Caffe. Several other Cino artists moved the outsider, particularly the sexual outsider, from the margins to the center, celebrating the previously unspeakable, unspeaking gay male body. Of all the work produced at the Cino, *The Clown* was Jonathan Torrey's favorite and was scheduled for a revival on his birthday in April 1967, though he died three months beforehand. The cast of *The Clown* included Lanford Wilson, fresh from Chicago, making his New York debut. His own first production *(So Long at the Fair)* would soon appear on the Cino stage.[127]

At least one other work from this period deserves mention: Michael Smith's *I Like It.* From most accounts, including Smith's own, the play itself was not particularly significant, though Smith's work with a production is important. Having studied at Yale University shortly before arriving in New York in the late 1950s, Smith volunteered to work in the offices of the *Village Voice,* then a small, unknown weekly newspaper of about twelve pages. After writing occasional reviews, he became a regular theatre critic and eventually became the entertainment editor. Though the use of the term *off-off-Broadway* generally is attributed to Smith's predecessor, Jerry Tallmer,[128] Smith contributed more to the discovery and popularization of the movement than any other critic. He was the first to give regular, serious attention to productions in coffee-houses, basements, churches, and similar venues.

Fundamental to the creativity (on stage and off) at the Cino was the examination of various forms of community and family. As Sally Banes has shown in *Greenwich Village 1963*, the early sixties was a time of exploration and reinvention of the meaning of "community." According to Banes, the Village saw an influx of artists from all parts of the country, with the artists attempting to create the rural village within the urban Village. As a result, they were "involved in self-consciously founding communities; and further, their sense of communitas was integral to the decade's revitalization of city life."[129] In her brief glance at the Caffe Cino, she notes that the Cino has been mythologized more as a family than as a collective, with the playwrights playing the role of the bad children, who would be spoiled by success.[130] This familial spirit of Cino artists is apparent in the reminiscences in which the word *family* appears repeatedly. Often the reference to family is literal as, for example, when used in reference to George and Ann Harris and their children, who worked at the Cino. Other references are to a family of choice (rather than kinship) or to a sense of community. Jean-Claude van Itallie noted that the Cino "was a clique, a family, an atmosphere in a small, dark place, special: fellow gay men, mostly gallantly trying to express their individuality at least ten years before gay consciousness became an active movement."[131]

From the beginning Joe Cino focused on the familial aspect of his coffee-house; he never intended it to be just or even primarily a theatre. By March 1965 productions were at their peak, and the coffeehouse would receive an Obie in only two months. Yet Cino repeatedly emphasized that his business was a cafe, not a theatre: "We're not off-off-Broadway," he told Michael Smith; "we're in-cafe."[132] It was a place for friends to gather and, in his words, to "do what you have to do"—and what they had to do was to create theatre. As long as theatrical productions served a communal need and as long as it brought the Cino family together, Joe Cino would continue to sponsor it. According to Charles Loubier, theatre did bring the Cino family together: "What happened at Cino's was you not only wrote a play, you became part of the family."[133] The familial atmosphere was fostered in part by the creation of an in-group language. According to Loubier,

> Cino and I invented a language based on how Sicilians speak English. He was American Sicilian. We had this mad tongue going. It was made

to titillate each other, but it got out of hand. It became a sort of Frankenstein. Everybody learned it. Love was made in that language—I guess it's a language. People laughed and fought in it. Ultimately, Joe probably died in it. *Phonocca,* which meant phony, was used all the time. . . . The word jet was short for jet black. We called ourselves the jet set long before there was a jet set. But Cino meant it *in miseria.*[134]

This secret language became one means of defining who was or was not a member of the Cino family.

In 1966 Nancy Lynch published an article based on interviews with coffeehouse owners and customers. Lynch found that the patrons tended to select one coffeehouse for their primary social outlet, banding together with others there to form "the Group," a circle of close friends. Quoting a coffeehouse patron (also named Nancy), Lynch notes, "The Group is exclusive. Nancy says: 'You don't bring your friends into it. . . .' It is loyal in its way. The actresses share leads on juicy parts in new plays. . . . Money is loaned back and forth. Confidences are exchanged." The Group served many of the same functions as a family: "The Group seems to provide a cozy, family-like pocket for young people who find New York cold and unfeeling. And the word 'family,' you notice, is one that is used by many habitues of Village coffeehouses when they talk about the attractions of their hangouts. Some speak crossly of the day 'they broke up the family table' at such and such a coffeehouse."[135] Coffeehouses became everybody's living room.

Years after that *Mademoiselle* article, Cino regulars still use terms such as *family* and *living room* when speaking of the Cino. Furthermore some of their fondest memories of Caffe Cino are of the times that various people would bring in neck bones or other inexpensive cuts of meat for Cino to throw into the large pot of stew on the little stove in the back of the Cino. The Cino family—Davies, Torrey, Burgess, Dodd, and others—would sit around the Caffe and enjoy the domestic gathering. A characteristic shared by many Cino regulars was a sense of being "other," some because of sex, others because of sexual orientation, and almost all because of their interest in alternative theatrical styles.

While the coffeehouses provided space for people to gather in a familial atmosphere, the art created in and around the gatherings helped define new communities. Critic Arnold Aronson argues that "[t]he search for new forms of language in the avant-garde theatre of the 1960s inevitably led to a concurrent attempt to create new myths and rituals in the belief (naïve as it turned out) that these ceremonial activities and quasi-religious enactments would create new communities that would serve as an antidote to the perceived failures of modern society."[136] Sally Banes shows that many artists of the sixties believed that art, particularly the urban "folk" work of such pop figures as Andy Warhol, both constitutes and is constituted by community.

[T]he groups that constituted the Greenwich Village avant-garde constructed themselves as a community. Since folk art may be defined as the art that a community makes for itself, perhaps it seemed to them that to make art that somehow resembled folk art could work backward, as an index of potent, productive communal bonds. That is, if community implies folk art, then to have what looks and feels like folk art must, in part, constitute community. In the paradox of avant-garde folklore, folk art was thought to create communal bonds, rather than vice versa.[137]

In addition to the pop aspects of work at the Cino (a characteristic evident as early as Doric Wilson's *And He Made a Her* but which became much more important in later years), the Cino artists used their productions to define themselves as a community. By challenging traditional theatrical standards through drawing from the new European movements, by instituting alternative production and management values, and by challenging traditional social values through their acceptance of homosexuality, female sexuality, and sadomasochism, Cino artists created a family, a community, a collective standing apart from the dominant culture. As Michael Smith proposed, theatre communicates most effectively to individuals who are within a group, thus affirming their membership within a community:

It is in the cities, and on this level, that the theatre is particularly needed today, when communities have become so large as to be inhuman, so subdivided as to be cliqueish [*sic*] and narrow, so interrelated that the consequences of any choice are immeasurable. Together with the virtual collapse of the family—at least as a source of values—the unchecked proliferation of abstract social units and the global nerve-network of communications make the individual feel totally connected (and "turned on") but undifferentiated—like just any synapse. Unable to accept any going system of morality, since all are rendered amoral by their pragmatic standards and expedient style, he has yet no means to identify his own. . . .[138]

In the modern-postmodern age with its media domination, fragmentation, disjointedness, incoherence, and collapse of metanarratives, theatre becomes a means to define and structure a community that relies more on choice than on geographical boundaries or class.

Perhaps most important, the Cino provided space both on its stage and in its house for gay men to model and enact new communal and individual performances of identity. Richard Dyer has noted that art provides an experience around which such identities can emerge.

> Works of art express, define and mold experience and ideas, and in the process makes [sic] them visible and available. They thus enable people to recognise experience as shared and to confront definitions of that experience. This represents the starting point for a forging of *identity* grounded in where people are situated in society, in whatever strata. This sense of social identity, of belonging to a group, is a prerequisite for any political activity proper, even when that identity is not recognised as political. This role for culture has perhaps a special relevance for gay people because we are "hidden" and "invisible."[139]

The Cino gave a body to the invisible and a voice to the silent not just for the individual gay men who performed there but also for a gay community that it helped create.

By the summer of 1963 a growing professionalism was evident in the productions at the Cino, as original work dominated the production calendar and Cino collected larger numbers of talented directors and actors. In the early fall of 1963 the Cino began its most successful period, introducing new works by Lanford Wilson, Sam Shepard, and other major writers.

Joseph Cino and *Village Voice* critic Michael Smith. James D. Gossage, Billy Rose Theatre Collection, The New York Public Library for the Performing Arts, Astor, Lenox, and Tilden Foundations.

Joseph Davies, Joseph Cino, and Judy Eckhardt inside Caffe Cino (date unknown, but sometime after rebuilding from the fire in 1965). James D. Gossage, Billy Rose Theatre Collection, The New York Public Library for the Performing Arts, Astor, Lenox, and Tilden Foundations.

Poster for James Howard's *Flyspray*, 1960, generally considered to be the first production of an original work at Caffe Cino. Billy Rose Theatre Collection, The New York Public Library for the Performing Arts, Astor, Lenox, and Tilden Foundations.

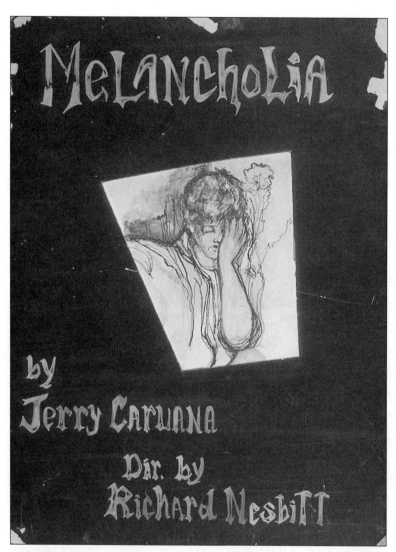

Poster for Jerry Caruana's *Melancholia,* 1962. Billy Rose Theatre Collection, The New York Public Library for the Performing Arts, Astor, Lenox, and Tilden Foundations.

Playwright Doric Wilson and cast during a rehearsal of *And He Made a Her,* 1961. Collection of Doric Wilson.

William M. Hoffman and Robert Patrick in Patrick's *Haunted Host,* 1964. Collection of Robert Patrick.

Joseph Cino holding a program for the benefit organized by H. M. Koutoukas for the burned Caffe Cino at Writer's Stage, March 1965. James D. Gossage, Billy Rose Theatre Collection, The New York Public Library for the Performing Arts, Astor, Lenox, and Tilden Foundations.

Poster for an adaptation of Diane di Prima's *Poet's Vaudeville* by Caffe Cino using La Mama, ETC's space after the 1965 fire. The work originally appeared at Judson Dance Theatre and was written for a dance piece created by James Waring and John Herbert MacDowell in 1965.

Billy Rose Theatre Collection, The New York Public Library for the Performing Arts, Astor, Lenox, and Tilden Foundations.

Henry Ansel, Renee Maugin (also known as Sylvia Maugin), Judy Eckhardt, and H. M. Koutoukas standing outside the renovated Caffe, May 1965. James D. Gossage, Billy Rose Theatre Collection, The New York Public Library for the Performing Arts, Astor, Lenox, and Tilden Foundations.

Cast and production team of H. M. Koutoukas's *With Creatures Make My Way,* May 1965 *(left to right from top row):* actor Warren Finnerty, Koutoukas, lighting and effects designer John P. Dodd, Charles Stanley. James D. Gossage, Billy Rose Theatre Collection, The New York Public Library for the Performing Arts, Astor, Lenox, and Tilden Foundations.

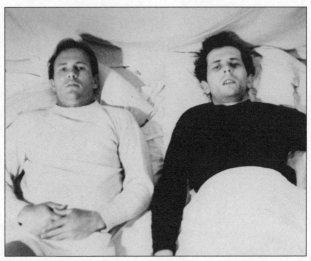

James Jennings and Walter McGinn in the original production of
Robert Heide's *The Bed*, 1965. From the Robert Heide collection.

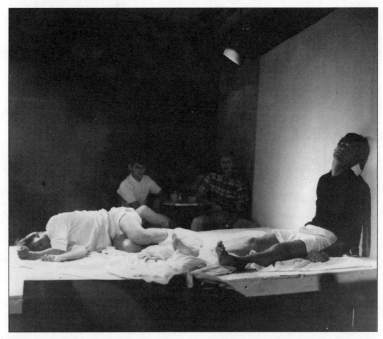

Jennings and Burns in Heide's *The Bed*, with audience members in the background, 1965.
From the Robert Heide Collection.

Backstage at H. M. Koutoukas's *All Day for a Dollar, or Crumpled Christmas.* Shown are Robert Dahdah, Ronald Link, Charles Stanley, and Candace Scott, January 1966.

James D. Gossage, Billy Rose Theatre Collection, The New York Public Library for the Performing Arts, Astor, Lenox, and Tilden Foundations.

Rehearsal of Haimsohn, Miller, and Wise's *Dames at Sea*, 1966. *Clockwise from lower left:* director Robert Dahdah, actress Bernadette Peters, composer Jim Wise, actor David Christmas, Gary Filsinger, unidentified, Donna Forbes (now Donna DeSeta), and unidentified (man facing away from camera in lower center). Billy Rose Theatre Collection, The New York Public Library for the Performing Arts, Astor, Lenox, and Tilden Foundations.

Joseph Cino, Eddie Barton, and H. M. Koutoukas, probably in 1966. Billy Rose Theatre Collection, The New York Public Library for the Performing Arts, Astor, Lenox, and Tilden Foundations.

James Jennings, Jacque Lynn Colton, Victor LiPari, and Jane Buchanan in the original production of Robert Heide's *Moon,* 1968. From the Robert Heide collection.

John Gilman and Robert Frink in the second production of Robert Heide's *Moon*, 1968.
From the Robert Heide Collection.

c
a
f
f
e
cino
presents

EMPIRE STATE

by Tom LaBar

direction by
Reynolds L.
Callender

with

MURRAY
STIRTON

DAVID
CHRISTOPHER

ROBERT
RODRIGUEZ

MARTIN
MEDEL

set and light
designer
Jim Hardy

assisted by
Robert Luyster

costumes
Kathy Iverson

assistant to
the director
Lynne Brodbeck

Cast and crew list for Tom La Bar's *Empire State,* January 1968. Billy Rose Theatre Collection,
The New York Public Library for the Performing Arts, Astor, Lenox, and Tilden Foundations.

EXCLUSION/EJECTION LIST IDENTIFICATION RECORD

STEPHEN ANTHONY CINO

Name/Aliases								
STEPHEN ANTHONY CINO						AKA:	Steve Cino, Steven Cino, Steve "The Whale" Cino	
Sex	Race	Height	Weight	Hair	Eyes	Build	Other Characteristics	
M	**W**	**68"**	**325**	**Gray**	**Green**	**Large**		
Date of Birth		Place of Birth		FBI			CII	
October 29, 1936		**Buffalo, New York**		**444216E**				
Last-known Address								
156 Tapatio, Henderson, Nevada 89014								
Date Last Update		Other Information						
Placed on List							Photo Date	
September 25, 1997							**1990**	

(9/97)

[42]

Entry for Stephen Cino, Joe's younger brother, in the *List of Excluded Persons,* published by the State Gaming Control Board, Nevada Gaming Commission.

3 Veiled Strangeness

On a Saturday night during February 1963, a small group sat sipping coffee, eating pastries or sandwiches, chatting to kill time, and waiting for the eleven o'clock performance. The play for the night was the second by David Starkweather to appear at the Cino and the first in which Starkweather worked with director Robert Dagny. Mr. Dagny neither had directed for the Cino nor had any association with it until Joseph Cino attended another theatre to see Mr. Dagny's production of *What Else Is There?,* a play by Robert Downey, the father of the movie star Robert Downey Jr. Later Cino went to Mr. Dagny and offered him a script to direct. When the director asked about the play, Cino refused to give him the title or any other information, saying only, "Read the play." He did so and leapt at the chance to direct it. The work that Mr. Dagny directed and that the February audience awaited was David Starkweather's *So, Who's Afraid of Edward Albee?* with Brandy Carson and Neil Flanagan in the cast. Having received rave reviews from the *Village Voice* and *Backstage,* in which the play, the direction, and the acting were all praised, the production was completely sold out three days after opening. As the audience sat anticipating the performance, some cast furtive and not so furtive glances at a young man at one of the small tables slightly stage right. He was, in fact, Edward Albee, the playwright who had influenced much of the theatre created at Caffe Cino and other underground theatres. His use of absurdist techniques pointed the direction for other playwrights in the United States, and his success with such one-act plays as *The Zoo Story* and *Sandbox* had helped rekindle interest in the form, still the staple of off-off-Broadway in 1963. Albee may very well have been lured to the Cino's production by reviews that referred to its "Albeean" quality.

On that February night, ten minutes or so after the scheduled performance time of eleven o'clock, a stocky, somewhat nondescript man sitting alone at a table near the stage became increasingly frustrated with the tardiness of the production, finally asking loudly, "When the hell is this thing going to start?" For most of the crowd, the delay simply was accepted as a typical late start in the disorganized world of off-off-Broadway. The man, however, became increasingly loud and obnoxious. As Lanford Wilson, who attended the production one evening, said, "You got annoyed with him because he was such a prick."[1] Only when the audience realized that the lights throughout the house had dimmed almost imperceptibly—all lights except an amber over the belligerent man's table—did many realize that the play had, in fact, started. The annoying prick at the table was actor Neil Flanagan, who was joined shortly by his date, a nurse played by Brandy Carson. The play was a dark comedy, set in a coffeehouse very much like the Cino, in which the two characters awaited the start of a production of a play by Edward Albee, the only overt reference to Albee in the play. Unable to navigate the intricacies of a relationship, the man berates his date, who has come to end their relationship. Unable to control her in "real" life, he creates a fantasy in which he exerts the control he cannot manage otherwise. But even in the fantasy scene that moves from the table onto the stage, he fails to master her, since she leaves him in the fantasy also.

To the disappointment of the cast, Albee did not react during the performance and left immediately afterwards without speaking to them. Like his producing partner Richard Barr, Albee visited the coffeehouse periodically. The Albee-Barr-Wilder producing team moved Lanford Wilson's *The Madness of Lady Bright* and other Cino shows into off-Broadway theatres. The group had been associated with the Cino from early in its history. They had persuaded Cino to give them the Caffe for the opening night party of the off-Broadway premier of Albee's *American Dream*. According to Barr the group did not normally have opening night parties but decided to do so for Albee's play. He arrived late in the evening, just as the party was becoming interesting. The first thing he saw when he walked into the Cino was actress Sudie Bond in the middle of the room on a table dancing the fandango. "And that's kind of the way," he commented, "we celebrated off Broadway openings in those days."[2]

The production of *So, Who's Afraid of Edward Albee?* is significant for several reasons. It attracted sizable audiences, including Edward Albee. It was among the first productions that aspiring playwright Lanford Wilson saw at the Cino and helped introduce him to avant-garde theatre; Wilson still vividly and fondly recalls the production. It established the talent of the reticent

Starkweather, whose previous play Michael Smith had called "a pretentious and tiresome amalgam of Thornton Wilder and the heavier sort of expressionism."[3] Even in these two very early works, Starkweather shows his fondness for adopting and toying with styles of other authors.

> [For] two weeks running the Cino . . . has given premiere productions of plays by David Starkweather. The current one, playing through Saturday, is a striking romp called *So, Who's Afraid of Edward Albee?* Obviously Mr. Starkweather is not, and he need not be. His one-act play gambols through the field of Albeean symbolism like a ram in spring. Scattering Absurd techniques right and left and blithely ignoring all rules of structure, he nonetheless manages to evoke hilarity, sympathy, and bizarre terror by turns.[4]

Albee established David Starkweather as one of the Cino's leading intellectual playwrights. It also led to his third Cino production when Joe Cino asked him for another work. The resulting play was *The LOVE Affair* (later retitled *The LOVE Pickle*), also directed at the playwright's request by Mr. Dagny. Like *Albee,* it was well received by critics.

Though *Albee,* along with most of Starkweather's other work, is now nearly forgotten, the playwright sometimes has been considered among the most innovative of the Cino writers, with experimentations in style, content, and form that often led him to draw from a variety of traditions, including those of Asian theatre. *You May Go Home Again* is subtitled *A Domestic Noh;* in one of his later, non-Cino works, he used a different style in each act: Kabuki for the first, Shakespearean for the second, and naturalistic for the third.[5] In *Contemporary Dramatists,* William M. Hoffman quotes Starkweather's philosophy of theatre.

> My current vision of theatre is a head, the bodies of the audience resonating chambers like the jugs beneath the stage in the classic Noh, feeling their behavioral imaginations. Sound surrounds but the eyes are in front perceiving SENSES in terms of each other. Vision is figure to sound's ground and vice versa because each word has an aural and visual component. A noun is a picture (visual/spatial) and a verb is a melody (aural/temporal) relation. The split between being and doing dissolves when nouns are just states verbs are in at a given moment. The central human art form is the spoken word.[6]

Hoffman argues that Starkweather's plays offer us a portrait of a man who once would have been considered a saint: the outsider, antihero "who leaves his society, goes into physical and psychical exile, searches for his god, and brings back the golden fleece to an indifferent world."[7]

Lanford Wilson's fondness for Starkweather's work is not particularly surprising, since both playwrights were concerned with many of the same issues. Though none of his work had been produced at the time, Wilson might easily have recognized in such Starkweather plays as *Albee, You May Go Home Again,* and *LOVE Affair* at least some themes common to his own Cino plays: the difficulties of communication and the risks of personal relationships. *LOVE Affair,* produced in May 1963, was typical of Starkweather at the time; Robert Dagny (who directed the play) described it as

> about a hippy couple who are so bored with everything and so blasé that they decide to go to a men's room to have a new experience; and in the course of having the experience, a man comes in who represents all the virile manhood in the world. You know, he is a symbol—he has no lines, but he is a symbol in the play. And, of course, she comes on to him, and they have this ritualistic coupling. And she uses the fact of this guy having . . . virility and so forth to beat verbally her date. At one point he [the date] tries to offer dental records and pictures of himself in various stages of undress, and she just laughs at him. So basically . . . both plays [*LOVE Affair* and *Albee*] dealt with men who were very neurotic, very high strung, and [who] had difficult relationships with women. And they were also brilliantly imagistic and brilliantly funny.[8]

Using effects such as contrasting images of impotence and virility, the play examines the dynamics of the relationship among the three characters, particularly the difficulties in the relationship of the hippie couple, much as Lanford Wilson often explores similar themes of isolation and discordant relationships in his early work.

As works by playwrights such as Lanford Wilson and David Starkweather became central to its production schedule, the Cino entered its most successful phase, financially and critically. Though the Caffe already was established as one of the leading venues of the avant-garde theatre scene, the period from 1963 to 1966 saw the emergence of some of the most accomplished individuals and director-playwright teams: actors Bernadette Peters and Harvey Keitel; playwrights John Guare, Robert Patrick, William M. Hoffman, and H. M.

Koutoukas; and the teams of Marshall Mason with Lanford Wilson and Ron Link with Robert Heide. These middle years, however, offered remarkable contrasts: extraordinary successes followed dismal failures, catastrophes brought a rush of community support, and shows canceled at the last minute were replaced by extemporaneous productions of remarkable creativity. The highs had their dark side. As the Caffe attracted more attention and as many Cino artists achieved commercial success, some bemoaned and avoided success, referring to it as the "bitch goddess" because of its fickleness.[9] But the lows had their positive side. The devastating fire in 1965 brought a community together to rebuild the coffeehouse. Perhaps no year in the period so effectively exemplifies the movement through the peaks and valleys of success as does 1965. Opening and closing with popular productions by quintessential Cino playwright H. M. Koutoukas, the year witnessed the devastating fire, the first Obie awarded to the Caffe, and the first significant coverage of off-off-Broadway by the *New York Times*.

Most of the works now remembered from the Cino come from this middle period: Lanford Wilson's *The Madness of Lady Bright,* Robert Patrick's *The Haunted Host,* and George Haimsohn and Robin Miller's *Dames at Sea.* The once infrequent reviews in the *Village Voice* became much more regular, and increasing attention came from other newspapers as well. More often than ever before, lines formed outside for the few available seats; patrons arrived in limousines, as well as by foot, taxi, and subway. Cino playwrights began to see their work in print, on television, and in commercial theatres. Two ominous shadows were largely overlooked: the increasing influence of city leaders such as Ed Koch who worked to close coffeehouses and the growing influence of drugs on the lives of Joseph Cino and Jonathan Torrey. Both these factors weighed heavily on Cino, with one threatening the continued legal existence of his coffeehouse and the other threatening his ability to manage it.

During this central period of Caffe Cino's history, playwrights and directors continued to explore the themes and styles typical of earlier years. Pop culture references common in the earliest Cino productions became central to playwrights such as Robert Patrick and to the "comic book productions," largely improvisational shows based on comic books; the camp stylistics of earlier Cino artists were taken to remarkable heights by H. M. Koutoukas and Tom Eyen; issues regarding sexual orientation, which had more often remained subtextual (though barely disguised) in early works, were treated with increasing frequency and explicitness in works by William M. Hoffman, Lanford Wilson, Robert Patrick, and Robert Heide.

In the spring and summer of 1963, Joe Cino seems to have been at his creative peak. In March he directed Tennessee Williams's *Auto da Fe* for La Mama after having directed the play a year earlier for Cafe Bizarre. In April, during the same week in which La Mama promoted its first production of a full-length play, the Cino advertisement proclaims "By Popular Demand: 2 One-Acts by Joe Cino & Neal Flanigan [*sic*]."[10] Whether the plays were written, adapted, or only directed by Cino and Flanagan is unclear, though Kathryn Ann Absher assumes that the two wrote the pieces.[11] The possibility that Cino may have written a one-act play is particularly intriguing, since the only written piece attributed to him is an introduction to a play in Michael Smith and Nick Orzel's *Eight Plays from Off Off-Broadway*. Both Cino and Flanagan offered the Caffe's audiences adaptations of other work, including Flanagan's version of Voltaire's *Candide* (April 1962) and Cino's version of Strindberg's *Miss Julie* (July 1963), which he retitled *Miss Julia*.

During the spring and summer of 1963, Cino directed an adaptation of Shakespeare's *As You Like It* (May) and *Miss Julia* (July). Though Clayton Delery suggests that *As You Like It* was performed in full,[12] that almost certainly was not the case. The advertisement notes that the piece is an adaptation,[13] and it played the traditional schedule of performances at nine and eleven p.m. and one a.m. As a quasi-postmodern blending of styles and texts, *Miss Julia* followed a trend well established at the Cino: intermingling contemporary references and slang from various periods. The production confused critic Arthur Sainer because of the blending of contemporary and Victorian styles, thought, and methods: "The adaptation seems at times to be set in modern-day Sweden and at other moments to be happening at the turn of the century, the characters mingle hip colloquialisms with Victorian rhythms, and the psychology is fuzzy." Ultimately, the production was dominated by the psychotic character of Julie, the changing social structure, and the boots of the master. As Sainer concludes in his review, "The only dominant feature of the Cino version is the existence of uncertainty."[14]

During the early months of 1963, attacks on coffeehouses by city officials and neighborhood groups continued, resulting in the formation in late spring of the Greenwich Village Cafe Theatre Association (GVCTA) by seven establishments that earlier had been members of a similar organization, the Greenwich Village Coffee House Association. GVCTA's members were the Bitter End, the Cafe Bizarre, the Gaslight Cafe, the Phase 2, the Thirdside, the Take 3, and the Café Wha? The Association developed and promoted a

"strict new self-policing code of ethics."[15] The code attempted to address the
basic concerns of neighborhood residents: "Briefly, it prohibits the use of
loudspeakers at cafe doors, all disturbing noise after 11 (and no undue noise
at any time), doormen acting as barkers, entertainers sitting in windows or
within fifteen feet of entrances, girl 'shills,' loitering in front of establishments,
misrepresenting of prices (price policy must be clearly displayed on the door,
or on menus and tables inside), and serving drunks."[16] To promote a better
relationship with the community, the GVCTA advertised in the *Village Voice*
that they agreed some action was needed to resolve the problems on Mac-
Dougal Street and pledged to join in the search for a solution. The advertisement notes an important distinction between the patrons of GVCTA establishments and patrons of other, less desirable locations of the area: "We'd like
the Villagers to discover and distinguish between the type people *(primarily
couples)* that frequent our establishments, and the undesirable loiterers on
MacDougal Street, whom we absolutely do not cater to" (emphasis added).[17]
By speaking of couples in the advertisement, the Association wished to distance itself from the roving groups causing so many problems in the neighborhood; it may also have wished to deny association with the gay men coming into the area.

The increased visibility of coffeehouses in the Village is evident from the
extent to which they were centered in popular cultural images. Appropriate
to his frequent recital of poetry before entering the ring, boxer Cassius Clay
(later known as Muhammad Ali) chose the Bitter End, a coffeehouse that featured readings of Beat poetry, as the site for a press event to publicize his
upcoming fight in Madison Square Garden. Yet he denigrated the typical
patrons of the coffeehouse when questioned by a reporter:

"Do you consider yourself a beat poet?"
"What do you mean? I'm a Country boy."
"You know, beatniks."
"Oh, you mean the guys who look like Castro, the ones who look
like the Smith Brothers? I'd like to get in a ring with one of them." And
he reminisced about an incident on Telegraph Hill in San Francisco, a
discussion he had had with a "beatnik." "He was so ugly, and I was tellin'
him about it."[18]

The attempt by coffeehouses to recuperate their image through such events
and the creation of a business organization had little success. The establishments

were increasingly becoming ensnared in the struggles between various political factions, notably that of future mayor and congressman Edward I. Koch (then representing the Village Independent Democrats) and his primary opponent, Carmine G. DeSapio (of the Tamawa Club).

Without a doubt the important event of 1963 for the Cino was the arrival of budding playwright Lanford Wilson and his actor friend Michael Warren Powell. Born in Lebanon, Missouri, Wilson moved with his family to the small town of Ozark, Missouri, when he was about fourteen, after his divorced factory-worker mother married an inspector at a dairy plant. When he graduated from high school in 1955, he went to visit his father in San Diego. He attended one year of college at San Diego State University while working full-time as a riveter in the aviation industry. At the end of the year, he left school and went back to Missouri and then to Chicago. He fell in love with Chicago and with city life. He found work in an advertising agency and began writing short stories, hoping that he could support himself through his writing while pursuing a career in art. As he comments, he hoped to write "stories to support my art habit."[19] One day while working on a story, he realized that it was "more play than story" and began rewriting it as a play.

His background in theatre was limited: he had been in two productions in high school (one one-act and one full-length) and had been assistant stage manager for a touring production for Southwest Missouri State University when he attended one term there. Despite the lack of experience, he became enamored of playwriting immediately: "I started writing the play and on page two said 'I am a playwright.' It was just as clear as day. It would always be a challenge. I would never be thoroughly happy with anything. And I had a real talent for writing dialogue and really enjoyed the process more than anything I've ever done." His first major project was a farce, though he had no idea what a farce was ("I thought, 'You just keep it funny'") and though he had chosen a setting (Fire Island) where "I had never been and knew nothing about." Without finishing the farce, he began work on a full-length play that was "so bad that I don't even tell anyone what the title was."

Realizing that he may need help to become a playwright, he enrolled in a course at the downtown center of the University of Chicago. Wilson was exhilarated by the course, in part because the structure of the class allowed him to hear his words in performance shortly after they had been written. The instructor began the course by saying, "Every play has to have conflict. . . . Read this scene of conflict and this scene of conflict. . . . Write a scene of conflict between . . . a man and a woman or between a man and a man or a woman and a woman." When the students returned with their completed scenes for the next class, a group of actors from the Goodman Theatre performed each scene: "You could tell who had written it by who squirmed. . . . That was my education in writing a play." With one course in playwriting, Wilson concluded, "Okay, so now I'm a playwright in Chicago where there is no original theatre. So the logical thing was to go to New York."

Wilson, Dean Morgan, and Michael Warren Powell decided to move to New York together. Before moving, however, Wilson threw one last party with his four Chicago roommates. The five had taken a four-bedroom, two-story apartment ("the best in Chicago") in an art deco building. Since Wilson was the only one of the group with a job at the time, he signed the lease: "We were there for three months without paying a nickel, except the first month's rent, and not even a security back then. So we owed two months' rent; we were certain that the Mafia owned the building and was going to kill us. We had no furniture. Everyone had brought a mattress, and sheets, and a blanket, and that was what we owned. There was this huge living room with no furniture in it." Powell, who was working in a display house, used the corporate credit card to rent "an outrageous number of plants." After decorating the house with the plants and display lights, the group went to all the touring companies in town, putting up big signs: "Big Party Tomorrow Night."

> Jammed. Jammed. Crushed. The best party you have ever been to in your life. The police were called three times. All three times, two policemen would come. You enter the door and go up this winding stairway to the living room. It's all enclosed until you get up to the living room. All three times about four chorus girls would meet them at the top. All three times they stayed. We had policemen with guns dancing, boogying all night long. It was just great. We had six policemen there. The party was over about five in the morning. It was summer—July. And we left everything right where it was, got on a bus and came to New York. Michael Powell and I [and] Dean Morgan all came.

The three men left for New York just before July 4, 1962. According to Powell, Morgan did not have money for the bus ticket to New York (the three having started the trip with total combined funds of about forty dollars), so Morgan decided to hitchhike and rejoin them in New York. On one of the first stops just outside Chicago, however, Morgan was waiting, his effort at hitchhiking having been unsuccessful. Wilson and Powell used much of their remaining funds to buy him a ticket, so they arrived in New York with only $7.20.[20] None of the three knew anyone in New York well. Wilson had visited the city the year before and had encountered an acquaintance, a "screaming queen."

I was [seated] outside a cafe in the Village and this screaming queen— there are no queens like Chicago Queens. I was appalled at the quality of the queens in New York when I first came here. I mean, they just didn't know how to do it. So this screaming Chicago queen screamed, "Lanford, darling, I have the most marvelous house here. It's just wonderful. You must call me." And that was the phone number I had in New York.

Unfortunately the three had not considered the holiday, so no one answered the telephone at the home of the screaming queen despite their repeated calls. With little money and no lodging, they spent the first night in a park, reaching Wilson's friend sometime the next day. When he greeted them at the door, he said that he remembered the friend who was with Wilson when they met the previous year: "'You know I could not remember who your friend was at all. And I just thought of who it was. It was this terrible queen who was here only one day. And if I had remembered who it was, I would have hung up on you. But I am very pleased to see you. . . .' Back then we were all gorgeous."

The three men soon found jobs and began making a home in New York: Morgan (who had managed a hotel in Chicago) quickly got a job at the Plaza and moved out of Wilson's life; Powell took a job with an upscale decorator and began acting; Wilson continued writing plays while working at various odd jobs. The two found a small apartment on Seventy-fourth Street on the block in which the cafe in Wilson's *Balm in Gilead* was located. The two men were under almost constant financial pressure. Once they were about to be thrown out of their hotel. As Powell noted, "So Lance [Wilson's nickname] wrote a play to be done at the Cino which would incorporate our bed and all of our possessions. After performing the play we would turn down the bed on stage and go to sleep."[21]

Wilson quickly found the local areas in which gay men cruised for sex, including a "wonderful cruising neighborhood" at Central Park West. Wilson remembers first meeting William M. Hoffman there; according to Hoffman, their first meeting occurred at a large party in the building in which Hoffman lived. When Wilson spoke of his interest in writing, either Hoffman or John Corigliano responded, "Oh you're a playwright; do you know the Caffe

Cino? That's where everyone starts out." Wilson was unable to go to the Cino that night; Powell went instead. The next day he told Wilson, "You've got to come down and see the outrageous show." Wilson went the next night. Though the precise time of the events is unclear, it seems likely that Wilson first attended the Cino early in January 1963 when Ionesco's *The Lesson* was playing. It was Wilson's introduction to Ionesco, to absurdism, and to the fledgling off-off-Broadway scene that became his theatrical base. He continued to attend productions at the Cino and was particularly impressed with David Starkweather's *You May Go Home Again* and *So, Who's Afraid of Edward Albee?* (both of which ran in February 1963).

Powell recalls the night that Wilson introduced himself to Joe Cino: "Lanford said to Joe, I want to be a writer and he [Powell] wants to be an actor. What should we do? 'Well,' Joe said, 'you write a play for him and do it here.' I was like 'Oh my god, isn't that brilliant.' You would have thought that something like that would be so . . . that we could have thought of it ourselves."[22] On August 25, 1963, Wilson's *So Long at the Fair* opened in a slot originally intended for *Home Free!* By the time Wilson persuaded Neil Flanagan to direct the latter show, however, he had submitted it to the Spoleto Festival, which considers only plays that have never been performed. When *Home Free!* was accepted for the festival, Wilson presented *So Long at the Fair* in its place. The work opened to a strong review by Michael Smith of the *Village Voice:* "Lanford Wilson's tense little comedy ends with one of the funniest single stage events I have ever witnessed. . . . What redeems Mr. Wilson's writing is the exactness and inner logic of his dialogue."[23] Some years later, the only copies of the manuscript were lost when Wilson sublet his apartment, leaving behind various materials (including the manuscripts for *So Long at the Fair* and *Sex Is Between Two People*). Some of the manuscripts recently have been returned to him, but the only copy of *So Long at the Fair* now known to exist predates that performed at the Cino.

Though all accounts suggest that *So Long at the Fair* was not equal to his later work, it was strong enough to attract favorable attention from Marshall Mason, who had already begun to gain a reputation for his skills as a director. After directing three plays by Claris Nelson at the Cino, Mason was, as he says, "full of myself."[24] With Nelson and seven other graduates of Northwestern University, Mason formed the unsuccessful Northwestern Productions, an endeavor that took him away from the Cino for some time. He returned to see the final performance of *So Long at the Fair*. Though he considered it "amazing, a wonderful play," he was most impressed with Powell's performance.[25]

Mason returned a few months later when *Home Free!* (January 1964) finally had its run at the Cino. It was probably Wilson's second production in the Caffe, although the record is somewhat confusing regarding the possible performance of an untitled play that began November 3, 1963. The off-off-Broadway section of the *Village Voice* for October 31, 1963, lists the untitled play as opening on November 3 (which, given the Cino's normal schedule, would suggest an ending date of November 9). Yet the listings for the following week in both the off-off-Broadway section and the Cafe–Coffee House section (dated November 7) show the current production as Lorca's *Don Cristobal.*

Though Powell was again "fabulous" in *Home Free!,* Mason was most impressed this time with the quality of the writing: "Not since Tennessee Williams had there been a writer like this. The first play, *So Long at the Fair,* was good, but what had struck me about it was Michael's performance. What struck me about *Home Free!* the minute I saw it was the *writing*" (emphasis in original).[26] On at least two points, the first version of the play differs markedly from that used in the August 1964 revival, the latter of which is the published version: the original uses a gyroscope instead of a Ferris wheel, and the revelation that the two characters are brother and sister occurs near the end of the play rather than at the beginning. In his interview with Jackson R. Bryer, Mason indicates dissatisfaction with the second, published version, noting that the first was a "tremendous experience," whereas the second was only "very good," reserving his primary criticism for the less magical staging of the second production as conceived by director William Archibald.[27] According to Wilson, Mason's response to the second version of *Home Free!* was significantly less favorable than Mason indicates in his interview. When Wilson asked him what he thought, Mason replied, "You've ruined it."[28]

The first meeting between Mason and Wilson occurred during the revival of *Home Free!* According to Mason, "Joe Cino said, 'Well, what did you say to Lance?' I said, 'I've never met Lance.' He said, 'You haven't met Lanford?' and I said, 'No.' He said, 'Sit down, I'll bring him out.' So he brought Lanford over and sat him down."[29] The meeting, of course, was one of the most important in recent theatrical history, resulting in a writer-director team of remarkable durability and productivity. Ironically, though the team was forged at Caffe Cino, only two of Wilson's plays at the Cino were directed by Mason, one of which *(The Sandcastle)* moved to the Cino only after premiering at La Mama. The notebook for the 1985 Lincoln Center exhibit seems to suggest that *Sandcastle* premiered at Caffe Cino in 1965 and was revived twice, once in 1966 with Robbie McCauley and William Haislip and again in 1967. According to Absher, *The Sandcastle* was scheduled to premier at the Cino under the title *Or Harry Can Dance,* though the production was canceled. It subsequently premiered at La Mama. It does seem to have played at the Cino benefit on March 15, 1965, some six months before it appeared at La Mama.

On May 18, 1964, the most successful of Wilson's Cino shows opened when Neil Flanagan stepped onto the stage as Leslie Bright, an aging drag queen going slowly mad in the solitude of his room. Wilson credits the production of Adrienne Kennedy's *Funnyhouse of a Negro* as his inspiration for *Lady Bright.* In part he was reacting to his dislike of Kennedy's play: "[T]alking about *Funny House* [*sic*] *of a Negro,* trashing it, seeing this silly black girl flip out in her room was the most uninteresting idea. I'd just as soon see some screaming faggot go mad, and I said, 'Wait a minute!'"[30] Wilson wrote *Lady Bright* while working at the reservation desk of the Americana Hotel. During a slow shift,

> I was down there, and I was thinking of a play by Adrienne Kennedy. And I called up, because it was still early, Neil Flanagan. "Neil what can we do at the Caffe Cino? I mean, what can we get away with?" He said, "What do you mean? As to what?" I said, "Well, can we write a play about a screaming queen going crazy alone in her room one afternoon?" "Write it and we'll see." And so I wrote *The Madness of Lady Bright* in a couple days on the typewriter down there in the bowels of that hotel. And took it in to him [at the Cino]. . . . He and his wife read it in his dressing room while the play [in which he was performing] was on. It was really a first draft.[31]

After reading the script, Flanagan came out to talk to the anxious playwright, who was not quite sure what to expect.

> "Well, you're going to have to get a very, very good director for this." I was crestfallen. I said, "Oh, I was hoping you would want to direct it." He said, "No, no. I'm going to play it." "Neil, you are not at all what I had in mind." "That's why you are going to have get a very good director."

Wilson selected Denis Deegan, who eleven months earlier had directed Michael Smith's first work, *I Like It.* One of Deegan's first comments after reading the play was to suggest the music, Mozart's twenty-third, second movement. It was, according to Wilson, the perfect music for *Lady Bright*. Response to the production was tremendous. In the *Village Voice,* Michael Smith observed that the work displays Wilson's "unmistakable talent for swift, biting dialogue," even though it "a few times slides toward sentiment and moralizing." He lauded Flanagan's performance as "expert and delightful, with a clear sense of modulations between joy and manic desperation."[32] Scheduled to run only two weeks (May 18 to May 31, 1964), the work was so popular that it was brought back two weeks later (though the Boy and the Girl, originally played by Carolina Lobravico and Eddie Kenmore, were replaced by Lucy Silvay and Tom Bigornia); it was revived frequently thereafter.

The subject matter was controversial, but the play seems to have offended relatively few audience members because, Wilson argues, of how beautifully it was done. Audience members often walked out of *So Long at the Fair* because of the language. In his naïveté, Wilson was unaware that the word *fuck* was avoided on the stage; and many in the audience objected to the incest of *Home Free!,* an objection that John Costopoulos suggests may have been shared by Cino and Flanagan: "Cino hated it [*Home Free!*]. When Wilson next showed it to Neil Flanagan, a Cino director, Flanagan said, 'Lance, I don't know. . . . I'm Catholic, and I'm not sure I can direct a play that's all about incest.'"[33] Wilson, however, believes that Flanagan's objection to the play was playful hyperbole and did not represent a serious objection. *Lady Bright* drew far less criticism than did the earlier two works. According to Wilson, audiences seemed to get what he was trying to say: "So many older women came to me and said, 'Your play is not about homosexuality, it's about loneliness.'"[34]

In the various revivals of the play, the structure changed, though precisely how fully is unclear. The scrapbook for the Caffe Cino exhibit in 1985 at Lincoln Center, reviews, advertisements, programs, and posters provide conflicting information. The most apparent difference between the various versions is in the number of characters involved, with the three possibilities being Lady Bright only, Lady Bright with a young man, and Lady Bright with a young man and a young woman. Table 1 summarizes the differences in number of actors and the source for the information. According to the scrapbook from Lincoln Center, the work again became a monologue when it appeared off Broadway at Theatre East; this assertion is supported by newspaper articles that announce the selection of the "sole actor" for the production[35] and by the program for the production.

Table 1. Number of Actors in *Madness of Lady Bright*

Date Performed (week of)	Scrapbook	Review or Advertisement	Program or Poster
May 18, 1964	1	3 *(Village Voice)*	—
June 15, 1964	3	3 *(N. Y. Post)*	3 (program)
July 13, 1964	2	—	—
October 18, 1964	2	—	2 (poster)
March 15, 1966	1	1	1 (program)
March 23, 1967	—	3 *(Village Voice)*	—

For Leslie Bright, madness is the consequence of loneliness. Sitting alone in his room, he is surrounded by memories of past sexual partners in the form of signatures on the wall—essentially hollowed-out, vacant signs of empty, one-night stands. Even the concept of "God" is emptied of meaning, being replaced by an anonymous recording on Dial-a-Prayer. Wilson strongly rejects any reading of the play that places homosexuality as the central issue of the play, suggesting that the play is about the effects of loneliness and an inability to form meaningful relationships.

> BOY *[faking a hurt voice]*. Well, you might consider—I looked over expecting you to be there—and there was nothing but loneliness.
> LESLIE *[to himself—listening in spite of himself]*. Loneliness. *[He is not looking toward them.]*
> GIRL. You were asleep when I came back.
> BOY. It's a terrible thing to wake up to loneliness. *[Leslie looks sharply toward him at the word repeated.]*
> LESLIE. You know nothing about loneliness.[36]

Leslie Bright is left with only imaginary companions—Dial-a-Prayer, the Boy and Girl, and the signatures on the wall, all meaningless or imaginary remains of past shallow relationships.

Wilson's Cino plays share several basic traits. They are less experimental in form and structure than were many of the productions at Caffe Cino and other off-off-Broadway venues. In discussing a group of Wilson's plays, Michael Smith describes them as "distinguished by flexible naturalistic speech that establishes characters expertly and precisely. . . . His works deal mostly in character rather than idea or image and are similar in impulse, if not in style, to many plays by Tennessee Williams."[37] Also, as Smith comments with some justification, Wilson's plays from the Cino period often fail to reach deeper meanings or emotions.

> Lanford Wilson is still operating among familiar and safe emotions: he has not yet dived down among the feelings within feelings, the nameless surges that lie behind a true tragic or comic vision. He is creating a flexible and promising technique. How far he can go with it depends on the extent and courage of his vision.[38]

Of the Cino plays, *The Madness of Lady Bright* and *This is the Rill Speaking* are the most complex and adventurous structurally. Probably the most frequent theme running through the plays relates to the difficulty and challenges of close relationships. In *Sex Is Between Two People* (1965), for example, two young men, played by Robert Dahdah and Neil Flanagan, meet at a gay bathhouse that probably was modeled on the old St. Mark's Baths. They part frustrated, having only nervously chatted with each other. They are unable to overcome the gulf that separates them. The more timid and naïve of the two dresses to leave; feigning sophistication and self-assurance, the second man initially decides to leave but changes his mind and goes to join an orgy in another part of the bathhouse. Ironically, their inability to relate to each other means that sex does not occur between the two people in the play.

Wilson's arrival in 1963 helped move Caffe Cino toward increasingly professional, polished productions. Like others involved in the off-off-Broadway movement, most at the Cino were not offended by a certain degree of amateurishness in their productions; many even valued that amateurishness. As journalist John Keating noted, off-off-Broadway "is amateur in just about every sense of the word. It is aggressively, sometimes self-consciously, amateur. . . ."[39] In many ways Joe Cino's idiosyncratic method of selecting plays only enhanced the nonprofessional appearance. Thus, for example, on October 7, 1963, he presented a play by a high school student whose name was variously listed as Kelly Davis and Kelly Smith. Cino was not particularly impressed with the work: "The youngster, Kelly Smith [*sic*], got a showing on Cornelia Street not because his play, *Flywheel*, was really great—for, in the opinion of Joe Cino, who decides what gets produced at his cafe, that's precisely what it wasn't. 'But,' Cino explains, 'the fact that the kid was so young and that he did have something to say made us fell [*sic*] there was a value in doing it.'"[40] Cino's reason for staging Davis/Smith's work seems central to his overall method of operating: he encouraged artists who had no other venue in which to perform because of age, sexuality, experience, or subject matter if they genuinely had something to say.

By the fall of 1963 new salvos were fired in the coffeehouse war. In 1962 the city had moved responsibility for licensing coffeehouses from the police department to the department of licenses, in large part because of charges of corruption within the police department. The move, however, brought no respite in the actions against coffeehouses. The efforts of the Cafe Theatre Association at self-policing had little effect on the operation of most coffeehouses (including some of its own members). In August the *New York Times* listed some of the ongoing abuses as poorly written menus with barely legible prices, dim lighting that made reading menus even more difficult, bothersome barkers who lured customers inside, admission prices of as much as $2.50 with an additional minimum order of one dollar, excessively high-priced drinks, and collections taken after performances.[41] Despite the continued actions by city officials, rulings by courts remained inconsistent. The city won a case in May 1963 when a court ruling reversed an earlier action and forced Cafe Figaro to discontinue its concerts. Less than a year later the city lost a case when Judge James Camerford dismissed a suit brought by the Department of Licenses against LeMetro Caffe Espresso for allowing poetry readings.

Aggressive action against coffeehouses and other arts establishments continued into 1964 as the city's building department ordered eleven coffeehouses (including Caffe Cino) to close[42]; the order was largely ignored. At the same time, the city seems to have increased enforcement of regulations that allowed the showing of films only if the venue was licensed by the New York State Board of Regents. Journalist Stephanie Gervis Harrington suggested that speculation about the cause of the city's more aggressive stance against avant-garde artists ranged from efforts by officials to clean up New York before the World's Fair to infighting within the license department to determine who would succeed former commissioner Bernard J. O'Connell. O'Connell had been appointed to the criminal court by Mayor Wagner; those who wished to replace him may have increased action against coffeehouses as an effort to "demonstrate their zeal for serving the people."[43] With the aggressive actions by the city in late March 1964, artists and patrons became increasingly discontent. Poet and playwright Diane di Prima described their concerns:

An epidemic has seized Manhattan Island, an epidemic of rage and fear and frustration. Bit by bit, all the life of downtown Manhattan is being turned off. The coffee houses have had to fight to keep going. The number of off-Broadway theatres has been lessened by four by the License Bureau. Screenings of experimental films—which were flourishing and had just developed a large audience—have stopped altogether. The Living Theatre has been seized, and the New York Poets Theatre has been effectively stopped. Painters and sculptors are again facing the possibility of losing their loft situation. . . . [44]

To protest, artists and activists planned a march for April 22, beginning at six p.m. at Forty-first Street and ending at Lincoln Center. Led by di Prima and Julian Beck, the march went much as planned, though participants were not allowed to carry a coffin labeled "Will Freedom Be Buried?" According to police, to do so would turn the march into a parade, which ironically required additional bureaucratic permission.

In the summer of 1964 Edward Koch renewed his efforts to force action against unlicensed coffeehouses and similar businesses in the Village, arguing that the city had thus far been unsuccessful in decreasing congestion in the MacDougal. Summonses and fines had proved useless, since the businesses simply considered them to be a part of their "rent" and remained open in violation of the law.[45] In July Koch began an effort that would be one of the most successful movements against the coffeehouses when he announced the formation of the MacDougal Street Area Neighborhood Association (MANA). At the organizational meeting for MANA, a spokesman for the Department of Licenses announced the problem to the group: "There are only six legal coffee houses in all of Greenwich Village. The rest are illegal"[46]; his department could do nothing about increasing fines for those facilities that operated illegally. He failed to note that coffeehouses blamed infighting between city departments and (perhaps intentional) inaction by the Department of Licenses for the fact that applications for licenses lay for month after month without resolution.

The coffeehouse war did nothing to curtail the productions at Caffe Cino. In February 1964 Ruth Yorck presented *Lullaby for a Dying Man*, the only one of her plays to be presented at the Caffe Cino, though Yorck was a significant figure there and at similar venues. Her *Happening at the Cafe* (1964) has sometimes erroneously been called *Happening at the Cino*, as occurred in her obituaries.[47] Yorck served as a link with an older, European avant-garde, having, according to Leo Lerman, "triumphantly nonconformed in '20s Berlin, '30s Paris/London, '50s–'60s New York."[48] Born Ruth Landshoff in Berlin in 1904, Yorck grew up at the center of European intellectual and artistic life, counting among her friends Ernst Toller, Bertolt Brecht, Thomas Mann, and Albert Einstein. As a young woman, before she had begun to study acting at the Reinhardt School, she appeared in several avant-garde films, including *Nosferatu* (1922), the landmark silent film about Dracula; she created something of a scandal by appearing nude in Carl Theodor Dreyer's *Die Gezeichneten* in 1922.

From a privileged background, Yorck enjoyed the decadent life of Berlin in the twenties, sneaking away from home to frequent one of the many gay bars: "I liked the soft, pretty boys. And they of course liked me. Because my hips were as narrow as they hoped theirs to be. I liked to dance with them. And listen to them. They liked to talk clothes. I was of course offered cocaine and was very excited and tried. It made my nose feel funny . . . but it made me sleepy and not high."[49] She occasionally cross-dressed, having "learned how to enhance my secondary male attributes. That is I learned to look more like a boy than nature intended me to."[50] Dressed as a boy and called René, she placed a tangerine in her left pants pocket to give the impression of male genitalia. One evening she met and danced with a new girl: "pretty of course, doelike brown gentle very thin and long legged."[51] Over the course of the night, she continued to dance and flirt with the young woman, having consequences that Yorck claims not to have expected: "Come home with me she said. Don't be a goose I said. She begged. I stopped dancing. She did not want to let go. Don't be silly I said. I am a girl. Don't you know that?"[52] The only way Yorck could convince her was to take her into the toilet and strip from the waist up. She showed no compassion for the distraught woman: "I had not been serious. How stupid to fall in love with me. The gril [*sic*] sat down on the lid of the WC and started to cry. I tries [*sic*] embarrassed to console her. For what. Ridiculous. She cried very hard. . . . What a bore."[53] Later Yorck donned male clothing to audition for the part of Lord Alfred Douglas in a play by Carl Sternheim; she did not get the part. Eventually she gave her men's clothing to her brother when he got his first engagement with an orchestra.

Through a short marriage to a member of German's nobility, Landshoff became Countess Ruth Yorck von Wurtenburg. Like her husband, Yorck opposed the rise of Hitler, ultimately fleeing to safety in the United States where she lived in comparative poverty and where she continued her opposition to Nazism. By the time she left Germany, she already had established a significant reputation for her novels and poems.

Decades before entering Caffe Cino, Ruth Yorck had violated and made fun of traditional gender codes—cross-dressing, dancing with "pretty boys" in bars, and flirting with "pretty girls" at parties. She had also discovered the fluidity of identity: "I was leading a double life. I was leading a triple life. Or changed my way of life twice a day or once a week. No I was I R[uth]. L[andshoff]. an image. I was the young well behaved daughter of a middle class family, a happy house. I was a call girl. My honest father's telephon [sic] number figured in many a small black book."[54] Issues of gender and identity appear in many of her American plays. *Lullaby for a Dying Man* centers on homoerotic attraction; in *Love Song for Mrs. Boas, Yorck suggests a lesbian* undercurrent to the relationship between Biblical figures Ruth and Naomi.

Lullaby for a Dying Man is the story of a condemned man (Victim) who has committed murder because of his inability to express love.[55] Sentenced to death, the Victim experiences an existential crisis in fearing that he will die without having ever lived: "I've never had anything happen in my whole life. I mean important things like hate or love or spending sprees or a trip to somewhere. A man has to create something special to fill his life. Make it worthwhile. I am short on time. I have got to cram an experience into my last minutes. Quickly."[56] The underlying significance seems to come from existential philosophy—the belief that (in the words of Robert G. Olson) "the commanding value in life is intensity, as manifested in acts of free choice, individual self-assertion, personal love, or creative work."[57]

As a prisoner who is being transported to his execution, the Victim has few options open to him in deciding how to "cram" experience into his life. He chooses what seems his only option, falling in love. In doing so, he chooses someone who is stronger, superior to himself, someone to whom he must submit:

I want to live before I die. What shall I do? What can I do? I have to fall in love. That's the least I can do. Who is there to fall in love with? This whole prison is full of men. Shouldn't I fall in love with a man? . . . perhaps a man behind bars, there are so many. My heart goes out to them. No, not really. They are broken, vanquished men, conquered men. Down in their luck. They demand compassion, not passion. No. I want a person who is not conquered. If I cannot conquer him, I will submit to him. I have to submit to make it love. And life is that: submission.[58]

Ignoring a priest's advice that he turn his thoughts to God, the Victim turns to love of the Guard; but the Victim does not want the Guard to become a murderer by participating in his (the Victim's) execution. To do so would mean that the Guard has fallen to the same level as has the Victim. His only means of preventing such a downfall is to murder the Guard before the execution: "I have to do this. You will be grateful. I have to save you. I love you. I cannot stand and watch you to be guilty of my death. I tell you it is hell being a murderer. You must not be a murderer. And for me it does not make any difference. I hold your sweet throat in the palm of my hand, your heart, your sweet life, my angel. I love you. There is a moment in love when a man dies a death of splendor."[59] By killing the Guard, the Victim allows him to die in innocence.

In addition to several plays, Yorck's literary output after her arrival in the United States includes a few novels, many poems, and several essays drawn from memory about the famous people in her life. She worked with Ellen Stewart during the early, difficult years of Cafe La Mama and shared her knowledge and experience with aspiring playwrights, directors, and actors. She told John Gruen that she had been discovered and rediscovered frequently: "I am rediscovered every year, but like Persephone, I always return underground."[60] She died January 19, 1966, while she and Stewart were at the Martin Beck Theatre awaiting the opening curtain for a matinee production of Peter Weiss's play *Marat/Sade*. Initially Stewart's cries for help brought no assistance because the audience, anticipating an avant-garde work, thought that the commotion was the opening scene of the production. At the time of her death, Yorck lived at 21 Cornelia Street, only a few doors from the Cino. One year after her death, Ellen Stewart offered Ruth Yorck's Golden Series, a presentation of nine full-length off-off-Broadway plays beginning with Leonard Melfi's *Niagara Falls*.

While Ruth Yorck linked the avant-garde of off-off-Broadway to the earlier European avant-garde, H. M. Koutoukas sought new directions in experimental theatre, often by infusing older, traditional forms with new meanings and perspectives. A prolific writer and winner of the National Arts Club Award, he had seen seventy-five of his plays performed by 1972, according to his biography in Michael Smith's collection *More Plays from Off-Off Broadway*; a press release in 1978 referred to *Too Late for Yogurt* as his 152nd play, though these numbers may be exaggerated.[61] Noted for his wild, campy style, his surreal, existential worlds, his highly poetic language, Koutoukas writes in a variety of styles, from the poetic *Tidy Passions, or Kill, Kaleidoscope, Kill* to the slightly more prosaic *With Creatures Make My Way,* from the outrageous camp of *Only a Countess May Dance When She's Crazy* to the gentle sentimentality of *A Letter from Colette.* Characteristic of his plays is the creation of a bizarre, inscrutable world in which characters attempt to construct or determine some meaning, both for the world at large and for their own lives in particular. His works are often less concerned with the interaction of characters than with one or a few characters' search for meaning and meaningfulness. Though Koutoukas was both popular and prolific, very few of his plays have ever been published. At the 2003 conference of the Association for Theatre in Higher Education (ATHE), he said that all of his "things are shredded" after performance. According to his friend and fellow playwright Robert Heide, Koutoukas has always hesitated to publish his works because he wrote for a specific moment and does not wish to allow publication to freeze them in time or to remove them from the context for which they were written.

Koutoukas's biography is not easily determined, since he, like many other off-off-Broadway figures, often told conflicting stories about himself. According to Jameson Currier, "The details of Koutoukas's early life are either sketchy or varied, preferably so, it seems, since the theatrical personality himself told a friend and interviewer for a gay newspaper in Manhattan in 1990, 'Let's just say I arrived in the Village.'"[62] Koutoukas was born June 4, 1947. His place of birth has variously been listed as Athens, Greece,[63] and Binghamton[64] or Endicott,[65] New York, with the last being the correct location. As a teenager he apprenticed in summer stock, working with Veronica Lake, Constance Bennett, and Margaret Truman. After studying at the New School for Social Research with such notable figures as Maria Ley Piscator (the wife of modernist theatre director Erwin Piscator and a notable theatre figure in her own right), he launched a career that included creating performance pieces with Yoko Ono long before her marriage to Beetle John Lennon, writing campy plays, and directing glittery productions that pioneered the style now known as genderfuck.

At the recent ATHE conference, Koutoukas spoke of his start as a playwright: "I was going to kill myself but I decided to write a play instead so that I could leave something behind that I had made with my bare hands. . . . Then I forgot to kill myself." Warhol actor Ondine suggested that Koutoukas submit his work to a competition. The play, *Last Triangle,* won. When a producer wanted to stage the work, Koutoukas met with him.

I went to his [a producer's] office and asked, "What can you do for me?"—that's what 20-year-olds are supposed to ask. He reached in his pocket and pulled out all this money. I pretended I had to go to the bathroom.

On the street, I ran into Joe Cino and decided I wanted to work someplace where money wasn't the first thing that came up. Now, age has taught me that it comes up no matter where you are.[66]

Koutoukas had moved to New York to "die for art. I didn't want money. I just wanted consumption."[67]

In his work Koutoukas frequently turns to traditional, classical structures for his experimentation: "But if you want to get wild or campy, you need the strength of the Classical structure. Then your teapots can have nervous break-downs."[68] As David Hirsh explains, Koutoukas merges the classical and romantic: "Classical structure becomes a common device supporting the weight of a Romantic inflection which is meant to bring down the stars. The Romantic and Classical are united by sexual longing at its most campy."[69]

Though many of the Cino playwrights and directors used camp in their productions, Koutoukas is the artist most closely associated with the style. His work is characterized by the use of glitter, cross-dressing, and outrageous styles, though his biography in *The Off-Off-Broadway Book* goes a bit too far in crediting Koutoukas with having invented camp. For gay men, camp was a means of covert communication and of publicly acknowledging their sexuality without the risk of an overt statement. In terms that apply to Koutoukas's plays, Michael Bronski describes how camp is used by gay men: "Gays have hidden themselves from oppressive straight society through circumlocution—camp—and defended themselves through wit. In gay life nothing is what it seems to be. By pulling the rug out from under usual gender expectations—is it a boy or a girl?—or sexual arrangements—what *do* they do in bed?—homosexual life and culture undermine patriarchal and heterosexist social assumptions."[70] At about the same time that Koutoukas's first play, *Only a Countess May Dance When She's Crazy,* was being performed (December 1964), Susan Sontag published her "Notes on 'Camp'" in the fall 1964 issue of *Partisan Review.* She defines camp as "love of the unnatural: of artifice and exaggeration. And Camp is esoteric—something of a private code, a badge of identity even, among small urban cliques."[71] Sontag's essay has proved particularly important in discussions of camp, with many subsequent writers refuting or trumpeting her various contentions.

In the midsixties, camp became a topic of debate in the *Village Voice,* when Vivian Gornick published an essay that seems to equate the rise of pop art and certain strains of sexism with the growing visibility and strength of homosexuals. Gay men, Gornick suggests, have taken over popular culture: "It [e.g., camp] is homosexual taste that determines largely style, story, statement in painting, literature, dance, amusements, and acquisitions for a goodly proportion of the intellectual middle class."[72] To Gornick, underlying the camp sensibility is a rejection of women. Furthermore she argues that the influence of camp has become so strong because "[w]e have become disheartened, demoralized, and finally hysterical—so intolerable is our circumstance. The world thus must be declared a topsy-turvy place, the banners of renunciation must wave."[73] Responding to Gornick, Suzanne Kiplinger argues that the characteristics of camp that Gornick attributes to homosexual men actually are the characteristics of the hipster, particularly Norman Mailer's superman-psychopath as described in "The White Negro." Kiplinger notes that "triviality, hatred of authority, impatience, exaltation of style, and so on" are characteristics of both camp and the hipster but that the emotional aloofness and charm attributed by Gornick to camp are actually the distinctive traits of the hipster psychopath.[74] In a period of increasing political activism, camp was seen as either politically ineffectual or disengaged. As Avery Corman argued in a letter to the editors of the *Voice* in which he decried the amount of coverage given to "zany, wacky stuff infused with pop, jazz, rock 'n' roll, vamp, and camp": "Direct your influence toward what is really needed in the theatre—scripts and writers with commitment, with vision, and with balls. Nobody is going to make the world a better place by giggling or waltzing through with butterfly nets."[75] The implication, of course, is that a politically engaged theatre is efficacious only if its commitment and vision are accompanied by austerity, severity, and masculinity.

Koutoukas's work can hardly be considered austere or severe. Michael Smith summarizes Koutoukas's style as

> flamboyantly romantic, idiosyncratic, sometimes self-satirizing, full of private references and inside jokes, precious, boldly aphoristic, and disdainful of restrictions of sense, taste, or fashion. Koutoukas is perhaps the last of the aesthetes. Underlying the decoration, his characteristic themes concern people or creatures who have become so strange that they have lost touch with ordinary life, yet their feelings are all the

more tender and vulnerable—the deformed, the demented, the rejected, the perverse.[76]

As a protégé of avant-garde filmmaker and performance artist Jack Smith, Koutoukas was influenced by works such as *Flaming Creatures* and by Smith's interest in actress Maria Montez. Though many critics spoke of Montez's limitations as a performer, Smith was fascinated by her. In "The Perfect Filmic Appositeness of Maria Montez," he wrote, "M. M. dreamed she was effective, imagined she acted, cared for nothing but her fantasy (she attracted the fantasy movies to herself—that needed her—they would have been ridiculous with any other actress—any other human being). Those who credit dreams became her fans."[77] *Cobra Woman* (1944), in which Montez appeared, proved particularly fertile ground for Koutoukas's imagination, so much so that references to cobra jewels appear in many of his works. Sometime after the demise of the Cino, he appeared in a work written specifically for him by Harvey Fierstein and entitled *In Search of the Cobra Jewels.*

While Koutoukas's Cino plays have no explicitly gay characters, they constantly challenge and transgress gender codes. Koutoukas was fascinated by the classical practice of men playing women's roles. Thus his work often was written with the intent of being played by either a man or a woman: Countess Olie Samovitch, for example, in Koutoukas's first Cino play, *Only a Countess May Dance When She's Crazy* (1964), initially was played by Carole Griffith but has since been played by both men and women; in the 1990 production Everett Quinton played the role. Shortly after the opening of *With Creatures Make My Way*, Elizabeth Davison, who played the sole character (Creature, sovereign of the sewers), was replaced by Warren Finnerty.

Koutoukas creates in his plays an absurdist world devoid of meaning but always on the verge of meaning, a nonsense realm threatening to achieve but never achieving clarity, as in *With Creatures Make My Way:*

> Come come and know the reason
> No promise can be kept
> For secrets are for knowing
> And voices are for the dumb.[78]

This world, in which basic signifying systems are sabotaged and understanding is always deferred, reflects the existentialist's understanding of existence. Philosopher Abraham Kaplan explains, "It is not in the least accidental that existentialism should have taken hold of the public mind some hundred years after it might have done so: its basic tenets were already quite clearly expressed in the nineteenth century. For today large parts of the earth's population feel that they are confronted with a world they never made, a world too vast and complex to yield to human urging and one which is indifferent—if not downright hostile—to human aspiration."[79] It is the skirting of meaning, the presentation of an indecipherable, paradoxical universe that so frequently leads to the linking of madness with Koutoukas's work: Robert Heide says, "His plays came out of an internal, psychic madness. It is as if he did not always know what he wrote—the plays came out of a dreamscape"[80]; similarly, John Gruen wrote in *Vogue* in 1969, "Koutoukas dwells on fantasy and madness, stretching reality toward points of no return."[81]

Among the most frequently discussed of Koutoukas's works is *Medea or Maybe the Stars May Understand or Veiled Strangeness,* a work influenced by a news story about a young woman in Harlem who killed her child. In quick succession, *Medea* premiered at La Mama, only days later opened at the Cino, and subsequently played at Theatre Genesis. At Theatre Genesis, *Medea* was played by a woman; at La Mama and Caffe Cino, under the direction of Koutoukas, the role was played by the bearded Charles Stanley, probably now best known for his pioneering work with Deborah Lee and Yvonne Rainer in postmodern dance. Though Koutoukas generally remains faithful to the overall concepts of the original myth, he takes many liberties, recreating and revising the story. He reduces the scope of his play, focusing on only the concluding scenes of the original work, reduces the number of children to one (making a cast of four characters: Medea, Jason, the child, and a Red Cross nurse), and presents Jason as weak and ineffectual. Perhaps most indicative of the style of the piece is the setting (a Laundromat). Koutoukas mingles the common with the exalted, the mundane with the sublime, the comedic with the tragic. In her fury Medea dashes bleach in Jason's face and kills their child by throwing him into a washing machine (not forgetting, of course, to include an appropriate measure of Oxydol detergent). In his review for the *Village Voice,* Michael Smith describes the play as being

> so eccentric as to be nearly unthinkable. The play is a straightforward enactment of the final terrible scene when Medea murders her child to avenge herself on Jason. The language is high-flown as befits tragedy, the tragic impulse is pursued without deviation, and Koutoukas has

injected a philosophical content of evident seriousness—the play is violently anti-logic, anti-Greek. Medea is the very heroine of old—fanatical, hideously wronged, ecstatically suffering.[82]

In Medea, Koutoukas may have captured the heroine of old, but he did so through a campy subversion of the traditional form of the tragedy. When Stanley performed as Medea, he did so with a full beard and with no effort to pass as a woman. Koutoukas suggests that Medea emerges from a position of rage, pain, and marginalization so great that she is outside or beyond terms such as *gender* and *sex,* that her emotions are so overwhelming as to defy containment within such traditional constructs. In his review Smith notes that "Charles Stanley is a grotesque Medea, in not quite the same way that Medea was a grotesque woman, but as the play goes on he becomes invidiously convincing." When Linda Eskenas played Medea at Theatre Genesis (opening just before Stanley's final performance in the role at the Cino), Smith seems to have found the introduction of a real woman's body into the role to have weakened and confused the production: "Linda Eskenas plays Medea more naturally, with less madness and ecstasy than did Charles Stanley. . . . One is more able to see the real woman inside this monster of suffering and vengeance, which is valuable. But the monster is diminished in the process, the mythical grandeur yields to comprehension, and the performance fails to accumulate the headlong force the play requires."[83] The actual presence of a woman's body, then, makes the performance too real, too understandable, too recognizable. Smith's analysis of Eskenas's performance echoes Goethe's comments in "Women's Parts Played by Men in the Roman Theatre": "We come to know this nature [of women] even better because someone else has observed it, reflected on it, and presents us not with the thing itself but with the result of the thing."[84] A distillation of "womanliness" presented by and through a male body has greater validity and clarity while also being more pleasurable to watch because it is removed from the real object. Both Smith and Goethe seem to mistake a socially coded performance and audience reception of gender with what they assume to be a real, essential gender. They are conflating gender as performance with gender as a reality tied to a specific type of body.

It was a position of absolute marginalization that intrigued Koutoukas and became central to many of his plays. Most of his characters are outrageous and bizarre. To be ordinary or mundane in Koutoukas's world is the great tragedy.

According to Koutoukas, we strive to be different, to be extraordinary, to be individuated from the mass of people, and not to be what Abraham Kaplan calls "a personified type without human personality."[85] As Clackety Clack says in *Awful People Are Coming Over So We Must Be Pretending to Be Hard at Work and Hope They Will Go Away* (a play written after the Cino closed), "I guess each man would like to find something a little different in his life; something that made his living a bit of a parable. Wouldn't it be nice to leave a little story of your life behind? It wouldn't have to say much, it would probably do more if it just gave others a chuckle."[86] Koutoukas's characters strive for the exceptional and the unique that Koutoukas values, a quality captured by Stanley in his performance (despite the "amateurishness" Smith found in the production).

Through his outrageousness Koutoukas became one of the most popular and unusual figures at the Cino. Even his calls for actors showed his particular flair; according to an unidentified clipping in the files of the New York Public Library, "Harry says he needs the following: one trained panther, a male-female dwarf chorus that can tap dance, and a sort of rough Dietrich-type male impersonator. Freaks of all kinds are also wanted, but they must be able to sing and/or dance." He directed most of his own plays and appeared in works by other playwrights, notably as Wonder Woman–Diana Prince in *The Secret of Taboo Mountain,* the first of the comic book productions. In 1966 Koutoukas won a special citation during the *Village Voice* Obie Awards presentation "for the style and energy of his assaults on the theatre in both playwriting and production."[87]

Koutoukas's arrival at the Caffe Cino late in 1964 helped shift the caffe's direction; about the same time, three other events helped shift the direction of the coffeehouse war. First, the newly formed Coffee House Employees Guild led a strike against the Why Not Cafe and Basement Cafe, both of which were owned by Harry Cropper. The union demanded a minimum wage of one dollar per hour plus tips for waiters, along with a guarantee of at least five dollars per day for performers. The *Village Voice* noted that Cropper cited several reasons for not meeting the salary demands, including the licensing problems: he was unable to pay entertainers, since he did not have a coffeehouse license; he could not obtain a license because of zoning problems; and those zoning problems were not likely to be resolved, since MacDougal Street merchants and residents were opposed to coffeehouses.[88] To show the degree of animosity some in the area felt toward coffeehouses, the *Voice* quoted a figure whose name often appears in opposition to the establishments: "Izzy Young, proprietor of the Folklore Center at 110 MacDougal Street, wants to see the owners 'extirpated.' They are animals,' he said, 'making a lot of money on underpaid kids who are being held up for the tourists to laugh at. They should be shot.'"[89]

The second event of the fall of 1964 was the continuing growth of the bohemian community in the East Village. For some time Stewart's La Mama had been one of the few arts venues on the east side, but new locations began to open and older establishments changed their operations to attract the young artists. Among the most significant of this latter group was Speedy Hartman's Old Reliable, a "funky, junky, divey bar on Third Street [. . . where] authentic lowlife—junkies, pimps, whores, pushers—cavorts at the bar over a gin or a 50-cent draft."[90] It had been a quiet Polish bar, depending on sales to afternoon drinkers and a boost in income from the occasional wedding reception. According to the *Voice,* Hartman decided to try to attract a different clientele. So he cornered a young "beatnik" walking by and asked how to turn his place into a Village bar. "'You need atmosphere,' said the beatnik. 'What's atmosphere?' asked Speedy. The beatnik thought for a minute and answered, 'More people like me.'"[91] Hartman installed a jukebox, brought in a few "hipsters" as bartenders, and began serving free french fries. In only a matter of weeks, the Old Reliable was so crowded that he had to turn away customers. With the poetry and arts scene migrating eastward, Hartman eventually converted his small dance floor in the back room into a theatre; after the Caffe Cino closed, Cino regulars such as Robert Patrick, Eric Concklin, Helen Hanft, William M. Hoffman, Bill Haislip, and Walter Michael Harris moved to the Old Reliable. From its first production in the summer of 1967 through its close in 1971, the Old Reliable functioned much like the Caffe Cino, though Hartman's disorganization seems to have exceeded even that of Cino.[92]

The third event in the fall and winter of 1964 that threatened coffeehouses was, yet again, renewed vigor in official actions against coffeehouses. Perhaps responding to MANA and Edward Koch's pressure, on Monday, November 2, city corporation counsel Leo Larkin ordered a crackdown on coffeehouses in the MacDougal Street area. Only a month later, however, Village coffeehouses received one of the few pieces of encouraging news in some time when a meeting of MANA concluded in a "hands-across-the-political-factions moment of good will."[93] Even the nemesis of coffeehouses, Edward Koch, expressed concern about the well-being of the Gaslight coffeehouse. He noted that then-existing laws and regulations made it difficult to distinguish between "good and bad" venues, with the Gaslight presumably being one of the good establishments.[94] The conclusion of the MANA meeting brought with it hope for a conclusion to the politically charged coffeehouse war.

By 1965 the reputation of Caffe Cino was expanding, and it was becoming particularly known for presenting gay or gay-friendly works. The Cino presented performances by and about gay men to a degree never before experienced, though according to William M. Hoffman the presentation of gay plays was not a central purpose of Caffe Cino: "Joe Cino became a play producer because many of his customers wanted to put on shows, and he and many of his customers were gay. Joe Cino did not have an obsession with homosexuality. He simply had an extraordinary largeness of spirit that allowed other people to explore, set other people aflame to express what they never had been allowed to before. So at the Cino we experimented with the theater in both straight and gay plays."[95] The central figures in its operation were gay or bisexual (Johnny Dodd, Jonathan Torrey, Kenneth Burgess, and Joe Cino), as were its primary artists (William M. Hoffman, Doric Wilson, Lanford Wilson, Roberta Sklar, Neil Flanagan, and Tom Eyen). Perhaps as a result, productions that did not have lesbian or gay characters reflected a gay sensibility when produced at the Cino: "Both gay plays and gay theater were pioneered at the Cino from the beginning. Early productions can only be described as homosexual in style: a vivid sexy *Deathwatch* (Jean Genet) and *Philoctetes* (André Gide)."[96] Descriptors that Hoffman associates with this style include "sexy," "drag," "frequent references to homosexuals," "campy," "witty," and "affirmed in a positive fashion the existence of gays."[97]

Some time ago Robert Patrick stirred up more than a bit of controversy with his pseudoautobiographical, romantic novel *Temple Slave,* in which he describes the gay orgies and drug abuse at Espresso Buono, a coffeehouse in Greenwich Village not unlike Caffe Cino. The work is fiction and clearly should not be taken as an accurate portrayal of any real persons or events. But some who were part of the Cino scene point to the novel as an accurate portrayal of the atmosphere at the Cino, while others strongly reject the portrait it contains. As Patrick has said,

> Except for the title character cooly observing Joe Buono's suicide, everything that happens in Temple Slave really happened. It didn't all happen in one place, and it certainly didn't all happen to one person. There were as many Caffe Cinos as there were people who came through

the door. There is no one simple truth about the place. No one knew everything that went on there. That is why my story is cast as fiction, and why I have encouraged each of its critics to write about his Cino— each of which would, believe me, seem as fictitious to me as mine does to them.[98]

The controversy over the novel centers on three questions: How prevalent was drug use at the Cino? To what extent was it a gay space? How common were orgies and similar activities? Definitive answers to the questions are difficult, since different Cino regulars provide sharply contrasting responses. To some degree, answers also depend on the particular time about which one chooses to speak.

Whatever the validity of his novel as a description of Caffe Cino, Patrick is certainly a significant figure in the history of the Cino, as well as in the histories of off-off-Broadway and gay theatre. As Hoffman suggests in his introduction to *Gay Plays,* the history of the Cino, the start of off-off-Broadway, and the emergence of gay theatre are bound to each other. Born Robert Patrick O'Connor on September 27, 1937, in Kilgore, Texas, Patrick grew up in an environment of relative poverty characterized by instability as his father moved from town to town seeking work in the oil fields. To escape from the turbulence of his childhood, Patrick turned to radio programs, movies, and other aspects of popular culture, an influence that is easily recognizable in his plays. Though he had never attended a live performance, he enjoyed reenacting movies he had seen or creating plays with his friends and sisters. Since his understanding of theatre was shaped by the movies he saw, he had no real concept of the aesthetic differences between the stage and film. Finally a roving theatre group was stranded near his home during World War II and had to raise funds so that they could continue to travel. Thus they hastily erected a tent to house a variety of entertainments, including a play, a puppet show, and an amateur contest. Shortly after this exposure to live theatre, Patrick gained his first real experience in the theatre when he participated in a school production in Roswell, New Mexico. As he matured as an artist, he became increasingly convinced of the political, social, and aesthetic power of the stage as compared with film, since the former is an experience shared between the actors and audience at the moment of creation: "Unlike films and literature, which record experiences that once happened, a play presents an event. Its *reality* makes it a powerful moral and psychological tool."[99]

After spending three years at Eastern New Mexico University in Portales, Patrick worked in the kitchen of a summer stock theatre. When the summer ended, he decided to go to New York for a short visit. During his first hour in the city, he went sightseeing in Greenwich Village, encountered a young man with what he called in *Temple Slave* an "ass of infinity,"[100] and followed him to Caffe Cino: "Two actors were rehearsing the 'muffin scene' from *The Importance of Being Earnest*. They would stop when they missed a line and go back. I thought *that* was the play, and I thought it the most brilliantly experimental work I'd ever seen. (I thought so 14 years later when Tom Stoppard did it in *Travesties*.)"[101] Enamored of the people, the atmosphere, and the productions, Patrick returned frequently, soon volunteering for various chores and becoming a self-described slave at the temple of Caffe Cino: "I didn't know that movement would be the most important, innovative, experimental theatrical event of the second half of the century. I just knew that I had found a lot of wonderful, gay people, an alternative to the dreary chain gangs of the bars and baths and streets, a breeding-place for gay dignity and wit."[102] Doric Wilson's work provided Patrick an introduction to the Cino and to gay-oriented theatre: "When I fell in love with the Cino's first playwright, Doric Wilson (a fact he will learn here for the first time) I didn't know he'd wind up a famous gay theatre manager and movement dramatist. I just knew he wrote wonderful, obscure, Absurdist plays."[103]

Associated with the Cino from 1961, Patrick did not write his first play until 1964. His interest in writing grew out of his fascination with theatre artists; it was a means for him to continue to fraternize with "those fascinating, deranged, charming characters called actors."[104] Though it took him a few years to develop an interest in writing, he has been remarkably prolific, so much so that Michael Feingold compared him to Spain's Lope de Vega.[105] When Patrick presented his first play, *The Haunted Host,* to Joe Cino, the coffeehouse entrepreneur initially tried to dissuade Patrick from becoming a playwright. Cino allowed the budding playwright to present his play only after Lanford Wilson, Tom Eyen, and David Starkweather intervened on Patrick's behalf.

The Haunted Host shows the personal growth of the writer Jay, who becomes strong enough to resist the demands of the opportunistic Frank. Jay has sacrificed his career to support that of his less-talented and now dead lover (Ed, the ghost referenced in the title of the play). Bearing a strong resemblance to the dead lover, Frank, an aspiring writer, turns to Jay for emotional and creative support in much the same way as had Ed, thus placing Jay again in the position of denying his needs and talent so as to nurture someone else. Despite being heterosexual, Frank seems prepared to enter into an emotional and perhaps physical relationship in return for Jay's support. In the end, however, Jay chooses self-protection, rejecting the advances of the younger artist.

For Patrick the play has two levels of meaning, one general to the gay male community and the other specific to Caffe Cino. By rejecting the parasitic relationship with Frank, Jay has overcome a harmful, demeaning relationship: that between a "heterosexual" male (often a prostitute) and a gay man. Patrick argues that *The Haunted Host* presents a fresh, stronger image of the gay man: the play centers on a new, stronger, freer gay man, one who "throws out an opportunistic hustler."[106] He also notes similarities between the relationship of Jay and Frank and those of Joseph Cino with the artists of his coffeehouse. Like Jay, Cino often neglected his own self-interest to provide financial, emotional, and aesthetic support to the actors, directors, and playwrights who worked at his Caffe. According to Patrick, the play is not modeled on the relationship between Cino and any specific individual; rather it reflects Patrick's concern about the extent to which a group of artists who sometimes, intentionally or not, abused Cino's generosity. Patrick does not exclude himself from this group.

Because of the subject matter of *The Haunted Host,* Patrick had difficulty recruiting actors for the first production. Thus he had to play Jay; William M. Hoffman played Frank. Patrick's pen name emerged from the production. Because he did not want the audience to know that he was both the writer of the work and an actor in it, he asked Marshall Mason to split his name in the program. Thus he became Robert Patrick, the playwright, and Bob O'Connor, the actor.[107]

Patrick vividly recalls a particular night when a young man attended the show with his parents; during the production Patrick overheard the man say, "You see, Mom, Dad? That's what I am. I'm a homosexual." That a young man could use his production as a means of coming out to his parents epitomizes for Patrick the importance of the stage as an educational tool and a means of building a gay community.

On March 2, 1965, Jean-Claude van Itallie's *War* opened at Caffe Cino, with Jane Lowry and Gerome Ragni as performers. Cino had encouraged Itallie to write a play for the coffeehouse even though the young playwright neither regularly attended performances there nor even was particularly fond of the place. His first exposure to the Cino (also his first exposure to off-off-Broadway) hardly impressed him: "I remember the first time I went to the Cino. I don't remember what was playing, but I know I thought it stank. At the end of the performance someone got up and said if we wanted more, we could go to the just newly opened La Mama Cafe. We laughed. Who wanted more?"[108] Though he came to appreciate La Mama and off-off-Broadway in general, Itallie was never particularly fond of the Cino: "That's okay—there were other places for me in '64: Open Theater, La Mama. . . . I was touched when Joe Cino asked me to do a play. . . . Cino offered me a place to work, his home in fact (Cino lived in his cafe)."[109]

Written in 1962, *War* had been performed prior to its opening at the Cino, though that production ran for only two nights. Itallie considered the coffeehouse's space hardly ideal for the play, since it was written for a proscenium stage and needed distance from the audience for the Edwardian dream-moments: "However providing ideal space or environment was not the point at the Cino—the Cino provided a space, that's all, and that was a lot. The existence of the Cino was for the barely born avant-garde theatre, and, in a more personal way, for Cino and his friends, a survival measure with some taste of desperation in it. (I hope I am fair, with hindsight and distance, in saying that.)"[110] Feeling depressed over the less-than-satisfactory production, Itallie was walking down Cornelia Street just a day or so after the March 2 opening "when Gerry Ragni rushed at me from the other direction, pushing the baby carriage in which he later carted around the unproduced script of *Hair*, yelling, 'It's burned down! It's burned down! The cafe's burned down!'" Initially Itallie dismissed Ragni's shouts as a prank, only to discover that in fact the Cino had been destroyed by fire.

As Itallie and Ragni surveyed the damage, Jonathan Torrey crossed the street and unlocked the iron grill across the door to allow them into the charred space. They gathered the surviving costumes and props, most of which had been borrowed from NBC for the production: "We formed a sad procession, a few of us, including Gerry with the baby carriage, others carrying a long harpoon, swords, a charred chest, a few wet costumes, single-file, to my apartment on Christopher Street, like defeated Goths, returning from *War* indeed."[111] Among the items destroyed in the fire seems to have been the curtain Eyen used for *Frustrata;* years after the fire his biography in the program for *Rachel Lily Rosenbloom and Don't You Forget It!* acknowledges Eyen's gratitude to Ellen Stewart for sewing another curtain after the fire.

Ironically the Cino burned on Ash Wednesday, March 3, 1965. Officially the cause was determined to have been a gas leak, though many believe that

Jonathan Torrey was responsible for the fire. On more than one occasion, Torrey and Cino had argued violently, resulting at times in extensive damage from Torrey's (perhaps drunken) rages. Whatever the cause of the fire, however, the result was devastating. As Michael Smith noted, the fire "completely destroyed the interior of the cafe. . . . Credit for containing the fire goes to the fireproof ceiling of the cafe, recently installed as part of a new lighting system."[112] Almost immediately friends and patrons throughout the city flocked to Cino's aid. Actor and playwright Donald Brooks did much of the reconstruction; leaders of the off-off-Broadway movement sponsored benefits to help offset construction costs and revenue losses; Ellen Stewart offered the use of La Mama's space on Sunday and Monday until Caffe Cino could move back into its regular space.

In the weeks after the fire, benefits were held at various theatres and coffeehouses. According to Tillie Gross, the benefits featured virtually all the major figures of off-off-Broadway, as well as artists from off Broadway and Broadway, including Julian Beck, Judith Malina, Al Carmines, Richard Barr, and Edward Albee. The Becks even submitted an application for a grant in Cino's name.[113] Cino always had avoided pursuing grant money, fearing that to do so would bring unwelcome changes to his caffe. He is reported to have received one grant of a thousand dollars, which he gave away,[114] but when or why he received the grant (and whether it was related to Beck's effort or even to this period at all) is unclear.

One of the most active in arranging benefits for the Cino after the fire, H. M. Koutoukas had even organized a benefit before the fire, presumably intended to help the struggling coffeehouse survive one of its periodic financial crises. At least until the reopening of the Caffe in 1965, Cino took none of the money collected from the audience after the show, allowing those involved with the production to split the day's take. He also began providing a small production budget. According to Gross, Cino tried various means to attain financial security for the Caffe: "Several methods were tried to collect enough money to cover these added expenses, such as affixing a tax to the food bill, which had not been done before, or a minimum order charge of fifty cents because people would stay for two shows. For a while, Cino tried to make the house into a club, charging a two-dollar membership fee for a year. But none of these efforts lasted long, and the people who considered themselves regulars felt insulted by these supplemental charges."[115] Included in the archives of the New York Public Library is a pledge card dated February 15, 1965 (a few weeks prior to the fire), asking for two, four, eight, ten, or fifteen dollars every month "in order that Mr. Cino may continue his vital work." One reward for making a pledge to this effort headed by Koutoukas was to have been a subscription to a monthly newsletter that would detail Cino events, though the newsletter seems to have been an unfulfilled plan, since no record of one exists.

After the fire Koutoukas organized a major benefit, given on March 15 at Writer's Stage on East Fourth Street in space donated by Edward Albee. Performances for the benefit included work by such veteran Cino writers as Michael Smith (*I Like It,* directed by Roberta Sklar), David Starkweather (*Chamber Play,* directed by Alec Rubin), Lanford Wilson (*Or Harry Can Dance,* directed by Michael Kahn), Koutoukas (*Pope Jean, or A Soul to Tweek,* directed by Koutoukas), Claris Nelson (*A Road Where the Wolves Run,* directed by Marshall Mason), Ruth Yorck (*Love Song for Mrs. Boas,* directed by Neil Flanagan), Paul Foster (*Madonna of the Orchard,* directed by Sydney Schubert Walter), and Oliver Hailey (*Little Tree Animal,* directed by Alec Rubin). Performers included such Cino veterans as Harvey Keitel, Claris Erickson (also known as Claris Nelson), and Michael Warren Powell. Otherwise involved in the benefit were such Cino regulars and theatre professionals as Jim Perkinson, Kenny Burgess, Robert Dahdah, Hope Stansbury, and Richard Barr.

The cover of the program for the benefit shows a double-headed eagle because of Cino's admiration for the symbolism of that creature. To try to capture the significance and spirit of the Cino, the program for the benefit includes a section in which five people provided short essays about the coffeehouse. Three are artists who worked there (playwright Claris Nelson, director Marshall Mason, and actor Michael Warren Powell); two (gallery curator Ed Brohel and an unidentified resident of an apartment above Caffe Cino) are persons affected by the Cino though "not related directly to the theatre, people with various skill and different cultures." The most moving and prophetic tribute is Nelson's statement: "The Cino is an island where our souls can play. There is no city there; only plays written over coffee under the Christmas lights; our own plays performed with freedom and love; actors, directors, theatre people who believe in magic; wild, . . . beautiful plays by other young playwrights that show us what's about to happen in the American theatre." The most unusual of the quotations and the one that reflected the opinion of many Village residents about coffeehouses in general was that given by the unidentified woman who resided above the Cino: "They should all be blown up—all coffee shops in the Village—every one of them. Why's the newspapers so interested, they should come up to my apartment, I'll tell them a thing or two. . . . weirdo's hang-out—children could have been killed— the FIENDS!" Her comment was given before she learned that the firewall installed by Cino had prevented the fire from spreading to the rest of the building.

Ronald Link, who was the assistant stage manager for *The Fantasticks,* organized two benefits, the first held on April 15 at the Village Gate, a well-known performance venue, and the second at the Sullivan Street Playhouse on April 26. Later he would credit his experience with the benefits as being the launching point of his career as a director.[116] The program at Sullivan Street Playhouse was composed of the following performances:

- *Humilities,* by Diane di Prima, starred James Waring and was directed by Jerry Benjamin;
- *Little Tree Animal,* by Oliver Hailey, starred Marion Herrod and was directed by James Struthers, designed by Whitney Blausen, and stage-managed by Glenn Johnson;
- *The Bed,* by Robert Heide, starred Donald Brooks and James Jennings and was directed by Robert Dahdah; and
- *Three Sisters Who Are Not Sisters,* by Gertrude Stein, starred Deborah Lee, Bill Hart, Louis Waldon, Diane Fisher, and Marva Abraham and was directed by Michael Smith, stage-managed by Nick Orzel, and included harp music by Tom O'Horgan.

The Bed became one of the Cino's most successful productions when it was given a regular run after the coffeehouse reopened.

Other benefits included a special performance of Gertrude Stein's *What Happened* at Judson Poets' Theatre on March 12, with the proceeds going to the Cino fund, and on Friday, March 26, from midnight until dawn, Caffe Gomad hosted a "Show Him You Luv Him" party to benefit "Joe Cino's World."[117] Probably the last benefit for the Cino was one entitled "The Cino's Not for Burning," held on Tuesday, June 29, at eight p.m. and midnight, more than a month after the May 18 reopening of the rebuilt coffeehouse. Along with emcee Ellen Stewart, the event featured the following performances:

- *The American Rainbow,* with words by Arthur Williams, music by John Herbert McDowell, and performances by Edward Barton and John Herbert McDowell; directed by James Waring;
- a medley by the Fugs;

- *The Customs Collector in Baggy Pants,* by Lawrence Ferlinghetti;
- a selection from Avital's Mimi Repertoire, with Virginia Allen and Abby Imber;
- *The Treasurer's Report,* a monologue by Robert Benchley, with John Herbert McDowell;
- a Judson medley (songs from Judson works, including *Home Movies, Promenade, Sing Ho for a Bear*), with Al Carmines "and friends"; and
- *Patter for a Soft Shoe,* by George Dennison, with Al Carmines and George Bartenieff.

Though this benefit seems to have been the last one held in relation to the fire damage, a few years later a similar effort was undertaken to help pay legal and other costs incurred during the final days of the coffeehouse's operation.

As friends, patrons, and fellow artists worked to rebuild the Caffe, some supporters encouraged Cino to expand it. According to Tillie Gross, he had no interest in expansion, though he did dream of owning a building in which he and his artists could live and work without economic pressure.[118] Cino never achieved this dream, but he continued rebuilding his coffeehouse. His only goal was to reopen as quickly as possible.

> I firmly believe that there is a definite place for cafe theatre . . . where hot coffee or hot anything may be spilled on an actor if he doesn't pay attention to the audience. It's very exciting to be working so close to people.
>
> The way we are doing things, there is no end to the possibilities of improvement. This is without becoming a theatre. . . . My only thoughts about expanding are not commercial but only to make it more difficult. Good always comes from what is supposedly bad. What we need now is the room, to be open again as soon as possible. I am very anxious to get open again and continue what we're doing. It is all worth it forever.[119]

While awaiting completion of the construction, Cino presented shows on Sunday and Monday evenings in space provided by Ellen Stewart. Cino seems to have followed La Mama's policy of admitting only members, since the advertisements include the warning "Members Only."[120] Shows produced by Cino at La Mama include Beat poet Diane di Prima's *Poet's Vaudeville* and poet Ruth Krauss's *Cantilever Rainbow.* Two shows were coproductions by the Cino and La Mama: Canadian playwright Mary Mitchell's *Who Put The Blood on*

My Long-Stemmed Rose? and an evening of two plays by Jean-Claude van Itallie). Like LeRoi Jones's *Dutchman,* Mitchell's *Who Put The Blood on My Long-Stemmed Rose?* is set in a subway train, though the plays are similar in few other details. Perhaps Mitchell's play is most significant for the difficulties that arose around Actors' Equity, which tried to prevent the production from running. A delegation from Cino and La Mama (probably including Paul Cranefield and actor-director Robert Dahdah, who played the Conductor in Mitchell's piece) went to Equity to try to resolve some of the problems. Though neither side was fully satisfied with the results, Equity decided not to proceed with an effort to close the show. Equity would be less forgiving with future productions.

As work on rebuilding continued, Cino and his colleagues began planning a reopening celebration. Cino selected *With Creatures Make My Way* by H. M. Koutoukas as the first production for the refurbished space. Somewhat to her surprise, Roberta Sklar was chosen to direct it. Sklar had directed several times at the Cino, mostly scenes from European absurdist work, though she also had directed what she has described as a "very traditional" version of the medieval cycle play *Flight into Egypt* during the Christmas season of 1963.[121] Despite having been acquainted with Neil Flanagan before working at the Cino, Sklar was not on particularly intimate terms with him, nor was she a part of the Cino inner circle. To Sklar the limitations of her friendship are indicated by the fact that neither she nor Flanagan revealed to the other his or her attraction to members of the same sex. Given her relative distance from the core Cino group, Sklar remains unsure why she was chosen to direct one of the most important and anticipated productions in the Caffe's history. To Koutoukas, however, the choice was simple: the quality of her work with past Cino shows made her the most logical person to direct his work. For the Cino the show was one of its most important, as it reasserted the presence of the Caffe on the theatre scene.

4 The Bitch Goddess

T he Cino reopened on the evening of May 18, 1965, with Elizabeth Davison in the role of Creature in H. M. Koutoukas's *With Creatures Make My Way.* The opening of the new Cino was one of off-off-Broadway's major events. From Lucy, Phoebe, Lance, and Bill (probably Lucy Silvay, Phoebe Wray, Lanford Wilson, and William M. Hoffman) came a telegram reading "All our best wishes and love." Mary Boylan and Robert Dahdah were somewhat more metaphoric, using a particularly apt image, "Here's to the New Cino. May it live longer than the Phoenix."[1] The next eighteen months were the most successful of the Cino's history, with productions that included Oliver Hailey's *Animal* and *Picture,* a revival of David Starkweather's *You May Go Home Again,* Robert Heide's *The Bed,* Sally Ordway's *A Desolate Place Near a Deep Hole,* and Lanford Wilson's *This Is the Rill Speaking.* William M. Hoffman's first produced work appeared, soon followed by two more; a John Guare play opened in August 1965, though the listing in the *Village Voice* credited authorship to Paul Guare.[2] Michael Smith explored the role and nature of the critic as he directed Sam Shepard's *Icarus's Mother.* Tom Eyen, H. M. Koutoukas, and Alan James presented popular, gender-bending productions. Marco Vassi, future proponent of free love, author of *Stoned Apocalypse* and *Metasex Manifesto,* contributor to *Penthouse,* and victim of AIDS, produced his play under the name "Fred Vassi" ("Marco" becoming his preferred name sometime after his work appeared at the Cino). And yet another poet saw his work on the stage of the Cino when Michael Benedikt's *Vaseline Photographer* was placed on a double bill with *Newsletters* by poet–children's writer Ruth Krauss.

With its similarities to the Caffe, *With Creatures Make My Way* was a particularly good choice to initiate productions in the renovated space. It is an "intensive camp" set "[w]hen the full moon rises and sewer grates are smoldering, about the time when insomniacs are screaming for sleep, and every corner proves a threat."[3] Long before the opening of the play, the Creature, Sovereign of the Sewers, had drunk a potion that gives eternal life, though he had inadvertently let one drop fall to the ground. The drop had been swallowed by a lobster, thus giving it eternal life. As Creature speaks in the play, he addresses a pearl-colored lump, telling it that some day he will find the lobster and that they will live together and know what not to say for eternity. The play ends with a joyous reunion as the pearl-colored object is revealed to be the lobster (its natural coloring having turned to pearl over many hundreds of years).

Though *Creatures* never refers specifically to Caffe Cino, it captures the spirit and evokes the atmosphere of the coffeehouse. Robert Patrick has suggested that Koutoukas was the only playwright to write specifically about the Cino:

> The Cino playwright asoluto [*sic*] was H. M. Koutoukas, a true poet who enshrined such Cino cult-objects as mirror-balls, cheap glitter, dyed feathers ("cobra feathers"), rhinestones, toy pianos, sequins, shattered mirrors, valentines, and all other forms of "tacky glamour."
>
> Lots of people wrote for the Cino, but only Harry wrote about it. In his feverish fantasies it became: a sewer where an immortal lived with a pearl-coated lobster; the basement of a mad scientist's tower; and the "Heaven of Broken Toys" in his lovely *All Day for a Dollar*.[4]

Patrick engages in a bit of hyperbole when he names Koutoukas as the *only* playwright to write about the Cino; various others, including Doric Wilson and Claris Nelson, incorporated aspects of Caffe Cino and its clientele in their work. Even Patrick himself acknowledges drawing from the Cino for his *Haunted Host*. Yet no other playwright so clearly creates the Cino magic or captures the essence of Cino camp as does Koutoukas; and few of his plays so clearly evoke this magic and essence as does *Creatures*. While recognizing that we should not overemphasize the similarities between Koutoukas's sewer and Cino's coffeehouse, we can note essential ones. Over the years leading up to the fire and in the years after, the walls of the Cino had become encrusted with layers of old posters, clippings from "muscle" magazines, photographs, and various memorabilia from Cino artists and patrons. That and the perpetual invasion by cockroaches gave the coffeehouse a cluttered, disorganized, never-quite-clean air reminiscent of Koutoukas's sewer. More significant, the setting reflects the mystic quality Cino regulars have often ascribed to the Caffe. According to the manuscript, the action takes place in a sewer, a "temple of pastey [*sic*] consistency with lighting of amber and mauve. It reminds us of the churches of the White Anglo Saxon Protestants,"[5] and, according to the program, the place is "[a] temple, deep within the curvatures of the sewers of Timisoara in Transylvania, where all that has been left to die congregate."[6]

The most important echo of Caffe Cino to reverberate through *Creatures* is that which centers difference, which challenges traditional gender-affectional roles, and which marginalizes the conventional. Initially played by Elizabeth Davison but replaced by Warren Finnerty shortly after the show's opening, Creature recognizes his uniqueness, his marginality, and accepts it as "just one of the aggregations of my being."[7] As a result, he chooses to live in a marginal world: "That's why I'm here with all the things that have been left to die— because they're they [*sic*] only things that understand me—or need me in a way that I can return. Here in mud and rot and death—I can remind and always show that death is just a release from getting bored."[8] Though *Creatures* can hardly be called a "gay play," it depicts a liminal world—a sacred sewer and a profane temple—in which one who is different finds companionship with an unlikely partner, an apt description for the Cino itself.

The size and layout of the program for *Creatures* indicate the production's importance, since it is one of the few to exceed one page. At a time and location in which programs were often handwritten and seldom consisted of more than a simple listing of credits, the program for *Creatures* consists of a graphic illustration on the cover page, a list of contributing artists and acknowledgments on page 2, and acting-directing credits with details of the play's setting on page 3. The list of contributing artists contains eleven names, including Cato Typing Service for program printing; the acknowledgments section lists sixteen names, including Joseph Davies, Tom Eyen, John Brooks, and Ruth Yorck—quite an extraordinary list for an off-off-Broadway program of the time. Also unusual for Caffe Cino, the program contains advertisements—a soul-food restaurant, a fur dealer, two art galleries, and a frame shop.

Among the noteworthy productions after *Creatures* is Robert Heide's *The Bed*. Heide first wandered into the Cino in 1960 after graduating from Northwestern University the year before. The first work he saw there was Robert Dahdah's version of *No Exit,* for which he was the sole audience member on the night he attended.[9] Heide's introduction to the Caffe came shortly after a disturbing experience that involved his *West of the Moon*. Presented by Lee Paton, it and *The Blood Bugle* by Harry Tierney Jr. were the inaugural productions of the New Playwrights Theatre, a venture intended to bring promising new playwrights to the public's attention. Given the work's frank and sympathetic discussions of homosexuality, sexual promiscuity, and substance abuse, *West of the Moon* elicited harsh criticism from some reviewers, including the suggestion from the critic in *Theatre Arts Magazine* that Heide "break his typewriter over his hands."[10] The acerbic reviews prompted Jerry Tallmer to use a part of his space in the *Village Voice* to defend Heide's work: "Butchery with an extraordinary amount of violence was committed last week in the daily papers against a girl named Lee Paton whose sole crime was to present two new one-act avant-garde dramas at the tiny playhouse she has taken over. . . . [T]he critical slaughter was unjust, hysterical, and vulgar."[11] Despite such defense, Heide was so disturbed by the response to *West of the Moon* that he considered abandoning writing for the theatre. It was about four years before another of his plays appeared on stage.

Soon after the production of *West of the Moon* came Heide's "illumination": "a first visit to the Divine Shrine—the mad mythic mystical Caffe Cino."[12] Then in 1963 he ran into Joe Cino at the counter of Riker's Coffee Shop in Sheridan Square. Having seen the production at New Playwrights, Cino encouraged Heide to write for his Caffe, saying, "I think it's about time you wrote that existentialist play. But make it a play for blond men. You know what I mean, Heide. It's time to get off your ass and write it. *Now*."[13] The resulting play was *The Bed*. In addition to its successful run at the Cino and, subsequently, off Broadway, it was made into a movie by Andy Warhol, but disputes over ownership of the film forced it off the market after a brief run at the Cinematheque in New York; later, footage from it was spliced into Warhol's *Chelsea Girls*.

The Bed was first performed on April 26 at one of the benefits after the fire; it opened for a full run in July 1965, with a revival the following September. A brief, two-character work, the play is set almost exclusively in a bed. Though the play became one of the most popular pieces performed at Caffe Cino, several early incidents threatened to end its run prematurely. Under Robert Dahdah's direction, the cast for the benefit was Donald Brooks and James Jennings; the cast for the full run at the Cino was to have been James Jennings and Walter McGinn, though director Dahdah had to replace McGinn at the last minute. The concluding scene of the work calls for McGinn's character to get out of bed, a point for which the actor could never find an acceptable motivation. Thus he refused to budge. Dahdah presented McGinn with alternatives as to why the character might get up: because he wants a cigarette, because he has to urinate. But McGinn was adamant that the character would not get out of bed. Growing increasingly frustrated, Dahdah pointed to the script and said, "You get up because it says so right here"; when that did not work, Dahdah turned to McGinn and said, "You get up because I'm the director and I say you get up."[14] Since neither physical or psychological motivation nor direct commands could coerce McGinn from the bed, he was replaced at the last minute by Larry Burns. Advertisements for the first week of the run already had been placed when the cast change occurred, so they still listed McGinn among the cast. The departure from the cast of *The Bed* hardly hurt McGinn's career, since he soon afterwards replaced Martin Sheen in Frank Gilroy's *The Subject Was Roses*.

A more serious threat to the production came from official concern over its content—a show in which two men spend virtually the entire time in bed drew the attention of legal officials, particularly given the "homosocial orientation" of many of the Cino's productions. Officials were so concerned about the work that agents from the FBI attended to ensure that in the words of Heide, no "homo-sex [*sic*] hanky-panky" was being presented.[15] Despite being confused by the production, the agents left without disturbing it: "One of the guys said he couldn't figure out what the hell the play was about anyway, since there was no plot and no jokes. They left in a state of befuddlement, but only after Joe had fed them puff pastries stuffed with rum custard and cappuccino—on the house."[16]

As the producing debut of Ron Link, the play focuses on two men whose relationship is crumbling because of too much boredom, alcohol, and drug abuse. The set of the production at the Caffe Cino was dominated by a bed that occupied virtually the entire, quite small stage. In his unpublished notes to the script, Heide indicates the complexity of the bed as an image: "As a symbol it could represent gravity-pull-limitation, a death slab in a morgue, a 'padded cell,' a coffin, sleep, sexuality, whatever problem the bed might represent itself to be to an audience."[17] The bed, then, signifies a broader context of human experience, one in which the existentialist crisis is paramount:

JIM. I feel nauseated. This process going on like some great senseless flux. On and on and on. You. Me. Sex is dead. No, it's God. God is dead. No, it's Neitzsche, Neitzsche [*sic*] is dead. No, I am alive, here, and yet . . .
JACK. Why don't you just drop dead?

As critic Elenore Lester has argued, the characters "are caught in the nightmare of living death. Time and space, as areas for meaningful action are annihilated. . . . The playwright clearly establishes that what we are witnessing here is the anguish of existence."[18] Thus Jim tells Jack, "We don't do anything. We're . . . . we're like two objects frozen in time, in space, not even on earth, really . . . . suspended. Weightless being. Occasionally we go to the john to pee or to take a crap. We shove food down our throats. . . . Basic functionalism."

Among the productions that came between the two runs of *The Bed* were two by a young employee of a Hill and Wang publishing company, William M. Hoffman. Hoffman no longer recalls precisely when he first visited the Caffe, though he does recall that the event occurred when John Corigliano took him there to see *The Boy Friend*. Thus most likely it was the summer of 1960, since the only known Cino run of *The Boy Friend* was August 20–22, 1960. Corigliano, with whom Hoffman was intimately involved, knew about the Cino because someone whom he had previously dated was working there. Hoffman had little interest in the theatre at the time, because most of it "bored the shit" out of him;[19] nor did he immediately become a regular at the Caffe. It was a few years later, after Lanford Wilson was on the scene, that Hoffman frequently visited Cornelia Street.

Hoffman's first stage role came in December 1964 when he appeared in Patrick's *Haunted Host;* the experience convinced Hoffman that he had neither the talent nor passion for acting. Though he considered himself a poet and had little interest in playwriting at first, he soon turned to writing for the stage, in part because he wanted to share some of the attention that Lanford Wilson and others were receiving: "I started to get jealous because all of my friends were getting attention. So, I think out of self-defense, I turned from poetry to playwriting, although I didn't know that's what I had done until Lanford told me a short story I had written was really a play."[20] Like Wilson, Hoffman converted a short story he had written into his first play. In a 1985 interview during the promotion of his play *As Is,* Hoffman was more explicit about his start as a playwright: "Bill shook his head, wryly, 'All my friends were writing plays. Suddenly my world changed from book publishing . . . to plays. I said, if they could do it, goddammit, then I could do it.'"[21]

In August 1965 Hoffman's first produced work *(Thank You, Miss Victoria)* appeared at the Cino. As the play opens, the only character, Harry Judson, has just started work for his father's business. According to critic Elenore Lester,

> Although he is young, attractive, the possessor of a substantial income and friends of both sexes who are ready and eager to go to bed with him,

he is in hell. He suffers from a wicked case of alienation d. t.'s, aggra-
vated by a Daddy hang-up. He is alcoholic, compulsive, manic, more
or less impotent and possibly suicidal—as are his friends.[22]

By intercom Judson instructs his secretary not to disturb him as he makes
various telephone calls. Most of the play is occupied with a call in response
to the following advertisement placed by Miss Victoria: "Aggressive New York
business woman will employ male secretary. Experience and accuracy required.
Telephone Miss Victoria, *Rector* 5-1296."[23] The call to Miss Victoria quickly
moves from a job interview to dominant-submissive sexual role play in which
Judson submits to the unseen Miss Victoria. As Lester notes,

> Out of the interesting fact that the language and quality of experience of
> intense sexual passion sometimes comes close to that of fiery religious ar-
> dor, playwright Hoffman has fashioned a funny and poignant little dra-
> matic piece about a man who makes a psychic journey from despair to
> ecstasy via a crackling telephone wire. . . . Harry's sterile Wall Street office
> is the equivalent of a Beckett tomb-room and his telephone is like one of
> those ambiguous windows or doors on the modern stage; it may open out
> to something, but we have a strong feeling that the something is unlikely
> to be any different from or better than whatever is in the room.[24]

Like other works at Caffe Cino, *Thank You, Miss Victoria* centers on transgressive sexuality, along with the complexities of communication in a technological, mediated age.

The play foregrounds Judson as both the desired and the controlled object. Miss Victoria never appears on stage. When he telephones her, she immediately assumes control of both the conversation and Judson's body, commanding, prohibiting, or permitting him to engage in certain actions: "Yes,
it's sweltering in here. May I open my shirt? (Starts to open shirt. Closes shirt
to top.) Thank you for not letting me do what I would like to do."[25] Throughout the play we do not so much see his desire for her as we see her desire for
him reflected through his physical and verbal responses. Thus desire is dis-
lodged from its site within a heterosexual construct to become a free-floating
force that washes over his body, structuring him as *the* sign of the desired
object. Ultimately his body is completely objectified: "I would like to strip
naked for your examination, for your use. I would like to have my disgusting
slave's body naked for your use. . . . I'd love to come crawling to you like a

dog, with a dog collar on my neck, by which you lead me where you will, guide me, mount me, and drive me like a horse. . . ."[26]

Though *Thank You, Miss Victoria* was Hoffman's first produced play, *Good Night, I Love You,* based on his short story, was the first play he wrote. Appearing in September 1965 at the Cino on a double bill with his *Saturday Night at the Movies, Good Night* centers on a telephone call between a man (played by Michael Griswold) and his girlfriend (played by Linda Eskenas) in which the man confesses that he is pregnant as a result of a same-sex relationship. Given this complex relationship between a gay man and heterosexual woman, the work now seems almost a prototype of television's *Will and Grace.* In his review of Hoffman's work, Michael Smith clearly reveals his distaste for realistic works: "Both plays [*Good Night, I Love You* and *Saturday Night at the Movies*] were attractively staged by Neil Flanagan. Hoffman's vision of people trying to break out of their isolation and self-indulgence is sweet and sometimes perceptive, but the derivative and commonplace naturalism of his method limits him to fairly routine results."[27] Hoffman's words to Smith for publication in *Contemporary Dramatists* echo those Smith wrote for the *Village Voice:* "Until now the themes that have interested me have been concerned with what might be called 'oneliness,' the singularity of people, the consequences of singularity. In my first plays I dealt with requited and unrequited love. . . . In my early plays joy was to be obtained in the almost hopeless struggle of people finding each other."[28] *Good Night, I Love You* and *Saturday Night at the Movies* were the last plays Hoffman presented at the Cino.

About two months after reviewing the two plays by Hoffman, Smith found his own work at the Cino reviewed in the pages of the *Voice* as he directed the premiere of Sam Shepard's *Icarus's Mother.* An inexperienced director, Smith found some parts of the script difficult to stage. Shepard, for example, calls for the cast to build a campfire and to send smoke signals, which Smith somehow was able to arrange despite the closed space and limited ventilation of the Caffe. Smith's job was complicated by his largely having cast the production from actors associated with Joseph Chaikin's Open Theatre. The match between actors and script was less than ideal because "[t]he Open Theatre emphasized physicalization and improvisation and Shepard is mainly verbal."[29] Despite the various problems, he and the cast "somehow blundered through to something that was quite powerful, or so I have always imagined."[30]

Along with critics such as Ross Wetzsteon, Smith was openly partisan in his support of Shepard. According to Leslie Wade, these critics, many of whom were affiliated with the *Village Voice,* "would claim Shepard as '*our* playwright'—cast the writer as the emblematic spearhead of an emerging alternative consciousness."[31] Wade recognizes the importance of Smith in promoting Shepard's career after critics had censured a performance of the playwright's one-acts. After the works had received bad reviews from several critics, Smith gave them a good review in the *Voice:* his "confirmation underscores how important support can be for a beginning dramatist."[32]

In addition to demonstrating his respect for Shepard, work on *Icarus's Mother* provided Smith a means for developing his assault on the traditional divide between artist and critic. Assuming the role of the passive spectator and of an idealized representative of the audience, he believed, makes the critic an enemy of theatre; such a position is "depersonalizing and false."[33] The best that can be achieved with this approach is "the work of a man like Walter Kerr, whose reviews fulfill the function he is paid for by expressing generally popular opinions in highly readable prose, but whose effect on the theatre is useful only in industrial terms."[34] In 1965, while Smith served on the judges' panel for the *Voice's* Obie Awards, not only were Caffe Cino and Cafe La Mama jointly awarded their first Obie but Kerr received an Anti-Obie for his "outstanding disservice to the modern theatre: for his determined resistance to the works of Ibsen, Strindberg, Chekhov, Pirandello, O'Casey, Brecht, Sartre, Ionesco, Genet, and Beckett; and for turning his skills instead to the promotion and maintenance of a commodity theatre without relevance to dramatic art, the imagination, or our age. . . ."[35] Fellow judges Gordon Rogoff and Richard Gilman may have been the instigators of the award to Kerr.

Smith advocated a more involved role for the critic, in which he or she participated in the creative process. Taking part in both the creation and critical evaluation of theatre helps the reviewer counteract the debilitating effects of isolation and practical inexperience. Without experience, the critic is limited in what she or he can either understand or address: "Apart from the discomfort of this isolation, I have felt often that I simply didn't know what I was talking about. I can discuss playwriting because I know what it feels like to write a play. But otherwise I have little experience in the theatre. I acted and designed sets in high school, designed lighting in college. . . . Then I happened to become a critic and did nothing for years but see plays and write and talk about them."[36] To compensate for his limited experience, Smith began working in the theatre, directing at Judson Poets' Theatre and Caffe Cino, acting at Cafe Au Go Go, writing for Caffe Cino and La Mama, and participating in experimental activities at Open Theatre. Rather than serving as "an unpredictable but necessary publicist" for theatres, the critic should, Smith argues, enter into a more generalized aesthetic discourse about works he reviewed, intended not for the audience-recipient but for the artist-creator: "I have tried to define a different role for the critic. . . . [M]y reviews are basically addressed to the artist. By discussing the work in terms of its creation, rather than the 'objective' terms of a judge, I provide one side of a hopeful dialogue." In an interview some years later, Smith explained his position while discussing the critic's responsibility to readers and viewers: "I've always felt that my main responsibility was to the artist and to the art of theatre, rather than to any readers, or a public opinion, or taste."³⁷ The critic, then, becomes not an objective, all-seeing, judging eye removed from the creative fray but rather a member of a creative process. His contribution may not equal that of the playwright, actor, or director, but he enters the discourse on very nearly equal terms, as an artist, drawing on his knowledge of and experience in theatre practice to discuss the artistic process and product with the other artists.

Though Smith, Wetzsteon, and others contributed greatly to the recognition of playwrights such as Sam Shepard, Robert Patrick accuses other critics of having unfairly and adversely influenced the careers of other writers. In the *Advocate,* Robert Patrick describes how a particular *Voice* reviewer treated gay-themed plays with condescension. As a result, some of the more ambitious playwrights "played straight": "One of the most famous Off-Off alumni begged us all not to tell our resident *Voice*nik he was gay. The *Voice*nik who worshipped straight playwrights (he wanted to be one, I guess) . . . gave this playwright (I'll call him Dirk) mounting raves for plays whose gay content was increasingly obscured. When Dirk produced an incredibly bad 'experimental' play . . . , the *Voice*nik went wild with ecstasy."³⁸ When the critic learned of "Dirk's" sexual orientation, his reviews became sharply critical. Furthermore, the critic chose not to review the comic book productions because the cross-gender casting and cross-dressing made them too overtly gay. According to Patrick, good reviews could be purchased with drugs and sex.

In December 1965 Tom Eyen's *Why Hanna's Skirt Won't Stay Down* opened the first of at least three runs at Caffe Cino with Helen Hanft in the title role (a part written specifically for her). Characteristic of Eyen's work from the period, the play includes numerous allusions to popular culture, including such figures as Marilyn Monroe. Despite the seeming allusion to the famous image of Monroe from *Seven Year Itch,* the inspiration for the play came from Eyen's experience at Coney Island. According to Hanft,

> Then one day in the summer of 1965, a very warm day, I met him in a place called Riker's on the corner of 7th Avenue South. It was a kind of coffeeshop. The food was cheap and good. I met him there and we were sitting at this table. Out of his pocket, he takes this crumpled piece of paper, all creased and folded. Typed. And he said, "Can you read this?" He had this monologue, "I come here every payday and stand over the breezehole." So I read it, and it was interesting. "I wrote this play called *Why Hanna's Skirt Won't Stay Down,*" he said; "I'm not quite finished with it, but this is the opening monologue. I'd like for you to do it." And I said, "Where does it take place?" And he told me. He said, "There's this woman standing over a breezehole, screaming. It's sort half of Marilyn Monroe standing over the grating and half of my going on a trip to Coney Island." It was a very, very hot summer. He had taken the subway out to Coney Island. He said he was in the funhouse; they had a big funhouse there. They had a breezehole too. He said, "I saw this breezehole and I saw this woman, this wild woman, standing over it, and I saw your face." He said, "And I saw your face. And that's how it started."[39]

Shortly after *Hanna's* premiere at La Mama, Eyen told Hanft that they were to present the play at the Cino: "I said, 'I don't want to work there. It's a small place. And who goes there?'" After the production at La Mama, Hanft had signed with an agent and had begun to think that she was too important to play such a small venue. She had not, however, attained the commercial success she had hoped, so she agreed to perform at the Caffe: "They loved it; it was very, very successful. Joe Cino loved that play."[40] The role with which Hanft, who was at the time a switchboard operator for United Jewish Appeal, became most closely associated, Hanna helped her gain the title "Queen of Off-Off-Broadway."[41] The play also helped launch the career of Bette Midler, who was performing in Eyen's *Miss Nefertiti Regrets* at La Mama (Midler's first significant role in New York) at the same time that Hanft was performing at the Cino. Midler saw Hanft and incorporated into her performance elements of Hanft's self-described "ballsy, lude [*sic*], brassy, Jewish woman."[42]

Part of the trilogy that Eyen, perhaps in an allusion to Chekhov, called the Three Sisters Trilogy, *Why Hanna's Skirt Won't Stay Down* has been described as a "verbal rock concert"[43]: unlike Monroe, "Hanna isn't a sex goddess. She is an average looking chick who likes sex. And the play is a put-on of our sex-conscious times written by a modern-day Neil Simon."[44] For nearly a decade, Hanft played Hanna repeatedly in venues in the Village, in Cincinnati, Ohio, and elsewhere. The off-Broadway premier of the play with Hanft in the lead did not occur until 1974 at the Village Gate. The play became so well known that Michael Feingold wrote, "'AHHHHHHHHHHH!' To anyone versed in the lore of Off-Off Broadway, that shrill scream, half anguish and half intense satisfaction, can mean only one thing: Hanna O'Brien is standing over her Coney island breeze hole again. . . ."[45] Hanft recreated the role of Hanna when she appeared at the Cino in the premier of *Who Killed My Bald Sister Sophie?*, the play that Eyen intended as the second act of *Hanna's Skirt*.[46]

Caffe Cino closed 1965 with two plays by Lanford Wilson, *Sex Is Between Two People* and *Days Ahead*. Lost until recently, the former play uses its bathhouse setting to relate the misadventures of two young, inexperienced men who have met there. More a sketch than a full play, *Sex* shows the inability of the two characters to communicate comfortably or freely:

> ROGER. I was at a party. Got pretty high. I mean I had to—it was the god-awfullest party anyone had ever seen. People just sitting around talking. Endlessly.
>
> MARVIN. Yea. God I hate those.
>
> ROGER. Me too. I kept thinking if someone would just start dancing or something. You know—*instigate* something.[47]

Roger and Marvin talk endlessly because neither is capable of initiating anything else between them. Unable to break the imaginary barrier that separates them, Roger and Marvin part frustrated, with Marvin dressed to leave and Roger going to an orgy in another part of the bathhouse.

By the end of 1965 off-off-Broadway had been "discovered." For several years, critics in a few small-circulation papers such as the *Village Voice* had closely followed the developments at Caffe Cino, Cafe La Mama, Theatre Genesis, the Bitter End, Café Wha?, Judson Poets' Theatre, and other underground performance spaces. *Show Business,* the *New York Post,* and other periodicals occasionally had published reviews of productions and discussions of the movement. In 1964, for the first time, off-off-Broadway made a significant showing in the Obie Awards for the 1963–64 season. The awards (given by the *Village Voice* for work off Broadway) previously had largely overlooked off-off-Broadway. In 1964 Judson Poets' Theatre dominated the event, winning for

- best production of a musical (Judson Poets' Theatre for *What Happened*)
- distinguished play (Rosalyn Drexler for *Home Movies*)
- distinguished direction (Lawrence Kornfeld for *What Happened*)
- best music (Al Carmines for *Home Movies* and *What Happened*)
- special citation "for its sponsorship of experiment and experimenters in the performing arts, through the Judson Poets' Theatre and the Judson Dance Theatre."[48]

Other important awards for the season include those given for distinguished performance to Taylor Mead (whose poetry readings had been popular in Village coffeehouses, the Caffe Cino among them) and for distinguished play to Adrienne Kennedy for *Funnyhouse of a Negro*. Awards for the 1964–65 season continued to recognize work by off-off-Broadway theatres, as Caffe Cino and Cafe La Mama were given a joint special citation for "creating opportunities for new playwrights to confront audiences and gain experience of the real theatre." It was the first of many awards for Caffe Cino and its artists. In the following year, H. M. Koutoukas won a special citation for "the style and energy of his assaults on the theatre in both playwrighting and production," and Sam Shepard won for distinguished plays for three works, including *Icarus's Mother*.

With the increasing acceptance of off-off-Broadway as a legitimate force in New York theatre, these small underground venues began to draw attention from publications outside the Village, including the *New York Times,* which had covered the fracas over the coffeehouses but virtually none of the productions being offered in those venues. On December 5, 1965, the *Times* released its first major piece about off-off-Broadway when it published *Voice* critic Elenore Lester's "The Pass-the-Hat Theater Circuit." The title, of course, refers to the tradition of "passing the hat" to collect donations at the end of productions.

Lester suggests that the intimacy of the venues contributed to the success of the works they produced. Audience members tended to feel that they were a part of the stage action, since the spaces were typically so small that most seating was at least partially in the stage light. Furthermore, actors and audience were so close to each other that spectators had to be very conscious of stage movement lest an actor accidentally jostle them, spilling their coffee. For many who attended the productions, this proximity contributed to their enjoyment of the productions. As Lester notes, they "claim that the sense of involvement and immediacy gives them a definite sensuous experience that can't be duplicated in ordinary theatre, even theatre-in-the-round, which still maintains a kind of formal barrier between stage action and audience response."[49] Whereas Norman Mailer's hipster lived in a world constantly threatened by nuclear annihilation, off-off-Broadway playwrights wrote from a point *after* the threat has become reality in at least a philosophical sense: they "write as though they were born into the world the day after some metaphysical H-Bomb exploded, and they accept this blasted world as the natural environment."[50] Lester continues, "Although these characters are disconnected from society, they are unlike the traditional American outcast heroes in the works of Eugene O'Neill or Tennessee Williams, who are oppressed by the hostile power of society. In this sense, the young writers seem 'farther out' than either Albee, whom they regard as an old master . . . or Le Roi Jones . . . who, despite his own youth, is generally regarded as an aging bohemian somewhat tainted by commercialism."[51] Physical or emotional alienation and isolation become central to many of the coffeehouse works. Losing its ability to carry or contain meaning, language has become incomprehensible. Similarly, traditional familial and relational structures have become hollow, ghostly reminders of past, paternalistic, capitalistic, repressive social structures. If terms such as *family* and *community* had become linguistic shells, they could be redefined to suit new desires, needs, and interests. One means of redefining relationships and of exploring the limits of alienation was through expressions of sexuality. Though for some, the period's kaleidoscopic sexual expression had little more significance than a rather juvenile pushing of the boundaries of free expression, others saw free love and the sexual revolution as fundamental to redefinition of relationship structures and to liberation from the oppression of the dominant culture.

Lester's article gives a fair amount of attention to Caffe Cino and its artists. In addition to referring to Joe Cino's background in Buffalo, she describes the financial difficulties that he had faced. She also briefly traces the Cino's development as a theatre from the initial play readings to "a full-scale dramatization of Voltaire's *Candide* [in which] [t]he actors, 16 in all, chased one another around the tables, for the stage was everywhere in the house." According to Lester, a part of the "sensuous" experience at the Cino and other venues was the hard chairs in which audience members had to sit. The Cino had its own special tribulations: "[A]udiences sit at precariously balanced tables pushed close together and risk getting coffee and actors in their laps."[52] Lester discusses not only Starkweather's *So, Who's Afraid of Edward Albee?* but also works by Robert Patrick, Sam Shepard, Robert Heide, Lanford Wilson, and Claris Nelson.

Not all of the Cino crowd were happy about their newly found recognition. Most off-off-Broadway artists took either of two positions on fame and commercial success: they shunned it or they worked for it, though often with little success. Some were openly motivated by career goals. While promoting her new television show *All's Fair* in 1976, Bernadette Peters told Tom Burke, "Sure I'm ambitious: I have no objection now to becoming 'big' in television . . ."[53]; Burke suggests that her ambition is not a recently acquired interest: "A former *Dames at Sea* cast member has maintained that Bernadette is quite calculating about her career. It's good to know she doesn't hide that quality."[54] Yet such calculating ambition offended many off-off-Broadway artists. Sally Banes has argued, "But for off-off-Broadway, graduating to off-Broadway—leaving the alternative home and the alternative community—was a fate to be avoided, for it altered the relations of production, turning artists into alienated labor."[55] Thus many in the circle derided those artists who chose to move from underground theatres to success in commercial venues. The driving force behind Theatre Genesis, Ralph Cook expressed the sentiments of many when he dismissed the significance of commercial, uptown success: "We couldn't care less about Broadway. We are aware that it exists somewhere uptown, no more."[56]

The world of off-off-Broadway could prove detrimental to those who hoped to move into commercial theatre. In introducing the movement to his readers, French journalist Bernard da Costa describes some of the problems, particularly that of uncritical support from friends.[57] He notes that whether or not a performance is successful, actors' friends will applaud them: "[A]ll her friends will be there to applaud her and to find her 'marvelous.' In place of making progress [in her career], she risks taking on 'bad habits.' It is the danger which lies in wait for the actors, the authors of OOB. One ages badly in Greenwich Village and the material conditions are so bad that everyone is willing to do anything to live a little better."[58] Similarly, William M. Hoffman notes that off-off-Broadway playwrights were significantly hampered by similar uncritical cliques who support their favored authors' works regardless of the quality.[59] Even as the styles and issues explored by those artists began to influence other theatres, those who had originated the styles or first explored the issues remained ignored as other artists recreated them for the commercial stage.

Animosity between those who sought and those who shunned success sometimes flared. Helen Hanft, for example, told da Costa: "I am a Stanislavskian actress . . . and I will leave off-off-Broadway one day to go to Broadway. OOB authors write too misogynist plays. . . . Off-off Broadway is a world of chickens who would like to pass for eagles."[60] Many artists were able to overcome the problems and dangers of off-off-Broadway to attain commercial success. In addition to having a collection of his plays published, Lanford Wilson, for example, was able to move several of his works into off-Broadway venues, though when *The Madness of Lady Bright* made the transition to off-Broadway, the director chose not to cast Neil Flanagan as Lady Bright. Works by Robert Heide, Robert Patrick, John Guare, Sam Shepard, and many others eventually appeared off Broadway, on Broadway, and in regional and international theatres.

Events of the late fall and winter of 1965 seemed to shift the focus of the coffeehouse war yet again. A *New York Times* news summary noted that the city council had increased fines for operating illegal coffeehouses from fifty dollars to $250, with second offenses being punishable by imprisonment.[61] Village coffeehouses were clearly the target of the change, since coffeehouses could continue to operate as restaurants but could not offer entertainment. An important part of the renewed effort at regulation was a revision of city codes, which went into effect on December 4, 1965, according to a handwritten note in the Cino files at the New York Public Library.[62] According to the new codes, a coffeehouse was

[a]ny room, place or space in the city, except eating or drinking places, which provide incidental musical entertainment either by mechanical devices or by not more than three persons playing piano, organ, accordion, guitar, or any string instrument, which is used, leased or hired out in the business of serving food or non-alcoholic beverages and has a permit issued by the commissioner of health to maintain or operate a restaurant and provides entertainment without a stage . . . and is restricted to instrumental music, folk, popular or operatic singing, poetry or other literary readings or recitals, dramatic or musical enactments and which does not permit dancing.[63]

Clearly a concession to those residents who complained of late-night and early-morning noise, the new code stipulated that coffeehouses must be closed from three a.m. to one p.m. on Sunday and from four a.m. to eight a.m. all other days.

Perhaps the most significant event of the period was the inauguration of John Lindsay as the new mayor. He appointed Joel Tyler as the license commissioner. Before assuming his duties, Tyler visited two unlicensed coffeehouses in the Village, one of which was Caffe Cino. He explained his purpose as that of "getting down to the needs of the individual citizen as far as licensing is concerned. This, to me, is the meaning of this election."[64] According to the *Voice,* Tyler enjoyed both establishments. He promised a study of departmental procedures in view of the difficulty the Cino had in obtaining a license despite never having been the subject of complaints. The change in administrations seemed to bode well for the position of the Village's coffeehouses.

The new year (1966) opened at the Cino with H. M. Koutoukas's *All Day for a Dollar, or Crumpled Christmas* with a cast that included Robert Dahdah, Ronald Link, Johnny Dodd, and Charles Stanley; even Joe Cino made one of his infrequent stage appearances, playing St. Peter. Reviews were generally glowing: "It seemed to me a perfect meeting of event and place, and within its confines it was a source of special pleasure"[65]; "the best Christmas play I have ever seen."[66] *All Day for a Dollar* was followed by a revival of David Starkweather's *The LOVE Pickle* (formerly *The LOVE Affair*) and a few weeks later one of Koutoukas's most sentimental pieces, *A Letter from Colette, or Dreams Don't Send Valentines (A Bittersweet Camp).* With a cast of many of the Cino's favorite stars (George Harris II, George Harris III, Robert Dahdah, Deborah Lee, and Mary Boylan), *The Easter All Star Spectacular* replaced an unexpected closing of Maurice Maeterlinck's *The Death of Tintagiles.*

A press release boasted that the Cino production of *Tintagiles* was the first major performance of the work since Katherine Cornell and Margaret Mauer appeared in it with the Washington Square Players, probably in 1916.[67] The Cino cast included Suzanne Caddic, who had appeared on Broadway in *The Lovers, The Tender Heel,* and *Talent 61,* as well as Jane Harris, a young member of a family in which both parents and all six children appeared in Cino and other off-off-Broadway productions. In the audience on Saturday, April 2, was H. M. Koutoukas, who was noted for his wild sense of humor. He would sometimes, for example, wait until the lights had gone down and actors were scurrying to their places to light his cigarette (with a lighter that seemed to have an unusually large flame), so that actors were caught in mid scurry by unexpected and unwelcome light. As he sat on April 2 watching *Tintagiles* during the one a.m. show, the playwright giggled repeatedly at inappropriate moments, particularly at points in which one actress was at her most serious. Increasingly disturbed by the laughter, the actress broke character, turned to him, and told him that either he had to stop or she would leave. She returned to character and continued the play. As the young Jane Harris stood waiting for her cue to enter the stage, she again heard giggles, then a sword being thrown down, and the actress storming out, not to return. The run of *The Death of Tintagiles* ended one week and one day early.

At about two thirty a.m. that night, Michael Smith stopped by the Cino on his way home from a production of his *The Next Thing* at La Mama. He helped organize a show to replace *Tintagiles.* As usual, Cino was determined that some show, any show must go on. Smith, Cino, Koutoukas, and Charles Stanley hurriedly assembled a group of skits, scenes, and short plays by anyone who was available. Stanley proposed recreating the role of Jean Harlow in a scene from Koutoukas's *Tidy Passions,* which he had first performed the prior summer; new to the work was to be John Berger as Narcissus. Composer John Herbert McDowell agreed to perform the monologue *The Treasurer's Report* by Robert Benchley. Lanford Wilson and Marshall Mason offered a brief play that Wilson had written sometime before. Al Carmines volunteered to sing if someone could provide him with an instrument; the next day Smith located a harpsichord for him. Someone asked Mary Boylan to join the show, though she had to supply her own material, since they had nothing for her to perform. Smith persuaded Joyce Aaron to perform *More! More!,* a play directed by Remy Charlip and written by Smith, Charlip, and Johnny Dodd. Dancer Deborah Lee agreed to operate lights.[68]

The next day, the new show opened in place of *Tintagiles* to full houses. Despite never having had a complete run-through, the production played as smoothly as if it had been fully rehearsed. Given this success, Cino asked the performers to continue the run for the following week. It was called the *Easter All Star Spectacular with All Star Cast* or, more aptly and simply, *Pot Luck.* Smith labeled the experience of creating the show "delightful": "an unstructured collaboration in which everyone was pleased to do what he could do well, and the result proved the virtue of the method. The production will continue through Sunday, with additions and omissions according to who's free when, and I recommend it for your pleasure."[69] The only major flaw, according to Smith, was in John Berger's undisciplined performance as Narcissus in the selection from Koutoukas's *Tidy Passions*. As a result, his role was eliminated and Stanley in the role of Harlow appeared alone for the next week's run.

The spring and summer of 1966 brought several skirmishes between the factions fighting over what had come to be called the "MacDougal Street mess,"[70] though neighborhood residents and business owners yet again reached a "temporary detente."[71] In March, building commissioner Charles G. Moerdler, with various aides and their wives, visited three Village coffeehouses (the Basement, Four Winds, and the Feenjon Café) in "dignified raids."[72] During the visits, none of the establishments violated coffeehouse regulations concerning public performances. When asked about music, the host at Four Winds, for example, replied, "No, Man, we can't have any of that, you know; it's like we haven't got the right license."[73] Though Commissioner Moerdler enjoyed his visit to Bohemia, he warned that Mayor John Lindsay had told him to clean up the area quickly. A few days later, according to reporter Eric Pace, a spokesman for the police department announced a top-priority crackdown on crime in the Village and the Times Square area, because those areas "have become magnets for some of the more disreputable elements of our society and require our immediate and urgent attention."[74] Among the moves he announced was a more aggressive search for building code violations in bars and coffeehouses.

At eight p.m. on Friday, March 18, policemen attempted to extend their crackdown on crime by cordoning off a fourteen-block area, preventing traffic into the Village. Thus they hoped to decrease crowds. The effort backfired, as headlines the next day touted the failure of the policemen to control hundreds of young people and newsreels showed the teenagers roaming through the streets shouting, "Down with cops!" As a result, Saturday, March 19, was even worse than usual, with a hoard of youngsters descending on the Village. To an area already overcrowded, the news coverage drew even greater crowds of young people, both the rebellious and the simply curious. According to columnist David Gurin, the crowds were as large as those for New Year's Eve in Times Square, with the primary difference being that those in the Village were "white and all young . . . channeled along the narrow sidewalks by the 'keep moving' orders of police."[75] For several hours that Saturday evening after the initial police action, complete chaos threatened to erupt.

In the aftermath of the "barricades botch," the different MacDougal-area factions again sought a compromise acceptable to all sides.[76] In a move supported by the MacDougal Area Neighborhood Association, Village district leader Edward Koch put forward a proposal that seemed to please both coffeehouse owners and residents: change zoning regulations so that coffeehouses could move into the commercial district, away from the residential area. With all sides agreeing that a solution had to be found and with Koch's plan as one possible solution, the groups settled into a period of relative peace. Though the Department of License continued to act against theatres and cinemas that presented sexually oriented material or certain politically oriented acts (such as flag burning), the truce in the MacDougal area seemed to hold, as residents and businessmen formed a four-person committee to discuss the problems.

In the summer of 1966 Caffe Cino opened its most successful show, when eighteen-year-old Bernadette Peters stepped onto the stage in her first adult role, Ruby in *Dames at Sea, or Golddiggers Afloat*. An affectionate spoof of the Busby Berkeley musicals of the thirties and forties, *Dames* continually refers back to those musicals with its naval setting, its militaristic-drill style, character names that echoed those of the stars of the Berkeley musicals (Ruby [Keeler], Dick [Powell], Frank [McHugh], and Joan [Blondell]), and even its title (Berkeley having staged numbers for or directed shows such as *Dames, Gold Diggers of 1933,* and *Gold Diggers of 1935*).

Because of a heated conflict between the show's writers and director Robert Dahdah, information about the work's origin and development is now somewhat hazy. The concept seems to have been a group effort among writer George Haimsohn, composer Jim Wise, and British author Robin Miller; Haimsohn told the *New Yorker,* "Jim [Wise] and I had had the same idea as Robin. . . . We were going to do something on the 'Gold Diggers' Movies, and when Robin met Jim, Robin said he felt he needed an American to work with. That's how the three of us came together."[77]

Though writing the work took only five days, locating a production opportunity proved more time-consuming and more frustrating. The group recorded the show, and Miller went to various venues with the recording, trying unsuccessfully to attract interest. According to Miller, "I remember playing it for Herb Jacoby, at the Blue Angel, one hot afternoon. He said what everybody said: 'Nobody knows about the thirties.' We tried and tried, and then we gave up."[78] Haimsohn submitted the script to his friend and occasional collaborator Andy Warhol, who was not interested. Sometime later Haimsohn left a copy of *Dames* with the owner of an art gallery across the street from the Cino; the owner gave the script to Cino, who placed it with a stack of other unsolicited and neglected scripts. One day Robert Dahdah walked into the coffeehouse to find Cino sorting through the stacks of scripts and other clutter, throwing away much of it. Deeply concerned about the waste of anything that might be useful, Dahdah started thumbing through the discarded manuscripts. From the trash can he pulled a slim manuscript, yellowing around the edges, and began to read. The work was *Dames at Sea,* at the time little more than a short nightclub sketch. But Dahdah recognized its potential. He took the script with him and approached Haimsohn and Miller to extend the show to about fifty-minutes. They were initially reluctant to add material, believing that fifteen minutes was all that the audience could take of the sketch. Dahdah, however, persuaded them to work with him. Changes that Dahdah suggested range from the relatively minor (such as changing role names: Admiral to Captain and the Producer to Director) to the more substantive (insisting that Haimsohn and Miller add the song "Raining in My Heart").

Casting was a problem from the start. According to a letter addressed to Richard Buck, who organized the 1985 exhibit of Cino material at Lincoln Center, someone with the production team asked Fredi Dundee to audition: "I was asked to come and audition for *Dames at Sea* after they had seen me do a French monologue, but I told them that my tap dancing was non-existent, but I should have 'faked' it. I went there to see the show and absolutely loved it. Congratulations to Robert Dahdah."[79] One of the most challenging roles to cast was that of Joan, for they needed an actress who could capture just the right degree of sarcasm. When they finally settled on Jill Roberts for the role, they began rehearsals with the following cast:

Ruby—Judy Gallagher
Frank—Joe McGuire
Dick—David Christmas
Joan—Jill Roberts
Mona—Norma Bigtree
Director and Captain—Gary Filsinger

As a novice actress, Gallagher became concerned about her ability to fill the role of Ruby, especially since she, like Dundee, could not tap-dance adequately. After she withdrew from the production, Dahdah began recruiting other actresses. Choreographer Don Price recommended Bernadette Peters, with whom he had worked in summer stock. Peters and another actress were scheduled for auditions at two and two thirty, respectively. Dahdah recognized immediately that the fresh-faced "kewpie-doll" was perfect for the role[80]; when the second woman was late, Dahdah quickly canceled her audition and gave the role to Peters. In many ways, she was the part: the young, innocent performer determined to become a star.

Born Bernadette Lazarra, Peters grew up in Queens, where her father delivered bread. She began taking tap lessons at the age of three and singing lessons shortly thereafter; her professional television debut came at age five in *The Horn and Hardart Children's Hour.* Though her mother encouraged her to pursue a career in performance, she was not, according to Peters, a stereotypical stage mother: "It was my mother put me in show business . . . but she wasn't an obnoxious mother and I wasn't an obnoxious child. I didn't resent it, and she never made me do anything I didn't want to do."[81] She told Bob Lardine, "But when I was a kid, she fulfilled herself through me. She put me into show business so she could get a taste of the life herself."[82] Her mother was even responsible for her name change; fearing that Lazarra might sound too ethnic and might result in typecasting, the young actress chose Peters, from her father's given name, as her stage name. Peters was cast in her first play, *This Is Goggle,* with Kim Hunter and James Daly, when she was only nine, but the production closed out of town. Prior to *Dames,* her only significant stage role came when at the age of thirteen she played Baby June in a road tour of *Gypsy.* After *Gypsy,* she did little performing until she was seventeen: "I think I was just waiting to grow up. I didn't like being a child and I couldn't wait for it to be over."[83] Then, at seventeen, she went to Lancaster, Pennsylvania, to perform in summer stock: "It was awful. . . . We slept in a broken down inn and when I learned there were a few bats loose in the building it was the end of any sleep."[84] During the summer, she met Don Price, thus leading to her role in *Dames.*

Even as a child, Peters enjoyed the musicals of the thirties and forties. In an interview with Jerry Tallmer, Peters recalled watching the old movies and mimicking their dance steps. Thus, even before going to the Cino, she could dance in the style of the Berkeley musicals. Relying on her love for the musicals of the thirties, her years of training, and her air of innocence, Peters gave a remarkable performance as Ruby. She remained in the role through all of June but left to tour with a production of *Riverwind,* whereupon her older sister, Donna Forbes, took over the role. Forbes appeared in the production until she left for a European tour of another production. Two days before her departure, the replacement lost her voice and could not appear. Thus Sandy Bigtree took over the role. According to a press release from Caffe Cino, "Miss Sandy Bigtree who took the next bus to New York and arrived Sunday night

. . . went into rehearsal Monday and did the show Tuesday at 9 pm. Never in the history of the American Theater has any actor or actress taken a part and did it as well as this young starlet, who only had a twenty four hour rehearsal for song, dance and acting."[85]

Sandy Bigtree completed the run of the show. The following list contains the names of all characters and the actors who played them during the run at Caffe Cino.

> Ruby—Judy Gallagher (never performed), Bernadette Peters, Donna Forbes, Sandy Bigtree
> Frank—Joe McGuire, Chris Barret, Paul McCarthy
> Dick—David Christmas, replaced by unknown person
> Joan—Jill Roberts
> Mona—Norma Bigtree
> Director and Captain—Gary Filsinger.

Of the twelve persons, only Peters and Christmas appeared in the off-Broadway production.

Like her younger sister, Donna Forbes (now Donna DeSeta, the owner and manager of Donna DeSeta Casting) recalls their mother as having been encouraging but not demanding in her support of the two girls' careers in performance. She recognizes the production of *Dames* at the Cino as a turning point in Peters's career if not in her own; Forbes notes that *Dames* has "never been as magical again,"[86] an opinion shared by members of the audience and cast. Several sources incorrectly indicate that Donna Forbes preceded Peters in the role of Ruby: "Oddly enough it was Bernadette's sister, Donna, nine years her senior, who played Ruby when *Dames at Sea* was tried out at Cafe Chino [*sic*]. . . . But Donna is married and has a baby, so Bernadette took over the role."[87] Perhaps drawing from the same source, her biography released by MGM for *Pennies from Heaven* notes that she "stepped into her older sister Donna's shoes for the role of Ruby" and misspells *Cino* as *Chino.*[88]

The night before *Dames* opened, George Haimsohn approached Dahdah and said, "You must get rid of Bernadette. She's Blah."[89] Far from being blah, Peters created the magic of which Joe Cino was so fond, and the production became one of the biggest hits in off-off-Broadway history. The production was so successful that Wise, who played the piano for the production, gave up a contract to teach summer session at Newark College of Engineering. Part of the fascination of the production at Caffe Cino was the degree to which a cast of six, led by an inexperienced teen, could recreate the effect of the Berkeley routines, most of which featured seventy or more dancers. Some credit clearly must go to the limited size of the space available; Caffe Cino's stage could barely accommodate the small cast, thus making the show seem more populous than it actually was. But primary credit ultimately must go to the ingenuity with which Dahdah staged the work. He selected flashy costumes, some made by Peters's mother, and taped small pieces of mirrored glass onto umbrellas so that when the umbrellas were twirled under the stage lights, they reflected specks of light back onto the walls in an effective simulation of rain during the "Raining in My Heart" sequence. Not all of Dahdah's ideas met with equal success; his original intent had been to sew pin flashlights rather than mirrors onto the umbrellas. Lighting designer Johnny Dodd vigorously opposed the idea. When Dahdah bought the flashlights anyway, the angry lighting designer stormed over to Dahdah, grabbed the flashlights, and threw them into a hole that someone had punched into one of the walls. The *Dames* flashlights are most likely still encased within the wall.

The dispute with Dodd was neither particularly intense nor harmful to the production. A much more serious disagreement, however, began to develop between Dahdah and the writing-composing team. At least one member of the team had not wanted to work with Dahdah, arguing that he was too much of a method director to handle *Dames* effectively. As the production moved from rehearsals to performances, the conflicts increased, particularly between Wise and Dahdah. Dahdah became convinced that Wise and his partners were attempting to force him out of any future earnings from the show. Dahdah had already met with a producer interested in moving *Dames* into a larger house, though he wanted to lengthen the work, since it was less than one hour long. Ultimately the group could not reach an agreement, and the negotiations with the producer collapsed.

In 1968, however, without Dahdah's participation, *Dames* opened off Broadway in the Bouwerie Lane Theatre under the direction of Neal Kenyon. For some, *Dames* had proved quite beneficial. Judy Klemesrud notes, for example, that Peters "became a hot commodity after her 'Dames' debut. She pulled down the lead in *The Penny Friend* off Broadway, which snagged her a nomination for the Vernon Rice Award in 1967."[90] Yet neither Joe Cino nor Robert Dahdah benefited from the initial off-Broadway run nor from subsequent productions, despite their investment in the piece. Dahdah and the Cino are typically minimized or even completely erased from histories of the work.

When it was revived in 1985, for example, the only mention that an article in *Stages* makes of Caffe Cino is to note that *Dames* "began as a small scale revue at the Caffe Cino in 1968. It was quickly expanded and moved to Off-Broadway where it was an enormous success."[91] The article makes no mention of Dahdah. Other discussions of *Dames* sometimes completely ignore both Caffe Cino and Dahdah.

Normally when a dispute arose within a production, Cino refused to take sides, canceling the show if the different factions could not resolve their dispute quickly. *Dames,* however, was bringing in more money than any production in the history of the Cino. Crowds lined up to see it, limousines regularly dropped off uptown patrons, house after house sold out, even when the run of the show had been extended repeatedly, making it the only production at the Cino to have an open-ended run. Given the financial success of the show, Cino refused to cancel it. Having been involved with many productions at the coffeehouse and having earned the Caffe its first review, Dahdah felt betrayed by his close friend Joe Cino. *Dames* was Dahdah's last show at the Caffe; he seldom returned even as a spectator afterward. His friendship with Cino was seriously harmed and began to recover only near the end of the proprietor's life.

After opening at the Bouwerie Lane Theatre for its off-Broadway premier, *Dames* moved to the Theatre De Lys (now the Lucille Lortel), though complaints arose regarding the cost of admission virtually from its first appearance off Broadway. As the organizers of the 1985 Cino exhibit make clear, almost any ticket price would have been excessive when compared to the admission charge at Caffe Cino: "Two letters to the editor of the New York Times protest the rising price of tickets to the show. Perhaps this was a legitimate complaint considering the original price of admission was no more than a cup of coffee and a cannolli."[92]

Dames clearly represents the commercial peak of Caffe Cino's work. Though it embodies many of the traits of other Cino productions, it shuns the more subversive style or content of the most significant work presented at the Caffe. In many ways, it represents the beginning of a trend that would become increasingly common in subsequent years: the commodification of the subversive strategies explored by Cino and other off-off-Broadway artists. H. M. Koutoukas created his mad, camp world by foregrounding issues of gender and sexuality; Andy Milligan presented sadistic, violent interpretations of plays by established authors; Tom Eyen, Doric Wilson, and Robert Patrick employed iconic figures from both popular and high culture to challenge heteronormative values and traditional concepts of identity construction. With *Dames,* Haimsohn and Wise emptied camp of its most subversive content.

One of the aftereffects of *Dames* may have been the growing presence of members of Andy Warhol's Factory, a group often blamed for the collapse of Caffe Cino. Precisely when the Warhol crowd became regulars is unclear, though many believe that it was late in the Cino's history, thus lending support to Dahdah's assertion on his cable television show *Chelsea Journal* that *Dames* attracted the group. Certainly several early Cino figures (such as Robert Heide) had connections with Warhol. And as early as October 27, 1964, drug-related death struck near the Cino when dancer Freddie Herko, star of Warhol's *The Thirteen Most Beautiful Boys* and *Rollerskate,* went to a friend's apartment on Cornelia Street, put on Mozart's *Coronation* Mass, and danced to his death out a fifth-story window while naked and under the influence of drugs. Like Ondine and other Warhol associates, Herko was closely associated with Cino regulars.

Though many who frequented the Cino do not recall seeing Warhol in the coffeehouse, we know that he occasionally went there. Asked when he met the artist, Warhol's painting assistant Ronnie Cutrone replied, "I guess 1965. . . . The first time I met him was at the Café [*sic*] Cino, and I was pretty slicked up. I was wearing a raincoat, and my hair was longer, and it was combed up. And I said to ———, 'Is that another one of your amphetamine queens?' And ——— said, 'No, that's [an] amphetamine glory.'"[93] Dates in personal reminiscences, of course, must be taken cautiously; Cutrone's guess could easily be off by a year or two. Thus it is possible that the meeting occurred before Herko's 1964 jump from the Cornelia Street window or in 1966, after the opening of *Dames.* Regardless of when they arrived, the Warhol crowd had sufficiently insinuated itself into the Cino cadre by November 1966 for Ondine (star of *The Chelsea Girls*) to appear in the *Thanksgiving (Jury Duty) Horror Show.* It was the first of several shows to feature Warhol figures.

Many Cino veterans blame Warhol and his followers for the escalating use of heavy drugs by Joe and his followers. Most of the artists involved in the early and middle years of the Cino argue that the drug problem surfaced only near the end of the Cino's history. Charles Loubier, for example, wrote,

> As always, with creativity, you get another side. Sometimes there's the need to be hyped, with both dope and drink, which is a false thing. I

knew it then, even as a drunkard I knew it. The young people were coming in with pills. That was new to us. Joe wasn't on pills. He wasn't a drunk either. When he drank, he drank like he ate, he drank the whole bottle. That was rare. There was no grass, not at that time. A lot of people had it, but it wasn't done in the shop, not until much later. . . . He had a manner, he could put you at ease in one split second. And it was genuine. He didn't need drugs or drink to come on that way.[94]

According to Tillie Gross, Cino even fired a waiter whom he suspected of selling drugs. Though Gross begins her discussion of drugs in the coffeehouse by noting that Cino veterans do not recall Joe's taking drugs or smoking marijuana at the Caffe in the early years, she then adds that the veterans acknowledge his use of amphetamine, benzedrine, and dexedrine to help control his weight and to help him stay awake; they also indicate that he used LSD and mescaline "for his own pleasure."[95] By the fall of 1966 drugs were unquestionably becoming a significant problem, affecting the relationship between Cino and Jonathan Torrey and threatening the health of both men. Justly or not, Warhol and his crowd have been blamed for introducing a toxic level of drug abuse. Paul Foster, for example, seems to refer to the group when he speaks of the Cino as Camelot.

> Then, into Camelot came the serpents, the Pop Art golems, spawned in a silver factory. When these slimy drug slaves entered the door they infected the place and made it unclean. These angels [of] death came with their Campbell soup cans filled with drugs and destroyed the Caffe Cino. They are directly responsible for the death of Joe Cino. No one knows how many other deaths these insect larvae have encompassed, but as I see it, it's just a short jump from this zombie horde to a Reverend Jones Kool-Aid party. They succeeded in their lethal work. The Caffe Cino is now a used furniture shop, and Camelot is no more.[96]

Andy Warhol's reputation for cruelty hardly speaks in his defense. When told of Herko's suicide, Warhol's only expressed regret was that Herko had not let him know of his intent to jump from the window. Had the dancer done so, Warhol would have filmed it.[97] Taylor Mead implies that his own move to Europe came about to keep from killing Warhol; Mead was furious at the artist for manipulating people, lying, and being "too cold-blooded."[98] Similarly, a friend of performer Jackie Curtis said,

Andy was a cocksucker, a venal man. He was not a nice person. Andy robbed Jackie Curtis. He never paid anyone. A little pocket money and all the drugs they wanted he acquired for them. Heroin. Amphetamines. For *Women in Revolt,* Jackie Curtis got $163. At the most. All the drugs and booze they wanted, and boys. He would acquire young men. For that purpose only, to fuck 'em or suck 'em, whatever, from sixteen to twenty-two, young and foolish and impressed by Andy Warhol. Andy Warhol, when you come down to the bottom line, was an unscrupulous bastard, and when you come down to it, he was a charlatan.[99]

Robert Patrick also has said that members of the Warhol crowd had only one goal: to recruit boys and girls who were passed around at orgies. When the recruits lost their appeal, Warhol threw them out on the streets, discarding them like so much rubbish. With the exception of the work by Soren Agenoux, Patrick is highly critical of Cino productions by members of the Factory, calling them "sterile, self-serving, incomprehensible."[100]

Whether he was part of the cause or merely a symptom of the increased drug use, Ondine became one of the Cino regulars. Born Robert Olivio, Pope Ondine as he was typically called took his stage name from the 1954 Broadway production that starred Audrey Hepburn. Warhol actress Mary Woronov (who appeared at the Cino in *Vinyl*) was a friend of Ondine and the "Mole People," members of the Warhol crowd noted for their heavy drug use. She describes Ondine in several passages in her memoir of her Factory years:

- [There was] nothing he wouldn't do in the area of drugs and perversion[101];
- My nights were spent with Ondine and our good friends, the Moles, and these nights always began the same way—with drugs[102];
- If you hung with the Mole People, somewhere, somehow, either their drugs, one of their thoughts, or just one of their little hairs got into your skin and burrowed deeper and deeper, quietly driving you insane. It was the law, and nobody escaped, not even Andy.[103]

If even Warhol could not escape the fate of those who hung with the Mole People, then certainly neither could Joe Cino nor Jonathan Torrey.

While the astonishing twelve-week run of *Dames* marked the commercial apex of Caffe Cino, the following months saw the beginning of the downward spiral that ended in the death of Joe Cino and the closing of his beloved coffeehouse. First, the drug addiction of Cino and Torrey reached a critical point, ultimately prompting the two men to leave New York briefly in an effort to overcome the problem. Second, the MacDougal Area Neighborhood Association launched a new action against coffeehouses. When the truce between the Village factions fell apart, MANA began its most successful effort to control coffeehouses and other Village businesses. Aggravating these and other problems and constantly weighing Cino down was his dissatisfaction with his own success. The bitch goddess, success, had struck. And the goddess was not always benevolent. As Robert Heide told Clayton Delery, "[S]uccess is a sort of bitch goddess. Sometimes, when you're not looking, she smiles on you and things go well. Later, when you try and court her, she turns her back."[104] Crowds flocked to the shows; money flowed in—certainly not enough to make anyone, least of all Joe Cino, wealthy but enough to keep the cafe functional. Cino's friends were doing what they wanted or had to do: creating theatre. Yet the cafe for which Cino had worked so hard, into which he had poured so many hours, had vanished in spirit if not in fact; his intimate coffeehouse had become a bustling business enterprise and a popular theatre. The pleasures of quiet conversations with friends and of a casual celebration of all aspects of creativity had been replaced by a focus on the logistics of managing audiences, scheduling productions, and tending to other mundane operational tasks.

5 The End of the Cobra Cult

hereas the spring and summer of 1966 offered promise for a compromise in the coffeehouse war, the fall saw an end to any real hope for such a truce. With opinions ever more sharply divided, the city increased efforts to control the crowds in the Village by issuing more summonses to unlicensed coffeehouses. As the *Village Voice* reported, "The Caffe Cino, the Feenjon, and the Grand Slam were given summonses during the week for operating without the cabaret licenses they cannot get under existing zoning laws. The Cino, on Cornelia Street, is not in the troubled MacDougal Street area."[1] Playing at the time was *Eyen on Eyen,* the show that immediately followed *Dames at Sea;* it was not to be the last time Tom Eyen saw one of his productions involved in a city action against the Cino. A compromise between the various MacDougal factions seemed impossible. In August 1966 the MacDougal Street Neighborhood Association (MANA) held what a reporter counted as their eightieth meeting in two years.[2] As had happened so often in the past, the meeting concluded with most MANA participants questioning the possibility of a solution to the neighborhood's problems. Though he continued to work for an end to the impasse, even Village district leader Edward Koch seemed pessimistic. Should the various parties in the dispute ultimately conclude that no solution agreeable to all could be reached, Koch emphasized, individual rights of residents must take precedence over the rights of coffeehouse owners. His position was strengthened by the fact that coffeehouses were for the most part operating illegally.

While Koch framed his dispute with the businesses in terms of concern over the congestion and other problems in the Village, many coffeehouse owners and patrons argued that the conflict represented a deeper cultural and political schism. A letter in the window of the Rienzi outlined some of the fundamental issues that separated the two groups:

To the living dead and MacDougal Street Society and Mr. Scrooge Koch:
You didn't like the way we dressed—You didn't like the way we
looked—You didn't like our guitars—You didn't like our long hair—
but my dear pretentious hypocritical prejudiced zombies—it was really
our zest and love of life that you did not like—we are not evil—it is
you who are evil—evil in your hate—evil in that you can see only your
little narrow world—Well, you might get rid of Rienzi's—You might
get rid of MacDougal Street, but you will never get rid of us. Remember, the children will bury you—You are the past—we are the future.
. . . May God have pity on your dead souls and we will dance and sing
on your graves.[3]

The coffeehouse war centered on a struggle over fundamental social values,
over essential political beliefs, and over basic issues of community (how "community" was to be defined, who was to comprise it, which sources of authority were legitimate within it, and which were to legitimate it).

As the city threatened coffeehouses from one direction, Actors' Equity
Association threatened from another, thus intensifying the dual threat that had
first surfaced six years earlier. In March 1966 Equity had decided to prohibit
its members from appearing in virtually any off-off-Broadway production. The
edicts were so broad, in fact, that a literal enforcement of them would have
prevented actors from appearing in the union's own showcase Equity Theatre,
which offered a full season of productions each year. For months the rules went
unenforced. Then, as La Mama prepared for a tour of Europe to present works
by off-off-Broadway playwrights, Ellen Stewart learned of new problems con-
fronting her theatre. In the first case of its kind, Equity had filed charges against
Marilyn Roberts and Patrick Sullivan for appearing without union contracts
in La Mama's production of Robert Heide's *Why Tuesday Never Has a Blue
Monday.* Equity argued that its actions were intended to force off-off-Broadway managers to pay a reasonable wage. Actors averaged only $2.60 per per-
formance for *Why Tuesday Never Has a Blue Monday,* with all income being
dependent on contributions from the audience.[4] Stewart, however, suggested
that the actions concealed an effort to protect the revenue of off-Broadway
theatres. According to Stewart, the union enforced its rules for showcase and
off-off-Broadway productions only after off-Broadway theatres complained
that La Mama engaged in unfair competition, since Stewart did not pay wages
and thus could afford to charge much less for admission than they could.[5]

Stewart was trapped: she could not pay Equity wages from the small revenue generated by La Mama, but she either would not or could not make the changes necessary to bring in sufficient revenue for such wages. As she said, "I refuse to turn La Mama into a commercial scene."[6] Complicating the situation was the $350 penalty assessed against Sullivan for appearing at La Mama. Stewart needed the actors and the actors needed the exposure and experience, but they risked penalties far in excess of any earnings potential if they appeared in such productions. Faced with these problems, Stewart decided to close La Mama. The theatre was dark beginning on October 12; Equity, it seemed, would manage to achieve what the licensing officials had not. No production appeared on the La Mama stage until November 9, 1966, when Bruce Kessler's *The Contestants* opened.

As the coffeehouse war and Equity battles raged in various parts of the Village, Caffe Cino continued a successful season, with Tom Eyen's *Eyen on Eyen*. Born in Cambridge, Ohio, Eyen claimed to have received various degrees from the Ohio State University, though his attendance there has yet to be documented. He studied at the American Academy of Dramatic Arts (1961–62), leaving without completing the program. At the academy he discovered that his interest was in writing rather than in acting. He was introduced to experimental theatre at Caffe Cino[7] but actually staged his first play, *Frustrata, the Dirty Little Girl with the Red Paper Rose Stuck in Her Head, Is Demented!* at Cafe La Mama on May 7, 1964. For the next few years, he and his Theatre of the Eye Repertory Company were closely associated with La Mama, though his work frequently appeared at the Cino as well. While promoting *The Dirtiest Show in Town,* his first major success, he expressed a preference for the by then defunct Cino: "I liked the working conditions at the Cino better; they were more intimate. Mama was more presentational. . . . It has sucked up the whole off-off Broadway movement."[8]

As a self-proclaimed pop artist, Eyen was part of and was influenced by the second wave of the avant-garde that began to emerge in the United States, which Arnold Aronson notes "drew inspiration from the raw energy, form, and content of American pop culture and iconography, the wonder and fear of new technologies and media, and from the conflicting chaos of urban society."[9] Even in his earliest work Eyen showed an interest in popular culture. One of the earliest of his known pieces is a fragment written while he was a student at Saint Benedict High School in Ohio. A parody of hit-parade radio programs, it opens with a commercial for Lucky Smokes cigarettes, in which he plays on several brand names: Lucky Smokes are rolled from tobacco grown in Chester's fields and are endorsed by the actor Phillip Morris. The use of commercials was a device that would continue even into Eyen's post-Cino work: the action of *2008½ (A Spaced Odyssey)* (1974), for example, breaks periodically for advertisements for such products as Sealtest Sperm Ice-cream and Aunt Cora's Come Remover. Despite his frequent use of mock advertisements, news shows, and such, Eyen's primary use of pop culture comes in his choice of characters and plots. In *Why Hanna's Skirt Won't Stay Down,* he draws from the lives of tragic actresses such as Marilyn Monroe. In other plays he uses images of Sarah Bernhardt, Lady Bird Johnson, Barbra Streisand, Cinderella, and Santa Claus. Even the world of off and off-off-Broadway, his artistic home, was not safe from his pillaging for characters and plots. *The Kama Sutra* parodies the work of the Living Theatre, and to celebrate La Mama's reopening after the dispute with Equity, Stewart's cafe presented *Give My Regards to Off-Off Broadway* in December 1966. Though the work is fiction, various characters clearly are meant to portray Helen Hanft, Joe Cino, Ellen Stewart, Al Carmines, and similar figures.

Just as popular culture provided Eyen with the characters and situations for virtually every one of his plays, television and cinema provided their structure, with such devices as quick scene shifts, voice-overs, and cross-fades. He called *Give My Regards to Off-Off Broadway* a "recorded, cinema, fantasy-happening in color." "A film for the stage," *Women Behind Bars,* written in 1974, a few years after the close of the Cino, recreates the world of the exploitation movies of the fifties and sixties that featured imprisoned women. In an interview Eyen said, "I've always written with stage techniques which translated into film. Even *Hanna* and *Women Behind Bars* are actually films. They're movies. *The Dirtiest Show* is totally a film, and I didn't rewrite it that much. Usually, plays don't transform to movies because they're too stagy. My work keeps on cutting and clipping from one montage to another. I've always known that secretly, but I was always scared of movies."[10]

Given Eyen's interest in film and popular culture, his plays typically focus on the individual situated within a mediated culture. Central to his work is the question of how identity operates when the individual is surrounded by mediated images. Thus in *The White Whore and the Bit Player,* the two characters are different aspects of one person, an actress who has committed suicide. According to Eyen's note to the published play, the characters represent the actress as "the nun-mind—what she imagines herself to be" and as "the whore-flesh—what the world saw her to be" as a result of her filmic images. Because of camp's emphasis on surface and appearance rather than content and because of its parodic qualities, that style of creative expression offered Eyen an ideal instrument for exploring the themes that dominate his work. By appropriating images from sources as diverse as pop artist Andy Warhol, avant-garde theatre groups, and the various popular media, Eyen created characters who are both produced by and trapped within mediated images.

With *Eyen on Eyen* at the Cino, Tom Eyen created a collage of his own work. His creativity appears not only in the campy, wild production but also in programs, posters, and advertisements. With an allusion to Peter Weiss's *The Persecution and Assassination of Marat as Performed by the Inmates of the Asylum of Charenton under the Direction of the Marquis De Sade,* the advertisement for *Eyen on Eyen* included the following lines: "From His Collected Works as Performed and Executed by the Inmates of the Asylum of Experimental Theatre under the Direction of his Chinese Half Brother, Tom Lee. . . . Due to surprising success (47 Buddhist nuns walking out) this program shall run until its scheduled California tour through Disneyland."[11] His biography in the program read, "Eyen O. Eyen (1908–62) wrote for *Vanity Fair* in it's [*sic*] hayday [*sic*]. A good friend of Dorothy Parker and ee cummings, the three could usually be seen at Martha's Vineyard picking grapes. Eyen has written only ten plays, all of which were before their time. He is survived by his wife Olga, and seven assorted children."[12] In other biographies he would claim to have a Puerto Rican wife named Mira and to be "the leading playwright of Sweden, and as clearly demonstrated by the quality of his work, has slept his way to the top."[13]

The period that followed the production of *Eyen on Eyen* is the only one for which we have a record of the shows that Joe Cino intended to run. In a notebook that contains, among other things, show-by-show receipts for several months, Cino had written the plans for August 30, 1966, through January 22, 1967. Table 2 shows Cino's plans, along with the shows that actually ran during the period. Why the changes in the planned schedule occurred is not always clear, though the Wilson piece scheduled to begin September 27, 1966, was probably not ready in time.

The first two productions ran as planned, with Alan Lysander James's *Dearest of All Boys* opening on August 30 and a revival of David Starkweather's *So, Who's Afraid of Edward Albee?* on September 13 under the direction of Phoebe Wray. On September 27, however, in a period intended for a work by

Table 2. Productions Planned by Joe Cino and Those That Actually Ran

Date	Planned	Actual
08/30/66	Oscar Wilde	*Dearest of All Boys* (a play referencing Oscar Wilde) by Alan Lysander James
09/06/66		
09/13/66	Starkweather	*So, Who's Afraid of Edward Albee?* by David Starkweather
09/20/66		
09/27/66	Lanford Wilson	*Indecent Exposure* by Robert Patrick
10/04/66		
10/11/66	Haimsohn *Psychedelic Follies*	*Psychedelic Follies* by George Haimsohn
10/18/66		
10/25/66	Sally Ordway	*Something I'll Tell You Tuesday* and *The Loveliest Afternoon of the Year* by John Guare
11/01/66		
11/08/66	Koutoukas	*Cobra Invocations & John Guare & Cobra Invocations* by H. M. Koutoukas
11/15/66		*GBS's ABC's from Annihilation to Ziegfeld: A Shavian Kaleidoscope* by Alan Lysander James
11/22/66		*Thanksgiving (Jury Duty) Horror Show* by H. M. Koutoukas
11/29/66	Eyen *Hanna* Part II	*Why Hanna's Skirt Won't Stay Down* by Tom Eyen
12/06/66		
12/13/66	Lanford Wilson	Probably either *Hanna's Skirt* or *White Whore and the Bit Player,* both by Tom Eyen
12/20/66	Koutoukas and *Crumpled Christmas*	*Chas. Dickens' Christmas Carol* by Soren Agenoux
12/27/66		
01/03/67	Heide	*Chas. Dickens' Christmas Carol* by Soren Agenoux
01/10/67		*The White Whore and the Bit Player* by Tom Eyen
01/17/67		

Lanford Wilson, Robert Patrick's *Indecent Exposure* opened; it is one of the few shows directed by Lanford Wilson. Sometime during the week of September 20, Phoebe Wray received a telephone call from Marshall Mason, who explained that the show scheduled to open on September 27 either had been canceled or was not ready. He asked her whether she would appear in the replacement show. When she asked Mason for the title of the work, he replied "I don't know, Patrick is writing it right now."[14] Patrick recently quoted Wray on the play: "Overnight Bob wrote a short, pungent little one-act called *Indecent Exposure*. I never knew the names of the other actors in it. I'm not sure I ever saw the whole cast. We did the show so fast I don't even remember how Lanford was as a director. We were a hit. . . . Joe, as usual, stayed out of the way to let us do our work."[15] *Indecent Exposure* is an antiwar play about a young man who shows his objection to the Vietnam War by taping his draft card to his wrist and walking the streets until he is arrested.

For the most part the remainder of the shows presented in 1966 were written by established Cino writers. With *Psychedelic Follies* (October 11), George Haimsohn shifted his attention to contemporary issues and culture, away from the old movies that had been the basis of *Dames at Sea*. With one of the early uses of *psychedelic* to refer to the burgeoning sixties drug culture, the production celebrated that culture through songs and skits about marijuana, acid, speed, and other drugs. Donna Forbes returned to the Cino to appear in the production, which featured music by John Aman. Ironically the play ran as drugs took an increasing toll on both Cino and Torrey.

Psychedelic Follies was followed by a double bill of John Guare's works, *Something I'll Tell You Tuesday* and *The Loveliest Afternoon of the Year*. Though the production received only fair reviews, Guare's work is significant in that a last-minute cancellation of one of his performances led to the start of the comic book productions. The announcement of *Cobra Invocations & John Guare & Cobra Invocations* immediately after *Tuesday* and *Afternoon* suggests that the comic book production followed those two plays. Yet it is entirely unclear whether an earlier Guare play, *A Day for Surprises,* ever played and thus could be the work that was canceled, prompting the start of comic book plays. *A Day for Surprises* was billed as being written by Paul Guare and was scheduled for August 1965. No review of the production is available, and sources list various initial production information for it, with dates ranging from 1967 to 1971 and venues ranging from the Cino to a theatre in London.

Whichever production was canceled, it left Cino with virtually no time to locate a replacement. He was frantic: soon people would arrive expecting to see a show, and he had nothing to present to them. In desperation he turned to the regulars who happened to be in the coffeehouse at the time. Someone suggested that they stage a work based on a comic book. Precisely who initially offered the idea has been debated, since several people have either claimed credit or been credited. The exhibit in 1985 relied on Charles Stanley's résumé to give him credit.[16] It seems much more likely, however, that the idea for the comic book production was a collaborative effort by playwright Donald Brooks, Robert Patrick, and Merrill Harris, also known as Merrill Mushroom, whom Patrick describes as "an impressive icon of the Lower East Side political and artistic scene—a figure to whom many of us showed our plays for approval."[17] A few days before the crisis over the Guare production, Harris had proposed covering a delay in a different production by performing a comic book, though the proposal was not acted on at that time. When Brooks proposed a similar strategy to cover the absence of the Guare work, Patrick sent someone around the corner to purchase "whichever comic the drugstore has the most copies of."[18] It turned out to be *Wonder Woman*. As the group was trying to sort out who would play which role, Koutoukas was given the role of Diana Prince–Wonder Woman. Other performers included Cino as a bear, Johnny Dodd as a cat, and Deborah Lee as an Amazon, with Charles Stanley reading all other parts. Known either as *Cobra Invocations & John Guare & Cobra Invocations* or *The Secret of Taboo Mountain,* it was the only comic book production presented during Joe Cino's lifetime.

The Secret of Taboo Mountain was staged with no rehearsal. Actors carried the books onstage, reading lines and improvising the action; Donald Brooks, the light operator, improvised lighting changes as well, on the basis of the action on stage and the parts of the script he managed to read. Though it played for at least a week, the script varied throughout the production. As Bernard da Costa comments on *The Secret of Taboo Mountain,* "The text changes each evening 'because a large part must be improvisation.'"[19] Given the success of the show, Cino would later warn playwrights who were being difficult that they could be replaced for the price of a comic book.

After *Wonder Woman,* both Koutoukas and Alan Lysander James returned to present their work, with James departing from his typical pieces about the life and work of Oscar Wilde to focus on George Bernard Shaw and with Koutoukas presenting the Thanksgiving show. As one of the Cino's most accessible, conventional, and least offensive shows, James's *G.B.S.'s A.B.C.'s from Annihilation to Ziegfeld: A Shavian Kaleidoscope* gave Cino the opportunity to invite his family to visit and watch one of his productions. Little is now known about either James's script or the Cino family's reaction to it.

Near the end of 1966, La Mama, the Cino, and other off-off-Broadway theatres received a reprieve from Equity. Though it had fined La Mama's actors earlier, Equity announced in November that it would relax its rules so that members could appear in off-off-Broadway productions without pay if the productions met certain criteria. Under the Showcase and Workshop Code, La Mama was required to meet the following conditions:

- no more than ten performances of the same play can be given within a three-week period;
- productions must be able to show that they are not making a profit;
- the original cast must be given the option to appear in professional productions that resulted from their showcase work; and
- no advertisements were permitted (announcements to members through listings in papers such as the *Village Voice* were allowed as long as they did not include location and similar information).

Ironically the Equity decision also mandated an end to soliciting donations from the audience (passing the hat), the sole means by which most off-off-Broadway theatres paid actors. Though the ruling applied specifically to La Mama, *Village Voice* journalist Stephanie Harrington suggested that the same rules would probably apply to Caffe Cino, "the oldest and one of the most vital, respected, and debt-ridden of off-off-Broadway institutions."[20]

The Cino production that closed 1966 and opened 1967 was *Chas. Dickens' Christmas Carol* by Soren Agenoux, the managing editor of Andy Warhol's *inter/VIEW* magazine. The play originated as a faithful rendition of Dickens's novel but, like so much else at Caffe Cino, ended as a campy, playful production, even toying with and commenting on its own self-referentiality. The opening paragraph of Ross Wetzsteon's review of the production clearly describes its style.

> There's something rather appealing about a pro-Scrooge interpretation of *A Christmas Carol.* . . . And even a homosexual interpretation of Scrooge isn't as preposterous as it might seem—if you read the story for double entendres ("they often 'came down' handsomely") you'd be surprised . . . ; and the visit of "the spirit of Christmas Past" really is, in a sense, an attempted heterosexual seduction; and the idea of Scrooge's

saving Tiny Tim's life for, shall we say, rather dubious motives, could be effective satire of the impulse to charity.[21]

Most of the remaining review focuses on the shortcomings that Wetzsteon noted in the production, primarily its in-jokes, self-referentiality, and refusal to take itself seriously. It winked at the audience and then made fun of, even winked at, its own winks: "But the trouble with Soren Agenoux's *Chas. Dickens' Christmas Carol* is that it includes itself in its mockery. If there's anything worse than taking oneself too seriously, it's taking oneself too ridiculously. For when self-mockery becomes compulsive, it isn't mockery any more."[22]

The production coincided with the peak of the drug problems at the Cino. Many of those associated with *Christmas Carol* were so heavily into speed and similar drugs that at least one person withdrew from the production out of concern for the toll that drugs were taking not only on the production but also on the Cino in general and on his friends. In the obituary for Ondine, Michael Smith wrote, "It has to be said that Ondine was very bad in the bad old days, outrageously irresponsible about giving drugs (mainly speed) to other people and wallowing in them himself. On the opening night of *Christmas Carol* he took LSD, and I had to go on in the role—a certain thrill, to be sure, though not to my taste."[23]

Robert Heide recalls the day about this time when Joe Cino told him to go to the restroom and look inside. When Heide did, he saw Ondine standing in front of the mirror, watching himself masturbate. (He was noted for his large penis.) Heide quietly closed the door and went back to talk to Cino; a few moments later, Ondine came out of the toilet, walked up to Cino, and without comment gave him an injection from a syringe.

By the end of 1966, even Cino could not ignore the toll that his addiction was taking on his body and his business. Probably because of the concern expressed by a doctor,[24] he decided to leave New York to spend time with his family in Buffalo while he battled his addiction; he convinced Jonathan Torrey that he too had to overcome his addiction by returning to his family in New Hampshire. To disguise his problem Cino told his family that the withdrawal symptoms he experienced were symptoms of pneumonia.[25] He stayed in Buffalo only a short time before returning to New York without overcoming his addiction.

Torrey never returned to the Cino. Over the years several stories have been offered to explain his sudden death in 1967. Douglas Gordy, for example, describes the events as follows:

Toward the end of 1966, Torry [*sic*] took a trip to New Hampshire to work on the lights for a stock production. What happened there is a matter of conjecture. Perhaps also high on drugs, Torry, who surely knew better, was not wearing gloves as he hung the lights. Whether he intentionally touched a live wire, as some believe, or whether a wrench he wore on his belt accidentally brushed against one, Torry was electrocuted and died instantaneously.[26]

Gordy's description of Torrey's death resembles that given by Michael Feingold and is largely incorrect.[27] Actually Torrey left New York for Jaffrey, New Hampshire, late in 1966 to spend time at the home to which Norman and Elizabeth Torrey had moved sometime in the fifties (both eventually died there); Jonathan Torrey himself had lived there, working at Bean Fiber Glass, Incorporated. After arriving in Jaffrey from Greenwich Village, Torrey returned to the job at Bean Fiber Glass, working in plant and machine maintenance. On Thursday, January 5, 1967, Torrey began repairs on a loom used in the manufacturing process. The repairs involved adding gears to the machinery, but to do so part of the frame had to be ground away. Torrey suggested that the grinding could better be done with a tool that he owned, so he went home, got the device, returned, and crawled under the frame of the loom. According to a local paper, the *Monadnock Ledger,* the grinder shorted out when Torrey turned it on. The malfunction electrocuted him because he was very nearly perfectly grounded, lying on a metal plate beneath the loom, with his head resting on a steel crosspiece. The current through Torrey's body was so strong and sudden that "no outcry was heard."[28] When other employees removed Torrey from under the loom, he was no longer breathing, though mouth-to-mouth resuscitation and a mechanical resuscitator brought a moment of hope when Torrey's pulse returned briefly. Despite the momentary hope, Torrey died while at the plant. As suggested by Gordy, some people have argued that Torrey intentionally exposed himself to the live current.

Cino was devastated by Torrey's death. He performed in public for the last time when he danced at Judson Church to Ravel's *Bolero* as a tribute to his deceased friend and companion. The performance failed, in part because Cino had not rehearsed.[29] A memorial program organized by Neil Flanagan and Marshall Mason was scheduled to occur some months later at the Cino on April 4, 1967. One of Torrey's favorite plays, Claris Nelson's *The Clown,* was scheduled for a revival in April in celebration of his birthday.

In the immediate aftermath of Torrey's death, the operation of the Cino continued much as before, though its proprietor became increasingly despondent. The first production of 1967 brought to the stage another Eyen work, *The White Whore and the Bit Player.* Eyen had written the piece for Marie-Claire Charba and Jacque Lynn Colton to take to Paris on a trip that slightly predates (but is often confused with) Ellen Stewart's first European tour. The production at the Cino featured Charba and Helen Hanft, whose relationship with Eyen was tempestuous despite their strong affection and respect for each other. According to Hanft, "I always went back to working with him [Eyen]. We were always fighting; every time I did another play with him, we'd have a fight. He and I were constantly arguing. I don't know what it was, but we would constantly have arguments. We would clash about everything."[30] The production of *White Whore* brought about one of their clashes. During a technical rehearsal for the production, Hanft stepped offstage to greet Al Pacino, who had recently performed at the Cino and who had stopped by to see her. After Pacino left, Hanft became upset at lighting designer Johnny Dodd because he "had me in this vomit-green light."[31] Hanft protested: "I know I'm a nun, but let's not make her repulsive." Suddenly she felt someone hit her in the back of her head "so hard the fall and most of my costume fell off." When she realized that it was Dodd, she yelled, "What the hell is wrong with you?" to which he replied, "You don't like the light? You think you're a star?" Expecting Eyen to support her in the argument, Hanft was surprised that he came over and started screaming at her also. When Hanft challenged Eyen with "Who the hell do you think you are?" he slapped her hard enough to draw blood. In turn she ripped his shirt. Hanft continues,

The actress playing the White Whore, who was fresh out of Saint Vincent's for a nervous breakdown, said, "Oh, no," and locked herself in the dressingroom. I ran to the coffee-shop on the corner of Cornelia Street and two burly cops were in there having dinner. I screamed, "A writer and a lighting-designer are trying to kill me!" They looked at this bloody half-naked nun and quietly set their coffee down, put on their jackets, strapped their guns to their hips, and walked back with me to the Cino. They took one look at Tom and Johnny—who were not, how shall I say it, specimens of machismo—and one of them said, "Look, buddies, I don't care what your problems are with women but don't hit 'em." Tom feebly responded by showing them his torn shirt.[32]

When one of the policemen asked whether she wanted to press charges, Hanft "suddenly became Little Mary Sunshine, the ingenue of all time," replying "Oh, no, officers; we have a show to do."[33]

On January 31, 1967, Jeff Weiss opened *A Funny Walk Home,* for which he won his first Obie, a special award that the *Voice* named after Joseph Cino. In a glowing review of the work, Ross Wetzsteon attempted to define not just what the play is about but also what it is. The play is "about" a young man (Weiss) in a "lobotomized state" returning home from an asylum.[34] In one of the few tender scenes in the play, Weiss attempts to seduce his younger brother (played by George Harris); much of the play is given to what critic Ross Wetzsteon calls "re-enacting his birth trauma—'sex and violence,'" as Weiss rapes his mother and assaults his father.[35] For Wetzsteon, determining what the play is becomes more difficult than determining what the play is about: "[T]he best I can come up with is this: it isn't 'personal statement about,' it's 'personal experiencing of.'" The play does not express Weiss's opinions about family life, homosexuality, or politics, but rather re-enacts his feelings: "He didn't remember these feelings, he seemed to re-experience them, and with such unrelieved honesty, that his play-performance at the Caffe Cino was not only enormously moving but almost terrifying."[36] Because the work seems so personal to Weiss, it could never, Wetzsteon argues, be performed as effectively by any other person. And whether Weiss was in or out of character seems not to have always been clear, as at the point in which he turned to the audience to engage in a verbal attack on the *Village Voice* critic who had disliked his only other performed piece (done at La Mama). Near the end of the work, an emotionally and physically exhausted Weiss again turned and talked directly to the audience. Moving downstage, wet with sweat and tears, he asked the audience, "Won't somebody please stop this? If anyone has been moved, if anyone has felt love or pity, won't somebody please stop this play?"[37] According to Wetzsteon, Weiss's need and desperation were so naked as to be embarrassing or intimidating. On several nights the production did end at this point at the request of patrons horrified by the events of the play.

Central to the work is an attempt to implicate spectators in the action. The effort to draw them into the action and to break down the barrier between spectator and actor began from the moment the production opened. The opening scene was of the Mother and Father passing out party hats to the audience, thus making spectators both observers and participants in a celebration that quickly goes awry. Critic Wetzsteon suggests that the work developed several images into significant metaphors.

> Several themes are building up: the way we bring up our children is equivalent to sending them to an asylum (education as lobotomy); our society values sterile "seriousness" over joyous laughter (the parents won't believe their son is "cured" until they see him in tears); all current political positions are rotten (the father is a Birchite, the mother an empty-headed liberal); our forms for expressing love and hate and emotional need have become grotesquely distorted.[38]

By demolishing the fourth wall, by integrating the audience into the performance, and by blurring the line between life and art, the work forces the audience into the position of recognizing its responsibilities for (and complicity with) many of the situations that it critiques. Breaking the action at a critical moment to ask someone to stop the production placed the responsibility for the outcome directly on the audience. As Claris Nelson, who used the stage name Mae Durnhelm in playing the mother, argued, "If no one said, 'Stop the play,' everyone [onstage] ended up being dead. If they said, 'Stop,' they are good people, and they may go home; if you see mayhem about to ensue you need to take some responsibility to say, 'Stop.'"[39]

Weiss is sometimes accused of being self-indulgent in his work. During his acceptance speech for the Obie for *A Funny Walk Home* and *And That's How the Rent Gets Paid,* he told the audience: "'To all those who've called my plays self-indulgent . . . schizophrenic . . . juvenile . . . paranoid,' he said, lingering lovingly over each word, then that stuttering giggle, looking out over the 500 people jammed into the Village Gate, 'all I have to say is, *I can only promise you more of the same*'" (emphasis in original).[40]

Immediately after *A Funny Walk Home,* Robert Heide opened *Moon: A Love Play Written Specifically for the Cino St. Valentine Centennial,* his last Cino work. *Moon* is quite different in style and tone from *The Bed* but employs a device used in the earlier play that was becoming a rather distinctive device in Heide's work: he brought the action of the production to a stop while he played a rock album. According to Michael Smith, the Cino production of *Moon* included three albums, two played before the action began and another played later.[41]

The action of the play focuses on two dysfunctional couples, Sally and Sam, who are recovering from a hangover from the previous night's party, and Ingrid and Harold, who attended the same party. While both couples have relationships that are unstable and acrimonious, a stable, nurturing relationship is introduced in the form of Christopher (originally played by Heide's partner, John Gilman) and his male roommate-lover. In his introduction to the published play, Michael Smith notes, "Robert Heide is preoccupied with the experiences of alienation and pointlessness and transmits them with exquisite intensity. His characters make contact only when they panic."[42]

Following *Moon* was Terry Alan Smith's *God Created the Heaven and the Earth . . . but Man Created Saturday Night,* with music by John Aman. When the work is contrasted with Jeff Weiss's *A Funny Walk Home,* the range of styles and political approaches of Cino productions becomes apparent. Whereas Weiss challenged both theatrical and political conventions, Smith challenged neither, even applauded both. In his review of the work, Michael Smith described it as "a right-wing protest play . . . [which] mocks unionism and women's suffrage, dramatizes the evils of alcohol, and ends with a rousing plea for God's stern justice, all within the framework of a Biblical morality pageant."[43]

God Created the Heaven and the Earth . . . but Man Created Saturday Night was the last original work presented during Cino's lifetime. On March 21, 1967, a new production of *The Madness of Lady Bright* opened with Neil Flanagan, Fred Forrest, and Brandy Carson in the cast under the direction of Lanford Wilson. Though it previously had run for 168 performances under different directors (including Denis Deegan and William Archibald), Michael Smith considered the March 1967 production to be the "definitive" version,[44] concluding, "Let this be a lesson: flamboyant theatricality and emotional realism are not incompatible."[45]

As Jonathan Torrey's birthday approached and as Cino sank deeper into depression, *Lady Bright,* with its tale of a lonely, aging, gay man seems the worst possible show for Cino to have had to watch every night, two or three times a night. Along with concerns about his weight and aging, he fought depression over the loss of Torrey. Charles Loubier reports the following exchange with Cino regarding Torrey:

> I was living in Boston when my brother told me Torrey died. . . . They were heavy into drugs when I came back. I spoke to Joe. He said, "They only made one of a kind." I said it was an accident, these things happen. Do what you have to do, but make a face. "I am making a face, but it's not worth it anymore," he said. He did every pill for 4 or 5 months. I didn't want to believe it. He said to me, "You're a drunk, I'm

a drug addict. Remember when we used to play funeral? Now it's true."
Then he laughed.[46]

After a distressing incident in a taxi in which he suffered a frightening hallu-
cination, Cino decided again to stop taking all drugs. According to Robert
Dahdah, at least in the early years, Cino never regularly used hard drugs but
had frequently taken amphetamines to boost his energy so that he could
maintain his hectic schedule. Dahdah believes that withdrawal from amphetamines exacerbated Cino's problems and ultimately contributed to his self-
destruction. Al Carmines recalls seeing the coffeehouse proprietor the night
before his attempted suicide: "I saw Joe Cino wandering the midnight streets
of New York the day before he committed suicide. He asked me to take a boat
trip to the Statue of Liberty with him. I was too busy. How I regret that business. The next time I saw him Ellen Stewart and I sat by his bedside in St.
Vincent's Hospital as he agonizingly died. . . . He gave till it hurt. He loved
till it killed him."[47] Later that night, an exhausted, distraught Cino arrived at
Dahdah's apartment on Forty-sixth Street. Though Dahdah had not worked
at the Caffe after the *Dames* problems, he reached out to support Cino after
Torrey's death. Their friendship had healed, and the coffeehouse owner occasionally spent the night at Dahdah's apartment. When Cino arrived the
evening before his suicide attempt, he was convinced that someone had been
following him, a paranoid delusion that had occurred before when he was
taking drugs heavily. Dahdah invited him in, tried to soothe him, and finally
got him to lie down to sleep. Without thinking about the recent loss of
Jonathan Torrey until he overheard Cino crying, Dahdah played an album with
the song "Where Are You" on it. The next day, assuming that Cino was sleeping, Dahdah left to work on a show; it was the last time he saw his friend
outside the hospital.

Apparently on Thursday, March 30, 1967, the day before his suicide attempt, Cino argued with a close friend, one of the playwrights at his coffeehouse. On Friday, March 31, Cino went with Johnny Dodd to visit a person
whom Charles Loubier calls "some Countess uptown."[48] Later in the evening
Dodd and Cino went to Flanagan's apartment to talk with him about the
argument of the previous day. When Flanagan was not home, Cino went alone
to Kenny Burgess's apartment on the Bowery (an apartment that Burgess had
taken over from Cino), but Burgess also was not home. Since several books
had been opened to his favorite passages, it is clear that Cino let himself in,

perhaps to wait for Burgess. Before Burgess returned, however, Cino left for his own basement apartment on Cornelia Street, a few doors from the Caffe. When Burgess came home, he telephoned Flanagan to ask whether he knew anything about the conflict between the playwright and Cino. As the two men talked, they became increasingly concerned about Cino, deciding to go look for him to see if he needed help. They never found him. It is unclear whether, as has been suggested, the events of the evening and night were complicated by someone having slipped acid to Cino.[49] Also, it is unclear whether someone was, as Gordy has suggested, in the Caffe daring Cino to kill himself.[50]

For Michael Smith the events of the early morning on which Cino attempted suicide began near dawn with a call from Cino for Johnny Dodd, with whom Smith shared an apartment on Cornelia Street. Dodd was asleep, so Smith answered the telephone. When Cino asked for Dodd, Smith tried to wake him but was hesitant to disturb him while he was sleeping soundly. Smith returned to the telephone, asking Cino, "Where are you? What's going on?" Cino's only reply was that he was dying and wanted to say goodbye to Johnny. When Smith pressed Cino to reveal his location, Cino refused, disconnecting the call. Smith woke Dodd: "Joe Cino called and he sounds like maybe he is killing himself. I don't know where he is." Dodd suggested checking the Caffe, so Smith grabbed Dodd's keys and ran down the block. After he opened the iron gate and door of the coffeehouse, he found Cino lying in a pool of blood in the back of the shop near his beloved coffee machine. Knives were on the floor nearby. Weak and covered in blood, Cino continued trying to stab himself. Smith tried to take the knife away from him but could not because the blood made Cino and the knife too slippery to grasp. Smith could never get a secure enough hold to take control of the knife. Though weakened by blood loss and injury, Cino was still powerful and his strength was enhanced by absolute determination. Unsure of what to do next but realizing the need for immediate action, Smith ran across Cornelia Street to Murray's Cheese Shop, asking them to call for help. When they ignored his plea, he went out again looking for someone to help or at least to call for help. Seeing a police car on Bleecker Street, he ran to it and briefly explained what had happened. They returned to the Cino and called an ambulance.

The gravely injured man was rushed to St. Vincent's Hospital, where a medical team struggled to save his life. News of the incident spread quickly. One of the first to arrive at the hospital as Cino regained consciousness was childhood friend Angelo Lovullo who, at the suggestion of the medical staff, sat beside Cino's bed, talking to prevent him from falling asleep (the doctors being concerned about shock and not wanting him to sleep at that point). Eventually running out of other things to say, Lovullo asked the first question that came to mind, "Are you hungry?" Lovullo then turned to the medical staff and said that Cino wanted soup. When he left the bedside, Lovullo called Buffalo and asked that a family member inform Cino's mother of what had happened and assist her in making the trip down from Buffalo. The family soon arrived, checking into the New Yorker Hotel.[51] Other friends began to gather at the hospital, many coming to give blood in support of Cino. When Ellen Stewart arrived, hospital personnel refused to allow her to see the dying man, even after Charles Loubier told them that Stewart was Cino's sister.[52] In her essay about Caffe Cino published in *Other Stages,* Mary Boylan describes her arrival at the hospital after she learned of what had happened:

> When I arrived at St. Vincent's Hospital early Friday morning, the first people I saw were Bob Dahdah and Ellen Stewart. They had been there all night. So began our three-day vigil: sitting in the hospital lobby, going and coming back, phoning the hospital, waiting, waiting for news. Joe was a strong man. He had been pronounced dead when the ambulance picked him up, but they opened his chest and massaged his heart and he lived for three more days. . . . Joe needed blood, and more blood donors came forward than the hospital had seen since the days of World War II.[53]

One of the many people who gave blood was a young actor, Steve Van Vost, who appeared at the Cino in Tom Eyen's *Why Hanna's Skirt Won't Stay Down.* Underage, he sat by anxiously awaiting his family's permission for him to donate blood.

For a brief period, Cino seemed to be gaining strength and recovering from his wounds, enough so that his condition was upgraded from critical. On Sunday, however, his condition worsened. The changes in Cino's condition came rapidly, creating confusion among his friends, Patrick recalls.

> Joe's family came [to the caffe], took his personal photos and one look at us freaks, and left. We got an announcement that he would recover and news of his death within seconds of each other: I phoned St. Vincent's and relayed to the stunned [Cino] staff the news that he was "doing nicely," I then popped out to get some groceries and met Maggie [*sic*] Dominic. . . . "I just called," said I, "Joe's doing fine."

"I was just there," she countered. "He's dead."

Second show that night was canceled because of the mourners: almost the only cancellation in Cino history.[54]

Late on the afternoon of Cino's death, Boylan returned to the hospital to find Dahdah speaking quietly to one of Cino's brothers. Dahdah said to Boylan, "Mary, an era has ended." Boylan continues, "And I knew Joe was gone. Joe's mother arrived and they took her away to tell her. I sat alone in the lobby. I heard someone ask, 'Is that boy with you?' I looked down the street and saw Marshall Mason leaning against a parked car, sobbing his heart out and not caring who saw him. Harry Koutoukas walked in, got the news from me and left again to 'break it carefully' to Charles Stanley, who was managing the Cino in Joe's absence."[55] Shortly afterwards, Dahdah and Boylan left the hospital, stopping to get a drink. As they sat talking, Dahdah told Boylan about the nun at St. Vincent's who comforted Mary Cino: "'She said, "Your son helped lots of people, directors, writers and people who thought they were actors." I wonder what she meant by that.' I said, 'I doubt if even she knew what she meant.' We looked at each other and suddenly realized that we were laughing. We were heartbroken, but we had to laugh. I think Joe would have laughed too."[56] Unlike some who wanted to close the Caffe because they could not imagine it without its founder, Boylan applauded those who took over the coffeehouse in its last days. For her, Joe Cino remained a presence in the coffeehouse even after his death.

Joseph Cino was buried in Buffalo, with services conducted on Friday, April 7, 1967, at nine o'clock in the Joseph Spano and Sons Funeral Home and at nine forty-five at the Holy Angels Church. According to Angelo Lovullo, he was permitted a full Catholic service despite his suicide attempt because he requested food while in the hospital, thereby showing a will to live. His death, then, resulted not from his own hand but from peritonitis.

On April 10, 1967, Al Carmines hosted a memorial service at Judson Church. The event featured numerous scenes, songs, and readings, most from popular Cino productions (including Tom Eyen's *Why Hanna's Skirt Won't Stay Down*, Alan Lysander James's *The Life of Oscar Wilde*, and Robert Heide's *Moon*), with performances by many of the Cino's central figures and supporters (Deborah Lee, Helen Hanft, Bernadette Peters, Tom O'Horgan, Remy Charlip, Robert Cosmos Savage, Robert Patrick, Claris Nelson, Marie-Clair Charba, Mary Boylan, Robert Dahdah, Phoebe Wray, and John Gilman).

The occasion also featured Al Carmines reading from "Requiem for Cino" by H. M. Koutoukas. Perhaps the most unusual and touching moment was the appearance of the actor Ed Barton, who had performed with Boylan in *A Letter from Colette, or Dreams Don't Send Valentines: A Bittersweet Camp:* "And when Ed Barton, his [nude] body covered with glitter, walked on his hands the length and breadth and up and down all the aisles of that large church, it was as though he were performing some ancient, sacrificial rite of mourning."[57]

Why Cino took his life is a matter of dispute among Cino regulars. Perhaps Mary Boylan put it best when she wrote, "Why did Joe do it? I don't think anyone really knows. Some said that he thought no one loved him; he could not have been more mistaken. They said he was grieving for his best friend, Joe Torres [sic], killed without warning in a tragic accident some months before. They said drugs were responsible. All I know is, Joe could not have been himself when he did it."[58] Though we can never know the exact reasons behind his act, it is worthwhile to consider some of the factors that may have contributed to Cino's actions. In her brief list Boylan covers the factors most frequently cited by Cino's friends: his concern about aging, his loneliness, his drug addiction, and his grief for Jonathan Torrey. Along with those concerns, at least two other issues were fundamentally significant to Joe Cino: the constant threat to Caffe Cino posed by city officials and his dissatisfaction over losing the intimate atmosphere of the Caffe as it became successful.

For almost ten years Cino had labored tirelessly to keep his coffeehouse in operation, often working a full-time job to raise operating money and, when necessary, skirting or directly violating laws and regulations to ensure the survival of the Caffe. According to Tillie Gross, Cino seldom took time away from his shop:

> The only times anyone can remember the Cino being closed were the six-week period in 1965 when it was closed for repairs, and on the night of President John F. Kennedy's assassination, when Cino placed a large picture of Kennedy, draped in black, in the window and closed the doors. When Cino became beleaguered by people wanting to work, summonses from the authorities, and other troubles, some of his closest friends would attempt to take him away from the cafe for at least a night. This was difficult to do as Ken Burgess found out when Cino refused tickets Burgess had bought to treat him to the opera one night.

Burgess did manage to convince Cino to attend the World's Fair one day in 1964. . . . [59]

At times Cino would lie down behind the counter during a show or go across to Mona's Roost for a drink, though Delery has suggested that his presence was so habitual that his absence was highly notable: "Two other times, Joe left during performances to have a drink at a bar across the street. On both occasions, the shows immediately became box-office hits because everyone flocked to see what could possibly be so bad that Joe Cino could not stand it."[60] Thus Cino was physically and emotionally exhausted by the time of his death, leaving him with no reserve to recover from the stress of the period. Robert Heide echoes the sentiment of many when he says, "He gave so much to everyone else, but when he needed help no one was there for him,"[61] though, most likely, few recognized how desperately Cino needed help. The situation was complicated by the fact that many who might have been able to offer help had been driven away by the drugs and the resulting changes at the Cino.[62] Furthermore Cino seems to have felt guilty at having sent Torrey away to meet his death.

By the time of Cino's death, his coffeehouse was significantly more financially stable than ever, but pressure from the city and the MacDougal Street Area Neighborhood Association continued unabated. Clearly no compromise seemed forthcoming. Caffe Cino operated within an area zoned only for local and limited retail; coffeehouses were assumed to violate that zoning. No chance for an exception seemed possible given the political climate; therefore Caffe Cino seemed destined to operate unlicensed until the issue of coffeehouses was resolved one way or another.

As Cino fought financial and legal difficulties to keep his coffeehouse in operation, another, more subtle factor weighed heavily on him: his dissatisfaction with the success of his shop. Articles about Caffe Cino had begun to appear around the world; certainly one of the most important was Bernard da Costa's "Les Jeunes Fous d' 'Off Off Broadway'" in *Réalités* in February 1967. Furthermore, the Caffe's productions won prestigious awards, its artists began appearing on major commercial stages and in film, the Caffe's houses were often full, and major stars attended productions (Marlene Dietrich, Edward Albee, Arthur Miller, and Tiny Tim). The problem for Cino, however, was that the Caffe had become something he had never really wanted, and he had lost what he had wanted. As he stressed in his interview with Michael Smith after the 1965 fire, his interest was in operating a coffeehouse where friends could gather for conversation; he had less interest in operating a theatre. The theatrical productions were the provisional complement to the coffeehouse, not the reverse. The coffeehouse in itself was sufficient; productions were to be offered as long as his friends and customers wanted and needed them but to be discontinued when they did not.

In a brief memoir written for the 1985 exhibition of Cino material, Waldo Kang Pagune (whose plays appeared in 1962 and 1964 at the Cino under the name Pagoon) described a demoralized Cino who "grumbled how tough it was to run the coffee house, surviving barely week by week. 'It's a bitch you love and hate,' he said. He wanted to get out of the coffee house business, but he did not see an easy way out."[63] Though Pagune's comments are not dated, internal evidence suggests that Cino's comments date from June 1964 when Pagune's *Between Yesterday and Tomorrow* was in rehearsal. One of Cino's closest friends, Joseph Davies, told interviewer Robert Dahdah on *Chelsea Journal* that Cino was never happy "when the theatre part took over." He was even more distressed by the intrusion into his sanctuary of reporters such as Elenore Lester and da Costa. In many ways the Caffe was spiraling out of control, just as Cino's own life and drug addiction were spiraling out of control. He could do nothing to stop the constant assault by the Department of Licenses or MANA, and now he had lost control of the very nature of what his coffeehouse was to be. He had given his patrons and friends what they wanted and needed at the expense of his own needs and interests.

In the aftermath of Cino's suicide, both Michael Smith and Johnny Dodd left New York, though before doing so they worked together on the Cino production of Soren Agenoux's *Donovan's Johnson* in late May. Shortly after the end of the production, Dodd went on a European tour for four months with a black theatre-dance troupe and later did the lighting for the La Mama Troupe at the Mercury Theatre in London. Smith stayed in New York to participate in the Obie awards and soon after left for California to visit his parents. From there he went to Pennsylvania, where he managed Sundance, a theatre festival established by Wolfgang Zuckermann. Dodd and Smith were not together again until the fall, when Smith went to London to take over the lights for the LaMama Troupe production while Dodd did *Black New World* in the West End.

With the death of Joe Cino, management of the coffeehouse passed to Charles Stanley, an actor and dancer who had been closely involved with the Cino for several years. Though only about twenty-seven years old when he took control, Stanley had already begun developing a reputation of some distinction. According to his obituary after his death in a bus accident in 1977 in Seattle, his "dances in the 60's and early 70's were expressions of a personal landscape that revealed a tormented sensibility with an irreverent, satirical attitude toward Establishment values."[64] In a body of work that Barbara Naomi Cohen-Stratyner considers "surprisingly large for a postmodernist," Stanley "meshed visual, aural, and dance elements to create canvasses of images from the past to refocus the present. . . . Stanley eased out of dance in order to work more frequently in theatrical productions."[65] An area of particular interest for him was breaking down the boundaries that separate dance from theatre.[66] Though he danced and acted with Deborah Lee and others in several important productions at the Cino and at Judson, his primary successes as a performer at the Cino were based on his exploration of genderfuck in such productions as Koutoukas's *Medea*.

Some details regarding precisely why and how Stanley became the leader of the Cino are unclear. Tillie Gross suggests that Joe Cino's mother asked Ellen Stewart to take over management but that she declined after Cino regulars objected. They feared that she would destroy the unique character of the establishment as she turned it into an extension of La Mama ETC. Though Cino and Stewart were close friends (he often having visited her in the early morning after he closed his business), a rivalry existed between certain members of the core group from each establishment—so much so that Cino seldom spoke of his late-night visits with his friend and competitor. With Stewart removed from consideration, Charles Stanley emerged as the person most likely to continue the Cino tradition.[67] Critic Dan Sullivan reported that Stanley claimed to have purchased the business from Cino's family; he quotes Stanley:

> The night we heard that Joe was dead, there seemed nothing else to do but keep on with what we were doing—folding napkins, whatever. Later some people said that they thought I should try to keep the place going.
>
> Joe's people in Buffalo (Mr. Cino was not married) said they realized there was something precious to a good many people here and promised to do whatever they could to help—which means that they agreed to sell the business to me, in installments, instead of to some delicatessen.[68]

Records of the transfer of ownership are not available, nor do the key figures around the Caffe at the time recall any such sale.

As Stanley took control, he relied on such "temple slaves" as Wally Andro-chuk, Kenny Burgess, and Robert Patrick to keep the enterprise going. They worked as waiters, janitors, dishwashers, doormen, and whatever other roles were needed. As Robert Patrick explains, "We were obsessed with keeping the place exactly as it was. We cleaned around floor crevices where glitter had accumu-lated during the run of Snow White." Receipts were kept in a box under the espresso machine and used only for such expenses as rent and supplies.[69]

Reporting a few months after Stanley took over management, Dan Sullivan suggested that their goal to continue Cino's work had succeeded: "Two recent visits to the tiny coffeehouse-theater at 31 Cornelia Street confirm not only its survival but also its continued artistic vitality."[70] Stanley's management style was quite similar to that of Joe Cino: "Like Mr. Cino, Mr. Stanley selects the plays that will be performed at the cafe on an intuitive and, at bottom, prag-matic basis. 'I'll look at anything that could happen in a space like this that there isn't room for anywhere else in New York.' . . ."[71]

Ironically, the weeks immediately following Cino's death saw some of the strongest and most public efforts by MANA to force the city to act on their grievances. On the night of April 6, several hundred Village residents marched to protest their "losing battle with the turned-on [MacDougal] street."[72] The significance of the protest was heightened by the recent murder of a marine in the area and by concern over the annual influx of hippies that came with warm weather. At a meeting after the march, speakers railed against the city for fail-ing to protect the residents' rights; priests from the Church of Our Lady of Pompeii described the area as a "jungle" and a "Sodom and Gomorrah"; and Edward Koch argued that the murder of the marine was "the straw that broke the camel's back." According to Koch, action against illegal coffeehouses was an essential element in any effort to make the area safer: "We believe that if the Mayor would close up the illegal coffee houses and cabarets, it would help. The city has brought seven cases against illegal coffee houses—all were dismissed. Either . . . the city is unwilling or incapable of preparing proper cases. MANA is going to bring private lawsuits against these illegal operations because . . . you have a right to come home at night."[73] In the meeting after the march, MANA's steering committee decided to picket Gracie Mansion, the mayor's official residence, if the city had not met its demands within thirty days.

In response to MANA, the police department began vigorously to enforce licensing laws, citing any unlicensed establishments whether or not they were in the troubled MacDougal Street area. Thus, less than three weeks after its founder's death, Caffe Cino was cited for operating without a license; neither the police department nor the Department of Licenses would reveal the names of any other coffeehouses issued summonses during the period. The Reverend Howard Moody, pastor of Judson Memorial Church, called the city's action a "phony solution," noting that licensed coffeehouses and cabarets "turn over many more people in an evening than the unlicensed ones."[74] Even Edward Koch argued that citing establishments such as the Cino "is not what MANA wants"; their objective, according to Koch, was action against unlicensed establishments in the MacDougal area only. The policemen who served the summons at Caffe Cino stayed to see the evening's production, Lanford Wilson's *The Madness of Lady Bright*.

Since Cino had planned a celebration of the Caffe's tenth year by bringing back some of its most popular and successful shows, all productions during the months immediately following his death were revivals of past productions. Claris Nelson's *The Clown* opened on April 11 for a one-week run, followed by Jacque Lynn Colton and Fred Forrest in Lanford Wilson's *This Is the Rill Speaking*. The production of *Rill* was part of the Lanford Wilson festival to which most of the spring was devoted. The festival concluded on May 21 when *Ludlow Fair*, with Brandy Carson and Sandy Lessin, closed. Six weeks passed after Cino's death before an original script, Soren Agenoux's *Donovan's Johnson*, appeared onstage at the Cino. Directed by Michael Smith, Agenoux's work ended abruptly when Stanley intentionally broke an essential prop. The show was replaced by the hastily assembled show called simply *Potluck*.

In June 1967 Robert Patrick returned with a production of a new work, the tripartite *Lights/Camera/Action*, advertised not by its title but simply as "New Works: 3 Mini Plays by Robert Patrick." The work explores the effects of technology on communication and on the development of self-identity. The first play, *Lights*, centers on the difficulties in communication that arise between a young artist and an older woman who is assisting him with his show. She points to the failure of communication and the collapse of meaning in her opening lines: "No, you don't understand. . . . Can you understand?"[75] By privileging the voice of the older speaker and critic over the voice of the younger person and artist, the play foregrounds questions of authenticity and power. Who assigns meaning, the creator or the interpreter? Who determines legitimacy? How does age factor into these questions?

For the stage of *Camera Obscura*, the second miniplay, Patrick and Neil Flanagan built a frame around a six-by-six-foot piece of Plexiglas that they had found, using it for the floor of the stage. According to Tillie Gross, Dodd installed fixtures under the Plexiglas that allowed illumination from underneath.[76] As the actors spoke, Dodd changed the color of the lights and included additional visual effects with a spotlight that was reflected by foil strategically placed throughout the room.

Patrick has said that *Camera Obscura* was significant because it was performed nude, making it one of the first times an entire play had been performed nude in a regular theatre. Andy Milligan, who sold his own clothing designs in a nearby shop, was the costumer but could produce nothing that worked: "There was very little time between plays [*Lights* and *Camera Obscura*] for actors to change elaborate clothes; there wasn't much space in the single tiny dressing-room; it would be clumsy for the boy, heavily dressed, to fumble his way through tables up to the front in the blackout between plays, and as actor David Gallagher put it, 'There isn't room on that little box for both me and that costume.'"[77] Thus Patrick and director Flanagan decided to dispense with costumes altogether. The decision not only resolved the issues of costume changes and between-play mobility but also conveyed the depersonalization of the machinelike state in which people would relate in such an impersonal way.[78] On opening night, as lights came up on the two nude actors, costumer Milligan whispered to Patrick, "Well, Bob, this proves what everybody says; I really can whip up a costume out of nothing."[79] By the end of the first week, the actors asked for a costume because the extreme closeness and gawking of many in the audience broke the mood of the piece. Much to the annoyance of a critic who had come intent on creating a scandal, the production opened its second week with actors wearing stylized bikinis and headbands of transparent vinyl.

Action, the last play in the trilogy, opens with two men ("Man" and "Boy") onstage. Each is engaged in writing a script that details the existence of the other. Thus the well-dressed, older Man writes about a young Greenwich Village writer in his underwear working at a typewriter, while the younger Boy, who is clothed only in his underwear, types a script about an older, wealthy Man dressed in an expensive smoking jacket, writing in an elegant leather portfolio. The play raises fundamental questions about the nature of reality and of how we determine what is real. Much as in M. C. Escher's *Drawing Hands,* in which two hands are shown drawing each other, *Action* creates a world that challenges such terms as *original, copy,* and *real.*

After *Lights/Camera/Action* came George Birimisa's antiwar play *Daddy Violet,* brought to the Cino by Michael Smith after he saw a production of it in a small theatre on Twenty-third Street. The production of *Daddy Violet* occurred during a difficult period of Birimisa's life. He had just ended an eight-year love affair, leaving him crushed and depressed; furthermore he found the homophobia at Theatre Genesis increasingly disturbing. Struggling with issues of sexual identity, homophobia, and grief, Birimisa was "a nervous wreck": "I was so crazy."[80]

Having attended many off-off-Broadway shows, Birimisa chose to work outside realism, which had been his style until then, deciding "I'm going to out avant-garde everyone else." The result was a short play entitled *Three Violets*, first performed at Theatre Genesis as part of their new play readings. Birimisa had some difficulty casting it: "When I first wrote it, and I tried to get actors to do it, they thought I was nuts. 'I'm not gonna do that! Are you crazy? With all the improvisation and everything.'" Other actors read a few pages and threw the script down: "I'm not going to do a fucking faggot play."[81] Finally he cast the three performers: an unnamed friend who was studying acting, Dan Leach, and Sylvienne Strauss. Strauss was a "girl about twenty-one who had never acted before. . . . She played this really dumb novice actress and it somehow worked with her." Although Strauss warned him that she lacked stage experience, it was her rawness and lack of conventional stage polish that appealed to Birimisa. One week before opening, Birimisa's leading actor dropped out of the production. The playwright quickly rewrote the play, changed the title to *Daddy Violet*, and, though not particularly comfortable on the stage, took over the part himself, adding the line "There's nothing symbolic about this beer—it's just that this is opening night and I'm nervous," because he was nervous and wanted the can of beer on stage with him.[82]

Birimisa was so tense before each performance that he took an upper just before walking on the stage "and washed it down with a can of beer; after I did *Daddy Violet* for 61 times [across the country], we were in San Francisco for the 62nd performance. I looked out at a sea of faces: 'Oh my God, I didn't take my upper'; so I stopped taking them after that." Though Birimisa was especially nervous, all three actors were tense during performances: "We were all scared. It was terrifying. We never knew what was going to happen since the play has so many pools of improvisation."

The play opens with the three actors moving about the space and performing routine functions such as distributing programs. The published version is based on performances at the Firehouse Theatre in Minneapolis and includes three characters named after the actors who played them: George [Birimisa], Dan [Leach], and Sylvienne [Strauss]. The action starts when George walks onto the stage, points out the props for Arthur Sainer's new play that was scheduled to open the following Friday, and begins to sweep. He calls Dan to check the music and Sylvienne to distribute the programs. As the stage directions for the printed version indicate, the improvisational nature of the show meant that it was transformed according to where it was played: "When *Daddy Violet* is performed it must be involved with the reality of where it is being performed—where it is 'happening.' The actors must accept the total reality of where they are and the total reality of the audience."[83] At Caffe Cino, the play opened as follows:

> People would be in the audience. I had a hammer. I would go around and be putting nails in the walls, another actor would be sweeping and another actor would have the programs. The actor with the programs would yell, "Should I pass out the program now?" We would do an improv on all that stuff. . . . The man who did the lighting, Charles Stanley, was a little upset with me because I didn't want any lighting. I didn't want any illusion at all. He would turn off the lights in the audience and I would ask him to turn them back on.[84]

After the opening sequence, the three actors start doing exercises based on the actor-training techniques of Michael Chekhov. After various improvisational games, Dan works on placing his center in different parts of his body: "When he starts he has his center in his chest, and he goes out to the audience and tries to date a woman . . . ; and I say, all right now, put your center in your mouth. He just transforms into a gay man. He runs out into the audience and makes a pass at a man. Thank God Dan was huge; otherwise he might have been belted. So I say to him, "Put your center back in your chest." He says, "No I won't.""[85] Birimisa chases him through the audience, yelling, "'Think of Warren Beatty'; Don says, 'Ooooooh. . . . I love it, I love it."

The actors then begin impersonating flowers, with Birimisa becoming Daddy Violet, Strauss becoming Violet, and Leach becoming Easter Lily. When they discover their roots in a mountain that overlooks Vietnam's Mekong Delta, the view of women and children being tortured and killed in the valley below causes them to lose their centeredness and their identity:

DAN: I feel so empty! Empty! Dear God. I can't . . .

SYLVIENNE: You've been working too hard. Doing your famous turkey must be a terrible emotional strain.

DAN: My center is gone.[86]

Without his center, he cannot remember who he is.

SYLVIENNE: You've got to remember. You're clear, cool and such an eggshell white. You're Easter Lily!

DAN: I am?

SYLVIENNE: Yes! Yes! Yes!

GEORGE: Now don't panic. Let me think. *(He twists Dan's head around until they are eyeball to eyeball.)* Dan? Dan?

DAN: Who?[87]

Only by convincing themselves that the Mekong Delta is actually the Salinas Valley can they overcome the problem, remember their names, and quickly conclude the play.

On July 4 Wallace Stevens's *Carlos among the Candles* with Deborah Lee opened on a double bill with *Opening July 4th for Joe,* written and performed by Charles Stanley. The production was followed by *The Sandcastle* (with Walter Michael Harris, Tanya Berezin, and Robbie McCauley, among others). That production originally had been performed at La Mama and moved to the Cino. It was Lanford Wilson's last work in the coffeehouse.

Also in July the coffeehouse war took yet one more new turn when Emanuel Popolizio, the chairman of and attorney for MANA, prepared to file a writ of mandamus against Mayor Lindsay, police commissioner Howard Leary, and commissioner of licenses Joel Tyler. The writ charged Lindsay and the commissioners with dereliction of duty because of their failure to enforce various laws, particularly those related to the licensing of coffeehouses, thus causing "an increase in acts of assault, murder, robbery, rape, purveying of narcotics and use of hallucinogenic drugs, prostitution and pandering and contributing to the impairment of morals of minors, and general deterioration of public morals and public peace."[88] Rather than refute the charges in the writ, city attorneys sought to have the suit thrown out of court, alleging that it was groundless, since the proper means of resolving the issue was through the political rather than judicial process. On August 24 the city lost its motion to end the suit when New York Supreme Court justice Charles Loreto ruled in favor of MANA. As the suit gradually worked its way through the court system that fall and winter, one significant victory came for theatres, cabarets, and similar establishments in September when the city abandoned its practice of requiring identification cards for and fingerprinting of performers and cabaret employees.

On August 8, 1967, the Cino opened *Snow White and the 7 Dwarfs*, the first comic book production to be given a regular run. The production originated as a last-minute replacement for a canceled show. Magie Dominic recalls walking up Cornelia Street around nine p.m. when Charles Stanley suddenly dashed out of the Cino, grabbed her by the arm, told her of the cancellation, and asked her to appear in the replacement show. On the way back into the Cino, she asked Stanley which part he wanted her to play; he replied, "Snow White":

> We leaped through the door (I was wearing a red, white and blue polka-dot dress from Lamston's), ran through a packed house down to the back of the Caffe where Harry Koutoukas was in make-up and costume as the Wicked Step-mother; Kenny Burgess had an entire costume of little birds and animals, twinkle lights and fur and feathers as the birds and animals of the forest; Bob Patrick was ready as Doc, and David Starkweather as Sneezy with a box of Kleenex; Wally Anderchauk [*sic*] was in royal robes as the Kind Hunter; the prince was handsome; Charles Stanley did the part of The Magic Mirror in a head dress. . . .[89]

The production was then scheduled to run during the second week of August. Even during the regular run, the production retained an improvisational quality, since the number of dwarfs varied each night depending on how many actors were available to play the roles. Patrick recalls in at least one show having played all seven dwarfs, with Doc's hat on his head and three hats on each arm.

On August 22, 1967, the Cino opened Charles Kerbs's *Phaedra*, the first of three plays by writers from New Orleans (two by Kerbs and one by Josef Bush). Kerbs moved to New York to become a painter but soon found the cost of painting supplies beyond his meager budget. He turned to writing because "writing was cheap."[90] When Kerbs began taking acting lessons, Joseph Chaikin recommended instructor Nola Chilton, who became one of the most important influences on his artistic development. While studying with Chilton ("an exceptional teacher"), he learned of Caffe Cino through other students, many of whom were involved with various off- and off-off-Broadway theatres. After seeing a few productions at the Cino, Kerbs decided to submit one of his plays for consideration: "It was marvelous. . . . You would go hand them a play and they'd read it and let you know." The work was accepted, and his

Phaedra opened on August 24, 1967. A loose, free-form interpretation of the classic work, the play has only two characters: the mother, played by Tina Nandes (acting as Gina Ginakos to prevent problems with Equity), and the stepson, played by Albert Sinkus. One of the devices Kerbs uses in the play was particularly popular with Cino audiences: when Phaedra can no longer bear listening to her stepson, she grabs a trumpet and begins to play: "And, of course, she couldn't play the trumpet, so she just made a horrible noise."[91]

Four weeks after the close of *Phaedra,* the Cino opened Kerbs's *Sleeping Gypsy.* A coming-of-age play, *The Sleeping Gypsy* tells of a man trying to initiate his son into adulthood; like *Phaedra* it is a two-character work, performed at the Cino by Sully Boyer, even then an actor of some reputation who went on to a successful film career, and William Faulkner, though of course not the novelist. The set consisted primarily of a large "cutout of a completely naked woman with huge breasts and big hips." As the father tries to initiate the son into adult sexuality, he points to the cutout and says, "See the naked lady see the naked lady; the naked lady loves you," resulting in terrible fights between the two men.[92]

Like Cino before him, Stanley gave artists wide latitude in presenting their work. According to Kerbs, "When it was your production, it was your production. I mean, you could've brought in dancing dogs to do the play and they would've let it happen." And houses were full, mostly with uptown people ("young movers and shakers").

Between the works by Kerbs were plays by Robert Patrick (*The Warhol Machine,* his last at the Cino) and Louisiana native Josef Bush, whose *French Gray,* a play about Marie Antoinette, was written for Phoebe Wray. *The Sleeping Gypsy* was followed by *Goethe's Faust,* the last of the advertised comic book productions. *Faust* has been credited to Charles Stanley and featured Haal Borske in the lead role.

On October 31, 1967, a group from Warhol's Factory returned to the stage of the Cino with a production of Ronald Tavel's *Vinyl,* the play on which Warhol based his film of the same name. Directed by Harvey Tavel (the author's brother) and choreographed by Ron Pratt, the production traced the actions of a sadistic man who "gets his kicks from random cruelty and buggery."[93] Dan Sullivan of the *New York Times* focused much of his review on the sadomasochism of the piece, describing the use of whips, chains, high-heeled boots, skin-tight black costumes: "Ribs are cracked, fingernails yanked, eyeballs squished." The "serpentine lady inquisitor" played by Mary Woronov tames "a hairy chested hood who loves to carve people up," played by Mike St. Shaw.[94] Michael Smith found the sadism heavily ritualized, becoming a "ceremonial of pain." Sometimes the use of violence was effective, but at others it "becomes too dancy and arty and just looks fake. Sado-masochism is ceremonial to begin with and needs real pain to connect it with reality."[95] Though the production was popular, it offended many people. On the basis of discussions with friends, critic Robert Pasolli attended, expecting the work to be both daring and shocking. He found it "abominable—a succession of badly faked beat-ups and stomp-ons complemented by the non-acting characteristic of the Warhol world."[96]

The Cino closed 1967 with a series of productions that, with the exception of Haal Borske's *The Brown Crown,* ran only one week each. One of the few original scripts of the period, *The Brown Crown* was directed by Neil Flanagan, with Walter Michael Harris in the cast. It tells of Zephyrus, god of the west wind, who was banished by Zeus and who is now the love object of a scientist who visits him. Smith describes the play: "It's a weird, even unaccountable subject for a play, and the style is equally weird—campy, downbeat, sarcastic, often funny. The play continually puts itself down and refuses to be taken seriously. . . . Borske is an original and already, apart from echoes of Koutoukas, speaks with his own voice."[97] The final production was Chekhov's *The Marriage Proposal,* presented by students of Mira Rostova, a production that Smith found refreshing because it showed the "joys of conventional, minor, trivial masterpieces."[98]

After eight months as manager, Charles Stanley was exhausted and could not continue. The demanding operating schedule, the ever-present financial pressures, and the continuing harassment from the city had taken their toll. It was about this time that Michael Smith returned from Europe and discovered that the Cino was in a state of advanced decline. Stanley was so overwhelmed with the responsibilities thrust on him that he spent much of his time secluded in his apartment on East Second Street, appearing at the Cino only in the middle of the night to tend to essential business. To Smith the condition of the Caffe was deplorable: "Everything was falling apart, tables and chairs, plumbing, dimmer board, coffee machine; the cork walls and legendary collage were teeming with cockroaches and stained with cockroach shit."[99] Though Smith did not have the financial resources necessary to revitalize the Caffe, Wolfgang Zuckermann, a harpsichord manufacturer, offered his assistance. The two men had worked together previously when Smith managed Sundance, a theatre festival in Pennsylvania sponsored by Zucker-mann. Thus, on New Year's Eve, the Cino closed its doors for three weeks of renovation. Though Johnny Dodd did not participate with Smith and Zucker-mann in the management of the Caffe, he used Smith's gold-sheathed sword to offer a ceremonial blessing of the transition in leadership.

At the end of December as the management transitions occurred at the Cino, Justice Charles A. Tierney ruled in favor of the members of the Mac-Dougal Area Neighborhood Association in their suit against Mayor Lindsay and his commissioners. Noting that the suit was "replete with dates, times and places of the illegal acts complained of," Tierney ordered "each and every com-plaint with respect to violation statutes, ordinance or regulation specifically made therein, remanded to respondents [the three city officials] for further effective and appropriate action."[100] After the ruling Lindsay announced that all but six of the twenty-five unlicensed coffeehouses operating in the area when he was elected had been forced to close or to comply with licensing laws. Frustrated coffeehouse owners and patrons charged that the lawsuit had less to do with the interests of neighborhood residents than with Edward Koch's political ambition and his effort to gain votes from the predominantly Italian wards in the South Village, areas often openly hostile to the bohemian ele-ment in the Village. Koch's political strength lay with middle-class professionals of the West Village; his support was weaker in the older, ethnic neighborhoods. The day after the *New York Times* reported Tierney's decision, the Cino re-ceived a summons for operating without a license. One month after Tierney's decision, Koch announced his candidacy for U.S. Congress.

As the controversy over the decision receded, Caffe Cino reopened on Janu-ary 23, 1968, presenting Tom La Bar's *Empire State* as the first production in the newly renovated space. Robert Pasolli used his review in the *Village Voice* to urge a new direction for the Cino, after he had railed against past produc-tions at the coffeehouse because of their "slap-dash" incompetence and "homo-social orientation."[101] If Cino productions were sometimes inferior in qual-ity, he argued, they were consistent in tone: "What one could go to the Cino for, however, was to dig its specialty: a barely bridled indulgence and an im-pulsive bizarrerie that only the Playhouse of the Ridiculous has outdone." The Cino presented perhaps too many gay plays: "The Cino has had what you might call a homosocial orientation, and has proliferated productions present-ing homosexuals at play."[102] Charles Stanley made the mistake of continuing and even heightening the homosocial orientation of the Caffe. Originally scheduled by Stanley but performed after he left, *Empire State* perpetuated the worst excesses of past productions: "And, as a whole, it was just the Cino doing its level worst while depicting homosociety at play."[103] Though it may have escaped Pasolli's notice, even the program foregrounds the homosocial orientation that he so disliked. The names and other information are carefully positioned so as to evoke the image of the Empire State Building, but they also form the head and shaft of a penis. Pasolli concluded, "The important thing is for Smith and Zuckermann not to go on with it. The old policy, or the old non-policy, which allows if not encourages this kind of work should be scuttled."[104]

Empire State features a somewhat mad but inspired "lady bum," an obnoxious boy of ten, and two queens who design windows for department stores.[105] It also features an obscenity that caused problems for the coffeehouse. When Zuckermann learned of the 1985 exhibit at Lincoln Center, he wrote Richard Buck about the event, "[T]wo inspectors dressed as hippies came and watched one of our plays *[Empire State]* containing what was then considered a dirty word, starting with 'mother.'"[106] Because the obscenity was said in front of a child performing in the play, Zuckermann and one of the actors who was also the boy's uncle were arrested on January 26, 1968, only three days after the Caffe's reopening. According to the arrest record, the criminal act was to "permit child to act in theratical [*sic*] production, acts and diolgue [*sic*] impair morals charge."[107] When officials returned the child to his home, his mother's first words were, "How come you're back so early?"[108] Police also issued a summons to the Cino for operating without a license.

In addition to ending the run of the production, the incident was deeply upsetting to Zuckermann, who as a child had fled the Nazis with his parents. Feeling oppressed in the United States, which seemed headed toward fascism, Zuckermann lost his enthusiasm for operating the Cino. The situation was complicated by many of the Cino regulars having greeted the businessman's involvement in the Caffe with suspicion if not outright hostility. Within a year of the incident with *Empire State,* Zuckermann had sold his business and moved from the United States.[109]

After a revival of Heide's *Moon* and a production of Tom Eyen's *Who Killed My Bald Sister Sophie?,* the Cino opened Diane di Prima's *Monuments* on March 5, 1968. The entire work consists of eight monologues, three of which were done for the performance each night. Changing the combination and order of monologues changed the story line. According to di Prima, the monologues were "written for the people as if I were pretending to be in their heads."[110] The device posed a problem for critic Ross Wetzsteon:

> At first glance, Diane di Prima's *Monuments* seems a very simple theatre piece—eight monologues written specifically for and in a sense about the people who perform them. But immediately a problem arises—are they performance pieces, or character sketches, or self-images, or Miss di Prima's images of the performers' self-images? This isn't merely a quibble of definition, for the answer determines the very mode of our response—by what criteria does one judge them?[111]

Unable to satisfactorily answer his questions, Wetzsteon devotes most of his review to an examination of the monologues as poetry, not as theatre.

The first of the monologues was written for James Waring (who codirected the production with Alan Marlowe). Originally performed at the Actors Studio, the piece prompted Lee Strasberg to comment, "You are such a good writer. Too bad you don't do realism."[112] In addition to a monologue for herself, di Prima included pieces for or about Deborah Lee, John Herbert MacDowell, John Braden, Freddie Herko, and others. All pieces were performed by the individuals for whom they were written except those for Deborah Lee (who was out of the country) and Herko (who was dead); di Prima performed under the stage name Myra Murk. One or two of the pieces were written for male lovers of di Prima's husband, and Herko's monologue was delivered by Lee FitzGerald, also a lover of di Prima's husband. Because of Deborah Lee's absence, several people performed her monologue, including Teresa King and Sierra Bandit.

Under Smith and Zuckermann's management, the Cino had revived somewhat, despite the onslaught of city officials who issued citations for operating without a license. During the run of *Monuments,* however, problems with the city reached crisis level. Facing numerous police citations, the two had exhausted every avenue open to them to keep the coffeehouse in operation. By March 10 the Cino faced seven trials for various summonses and fines of up to $1,750.[113]

Zuckermann sought Edward Koch's assistance in resolving the problems with New York, since "it was his and MANA's actions, and that action alone, which (even if unintentionally) loosed the city's fury on us." Koch refused to help, arguing, "Do you think you are above the law? Only in a dictatorship does the law make individual exceptions."[114] In response to a letter regarding the Cino, Koch explained,

No one objects to off-Broadway theatres, and Café [*sic*] Cino's contributions to our cultural life is unquestioned. However, when an off-off Broadway theatre intentionally and in violation of laws moves into a block which is zoned for residential use only, in all fairness, it cannot request special treatment.

Café Cino can function on almost any avenue in the Village legitimately or, for good cause, it can apply to the Board of Standards and Appeals for a zoning variance. The owners have refused to take either alternative.[115]

The dispute became public when Smith used his column in the *Village Voice* during the week of March 14, 1968, to suggest that Koch's actions were intended to win votes in his congressional campaign. Koch fired back, "Mike's fantasies bear no resemblance to the facts. The South Village community which he refers to, the area below Washington Square, is not in the Congressional area in which I am running for election. It undoubtedly will be difficult for him to accept the fact that a politician would continue to assist people who cannot vote for him."[116] According to Tillie Gross, even the owner of the *Village Voice,* who claimed Koch as a friend, had met unsuccessfully with the politician to try to resolve the problems.[117]

Robert Patrick has described the complex legal issues that plagued the Cino during its last days as a "revolving door of twisted mirrors."[118] Given the convoluted legal situation, supporters of the Caffe presented three sets of photographs, hoping that the court would find one acceptable and thereby rule in their favor. The first set showed the interior of the Caffe without a performance area, thus proving that the establishment was only a coffeehouse eligible for a restaurant license. The second set showed a proscenium stage in the space, thus suggesting that the Caffe should be given a theatre license. The final set showed it with an unconventional stage in the center of the space, thus establishing that it was an important experimental performance space worthy of status as a private club. During the unsuccessful hearing, Patrick sat in court quietly reading *Rosemary's Baby* "to keep sane."[119] Other alternatives, such as relocating or applying for a zoning variance, entailed expenses and difficulties that Smith and Zuckermann could not meet.

One possibility that Smith mentions in his "Theatre Journal" for the *Village Voice* is that of forming a private club, much like that formed by Stewart for La Mama. As reporter Josh Greenfeld described, the process for attending a production could be confusing.[120] Performances at La Mama were open only to members. To become a member, a person had to go to the theatre and complete the application form, at which time the theatre issued a membership card. The new member could not, however, immediately attend a production, since attendance required that a member call in advance to make reservations. Information about an evening's bill was available through the *Village Voice,* in which La Mama ran a weekly advertisement. The advertisement, however, included neither address nor telephone number. That information was printed on membership cards. But to have the membership card, a person must first have found a theatre for which no contact information was given.

Though it is now unclear who was responsible, efforts were begun to reorganize the Cino as a private club. A "Certificate of Incorporation for Club Cino for the Advancement of the Theatrical Arts, Inc.," dated March 1968, states the purpose of the club: "To cultivate, promote, foster, sponsor, and develop among its members the appreciation, understanding, taste, and love of the theatrical, musical, film, and allied arts; to increase cooperation among and advancement of artists . . . ; to provide an opportunity for its members to produce and view new talent in the arts; to promote the improvement and advancement of the arts."[121] Though the certificate of incorporation is unsigned, the last advertisement placed by the Cino (still, as always, in the "Coffee House" section) includes the words *Arts Club* after the cafe's name.

All of these efforts, however, failed, and Caffe Cino closed abruptly on Sunday, March 10, 1968, during the run of *Monuments.* Both Dr. Paul Cranefield and Ellen Stewart were in the Cino on that night. As the contents of the coffeehouse were subsequently divided, Cranefield received an original poster for *This Is the Rill Speaking* and Stewart accepted several posters, as well as the new light board installed during the recent renovation.

Many who were involved in the operation of the Caffe Cino have suggested that the plight of the coffeehouse cannot be attributed solely to the actions of Koch and MANA. In the words of one person, a WASP and a Jew were an unwelcome combination to operate a business in a strictly Italian community. And one of the questions about the Caffe Cino that have lingered over the years is how Joe Cino was able to avoid much of the legal action to which other coffeehouses (Phase 2, Gaslight, Take 3, and Bizarre) were subjected. Part of the answer lies in location; city officials concentrated their action in the MacDougal Street area, that part of the Village that had become impossibly congested with tourists and young people. The Cino was removed from that scene. Furthermore it never employed a barker, it kept prices reasonable, and it otherwise operated so as not to attract the ire of neighbors or customers. Finally some people may tend to minimize the number of summonses actually served on the Caffe during its founder's life, for it was far from exempt from legal action. Before Cino's death the Caffe's name appeared in articles about summonses issued to coffeehouses; the archives of the New York Public Library include at least one summons issued for not having a coffeehouse license and several copies of health inspection reports that note various violations.

If the Caffe was subjected to less official action than comparable establishments, part of the reason may have been friendship and ethnic solidarity. Furthermore many believe that Cino received protection because of his family's ties with organized crime. Doric Wilson, for example, describes an incident in which an agent of the FBI questioned him regarding Cino; when Wilson met the agent by chance later (somewhat surprisingly, in a gay bar), the agent said that Cino's family was closely associated with a major Mob organization. Wilson is far from alone in speaking of the Cino family's association with the Mafia; Joe Cino himself sometimes claimed that his father had a connection with the Mafia, perhaps, as Douglas Gordy has suggested, accounting for the Cino family's reticence in sharing information with researchers about Joe or the family.[122]

Other persons close to Cino vehemently deny the rumors about the Mob, suggesting that they are based solely on ethnic stereotype and bias. Certainly one should not discount the potential ethnic bias in suggesting Mob ties for a person of Sicilian descent engaged in a somewhat unsavory business in New York City. Even with this limitation noted, sufficient evidence exists to suggest that Cino's brothers may indeed have had significant involvement with organized crime. In 1989 the *Buffalo News* reported the arrest of Gasper ("Gabby") Cino for violating the Racketeer Influenced Corrupt Organizations Law.[123] Though nothing in the article directly ties the arrested figure to Joe Cino's older brother, the age, name, and location are certainly suggestive of such a relationship. With Stephen ("Stevie the Whale") Cino there seems even less doubt of his relationship to Joe. When Stephen was on trial in September 1999 for several Mob-related charges, including contracting for murder, he was denied the opportunity to attend his brother Richard's funeral; according to the *Las Vegas Sun,* "The brothers, Stephen Cino's attorney T. Louis Palazzo said, 'shared a special bond ever since their father, Joseph, died in 1941.' At the time Stephen was 4, Richard was 12 and their brother, Gasper Cino of

Buffalo, N.Y., was 13."[124] Now reportedly associated with the Milano family from Los Angeles, Cino was among a group to be convicted in 1988 on racketeering charges. In September 1999 he was sentenced to fifteen years in prison for conspiring to extort longtime mob figure Herbert "Fat Herbie" Blitzstein; the Buffalo native was acquitted of murder-for-hire charges in the death of Blitzstein. Because of his convictions on these and other charges and because of his association with the Milano family, as documented in Jay Robert Nash's *Encyclopedia of World Crime,* his name was added to the Nevada Gaming Commission's "Black Book" on September 25, 1997. Officially known as the "List of Excluded Persons," the Black Book contains the names of those persons who are excluded from licensed gaming establishments because of prior conviction for certain crimes or because of their "notorious or unsavory reputation which would adversely affect public confidence and trust that the gaming industry is free from criminal or corruptive elements."[125]

Despite the possible association of Cino family members with the Mafia, nothing indicates that Joe Cino himself had any association with organized crime. As Feingold notes, he seems to have been estranged from his brothers; several close to the coffeehouse proprietor suggest that the Cino family preferred to keep him away from Buffalo and away from their Mob associates because of his sexual orientation. Gordy, for example, says, "When there was a shortfall, Joe often told friends, his family, embarrassed by their gay offspring, sent supplemental funds to keep him far from Buffalo."[126]

Whatever Joe Cino's relationship with his family and their supposed Mafia associates, it seems very clear that he (like other coffeehouse proprietors) paid protection money to law-enforcement officials. According to Robert Patrick, "I used to see Joe slip bills to some of the neighborhood cops. Others he'd take . . . in the back and they'd come out red-eyed and sniffling, or zipping their flies. The cops never bothered us while Joe was alive."[127] Paul Foster suggests that knowledge of such payoffs was so widespread that Cino would even include it in his introduction of plays: "Tonight, we dedicate this performance to . . . la luna and the rockettes, oh, and to the cop who just took the last ten in the drawer to let us perform."[128]

As the battle between the coffeehouses and the city grew heated in 1961, John Mitchell, owner of the Gaslight Cafe, charged that various policemen solicited bribes of five to seven dollars a week. When he stopped paying the bribes, he was given summonses that alleged various infractions in the operation of his coffeehouse. On May 1, 1961, Patrolman Edward L. Balfe was suspended for soliciting and accepting bribes from both the Gaslight and the Commons. Patrolman John N. Schneider replaced Balfe but also soon was charged with soliciting bribes. Sergeant John P. Griffin subsequently was charged with soliciting a monthly gratuity to "control service of summonses" on the coffee-houses.[129] The State of New York investigated the charges and turned over to police commissioner Michael J. Murphy a report that detailed these and other indications of corruption in the police force. Though quietly dropped soon afterwards, the charges against the policemen lend credibility to the assumption that Cino paid protection money to prevent legal problems.

Thus perhaps the Cino was forced out of business because neither Smith nor Zuckermann made payments to police officers and other city officials; neither even knew how to broach the subject. Having lost protection afforded by bribes and, perhaps, organized crime connections, the operators of Caffe Cino may have lost its only shield at a time when it was most needed. Once the doors were closed, little could be done to reopen them. As Smith said in his "Theatre Journal," "[M]aybe the Cino is tired. Maybe it's a relic of less up-tight Village days. Maybe what I loved was not the Cino but simply Joe, maybe his was the life of the room, maybe this new life was artificial, backward facing, forced, the effort to live it cowardly, not brave. Maybe Joe Cino is dead."[130] Like many, Tom Eyen lamented the lack of response to the closing of the Cino, particularly given the extent of support for the Cino after the fire in 1965.

> What amazes me, aside from the politics of this fun city (which shall never fail to amaze me) is the cool reaction, both artist and public, to the shut-out of the Cino—which has been in the planning since it opened, back whenever.
>
> [After the 1965] Fire . . . everyone screamed, "Benefit time." And a front page of the *Voice* was devoted to the item. Being burned down by a blazing fire and being shut down by numerous summonses are two separate entities. . . . No *Village Voice* headlines, no gala benefits, just a sad little comment in an article about it.[131]

Though fund-raising efforts for the Cino in the spring of 1968 hardly parallel those after the 1965 fire, some people did attempt to raise money to help off-set existing legal expenses. On Monday, April 15, a benefit was held at the Village Gate. A high point of the event was the performance of a scene from

Robert Dahdah and Mary Boylan's *Curley McDimple,* the musical forerunner of *Annie.* Some confusion surrounded the benefit, since Smith and others saw it as a means of obtaining funds to help pay off legal expenses, while Dahdah thought that they were working to assist in the reopening of the Cino.

The closing of the Cino stands as an important symbol in the history of off-off-Broadway, in many ways marking the end of an era. The cafe, underground, off-off-Broadway movement was changing, losing its rebellious position as a theatrical, cultural, and political movement at the margins. As John Gruen argues, experimental theatre had

> ceased to be the province of the underground few. It is now the taken-for-granted cultural commodity of the mass-media many. . . . If the underground has nothing to work *against,* if success comes to those who have worked hard to make success irrelevant, then the character of this underground changes radically. Now, its belligerent stance has unwittingly and ironically become catnip overground to the press, to foundations, to the public, and to mass-media entrepreneurs, many of whom have found its products attractively perverse. Indeed, the underground is like an international subway on which everybody is riding.[132]

Underground theatre was becoming mainstream, being regularly recognized at various award ceremonies, receiving grants from foundations, attracting awards from universities.

This pivotal moment in off-off-Broadway's history had been foreseen by some in the movement. In 1966 Sam Shepard seemed to predict that popularity could bring the end of off-off-Broadway: "It might turn out as popular as Off Broadway, and then die out. Then Off Off Off Broadway would start and it could go on and on like that—that's not bad."[133] Even as Shepard spoke, the popularity of off-off-Broadway was surging; as it found favor among a larger and more diverse audience, the movement also edged more toward gentrification and domestication. As Douglas Davis noted in 1967, "It had to happen and it did. [Off-off-Broadway's] face is cleaner, healthier than the old, presenting a gloss not entirely welcome for the pioneers who went into the downtown lofts and coffeehouses of the East Village seven years ago in determined flight from Broadway and Off-Broadway."[134] As its innocence, adventurism, and experimental edge waned, off-off-Broadway became for many little more than the proving ground for commercial theatre. The Cof-

fee House Association had suggested such a role years earlier when they defended their businesses by arguing that they offered new performers an opportunity to gain experience and recognition; yet some of the most ardent
supporters of cafe theatre rejected that role, hoping, perhaps naïvely, to build
instead an alternative noncommercial theatre.

6 The Magic Lives On

affe Cino ceased operation just as the events and movements most closely associated with the sixties were reaching their peak: political movements became increasingly divisive and violent; differing opinions about the war in Vietnam tore communities and families apart; the psychedelic generation turned on, tuned in, and dropped out in increasing numbers; the sexual revolution with its free love, women's rights, and even first inklings of gay liberation appeared ready to transform morals and relationships; the nonviolent resistance of the early Civil Rights movement seemed on the verge of giving way to violent turmoil as the passive Negro was transformed into Malcolm X's roaring lion. The Cino had served many roles during the period in which these tensions were emerging. It was a place to escape, to frolic in the camp excesses of Tom Eyen and H. M. Koutoukas, to encounter the violent, sadistic world of Andy Milligan, to pay homage to the Busby Berkeley musical. It brought together a community of men and women, gay and straight. It was a place to experiment, to challenge, to question gender, social, and theatrical conventions. For the most part, however, it was not a center of direct political action. One did not go there for radical agitprop.

Clayton Delery describes the work at the Cino as being linked by a common reaction "against convention, institution, the parent society, and the social codes of the time."[1] The Cino explored styles of resistance and transgression without committing to any particular political narrative or agenda. According to director Roberta Sklar, the artists there were more interested in exploring cultural issues and cultural or aesthetic change than in promoting any particular political issues. In these explorations they drew from or fashioned methods that would be incorporated into postmodern theatre: they created pastiches and verbal collages (much like Kenny Burgess's graphic collages that decorated the walls of the Cino) involving a free play of texts drawn from high art, popular culture, inside jokes, and references to the Cino culture. They displaced the boundaries of space and linear time by intermingling, in one Doric Wilson play, Helen [of] Troy, General Hector, Saint Augustine, and Agrippine Caesar with characters of contemporary Greenwich Village; setting *Medea* in a laundromat; and placing a pseudoclassical priest alongside a movie star, a Greek god, and a dove that thinks it is dying but is only molting. They drew their inspiration and images from popular culture, using comic books as scripts and turning to the lives of popular stars and other famous people for material. They subverted sex and age, casting H. M. Koutoukas as Diana Prince–Wonder Woman in the first comic book production and casting bearded Charles Stanley as Tiny Tim in a version of *Christmas Carol* that owes as much to Disney's Scrooge McDuck as it does to Charles Dickens's novel. They explored sexuality in virtually every form imaginable, with plays about sadomasochism, telephone sex, homosexuality, and masturbation.

The intermingling of existing texts with original ones and of literary characters with "real" people of different periods goes back to the earliest original plays produced at the Cino. Doric Wilson's *Now She Dances!* (August 1961) brings together Lane from *The Importance of Being Earnest,* Salome from the Oscar Wilde play, events in Wilde's life, and autobiographical details from Wilson's life. Wilson describes the play as recently revised:

> Operating on three main levels, *Now She Dances!* is a metaphor for this [Wilde's] trial, blending characters from Wilde's *Salome* and *Earnest* with a Post-Modernist America. The denizens of Herod's decayed and corrupt court discover themselves constrained in the lace and frippery of a polite Victorian comedy of manners where they sit in judgement on a contemporary stand-in for Wilde. The proceedings of this play are ruled over by Moloch, a deity who demanded of parents that their children be burnt in sacrifice.[2]

Like much else at the Cino, the history of *Now She Dances!* is linked to a story of transgressive sexuality, since the play emerged from Wilson's experience of being falsely accused of propositioning a plainclothes policeman.[3]

Work at the Cino explored other trends in theatre and performance that both were central to the period and would become increasingly influential over the next decades. In particular, Caffe artists challenged the boundary between fine and popular art. An important theorist of the period, Susan Sontag argued for a "new sensibility" that "understands art as the extension of life—

this being understood as the representation of (new) modes of vivacity."[4] An important consequence of the new sensibility outlined by Sontag is the abandonment of the "Matthew Arnold idea of culture" and thus the challenge of the distinction between high and low culture.[5] Leslie Fiedler championed a similar sensibility in literature. According to Perry Anderson, Fiedler "celebrated the emergence of a new sensibility among the younger generation in America, who were 'dropouts from history'—cultural mutants whose values of nonchalance and disconnexion, hallucinogens and civil rights, were finding welcome expression in a fresh postmodern literature."[6] The Cino reflected this leveling of culture. According to Albert Poland and Bruce Mailman, "He [either Joe Cino or H. M. Koutoukas, or both] saw value in seemingly opposite things; he considered *Looney Tunes* and *Thaïs* equally important and comparable artistic achievements. The highest compliment Joe Cino could pay a performer was to call him a Rockette; he thought the Rockettes were sheer genius."[7]

As playwright Robert Patrick has noted, the artists of the Cino generation were the first to mature during the enormous increase in media outlets in the first half of the twentieth century,[8] which led him to describe himself as a "media mutant."[9] Not only did these artists grow up under the influence of radio, film, television, and newspaper, the increase in the number of libraries and the widespread availability of inexpensive paperback books meant that they had ready access to copies of the works of canonical writers and philosophers. The great classics sat on bookstore shelves next to popular publications, all at affordable prices; if commercial price speaks to aesthetic worth, then in literature and philosophy the great and the popular had become of equal value. Thus economic forces supported the work of critics such as Susan Sontag to erase the distinction between high and low art, as well as between the definitions of "good" and "bad" art.

One aspect of this emphasis on popular culture was an exploration of the effects of technology on our lives. According to Theodore Roszak, the youth movement of the sixties rebelled against the technocratic society that not only depended on advances in technology but also operated in a machinelike way. Such a society was hierarchical, benefiting certain classes while depriving others of freedom and financial resources; it employed various methods of surveillance and control to ensure perpetuation. In their rebellion the youth challenged the technocracy by challenging the scientific worldview on which it is based.[10]

The world created by H. M. Koutoukas often has a postapocalyptic feel; it is a world in which technology seems to have brought destruction and death to people and social institutions. *Tidy Passions* takes place in a Cobra Temple, with the set being made of found objects: "It is important that the setting be made of remnants of glass, cellophane, etc. It is vital that no part of the setting or costumes be bought; the designer of costumes and sets must spin them of remnants of castaway items."[11] *With Creatures Make My Way: An Intensive Camp* is set "deep in the curvature of the sewer."[12] *Only a Countess May Dance When She's Crazy* takes place in an underground bunker, below the laboratory of Dr. Till. Responding to a telephone call, the countess reveals the conditions of the world: "Well I don't think that just because you people are the last survivors of a world shaking, mushrooming event that it's any reason to disturb him in his quest for *truth* and eternal life. What do you mean his last experiment killed the world. Don't you know the ancient laws of glitter . . . many must suffer for the few."[13]

In creating pastiches from popular and classical texts, in challenging the high-low art duality, and in examining the effects of technology, these sixties artists had begun pointing the direction for future playwrights who would ultimately bear the label "postmodern." Denizens of the Cino began an exploration of sexual and gender identity that would serve as a foundation for many who followed them, laying the groundwork for a specifically gay theatre and promoting the development of a camp stylistics. The Caffe not only was the first venue to regularly offer gay plays but also was the training ground for such figures as William M. Hoffman, who edited *Gay Plays: The First Collection,* and Doric Wilson, whose The Other Side of Silence is often considered the first professional theatre group in the United States formed specifically to produce works by and for those who were gay.

During the years in which the Cino operated, fundamental shifts in the political and social structures affected gay men and lesbians. A community and a distinctively gay (as opposed to homosexual) social identity began to emerge, fostering businesses that catered to a large population who publicly acknowledged their sexual orientation. As a new generation of activists looked to the Civil Rights movement for a model of a more aggressive and confrontational style of activism, many gays and lesbians became discontent with the conservative direction of such homophile organizations as the Mattachine Society.

It is an oversimplification to conclude as many do that the Cino was totally apolitical simply because (in Tillie Gross's words) it was a place for the alienated "to hide and to escape to, because here they were accepted."[14] That they were "accepted" is the very basis of the Cino's most effective political engagement. The importance of embodying and expressing a gay-queer position is the basis of William M. Hoffman's statement, "I wasn't looking to do anything political; I just wanted to write about *all* the kinds of people I knew and loved, and that turned out to be very political."[15] Elsewhere Hoffman underscores the power of gay theatre by arguing that it "will publicize ways of being that have been denied legitimacy."[16] Thus theatre became for the Cino regulars a means of enabling and affirming alternative performances of self for both the individual and the community. We may not be able to show a direct correlation between the existence of venues such as Caffe Cino and the rise of the gay political-social movement, but such a movement, according to Doric Wilson, would be "unthinkable" without those sites.[17] Edward Rubin goes a bit farther, suggesting that "the birth of off-off-Broadway [and] the emergence of gay culture in this country . . . are intricately intertwined." Though he confuses a more recent and still operating venue with Caffe Cino, Rubin gives much of the credit for both to "the father of off-off-Broadway, Joe Cino and his long-gone Cornelia Street Café [*sic*]."[18]

Representations of gay characters in plays prior to the 1960s typically take four forms, according to William M. Hoffman: silence (the total invisibility of gay and lesbian characters); false accusation (ostensibly heterosexual characters accused of homosexuality); stereotyping (swishy men, butch women who are often mentally disturbed or evil); and exploitation (sensational use of gay men and lesbians, perhaps for "local color").[19] In contrast to these earlier representations of gay men, productions at the Cino provided a space in which to center the gay male body as an object of desire. Such positioning of the male body, however, tends to subvert the traditional structure of the theatrical gaze, particularly when that body is framed to be desired by other men. As Laura Mulvey and others have noted, desire in traditional narrative forms originates from (rather than points to) the male. Man is the desiring subject, woman the desired object of the idealized spectator-actor on stage and, through him, of the less ideal(ized) audience. Cino productions often undermined this traditional position of masculine authority, subjecting the male body to the gaze that it has traditionally generated and controlled.

One of the Cino artists' most important contributions is their destabilization of sex and gender codes and thus of the identities based on those codes. David Starkweather, for example, has been interested primarily in writing from a bisexual "class" perspective in which he focuses on the oppression of bisexuals by not only heterosexuals but also gay men and lesbians.[20] In bisexuality he finds increased democratization. In the work of many Cino artists, identity is freed from the sexed body and becomes an object for play, teasing, parody. Medea can be played by a man in a dress, and *Only a Countess* is a "tour-de-force for one actor, male or female." To borrow a phrase from Michel Foucault, the artists at Caffe Cino were actively engaged in strategies through which alternative identities are "put into discourse."[21] For many Cino playwrights camp became the fundamental strategy through which these identities could be explored. Through camp they valorized and centered the outsider, the marginalized, the "other," while constructing the male body as an object of (male) desire and establishing a safe space within which alternate identities could be rehearsed.

Camp served both as an expression of identity and as an additional means of breaking the barrier between high and low art, for as Susan Sontag explains, the "whole point of camp is to dethrone the serious."[22] And, of course, camp provided a basis for challenging traditional gender constructions. Sontag says of camp, "What is most beautiful in virile men is something feminine; what is most beautiful in feminine women is something masculine. . . . Allied to the camp taste for the androgynous is something that seems quite different but isn't: a relish for the exaggeration of sexual characteristics and personality mannerisms."[23] References to the camp atmosphere of the Cino begin with the first published review, in which Seymour Krim refers to faggots camping, and continue throughout the Caffe's history. William M. Hoffman alludes to camp when he notes that the early Cino productions "can only be described as homosexual in style."[24] The critic Robert Pasolli describes Cino productions as "romps conceived in the spirit of mockery."[25] It is in fact these "romps" with their mockery that seem to have been objectionable to Jean-Claude van Itallie: "The atmosphere at Cino's was never exactly my own style. . . . Cino seemed to me too full of sequins, fishnets, and a general swishy loudness. Bernard da Costa, the young French journalist, describes the Cino as follows: "They sing opera, they worship knickknacks, glass trinkets, by-gone stars, the eccentric and certainly parodic plays. They serve too-sweet pastries, chantilly cream in coffee, chantilly cream in beer, chantilly cream everywhere." Da Costa then describes a production of *Wonder Woman*, one of the comic book plays performed at the Cino, noting in particular the gender inversion in the piece: "The author, Harry Koutoukas, dresses his players in prehistoric costumes, inverts the sexes, mixes reality and fiction, memories of television and political allusions, laughs at his own jokes."[26]

H. M. Koutoukas, the Cino playwright most successful in using camp to center the marginalized, created in his plays an odd, mad, cluttered world inhabited by the eccentric, the different, the marginal. Thus the Creature in *With Creatures Make My Way* recognizes and accepts his uniqueness, choosing to live in a marginal world. Countess Olie Samovitch in *Only a Countess May Dance When She's Crazy, a Historical Camp* (in a later revival, *An Almost Historical Camp*) occupies a similar position. She faithfully serves the unseen Dr. Till in a world where it is difficult to determine which is crazier, the Countess or the world she inhabits. Everything about the Countess is unstable, indeterminate, packed with multiple meaning-identities or with none at all. As Dan Sullivan wrote in his review of the 1968 revival of the play: *Only a Countess* "is dead serious at the core. Like the lady doing the talking . . . it seems to want desperately to make sense, but cannot—which, one imagines, is precisely how it feels to be mad."[27]

Through camp and particularly through placement of the gay male body on stage, Cino artists contribute to a process of reinterpreting and rewriting space. Because bodies exist within space and use and manipulate space in the performance of identity, we remap, reinvent, and rewrite space to reflect our own interests, beliefs, values, and being. But the relationship between self and space is not a unidirectional movement; as Tim Cresswell has argued, "I insist that the social and the spatial are so thoroughly imbued with each other's presence that their analytical separation quickly becomes a misleading exercise."[28] To "social" we should add "personal," since the creation of self, the formation of community, and the writing of space are coproductive.

We can see the personal-social written into the spatial at Caffe Cino through the interplay of influence among Caffe Cino, its artists and patrons, and Greenwich Village. Once a haven from the plague and other dangers of New York City, Greenwich Village had earned a reputation as "America's Paris" by the end of the nineteenth century.[29] By World War I the area had begun to symbolize a repudiation of traditional American values, a reputation that would increase during the middle of the century into the present. According to Heide and Gilman, sexual freedom and experimentation were nothing new for the Village even in the 1950s and 1960s: "The freedom to be who and what you are in terms of one's sex or sexuality was always a prerogative of Village life."[30] Joe Cino opened his coffeehouse in the heart of this bohemian area, not far from the point at which John Reed, Marcel Duchamp, and John Sloan had declared the Village a free republic and a new Bohemia in 1916. The Cino was within easy walking distance of the future location of the Stonewall Inn, the gay bar made famous during the Christopher Street riots of 1969. The Caffe reflected the social and historical nature of the Village. Like the Village itself, the Cino was home to many avant-garde writers and to lesbians and gay men.

If the location in the Village helped define Caffe Cino, the Cino helped define the Village. Only a child when he first went to the Cino, Walter Michael Harris describes the coffeehouse in which he, his parents, and his five siblings would perform over the years:

> We could see it from the end of the block—twinkle lights and a warm orange glow spilling out into Cornelia Street in the night air. Inside was a world of wonder. The delicious aroma of coffee, the lilt of opera, the strange hissing sound of Joe's [*sic*] Cino's magic espresso machine and millions of colorful twinkle lights gave the place the air of Charlie's Chocolate Factory, or Café Society in Paris. The efficient, effeminate waiters deftly maneuvered around the tiny tables, swishing by with giant platters of food and exotic drink. The tiny stage in the middle of the room made us feel right at home.[31]

The space, then, became one in which effeminate waiters could intermingle with the straight and gay audience and in which theatre productions could give physical presence to the gay male body. In turn these performances (both the "real" and the staged) manifested themselves in part by writing onto the space itself, through the photographs of youths that adorned the walls, through the glitter (used often in H. M. Koutoukas's campy shows) that covered everything, and through the twinkling lights. As Harris's reminiscence of the Cino suggests, the world of the Cino spilled out of the confines of 31 Cornelia Street into the Village itself. In many ways, the emergence of sites such as Caffe Cino and areas such as Greenwich Village and the Castro district represent a remapping of the civic body in much the same way that camp and leather represent a remapping of the individual body. That the civic and private bodies were being remapped simultaneously seems to destabilize the accepted, neat distinction between the two.

The greatest influence of Caffe Cino has been its introduction of new theatrical styles, management practices, and artists. Though individual figures from the United States such as Eugene O'Neill had attained international acclaim, influential movements had more often than not moved from Europe to the United States rather than the reverse. Never had our theatre launched a movement of as great an international significance, particularly in terms of theatre operation and management.

For many of the artists who worked there, the Cino was both an artistic home and a training ground. Having staged *Melancholia* and several other plays at the Cino while pursuing his full-time occupation as a license inspector, Jerry Caruana wrote a letter to the *Village Voice* shortly after Joe Cino's death that is a moving tribute to the man. Caruana attempts to speak for the "hundreds" who never would have "gotten a taste of the joys and miseries of 'the theatre'" had it not been for Cino. He concludes that Cino's "influence on the theatre and on those who worked with him, and whom he helped is so enormous, and so alive right now that only a perfect fool would try to take its measure at the present time."[32]

The Cino influenced both mainstream and avant-garde theatre. For mainstream theatre *Dames at Sea* helped launch the nostalgia craze that swept through theatre in the 1970s. Robert Dahdah recalls meeting producer Harry Rigby in Jimmy Ray's Bar sometime after *Dames* had moved to off Broadway. Speaking to Dahdah, Rigby said that he had planned to produce *Divorce Me Darling* until Dahdah and *Dames* reawakened an interest in Ruby Keeler and the productions and stars of the 1920s and 1930s. Rigby then dropped *Divorce Me Darling* and turned to *No, No, Nanette,* a production that saw Keeler's triumphant return and placed the nostalgia movement squarely on Broadway.[33]

In many respects the Cino and the movement of which it was a part represented a fundamental breach with past theatrical activity in the United States, and little was more indicative of that breach than the refusal of the Cino to become ensnared in commercialism. As Randy Gener makes clear, creativity, not finances, drove the work at the Caffe:

The random logic of creativity ruled. Folks were free to succeed or screw up because they weren't worried about economic risk and compromise. Magnanimous to the worthy and the worthless, Cino brought to bear Mother Teresa instincts: he fed people, . . . he provided space and nifty lighting equipment, he scheduled dates for your next one-act. It's not written yet? That's okay. "Do what you have to do" was his mantra. After weeks of trying, still no cigar? No problem. Neil Flanagan will read and perform comic books; they only cost 12 cents. *Finally* the fucking play is done, but there's not a single sonuvabitch in the house! Hey, man, cool it. We'll do it for the room, for the experience of *doing* it. Joe Cino put on a show without paperwork, subsidies, or corporate grants. He believed in no aesthetic theories, no movements, no pressure.[34]

Budgets for shows were minuscule and often came exclusively from the playwright or director. Claris Nelson's *The Clown,* described by the New York Public Library as "one of the most opulent productions ever staged in a cafe theatre" cost only $328 to stage[35]; for many shows, the total costs equaled only the price of the coffee and pastries that Joe Cino gave the cast. In addition to the inexpensive productions, costs at the coffeehouse were minimal, since Joe Cino required little for his livelihood. As Charles Loubier said, "Material things didn't mean a goddam thing to Joe. His waiters always made more than he did."[36] When his financial condition was especially bleak, he would give up his apartment and sleep on a mattress in the back of his shop. For Patrick (as for many others), the lack of financial constraints offered a tremendous burst of freedom: "For the first time a theatre movement began, of any scope or duration, in which theatre was considered the equal of the other arts in creativity and responsibility; never before had theatre existed free of academic, commercial, critical, religious, military, and political restraints. For the first time, a playwright wrote from himself, not attempting to tease money, reputation, or licences from an outside authority."[37] Phoebe Mooney found in the rejection of commercialism a freedom to take risks and to experiment; as she notes, "The Cino was a place to make mistakes."[38]

Fueled by the increased generosity of foundations and governmental organizations and the influence of venues such as the Cino, nontraditional theatres grew rapidly during the 1960s and 1970s. Though many relied on public funds, others operated on small budgets without such support. These were often targeted at specific sexual or ethnic groups: the Glines, Medusa's Revenge, and Spiderwoman in New York, the Gay Men's Theatre Collective in San Francisco, and similar theatres around the country. Undoubtedly many of those starting such theatres knew little (if anything) about Caffe Cino, but Merrill Harris has suggested that the Cino's influence was felt in various parts of the country:

> The spirit of the Caffe Cino remained with many of us over the years and was a motivating force in the formation of many similar cafe/theatres around the country. The women's coffeehouses in Knoxville, Tennessee, and in Nashville—both of them started in the 70's—owe their origins to the Caffe Cino; and even though the Knoxville coffeehouse

closed years ago, the one in Nashville is still going. And even though the beverages are now beer and soft drinks, and most of the performances are by musical artists, the spirit of community is what keeps it all going. For this, thanks to Joe Cino, wherever you are.[39]

Some people consider Theatre for the New City (which named a room after Joe Cino) to reflect the operating style of the Cino, but one of the direct descendants of the movement started at the Caffe is the Circle Repertory Theatre Company (1969 to 1996), founded by Marshall Mason, Lanford Wilson, Tanya Berezin, and Rob Thirkield.

According to Phillip Middleton Williams, "Berezin and Thirkield had met while performing in small theatres such as the Caffe Cino, and it as [sic] at this Greenwich Village coffeehouse that Mason and Wilson first met. . . ."[40] In addition to the Cino's influence on La Mama (where Mason and the others worked together) and on the Circle Rep itself, most of the founders of the company had Cino connections. Wilson and Mason, of course, worked on numerous productions there. Berezin appeared in both Maeterlinck's *Death of Tintagiles* (March 1966) and Wilson's *This Is the Rill Speaking* (April 1967). Actor Michael Warren Powell, who appeared in several Cino productions, became the director of the Circle Repertory Lab (subsequently the LAB Theatre Company of which he remains artistic director). The first production of Circle Rep was *A Practical Ritual to Exorcise Frustration after Five Days of Rain* by veteran Cino playwright David Starkweather. Other playwrights to work in both spaces include Claris Nelson (*A Road Where the Wolves Run* in the 1972–73 season) and William M. Hoffman (*As Is* in the 1984–85 season). Like Caffe Cino, Circle Rep offered an opportunity for less-experienced playwrights, actors, and directors.

Through figures such as George Harris III, the Cino style entered the glam rock scene. A member of a remarkable, quintessential off-off-Broadway family, Harris appeared in numerous productions at the Cino. His father moved to New York from their home in Florida to pursue a career in acting, often writing hasty notes home on the back of programs from the Cino. Soon Ann Harris and the children joined the elder George, with all becoming regulars at Caffe Cino, La Mama, Judson, and similar venues. In the late sixties at age seventeen, George III drove across the country with the poet Peter Orlovsky, who is perhaps better known as the lover of Alan Ginsberg than as a poet; when he reached San Francisco, young George joined Irving Rosenthal's commune. While engaged in chores, an idea occurred to him: "One day I was scrubbing floors in the commune . . . and I said, 'Why don't we do shows? We'll call ourselves The Kitchen Sluts and travel from commune to commune doing free shows.'"[41] Thus in 1969 he formed a troupe that became The Cockettes, with their breakthrough performance coming on New Year's Eve in 1969. Drawing from the outrageous, campy productions at the Cino (such as Koutoukas's *Medea,* in which a bearded Charles Stanley played the title role) and Judson (including Ronald Tavel's *Gorilla Queen*), George transformed himself into Hibiscus, often wearing a dress, elaborate headdress of fruit or flowers, garish makeup, and full beard. According to John Bell, ". . . Harris was not, like some '60s theater-makers, inspired by Artaud, Brecht, or Grotowski, but by Busby Berkeley and Radio City Music Hall. . . ."[42] Through figures such as disco singer Sylvester James (who was a member of the Cockettes for several years) and John Waters's film star Divine (who performed in at least one of their shows), the spirit and style that characterized the Cockettes attained a broad popularity. Near the end of his life, he formed Hibiscus and the Screaming Violets, a glam rock group that included his brother Fred and sisters Lulu Belle, Eloise, and Jayne Anne. In addition to his work in the theatre, Harris is remembered as the young blond man in a white sweater slipping a flower into the rifle of a soldier outside the Pentagon during a 1967 protest against the Vietnam War.[43]

In an essay Robert Patrick suggests the extent of the international influence of Caffe Cino, arguing that hundreds of theatres around the world have been influenced by Joseph Cino's work. Wherever he travels, a mention of the Cino evokes immediate interest among those working in fringe theatre. He mentions having found versions of the Cino in Canada, France, Holland, Austria, Venezuela, and elsewhere; when he went to the only theatre in South Africa that was open to persons of all races, he found that Paul Foster, Lanford Wilson, and Sam Shepard were playing.[44] To Patrick much contemporary theatre would have been unthinkable had it not been for Caffe Cino: "Some [well-known playwrights] would never have been playwrights without the latitude Joe extended. One who extended the bounds of dramatic imagination, and without whose exuberant example the world would never have been ready for Harvey Fierstein or Charles Busch or *The Rocky Horror Picture Show,* was H. M. Koutoukas, who I consider our finest playwright since Tennessee Williams."[45] Thus the influence of the Cino can be found both in what is on the stages of theatres around the world and in the management of such venues as Le Royal Café in Paris and the Bush in London.

Central to extending the influence of off-off-Broadway were the tours conducted by Stewart's La Mama in 1965 and 1967. In both cases some of the plays and many of the performers were closely associated with the Cino. The 1965 tour, for example, included several plays that first appeared at Caffe Cino: Lanford Wilson's *This Is the Rill Speaking* and William M. Hoffman's *Thank You, Miss Victoria.* The tour also featured actors who were veterans of Cino productions, including Michael Warren Powell. The plays that toured in 1967 again included Wilson's *This Is the Rill Speaking,* with such Cino performers as Victor Lipari, Marie-Claire Charba, Claris Nelson Erickson, and Jacque Lynn Colton. Ingmar Bjorksten notes that few people in Sweden knew about off-off-Broadway prior to Stewart's tour in 1965; because of the tour, La Mama, Caffe Cino, and the Open Theatre were heralded "as prophets from a new land of theatre."[46] Thus heavily influenced by Cino herself, Stewart helped extend the Cino's influence.

The influence of off-off-Broadway on international theatre came not only through Stewart and others who took the new theatre abroad but also through visits to New York by people who took the practices and styles of off-off-Broadway back to their countries. A significant figure in London's fringe theatre, Roland Rees, spent time in New York pursuing academic research. He discovered an exciting theatrical and cultural scene that changed the direction of his life.

In 1965, America, and New York in particular, was the place where major cultural and artistic upheavals were happening. Experiments in film, theatre, the visual arts, contemporary music and the fusion of these forms . . . the Feminist movement, and experiments in collective and personal life styles, all made a lasting impact during my two years in that city. The energy of New York taught me that you can step out of tradition, start your own and "Go for it!" I did not need much nudging to give up my academic future and start work in theatre.[47]

When he returned to London two years later, he found that the spirit of off-off-Broadway had just begun to appear in London: "New York had pioneered and London was to follow."[48] Influenced by his experiences in New York, Rees cofounded the Foco Novo company in 1972.

Other means through which the influence of off-off-Broadway spread to England were artists from the United States who traveled abroad. As Rees notes, "If much of the inspiration for the work was American, so were many of the actors, directors and writers. Whether it was for reasons of avoiding the draft or the atmosphere of America . . . , there were lots of American actors and directors in London."[49] Among those who traveled from the United States to London was Charles Marowitz, who cofounded the Open Space Theatre and London Traverse Theatre. According to Marowitz,

> Caffe Cino produce[d] a kind of theatrical fare which was new to New York—plays by marginal types, mavericks, and non-belongers that made up the Greenwich Community of the late 50's and early 60's. The new ambiance spawned a new kind of play; not only a new way of experiencing a play, but material which reflected experience peculiar to the denizens of the world that created it. So Cino has two great claims to fame: it created a place and it created an oeuvre. There are innumerable theatres that are part of its progeny—in England, the King's Head, The Bush, the Traverse Theatre Club, the Arts Lab in Covent Garden, and virtually all the fringe theatres that combine playgoing and dining.[50]

Among the figures influenced by Caffe Cino was Bernard da Costa. Fresh from Bordeaux in the mid-1960s, da Costa attempted to make his mark as a journalist and playwright, having arrived in Paris with several plays that he thought would help him move into the city's artistic and literary circles. He quickly discovered, however, that few opportunities existed for a beginning playwright. Thus as Pierre Merle notes, "In the end and as a last resort, one lone solution presented itself to him: to draw inspiration from what had been happening in New York for sometime already (and with a certain success), off-off-Broadway. . . ."[51] Merle posits da Costa's reasoning as follows: "If there are no theatres ready to welcome plays by new authors, there will be proprietors of cafes . . . which will accept them, although not officially licensed to present performances, to let us play in a corner of their establishment."[52] Thus on February 26, 1966, on Raspail Boulevard in Paris, Le Royal Café began offering works by writers such as Philippe Adriene and da Costa.

The Cino's mark can also be seen in television and film. Before working with Michael Bennett on Broadway's *Dreamgirls,* Tom Eyen brought the campy, pop-culture-laced humor of the Cino to television when he wrote for *Mary Hartman, Mary Hartman.* Lee Kalcheim, whose *Party for a Divorce* and *Morning After* appeared at the Cino, has worked on a number of television series, including *The Odd Couple* and the *Partridge Family* spin-off *Getting Together.* After Doric Wilson's *And He Made a Her,* Paxton Whitehead went on to a long career as an actor for television and film, appearing in numerous works, such as the 1993 production of *The Adventures of Huck Finn*. Similarly, after his plays *Episode* and *Vignette* appeared at the Cino, Ronald Colby continued a lengthy career in which he worked in or produced some of the *Godfather* films and numerous other works.

Thus directly or indirectly, Caffe Cino influenced film and theatre in the United States and in other countries, in part by allowing previously taboo topics onto the stage (such as homosexuality and sadomasochism), in part by exploring alternative production styles (notably camp), and in part by pioneering a unique management style that allowed playwrights, directors, and performers freedom to explore their own voices. By becoming, in actress Shirley Stoler's words, "a place where you were not only encouraged, you were required, to express every bit of madness you ever had," the Cino contributed to a remarkable period of creativity in American theatre.[53]

In their landmark study of off-off-Broadway, Bruce Mailman and Albert Poland compared Cino to his "room"; both were "complex, dirty, and brilliant."[54] Both were also eccentric and inscrutable. Cino's ultimate guiding principles were "say what you have to say, do what you have to do." The ultimate taboos were pretentiousness and experimentation for the sake of experimentation. Playwright William M. Hoffman told S. Isenberg, "It was a place of experiment but it didn't reject the past. It didn't say we were going to make something new just because new was good. . . . Joe had no patience with the bogus. . . . He could put up with anything but the pretentious. So we were not going to get tight little anythings there; it was not a place for that kind of theatre."[55] So long as a playwright seemed to genuinely have something to say—even if the playwright was untested, even if he was a high school student with a not very good play—Cino offered his space, finding room for a diverse list of works: unrehearsed actors improvising to lines in comic books; relatively traditional productions of the classics; camp spoofs that merged classical and popular art. As Larry Loonin notes, even the naturalistic had an element of the surreal: "I would like to discuss with you at some point a vision I have of the Cino. It has to do with fitting so much into such a space and the surrealistic look everything would end up having. Many plays that now seem naturalistic in the setting of the Cino were absolutely surreal."[56]

Perhaps Mary Boylan and Robert Patrick are correct when they suggest that Cino's suicide might have been influenced by the fact that no one was available for him when he needed them. Yet more than three decades after his death, the survivors of Caffe Cino remain remarkably devoted to his memory. Ellen Stewart acknowledges his pioneering role in American theatre; major play-wrights such as Lanford Wilson cite their debt to him and to the off-off-Broad-way movement that he helped launch; numerous actors and directors speak of the importance of Caffe Cino to their professional and artistic development. Each year on November 20, the date of Cino's birth, and on April 2, the date of his death as well as of Jonathan Torrey's birth, a small group gathers in a coffeehouse near the former location of Caffe Cino to remember the short, fat Italian who brought them together. Over the years, the group also has gathered repeatedly to mourn the death of one of their members, as they did during the summer of 1999 at the Cornelia Street Cafe (next door to the old Cino) to acknowledge the death of Ron Link. Sadly, such deaths have come all too frequently.

One of New York's most important cultural assets and symbols of freedom of the arts disappeared with the Cino. Only weeks before the Caffe closed, the U.S. Overseas Information Agency sent a request to the coffeehouse seek-ing permission to film it as part of a documentary on our "cultural assets and the freedom of the Arts in our democracy."[57] Many who experienced the Cino magic share Helen Hanft's feeling of loss: "There is nothing like it and there never will be again."[58] Hanft delivered her most moving tribute to Caffe Cino and playwright Tom Eyen when she spoke at the conference of the Associa-tion for Theatre in Higher Education in 2003: "If it were not for the Cino, if it were not for Tom Eyen, I would probably not be where I am. I am glad it happened to me. . . . I feel I was very lucky and very charmed to meet these two men, Cino and Eyen . . . because they did take me and put me together and make me an actor."[59] Equally moving, Ellen Stewart spoke in 1985 of the importance of Joe Cino: "Remember that what came from his soul, what came from his heart, what came from his mind contributed in a large degree to everything that we are doing today."[60] In his management of ArtsWest in Se-attle, Walter Michael Harris draws from what he learned at the Cino and La Mama, "You don't need a lot to create something of value artistically. All you really need is space, something to say, and somebody to hear you say it. . . . You can create good art and good theatre almost by spinning straw into gold. I have something that is valuable to me, which is the ability to create art out of thin air. That's what we were doing at the Cino."[61] Though the Overseas Informa-tion Agency was too late to film the Cino, the memory of a short, fat dancer and his cluttered coffeehouse remains fresh, their legacy influencing and inspiring artists who have never heard of either. Now that nearly four decades have elapsed since an actor has appeared on the stage at 31 Cornelia Street, perhaps we can begin to assess Joseph Cino's contribution to our theatre.

Notes
Index

Notes

Introduction

1. Freddie Herko quoted in Jimmy McDonough, *The Ghastly One: The Sex-Gore Netherworld of Filmmaker Andy Milligan* (Chicago: A Cappella Books, 2001), 56.
2. Arthur Alpert, "Cafe [*sic*] Cino Has *Alice* in One Act," *New York World-Telegram and the Sun,* January 26, 1962, n. pag., Mooney clipping file, Billy Rose Theatre Collection, New York Public Library.
3. Albert Poland and Bruce Mailman, *The Off-Off-Broadway Book: The Plays, People, Theatre* (New York: Bobbs-Merrill, 1972), xvii.
4. Paul Cranefield, interview by author, December 2001.

1. Background and Context

1. Julie Stephens, *Anti-Disciplinary Protest: Sixties Radicalism and Postmodernism* (Cambridge: Cambridge University Press, 1998), 11.
2. Theodore Roszak, *The Making of a Counter Culture: Reflections on the Technocratic Society and Its Youthful Opposition* (Garden City, NY: Anchor Books, 1969), 11.
3. Arthur Schlesinger, "The New Mood in Politics," in *The Sixties: Art, Politics, and Media of Our Most Explosive Decade,* ed. Gerald Howard (New York: Marlowe, 1982), 44, 45, 47, 49.
4. Schlesinger, "New Mood in Politics," 51.
5. Schlesinger, "New Mood in Politics," 45.
6. Schlesinger, "New Mood in Politics," 55.
7. Roszak, *Making of a Counter Culture,* 56.
8. Stephens, *Anti-Disciplinary Protest,* 22.
9. Dale Lewis, "Digging the Diggers: The New Left at Bay," *Village Voice,* July 6, 1967, 11.
10. Lewis, "Digging the Diggers," 20.
11. Marlene Nadle, "The Power of Flower Vs. the Power of Politics," *Village Voice,* June 15, 1967, 1.
12. Stephens, *Anti-Disciplinary Protest,* 25.
13. Jerry Rubin quoted in Stephens, *Anti-Disciplinary Protest,* 40.
14. Tillie Gross, "Parallels in the Development of London's Royal Court, New York's Caffe Cino, and Cafe La Mama" (PhD diss., New York University, 1994), 164–65.

15. Herman Shumlin quoted in Stuart W. Little, "A Dollar and Cents View," *Theatre Arts* 45, no. 5 (May 1961): 15.

16. Joshua Logan, "What's Right, What's Wrong," *Theatre Arts* 45, no. 5 (May 1961): 8.

17. Harold Clurman, "The Frightened Fifties Onward . . ." *Theatre Arts* 45, no. 3 (March 1961): 12.

18. Stuart W. Little, *Off-Broadway: The Prophetic Theater* (New York: Coward, McCann, and Geoghegan, 1972), 229.

19. Henry Popkin, "It's Big on Bleecker Street," *Reporter,* July 9, 1959, 46.

20. Robert Brustein, "Off Broadway's Trials and Triumphs," *New Republic,* March 6, 1961, 21.

21. Brustein, "Off Broadway's Trials," 21.

22. Barbara La Fontaine, "Triple Threat On, Off, and Off-Off Broadway," *New York Times Magazine,* February 25, 1968, 42.

23. Al Carmines, "How It All Began: The Flowering of Off-Off Broadway," clipping from unidentified periodical, October 1982, Jerome Lawrence and Robert E. Lee Theatre Research Institute, Ohio State University, 7.

24. Little, *Off-Broadway: Prophetic Theater,* 14.

25. Michael Feingold, "Caffe Cino, 20 Years after Magic Time," *Village Voice,* May 14, 1985, 50.

26. Ellen Stewart quoted in Josh Greenfeld, "Their Hearts Belong to La Mama," *New York Times Magazine,* July 9, 1967, 20.

27. "The Alluring Cupful," *Newsweek,* October 8, 1956, 87.

28. "Alluring Cupful," 86.

29. J. R. Goddard, "Coffee Houses: Many Things to Many Men," *Village Voice,* November 30, 1961, 1.

30. Jack Diether, "The Coffee House War," *Musical America* 81 (December 1961): 45.

31. Douglas W. Gordy, "Joseph Cino and the First Off-Off Broadway Theater," in *Passing Performances: Queer Readings of Leading Players in American Theater History,* ed. Robert A. Schanke and Kim Marra (Ann Arbor: University of Michigan Press, 1998), 303–4.

32. To distinguish father from son, I will refer to the older man as "Joseph" and the younger as "Joe."

33. Robert Heide, "Magic Time at the Caffe Cino: A First-Hand Account of the Birth of Off-Off-Broadway—and Gay Theater," *New York Native,* May 19, 1985, 30.

34. Palazzo quoted in Ed Koch, "Blitzstein Murder Case Figure Cino Kept from His Brother's Funeral," *Las Vegas Sun,* September 8, 1999,

http://www.lasvegassun.com/sunbin/stories/archives/1999/sep/08/
509277664.html?Cino (accessed February 7, 2000).

35. Feingold, "Caffe Cino, 20 Years," 50.

36. Angelo Lovullo, interview by author, July 22, 1999.

37. Michael Smith, "Joe Cino's World Goes Up in Flames," *Village Voice,*
March 11, 1965, 1.

38. Charles Loubier, "Caffe Cino: Part VII," *Other Stages,* June 14, 1979, 8.

39. Smith, "Joe Cino's World," 14.

40. John Martin, "The Dance: Accent on Brooklyn," *New York Times,*
December 9, 1956, 17.

41. Gordy, "Joseph Cino," 304.

42. Cino quoted in Smith, "Joe Cino's World," 14.

43. Robert Heide, interview by author, June 22, 1998.

2. Finding and Forming Community

1. *Excerpts from the Opening Night Celebration of the 'Caffe Cino and Its
Legacy Exhibition and Portions of the Formal Program,* VHS, 1985, Billy Rose
Theatre Collection, New York Public Library.

2. Joe Cino quoted in Michael Smith, "Joe Cino's World Goes Up in
Flames," *Village Voice,* March 11, 1965, 14.

3. Nancy Lynch, "The Square Root of Bohemia," *Mademoiselle,* March
1966, 137.

4. Smith, "Joe Cino's World," 14–15.

5. "Scrapbook of New York Public Library Exhibit of Caffe Cino Material," file Caffe Cino (NYC) Scrapbook RE NYPL Exhibit, March 5–May 11,
1985, no. 20, 1985, Billy Rose Theatre Collection, 8-MWEZ+n.c. 27646, New
York Public Library, 118.

6. Robert Patrick quoted in Douglas W. Gordy, "Joseph Cino and the First
Off-Off Broadway Theater," in *Passing Performances: Queer Readings of Lead-
ing Players in American Theater History,* ed. Robert A. Schanke and Kim Marra
(Ann Arbor: University of Michigan Press, 1998), 306.

7. Matt Baylor to the author, March 12, 2004.

8. "Scrapbook," 119.

9. "Scrapbook," 118.

10. "Scrapbook," 107.

11. Tillie Gross, "Parallels in the Development of London's Royal Court,
New York's Caffe Cino, and Cafe La Mama" (PhD diss., New York University, 1994), 178.

12. John Costopoulos, "Homosexuality on the New York Stage: Its Critical Reception, 1926 to 1968" (PhD diss., New York University, 1985), 354–55.

13. Cino quoted in Smith, "Joe Cino's World," 14.

14. Lucy Silvay, interview by author, April 29, 2000.

15. Robert Heide quoted in Michael Feingold, "Caffe Cino, 20 Years after Magic Time," *Village Voice,* May 14, 1985, 117.

16. Charles Loubier, "Caffe Cino: Part VII," *Other Stages,* June 14, 1979, 8.

17. Walter Michael Harris, interview by author, May 19, 2004.

18. Robert Heide, "Cockroaches in the Baubles," *Other Stages,* February 8, 1979, 8.

19. Robert Heide, interview by author, December 18, 1997; Lanford Wilson, interview by author, June 29, 1999; Helen Hanft, interview by author, November 23, 1998.

20. Richard Smithies quoted in Robert Patrick, "Caffe Cino: Memories by Those Who Worked There," *Los Angeles Theatres Magazine,* November 1994, 20–21.

21. Hanft, interview.

22. *Excerpts from the Opening Night Celebration.*

23. Jimmy McDonough, *The Ghastly One: The Sex-Gore Netherworld of Filmmaker Andy Milligan* (Chicago: A Cappella Books, 2001), 31.

24. Gross, "Parallels," 179.

25. Robert Pasolli, "The New Playwrights' Scene of the Sixties: Jerome Max Is Alive and Well and Living in Rome," *Drama Review* 13, no. 1 (Fall 1968): 154–55.

26. Michael Smith, "John P. Dodd, 1941–1991," obituary, *Village Voice,* August 6, 1991, n. pag., Dodd clipping file, New York Public Library.

27. Johnny Dodd quoted in Gross, "Parallels," 179.

28. McDonough, *Ghastly One,* 31.

29. McDonough, *Ghastly One,* 31.

30. Gross, "Parallels," 177.

31. "Scrapbook," 101.

32. Gross, "Parallels," 167.

33. Gross, "Parallels," 179.

34. Clayton Delery, "Caffe Cino: The Drama and Its History" (master's thesis, University of Lafayette [formerly University of Southwestern Louisiana], 1981), 10.

35. Robert Heide, "Magic Time at the Caffe Cino: A First-Hand Account of the Birth of Off-Off-Broadway—and Gay Theater," *New York Native,* May 19, 1985, 30.

36. Gross, "Parallels," 167.

37. Loubier, "Caffe Cino: Part VII," 8.

38. Sally Kempton, "Taylor Mead: The Homosexual Clown as Underground Star," *Village Voice,* November 30, 1967, 19.

39. Lanford Wilson quoted in Mary S. Ryzuk, *The Circle Repertory Company: The First Fifteen Years* (Ames: Iowa State University Press, 1989), 38–39.

40. "Scrapbook," 107.

41. Smith, "Joe Cino's World," 14.

42. Angelo Lovullo, interview by author, July 22, 1999.

43. Elliott Levine to Richard Buck, New York Public Library, 1985, 8-MWEZ+n.c. 27646 #21, Caffe Cino, Billy Rose Theatre Collection, New York Public Library.

44. Harlan Ellison, "Coffee Houses Are Cabarets, Police Say; Owners Deny It," *Village Voice*, September 1, 1960, 1.

45. "Learning," *New Yorker*, July 1, 1961, 21.

46. Edith Evans Asbury, "Greenwich Village Argues New Way of Life: Coffeehouses Arouse Fresh Controversy over Carnival Air," *New York Times*, August 4, 1963, 62.

47. Len Chandler quoted in J. R. Goddard, "The MacDougal Scene: II. Modern Version of a Bosch Painting," *Village Voice*, June 20, 1963, 6.

48. Asbury, "Greenwich Village Argues," 62.

49. Alex Atkinson, "The Antic Art: Innocents Off-Broadway," *Holiday*, September 1961, 90.

50. Homer Bigart, "Mayor Aids Drive on 'Village' Cafes," *New York Times*, April 3, 1965, 31.

51. Bernard Weinraub, "Nightmare Hours: Saturday Night on MacDougal Street," *New York Times*, April 12, 1965, 37.

52. Click advertisement, *Village Voice*, June 16, 1966, 15.

53. "'Hideaway' Loses License," *Village Voice*, November 11, 1959, 1.

54. Robert Heide quoted in Mel Gussow, *Edward Albee: A Singular Journey* (New York: Simon and Schuster, 1999), 79.

55. "Fawn Restaurant Regains License by Judge's Order," *New York Times*, January 7, 1964, 39.

56. Thomas A. Johnson, "3 Deviates Invite Exclusion by Bars," *New York Times*, April 25, 1966, 43.

57. Howard Smith, Scenes, *Village Voice*, March 7, 1968, 25.

58. J. R. Goddard, "Coffee Houses: Many Things to Many Men," *Village Voice*, November 30, 1961, 14.

59. "The Police and the Poets," *Commonweal* 70 (June 19, 1959): 294.

60. Henry Hewes, "Fresh Grounds for Theatre," *Theatre Arts* 45, no. 4 (April 1961): 20.

61. Asbury, "Greenwich Village Argues," 62.

62. Jack Diether, "The Coffee House War," *Musical America* 81 (December 1961): 46.

63. Leticia Kent, "The Desperate Mr. Z. and the West Village Grab," *Village Voice,* January 11, 1968, 1.

64. William Ames quoted in "Police Take Heat Off Cool Poetry," *New York Times,* June 9, 1959, 31.

65. Ames quoted in "Police Have Heart for Art, Poets Say," *Village Voice,* June 17, 1959, 1.

66. Joe Cino quoted in Smith, "Joe Cino's World," 14.

67. Gordy, "Joseph Cino," 308.

68. Phoebe Mooney, interview by author, March 13, 2004.

69. Cino quoted in Smith, "Joe Cino's World," 14.

70. S[andra] S[chmidt], "Cafe Theatre: *Herrengasse,*" review of *Herrengasse,* by Story Talbot, *Village Voice,* February 2, 1961, 12.

71. Robert Patrick, "The Other Brick Road," *Other Stages,* February 8, 1979, 3.

72. Waldo Kang Pagune, "Remembering Joe Cino," correspondence file 8-MWEZ+n.c. 27646 #21, Billy Rose Theatre Collection, New York Public Library.

73. Kenny Burgess quoted in McDonough, *Ghastly One,* 38.

74. Johnny Dodd quoted in McDonough, *Ghastly One,* 40.

75. Dodd quoted in McDonough, *Ghastly One,* 40.

76. Dodd quoted in McDonough, *Ghastly One,* 40.

77. Joe Cino quoted in Robert Dahdah, interview by author, November 24, 1998.

78. Cino quoted in Dahdah, interview.

79. Unidentified clipping provided by Robert Patrick.

80. Neil Flanagan quoted in Gross, "Parallels in the Development," 170.

81. Michael Smith, "The Caffe Cino: Homage to a Patron of the Arts," *Day* [New London, CT], March 24, 1985, 13.

82. John Guare quoted in Gene A. Plunka, *The Black Comedy of John Guare* (Newark: University of Delaware Press, 2002), 29.

83. McDonough, *Ghastly One,* 32.

84. Kevin Norris, "Review of *Blow Away,*" *Best Sellers* 39 (July 1979): 133.

85. Gregor A. Preston, "Review of *Blow Away,*" *Library Journal* 104, no. 1 (January 1, 1979): 101.

86. Dean Selmier and Mark Kram, *Blow Away* (New York: Viking, 1979), 12.

87. Selmier and Kram, *Blow Away,* 4.

88. Jeremy Johnson, interview by author, April 12, 2000.

89. J. R. Goddard, "Lights Are Dimmed along MacDougal St.," *Village Voice,* June 16, 1960, 1.

90. Diether, "Coffee House War," 46.

91. Doric Wilson, "Everything But the Dates," *Other Stages,* March 8, 1979, 7.

92. Feingold, "Caffe Cino, 20 Years," 66.

93. Gordy, "Joseph Cino."

94. Diether, "Coffee House War," 46.

95. Johnny Dodd quoted in Gross, "Parallels in the Development," 175.

96. Seymour Krim, "Cafe Theatre: *No Exit* on Cornelia," *Village Voice,* December 15, 1960, 11.

97. Krim, "Cafe Theatre," 11.

98. Krim, "Cafe Theatre," 11.

99. Mary Boylan, manuscript, Boylan clipping file, Billy Rose Theatre Collection, New York Public Library.

100. S[chmidt], "Cafe Theatre: *Herrengasse,*" 12.

101. Hewes, "Fresh Grounds for Theatre," 20.

102. Wilson, "Everything But the Dates," 7.

103. "Scrapbook," 108.

104. Wilson, "Everything But the Dates," 7.

105. Doric Wilson, *And He Made a Her,* original sound recording of a production at Caffe Cino, March 1961.

106. Doric Wilson, *And He Made a Her,* typescript, Billy Rose Theatre Collection, New York Public Library.

107. Delery, "Caffe Cino: The Drama," 95.

108. Wilson, "Everything But the Dates," 7.

109. Unidentified clipping supplied by Doric Wilson.

110. Wilson, *And He Made a Her,* typescript, 25.

111. Wilson, *And He Made a Her,* typescript, 28.

112. "Learning," 19.

113. "Learning," 20.

114. "Learning," 20.

115. "Learning," 21.

116. "Learning," 21.

117. Program for *Now She Dances!,* by Doric Wilson, supplied by Wilson.

118. Wilson, "Everything But the Dates," 7.

119. Gordy, "Joseph Cino," 305.

120. Randy Gener, "Back to the Cino: Remembering the Cafe Where Gay Theatre Came Out," *Village Voice,* June 21, 1994, 5.

121. Patrick, "Other Brick Road," 3.

122. M[ichael] S[mith], "Off Off-B'way: 2 at the Cino," *Village Voice,* August 16, 1962, 6.

123. Arthur Sainer, "Theatre: *The Clown*," review of *The Clown*, by Claris Nelson, *Village Voice*, October 11, 1962, 12.

124. Sainer, "Theatre: *The Clown*," 12.

125. Claris Nelson, *The Clown*, unpublished typescript, provided by Nelson.

126. Nelson, "The Clown," 30.

127. Feingold, "Caffe Cino, 20 Years," 117.

128. Oscar Gross Brockett, *Century of Innovation: A History of European and American Theatre and Drama since 1870*, Prentice Hall Series in Theatre and Drama, ed. Oscar Gross Brockett (Englewood Cliffs, NJ: Prentice-Hall, 1973), 710.

129. Sally Banes, *Greenwich Village 1963: Avant-Garde Performance and the Effervescent Body* (Durham, NC: Duke University Press, 1993), 31.

130. Banes, *Greenwich Village 1963*, 47.

131. Jean Claude van Itallie, "'War' and 'We,'" *Other Stages*, May 17, 1979, 6.

132. Smith, "Joe Cino's World," 15.

133. Loubier, "Caffe Cino: Part VII," 8.

134. Loubier, "Caffe Cino: Part VII," 8.

135. Lynch, "Square Root of Bohemia," 127.

136. Arnold Aronson, *American Avant-Garde Theatre: A History* (London: Routledge, 2000), 83.

137. Banes, *Greenwich Village 1963*, 95.

138. Michael Smith, Theatre Journal, *Village Voice*, December 30, 1965.

139. Richard Dyer and Derek Cohen, "The Politics of Gay Culture," in *The Culture of Queers*, ed. Richard Dyer (London: Routledge, 2002), 15.

3. Veiled Strangeness

1. Lanford Wilson, interview by author, June 29, 1999.

2. *Excerpts from the Opening Night Celebration of the 'Caffe Cino and Its Legacy Exhibition and Portions of the Formal Program*, VHS, 1985, Billy Rose Theatre Collection, New York Public Library.

3. M[ichael] S[mith], "Theatre: Caffe Cino," review of *So, Who's Afraid of Edward Albee*, by David Starkweather, *Village Voice*, February 28, 1963, 15.

4. S[mith], "Theatre: Caffe Cino," 15.

5. Robert Dagny, interview by author, September 10, 2000.

6. William M. Hoffman, "David Starkweather," in *Contemporary Dramatists*, ed. James Vinson, 2nd ed. (New York: St. Martin's, 1977), 751.

7. Hoffman, "David Starkweather," 752.

8. Dagny, interview.

9. Robert Heide, "Cockroaches in the Baubles," *Other Stages*, February 8, 1979, 9.

10. Caffe Cino, advertisement in Cafes & Coffee Houses, *Village Voice,* April 25, 1963, 10.

11. Kathryn Ann Absher, "Caffe Cino: The Cradle of Lanford Wilson's Career" (master's thesis, University of Nebraska at Omaha, 1990), 49.

12. Clayton Delery, "Caffe Cino: The Drama and Its History" (master's thesis, University of Lafayette [formerly University of Southwestern Louisiana], 1981), 51.

13. Caffe Cino, advertisement in Cafes & Coffee Houses, *Village Voice,* May 23, 1963, 16.

14. Arthur Sainer, "Theatre: *Miss Julia,*" *Village Voice,* July 18, 1963, 10.

15. J. R. Goddard, "MacDougal Cafes Open 'Operation Housecleaning,'" *Village Voice,* May 30, 1963, 3.

16. Goddard, "MacDougal Cafes," 16.

17. Greenwich Village Cafe Theatre Association, advertisement, *Village Voice,* July 11, 1963, 3.

18. Stephanie Gervis, "No Lean and Hungry Look on Coffee-House Cassius," *Village Voice,* March 14, 1963, 1, 25.

19. L. Wilson, interview.

20. Michael Warren Powell, interview by author, November 23, 1998.

21. Michael Warren Powell quoted in Jan Stuart, "Remembering Caffe Cino: Off-Off Broadway's Beginnings Are Evoked in a Lincoln Center Exhibit," *American Theatre* 2, no. 3 (June 1985): 36.

22. Powell, interview.

23. Michael Smith, "Theatre: *So Long at the Fair,*" *Village Voice,* August 29, 1963, 6.

24. Marshall Mason quoted in Jackson R. Bryer, "A 'Shared Vision' of 'the Human Scale of Life on Stage': An Interview with Marshall W. Mason," in *Lanford Wilson: A Casebook,* ed. Jackson R. Bryer (New York: Garland, 1994), 212.

25. Mason quoted in Bryer, "'Shared Vision,'" 213.

26. Mason quoted in Bryer, "'Shared Vision,'" 214.

27. Bryer, "'Shared Vision,'" 214.

28. L. Wilson, interview.

29. Marshall Mason quoted in Bryer, "'Shared Vision,'" 214.

30. L. Wilson quoted in Mary S. Ryzuk, *The Circle Repertory Company: The First Fifteen Years* (Ames: Iowa State University Press, 1989), 45.

31. L. Wilson, interview.

32. M[ichael] S[mith], "Theatre: *The Madness of Lady Bright,*" review of *The Madness of Lady Bright,* by Lanford Wilson, Caffe Cino, New York, *Village Voice,* May 21, 1964, 12.

33. John Costopoulos, "Homosexuality on the New York Stage: Its Critical Reception, 1926 to 1968" (PhD diss., New York University, 1985), 359.

34. L. Wilson, interview.

35. "Three Actors," *Tribune* [city unidentified], February 16, 1966, n. pag., Lanford Wilson clipping file, Billy Rose Theatre Collection, New York Public Library; "Hunt Picks Casts for Wilson Plays," *New York Post,* February 11, 1966, n. pag., Wilson clipping file, Billy Rose Theatre Collection, New York Public Library.

36. Lanford Wilson, *The Madness of Lady Bright, The Rimers of Eldritch and Other Plays* (New York: Hill and Wang, 1967), 82.

37. Michael Smith, "Theatre: Two by Wilson," *Village Voice,* February 11, 1965, 13.

38. Michael Smith, Theatre Journal, review of *The Sandcastle,* by Lanford Wilson, La Mama ETC, New York, *Village Voice,* September 30, 1965, 30.

39. John Keating, "Making It Off Off Broadway," *New York Times,* April 25, 1965, section 2, X3.

40. Joe Cino quoted in Stephanie Gervis Harrington, "Dimly Lit Room Produces Hundreds of New Plays," *Village Voice,* April 23, 1964, 3.

41. Edith Evans Asbury, "Greenwich Village Argues New Way of Life: Coffeehouses Arouse Fresh Controversy over Carnival Air," *New York Times,* August 4, 1963, 62.

42. Martin Gansberg, "15 'Village' Shops Ordered to Close," *New York Times,* March 25, 1964, 81.

43. Stephanie Gervis Harrington, "City Puts Bomb under Off-Beat Culture Scene," *Village Voice,* March 26, 1964, 14.

44. Diane di Prima, letter to the editor, *Village Voice,* April 16, 1964, 4.

45. Stephanie Gervis Harrington, "Koch Enlists City Aid on M'Dougal St. 'Mess,'" *Village Voice,* July 2, 1964, 1.

46. Susan Goodman, "South Villagers Cheer Koch Move on McD. St," *Village Voice,* July 30, 1964, 9.

47. Susan Sherman, "An Appreciation: Ruth Yorck," Obituary of Ruth Yorck, *Village Voice,* January 27, 1966, 14; "Ruth Yorck, Wrote Novels and Plays," Obituary, *New York Times,* January 20, 1966, 35.

48. Leo Lerman, "The Third Stream of Off Off Broadway," *Mademoiselle,* March 1966, 146.

49. Ruth Yorck, unpublished autobiography, typescript, box 1, Department of Special Collections, Boston University, 87.

50. Yorck, unpublished autobiography, 178.

51. Yorck, unpublished autobiography, 179.

52. Yorck, unpublished autobiography, 179.

53. Yorck, unpublished autobiography, 180.

54. Yorck, unpublished autobiography, 213.

55. Susan Sherman, "Theatre: La Mama, E.T.C.," review of *Lullaby for a Dying Man,* by Ruth Yorck, La Mama, ETC, New York, *Village Voice,* August 12, 1965, 12.

56. Ruth Yorck, *Lullabye for a Dying Man,* typescript, box 47, Department of Special Collections, Boston University.

57. Robert G. Olson, *An Introduction to Existentialism* (New York: Dover, 1962), 19.

58. Yorck, *Lullabye,* 6.

59. Yorck, *Lullabye,* 20.

60. Ruth Yorck quoted in John Gruen, "The Pop Scene: Series of 9 Plays Commemorates a Singular Lady of New Bohemia," *World Journal Tribune* [New York, NY], January 19, 1967, n. pag., Wilson clipping file, Billy Rose Theatre Collection, New York Public Library.

61. "Scrapbook of New York Public Library Exhibit of Caffe Cino Material," p. 116, file Caffe Cino (NYC) Scrapbook RE NYPL Exhibit, March 5–May 11, 1985, no. 20, 1985, box Caffe Cino 8-MWEZ+n.c. 27646, Billy Rose Theatre Collection, New York Public Library.

62. Jameson Currier, "H. M. Koutoukas," unpublished typescript, forthcoming in *The Gay and Lesbian Theatrical Legacy,* ed. Robert A. Schanke, Kim Marra, and Billy J. Harbin (Ann Arbor: University of Michigan Press).

63. John Gruen, "Chamber Theatre, 'Touring Living Rooms,'" *Vogue,* March 1, 1969, 114; Michael Smith, "H. M. Koutoukas," in *Contemporary Dramatists,* ed. James Vinson (New York: St. Martin's, 1977), 456.

64. Author biography in H. M. Koutoukas, *When Lightning Strikes Twice* (New York: Samuel French, 1991).

65. "Koutoukas, H. M," in *Contemporary Authors, New Revision Series,* ed. Pamela S. Dear, vol. 47 (Detroit: Gail Research, 1995), 255.

66. H. M. Koutoukas quoted in David Hirsh, "The Poets Are Right Again: H. M. Koutoukas Talks about His First Play in Five Years," *Stonewall News* [New York, NY], October 12, 1992, 5.

67. H. M. Koutoukas, panel participant, "Recovering the Past, Transforming the Future: The Story of the Caffe Cino from Those Who Lived It" (forum, Association for Theatre in Higher Education annual conference, New York, August 2, 2003).

68. H. M. Koutoukas quoted in Hirsh, "Poets Are Right Again," 5.

69. Hirsh, "Poets Are Right Again," 5.

70. Michael Bronski, *Culture Clash: The Making of Gay Sensibility* (Boston: South End, 1984), 46.

71. Susan Sontag, "Notes on 'Camp,'" in *Camp: Queer Aesthetics and the Performing Subject,* ed. Fabio Cleto (Ann Arbor: University of Michigan Press, 1999), 53.

72. Vivian Gornick, "Pop Goes Homosexual: It's a Queer Hand Stoking the Campfire," *Village Voice,* April 7, 1966, 1.

73. Gornick, "Pop Goes Homosexual," 21.

74. Suzanne Kiplinger, "Speak Out the Arts: Culture and the Psychopath," *Village Voice,* May 5, 1966, 18.

75. Avery Corman, letter to the editor, *Village Voice,* April 15, 1965, 4.

76. Smith, "H. M. Koutoukas," 457–58.

77. Jack Smith, "The Perfect Film Appositeness of Maria Montez," *Film Culture* 27 (Winter 1962–63), 35, reprinted in *Wait for Me at the Bottom of the Pool: The Writings of Jack Smith,* ed. J. Hoberman and Edward Leffingwell (New York: High Risk Books).

78. H. M. Koutoukas, *With Creatures Make My Way,* typescript, Billy Rose Theatre Collection, New York Public Library.

79. Abraham Kaplan, "Lecture Three: Existentialism," in *The New World of Philosophy* (New York: Vintage Books, 1961), 98.

80. Robert Heide, interview by author, June 22, 1998.

81. Gruen, "Chamber Theatre," 116.

82. Michael Smith, Theatre Journal, review of *Medea* by H. M. Koutoukas, Caffe Cino, New York, *Village Voice,* October 21, 1965, 22–23.

83. Michael Smith, Theatre Journal, review of *Medea,* by H. M. Koutoukas, Judson Poets' Theatre, New York, *Village Voice,* November 11, 1965, 27.

84. Johann Wolfgang von Goethe, "Women's Parts Played by Men in the Roman Theatre," trans. Isa Ragusa, in *Crossing the Stage: Controversies on Cross-Dressing,* ed. Lesley Ferris (New York: Routledge, 1993), 49.

85. Kaplan, "Lecture Three: Existentialism," 103.

86. H. M. Koutoukas, *Awful People Are Coming Over So We Must Be Pretending to Be Hard at Work and Hope They Will Go Away, When Lightning Strikes Twice* (New York: Samuel French, 1991), 18.

87. "OBIES Search Results, 1965–66," *Village Voice,* http://www.villagevoice.com/cgi-bin/obies/obies_year.cgi?year=1965-66 (accessed March 25, 2004).

88. Ken Burrows, "New Militancy Makes the MacDougal Scene," *Village Voice,* August 20, 1964, 8.

89. Burrows, "New Militancy," 8.

90. Poland and Mailman, *The Off Off Broadway Book: The Plays, People, Theatre,* lvii.

91. Sally Kempton, "Baby Beatniks Spark Bar Boom on East Side," *Village Voice,* September 10, 1964, 1.

92. Albert Poland and Bruce Mailman, *The Off-Off-Broadway Book: The Plays, People, Theatre* (New York: Bobbs-Merrill, 1972), lvii.

93. Mary Perot Nichols, "'Mess on MacDougal' to Be Toned Down," *Village Voice,* December 3, 1964, 8.

94. Nichols, "'Mess on MacDougal,'" 8.

95. William M. Hoffman, "Introduction," in *Gay Plays: The First Collection,* ed. William M. Hoffman (New York: Avon, 1979), xxiii–xxiv.

96. Hoffman, "Introduction," xxiv.

97. Hoffman, "Introduction," xxiv–xxv.

98. Robert Patrick, e-mail to author, May 20, 2004.

99. Robert Patrick quoted in "Patrick, Robert," in *Contemporary Authors: New Revision Series,* ed. Ann Evory, vol. 1 (Detroit: Gale Research, 1981), 498.

100. Robert Patrick, *Temple Slave* (New York: Masquerade, 1994), 19.

101. Robert Patrick, "Off Off Broadway—A Personal History," *Off Off Bway Theatre Choice,* July 19, 1978.

102. Robert Patrick, "Robert Patrick on Caffe Cino: Laughs, Critical Gaffes," *Advocate,* May 17, 1979, 41.

103. Patrick, "Robert Patrick on Caffe Cino," 41.

104. Patrick quoted in Maggie Hawthorn, "Robert Patrick: Theater's Maverick Urchin," in *Authors in the News,* ed. Barbara Nykoruk (Detroit: Gale Research, 1976), 216.

105. Michael Feingold, "Can a Kid from the Caffe Cino Be Really Big, Baby?" *Village Voice,* November 17, 1975, 116.

106. Robert Patrick, "Where Gay Plays Began," *Other Stages,* February 8–21, 1979, 26.

107. Leah D. Frank, "Robert Patrick," in *Contemporary Dramatists,* ed. D. L. Kirkpatrick, 4th ed. (Chicago: St. James, 1988), 420; Robert Patrick, interview by author, December 11, 1999.

108. Jean Claude van Itallie, "'War' and 'We,'" *Other Stages,* May 17, 1979, 6.

109. van Itallie, "'War' and 'We,'" 6.

110. van Itallie, "'War' and 'We,'" 6.

111. van Itallie, "'War' and 'We,'" 6.

112. Michael Smith, "Joe Cino's World Goes Up in Flames," *Village Voice,* March 11, 1965, 1.

113. Tillie Gross, "Parallels in the Development of London's Royal Court, New York's Caffe Cino, and Cafe La Mama" (PhD diss., New York University, 1994), 189.

114. Gross, "Parallels in the Development," 164.

115. Gross, "Parallels in the Development," 182.

116. Grant Duay, "The Missing Link," *Gay,* October 12, 1970, 11.

117. Caffe Gomad, advertisement, *Village Voice*, March 25, 1965, 23.

118. Gross, "Parallels in the Development," 189.

119. Joe Cino quoted in Smith, "Joe Cino's World," 15.

120. Caffe Cino at La Mama, advertisement, *Village Voice*, April 8, 1965, 20.

121. Roberta Sklar, interview by author, April 21, 2000.

4. The Bitch Goddess

1. Telegrams on reopening of Caffe Cino, 1965, 8-MWEZ+n.c. 27646, folder 2, correspondence, May 1965, re: congratulatory messages, Billy Rose Theatre Collection, New York Public Library.

2. Caffe Cino, advertisement in Cafes and Coffee Houses, *Village Voice*, August 12, 1965, 10.

3. Program for *With Creatures Make My Way*, by H. M. Koutoukas, 1965, clipping file, Billy Rose Theatre Collection, New York Public Library.

4. Robert Patrick, "The Other Brick Road," *Other Stages*, February 8, 1979, 3, 10.

5. H. M. Koutoukas, *With Creatures Make My Way*, typescript, Billy Rose Theatre Collection, New York Public Library, 1.

6. Program for *With Creatures*.

7. Koutoukas, *With Creatures*, 7.

8. Koutoukas, *With Creatures*, 8.

9. Michael Feingold, "Caffe Cino, 20 Years after Magic Time," *Village Voice*, May 14, 1985, 117.

10. Robert Heide, "Magic Time at the Caffe Cino: A First-Hand Account of the Birth of Off-Off-Broadway—and Gay Theater," *New York Native*, May 19, 1985, 29.

11. J[erry] T[allmer], "Theatre: New Playwrights," review of *West of the Moon* by Robert Heide, *The Blood Bugle* by Harry Tierney Jr., New Playwrights Theatre, New York, *Village Voice*, July 6, 1961, 9.

12. Robert Heide, *At War with the Mongols*, vol. 4, *New American Plays*, ed. William M. Hoffman (New York: Hill and Wang, 1971), 73.

13. Heide, "Magic Time," 30.

14. Robert Dahdah, interview by author, November 24, 1998.

15. John Costopoulos, "Homosexuality on the New York Stage: Its Critical Reception, 1926 to 1968" (PhD diss., New York University, 1985), 361.

16. Heide, "Magic Time," 30.

17. Robert Heide, *The Bed*, typescript, supplied by Robert Heide.

18. Elenore Lester, "Theatre: *The Bed*," review of *The Bed*, by Robert Heide, Caffe Cino, New York, *Village Voice*, July 8, 1965, 10.

19. William M. Hoffman, interview by author, July 12, 1999.

20. Hoffman, interview.

21. William M. Hoffman quoted in S. Isenberg, "Tale of Hoffman: *As Is* Completes a Circle," *Stages,* March 1985, 35.

22. Eleanor [Elenore] Lester, "Theatre: Caffe Cino," review of *Thank You, Miss Victoria,* by William M. Hoffman, Caffe Cino, New York, *Village Voice,* August 26, 1965, 10.

23. William M. Hoffman, *Thank You, Miss Victoria,* vol. 3, *New American Plays,* ed. William M. Hoffman (New York: Hill and Wang, 1970), 159.

24. Lester, "Theatre: Caffe Cino," 10.

25. Hoffman, *Thank You, Miss Victoria,* 165.

26. Hoffman, *Thank You, Miss Victoria,* 167.

27. Michael Smith, Theatre Journal, review of *Saturday Night at the Movies* and *Good Night, I Love You,* by William M. Hoffman, Caffe Cino, New York, *Village Voice,* September 16, 1965, 24.

28. Michael Smith, "William M. Hoffman," in *Contemporary Dramatists,* ed. James Vinson, 2nd ed. (New York: St. Martin's, 1977), 395.

29. Michael Smith, "The Caffe Cino: Homage to a Patron of the Arts," *Day* [New London, CT], March 24, 1985, 13.

30. Smith, "Caffe Cino: Homage," 13.

31. Leslie A. Wade, *Sam Shepard and the American Theatre* (Westport, CT: Praeger, 1997), 21.

32. Wade, *Sam Shepard,* 21.

33. Michael Smith, Theatre Journal, comments on Smith's production of *Icarus's Mother,* Caffe Cino, New York, *Village Voice,* December 2, 1965, 19.

34. Smith, Theatre Journal, comments, 19.

35. "Anti-Obie," *Village Voice,* May 27, 1965, 17.

36. Smith, Theatre Journal, comments, 19.

37. Michael Smith quoted in Judith Searle, "Four Drama Critics," *Drama Review* 18, no. 3 (September 1974): 7.

38. Robert Patrick, "Robert Patrick on Caffe Cino: Laughs, Critical Gaffes," *Advocate,* May 17, 1979, 41.

39. Helen Hanft, interview with author, December 7, 2001.

40. Hanft, interview.

41. Michael Lachetta, "Hanna's Skirt Rises Off-Broadway," *Daily News,* July 16, 1974, p. 46, box 40, Eyen Collection, Robert E. Lee and Jerome Lawrence Theatre Research Institute, Ohio State University.

42. Helen Hanft, "His Eye Is on the Sparrow Helen" (interviewer unknown), *Michael's Thing,* September 9, 1974, 30.

43. Lachetta, "Hanna's Skirt Rises," 46.

44. Lachetta, "Hanna's Skirt Rises," 46.

45. Unidentified clipping, box 47, folder 8, Eyen Collection, Robert E. Lee and Jerome Lawrence Theatre Research Institute, Ohio State University.

46. Handwritten note, box 47, folder 8, Eyen Collection, Robert E. Lee and Jerome Lawrence Theatre Research Institute, Ohio State University.

47. Lanford Wilson, *Sex Is Between Two People,* typescript, supplied by Wilson.

48. "OBIES Search Results, 1963–64," *Village Voice,* <http://www.villagevoice. com/cgi-bin/obies/obies_year.cgi?year=1963-64 (accessed March 25, 2004).

49. Elenore Lester, "The Pass-the-Hat Theater Circuit," *New York Times Magazine,* December 5, 1965, 98, 100.

50. Lester, "Pass-the-Hat Theater," 100.

51. Lester, "Pass-the-Hat Theater," 100.

52. Lester, "Pass-the-Hat Theater," 100.

53. Tom Burke, article about Bernadette Peters (title missing), *TV Guide,* October 9, 1976, p. 30, Peters clipping file, Billy Rose Theatre Collection, New York Public Library.

54. Burke, article about Bernadette Peters, 30.

55. Sally Banes, *Greenwich Village 1963: Avant-Garde Performance and the Effervescent Body* (Durham, NC: Duke University Press, 1993), 46.

56. Ralph Cook quoted in Douglas M. Davis, "The Expanding Arts: Success for 'Off-Off Broadway,'" *National Observer,* April 10, 1967.

57. My reference is to a copy of an article in *Réalités* available from the Jerome Lawrence and Robert E. Lee Theatre Research Institute at Ohio State University; since pagination is not always clear in the copy, page numbers in my citations are approximate. This and all other references to da Costa are my translations from the original French.

58. Bernard da Costa, "Les Jeunes Fous d''Off Off Broadway,'" *Réalités,* February 1967, 85.

59. William M. Hoffman, "Theatre Off-Off and Off-Broadway," *Status,* October 1966, 35.

60. da Costa, "Jeunes Fous," 87.

61. "A Summary of International and Domestic News During the Newspaper Strike," *New York Times,* October 11, 1965, 60.

62. Coffeehouse codes with handwritten note, 8-MWEZ x n.c 27646 #18, Billy Rose Theatre Collection, New York Public Library.

63. Coffeehouse codes.

64. Joel Tyler quoted in Stephanie Harrington, "New Man on Licenses Gives Aid & Comfort to the Avant Garde," *Village Voice,* December 30, 1965, 1.

65. Michael Smith, Theatre Journal, review of *All Day for a Dollar,* by H. M. Koutoukas, Caffe Cino, New York, *Village Voice,* January 13, 1966, 16.

66. Caffe Cino, advertisement for *All Day for a Dollar, Village Voice,* January 6, 1966, 18.

67. Press release for *Death of Tintagiles,* Caffe Cino clipping file, Billy Rose Theatre Collection, New York Public Library.

68. Michael Smith, Theatre Journal, comments on the closing of *The Death of Tintagiles,* Caffe Cino, New York, *Village Voice,* April 7, 1966, 27.

69. Smith, Theatre Journal, comments, 28.

70. Susan Goodman, "SRO Audience Views MacDougal St. 'Mess,'" *Village Voice,* August 8, 1963, 1.

71. "Marcus Gets Backing of MacDougal Factions," *Village Voice,* May 26, 1966, 9.

72. "3 Dignified 'Raids' on 'Village' Cafes Find Nary a Song," *New York Times,* March 5, 1966, 18.

73. Unknown man quoted in "3 Dignified 'Raids,'" 18.

74. Eric Pace, "New Police Drive Waged in 'Village' and Times Sq. Area," *New York Times,* March 16, 1966, 1.

75. David Gurin, "McD: A Losing Battle with a Turned-On Street," *Village Voice,* March 24, 1966, 1.

76. Stephanie Harrington, "'Street' Simmers Down, So Do the People," *Village Voice,* March 31, 1966, 3.

77. "From Off Off to Off," *New Yorker,* February 8, 1969, 29.

78. Robin Miller quoted in "From Off Off to Off," 30.

79. "Scrapbook of New York Public Library Exhibit of Caffe Cino Material," p. 142, file Caffe Cino (NYC) Scrapbook RE NYPL Exhibit, March 5–May 11, 1985, no. 20, 1985, box Caffe Cino 8-MWEZ+n.c. 27646, Billy Rose Theatre Collection, New York Public Library, 142.

80. Emory Lewis, "The Star Who Plays Stars," *Bergen County (NJ) Sunday Record,* October 20, 1974.

81. Bernadette Peters quoted in Jerry Tallmer, "Ruby from Ozone Park," *New York Post,* January 1969, Bernadette Peters clipping file, Billy Rose Theatre Collection, New York Public Library. Some bibliographic information is illegible.

82. Bob Lardine, "'Fair' Lady," *New York News Magazine,* October 24, 1976, 25.

83. Bernadette Peters quoted in unidentified clipping, Peters clipping file, Billy Rose Theatre Collection, New York Public Library.

84. Peters quoted in unidentified clipping, Peters clipping file.

85. Press release for *Dames at Sea, Dames at Sea* clipping file, Billy Rose Theatre Collection, New York Public Library.

86. Donna Forbes DeSeta, interview by author, July 22, 1999.

87. Robert Wahls, "Songs of Bernadette," *New York Daily News,* January 5, 1969.

88. Bernadette Peters biography released by MGM for *Pennies from Heaven,* Bernadette Peters clipping file, Billy Rose Theatre Collection, New York Public Library.

89. Haimsohn quoted in *Excerpts from the Opening Night Celebration of the 'Caffe Cino and Its Legacy Exhibition and Portions of the Formal Program,* VHS, 1985, Billy Rose Theater Collection, New York Public Library.

90. Judy Klemesrud, "Dame at Sea—or on the Way Up," *New York Times,* February 9, 1969, D3.

91. Frank Scheck, "These Are Dames to See," *Stages,* September 1985, 5.

92. "Scrapbook," 113.

93. Ronnie Cutrone quoted in Patrick S. Smith, *Warhol: Conversations about the Artist* (Ann Arbor, MI: UMI Research, 1988), 343.

94. Charles Loubier, "Caffe Cino: Part VII," *Other Stages,* June 14, 1979, 8.

95. Tillie Gross, "Parallels in the Development of London's Royal Court, New York's Caffe Cino, and Cafe La Mama" (PhD diss., New York University, 1994), 186–87.

96. Paul Foster, "A Nurse in a Madhouse," *Other Stages,* March 22, 1979, 7.

97. Victor Bockris, *Warhol* (London: Frederick Muller, 1989), 208.

98. Taylor Mead quoted in Bockris, *Warhol,* 208.

99. Bockris, *Warhol,* 332.

100. Patrick, "Other Brick Road," 10.

101. Mary Woronov, *Swimming Underground: My Years in the Warhol Factory* (Boston: Journey Editions, 1995), 106.

102. Woronov, *Swimming,* 149.

103. Woronov, *Swimming,* 169.

104. Clayton Delery, "Caffe Cino: The Drama and Its History" (master's thesis, University of Lafayette [formerly University of Southwestern Louisiana], 1981), 8.

5. The End of the Cobra Cult

1. Marlene Nadle, "Tug-of-War on Again on Coffee-House Area," *Village Voice,* August 25, 1966, 2.

2. Nadle, "Tug-of-War," 25.

3. Nadle, "Tug-of-War," 25.

4. "Equity Files Charges," *New York Times,* August 18, 1966, 28.

5. Julius Novick, "New Crisis at La Mama: Equity Picks Up Where License Dept. Left Off," *Village Voice,* September 8, 1966, 16.

6. Ellen Stewart quoted in "La Mama Theatre Club: Equity Writes Last Act," *Village Voice,* October 20, 1966, 23.

7. Roland Rees, "Tom Eyen on Tom Eyen and *The Dirtiest Show in Town,*" *Time Out* [London], May 7, 1971, 37.

8. Tom Eyen quoted in Rees, "Tom Eyen on Eyen," 37.

9. Arnold Aronson, *American Avant-Garde Theatre: A History* (London: Routledge, 2000), 17.

10. Tom Eyen quoted in Jodie Olbrych, "New York to Houston: Experimental Theatre," *Inner-View,* May 1980, 4.

11. Caffe Cino, advertisement for *Eyen on Eyen, Village Voice,* August 18, 1966, 12.

12. Tom Eyen, program for *Eyen on Eyen* at Caffe Cino, posters and promotional materials (misc.), box 31, Eyen Collection, Jerome Lawrence and Robert E. Lee Theatre Research Institute, Ohio State University.

13. Tom Eyen, program for *Four No Plays* by Theatre of the Eye Repertory Company at Extension, Etc., Eyen Collection, Jerome Lawrence and Robert E. Lee Theatre Research Institute, Ohio State University.

14. Phoebe Wray, interview by author, June 8, 2000.

15. Phoebe Wray quoted in Robert Patrick, "Caffe Cino: Memories by Those Who Worked There," *Los Angeles Theatres Magazine,* November 1994, 21.

16. "Scrapbook of New York Public Library Exhibit of Caffe Cino Material," p. 115, file Caffe Cino (NYC) Scrapbook RE NYPL Exhibit, March 5–May 11, 1985, no. 20, 1985, box Caffe Cino 8-MWEZ+n.c. 27646, Billy Rose Theatre Collection, New York Public Library.

17. Patrick, "Caffe Cino: Memories," 13.

18. Robert Patrick, e-mail to author, March 10, 2004.

19. Bernard da Costa, "Les Jeunes Fous d'`Off Off Broadway,'" *Réalités,* February 1967, 87.

20. Stephanie Harrington, "O-O-Broadway Lives, Equity Relaxes Rules," *Village Voice,* November 24, 1966, 24.

21. Ross Wetzsteon, "Theatre: *Chas. Dickens' Christmas Carol,*" review of *Chas. Dickens' Christmas Carol,* by Soren Agenoux, Caffe Cino, New York, *Village Voice,* December 29, 1966, 17.

22. Wetzsteon, "Theatre: *Chas.,*" 17.

23. Michael Smith, "Ondine," obituary, *Village Voice,* May 16, 1989, 102.

24. Robert Heide, "Magic Time at the Caffe Cino: A First-Hand Account of the Birth of Off-Off-Broadway—and Gay Theater," *New York Native,* May 19, 1985, 31.

25. Tillie Gross, "Parallels in the Development of London's Royal Court,

New York's Caffe Cino, and Cafe La Mama" (PhD diss., New York University, 1994), 191.

26. Douglas W. Gordy, "Joseph Cino and the First Off-Off Broadway Theater," in *Passing Performances: Queer Readings of Leading Players in American Theater History,* ed. Robert A. Schanke and Kim Marra (Ann Arbor: University of Michigan Press, 1998), 319.

27. Michael Feingold, "Caffe Cino, 20 Years after Magic Time," *Village Voice,* May 14, 1985, 117.

28. "Low Voltage Shock Fatal to Torrey," *Jaffrey (NH) Monadnock Ledger,* January 12, 1967, 1.

29. Gross, "Parallels in the Development," 191–92.

30. Helen Hanft, interview by author, December 7, 2001.

31. Hanft quoted in Patrick, "Caffe Cino: Memories," 20.

32. Hanft quoted in Patrick, "Caffe Cino: Memories," 20.

33. Patrick, "Caffe Cino: Memories," 20.

34. Ross Wetzsteon, "Theatre: *A Funny Walk Home,*" review of *A Funny Walk Home,* by Jeff Weiss, Caffe Cino, New York, *Village Voice,* February 16, 1967, 23.

35. Wetzsteon, "Theatre: *A Funny Walk Home,*" 23.

36. Wetzsteon, "Theatre: *A Funny Walk Home,*" 23.

37. Wetzsteon, "Theatre: *A Funny Walk Home,*" 23.

38. Wetzsteon, "Theatre: *A Funny Walk Home,*" 23.

39. Claris Nelson, interview by author, July 22, 2002.

40. Jeff Weiss quoted in Ross Wetzsteon, "The Spirit of Off-Off Broadway: Underground Legend Surfaces," *Village Voice,* April 26, 1976, 111.

41. Michael Smith, *Theatre Journal: Winter 1967* (Columbia: University of Missouri Press, 1968), 27.

42. Michael Smith, introduction to *Moon,* by Robert Heide, in *The Best of Off Off Broadway,* ed. Michael Smith (New York: E. P. Dutton, 1969), 47.

43. Michael Smith, Theatre Journal, review of *God Created the Heaven and the Earth . . . but Man Created Saturday Night,* by Terry Alan Smith, Caffe Cino, New York, *Village Voice,* March 16, 1967, 26.

44. Michael Smith, Theatre Journal, review of *The Madness of Lady Bright,* by Lanford Wilson, Caffe Cino, New York, *Village Voice,* March 30, 1967, 31.

45. Smith, "Theatre Journal," 38.

46. Charles Loubier, "Caffe Cino: Part VII," *Other Stages,* June 14, 1979, 8.

47. Al Carmines quoted in Patrick, "Caffe Cino: Memories," 21.

48. Loubier, "Caffe Cino: Part VII," 8.

49. Clayton Delery, "Caffe Cino: The Drama and Its History" (master's thesis, University of Lafayette [formerly University of Southwestern Louisiana], 1981), 25.

50. Gordy, "Joseph Cino," 319.

51. Angelo Lovullo, interview by author, July 22, 1999.

52. Loubier, "Caffe Cino: Part VII," 8.

53. Mary Boylan, "Take the IND to 4th Street," *Other Stages,* April 19, 1979, 3.

54. Robert Patrick, "The Other Brick Road," *Other Stages,* February 8, 1979, 10.

55. Boylan, "Take the IND," 3.

56. Boylan, "Take the IND," 3.

57. Boylan, "Take the IND," 3.

58. Boylan, "Take the IND," 3.

59. Gross, "Parallels in the Development," 186.

60. Delery, "Caffe Cino," 13.

61. Robert Heide, interview by author, June 22, 1998.

62. Gross, "Parallels in the Development," 192.

63. Waldo Kang Pagune, "Remembering Joe Cino," correspondence file 8-MWEZ+n.c. 27646 #21, Billy Rose Theatre Collection, New York Public Library.

64. Don McDonagh, obituary for Charles Stanley, *New York Times,* September 18, 1977, sec. 2, 44.

65. Barbara Naomi Cohen-Stratyner, *Biographical Dictionary of Dance* (New York: Schirmer, 1982), 838.

66. McDonagh, obituary, 44.

67. Gross, "Parallels in the Development," 193–94.

68. Dan Sullivan, "Caffe Cino Plays Bask in New Light," *New York Times,* July 28, 1967, 17.

69. Patrick, e-mail, March 10, 2004.

70. Sullivan, "Caffe Cino Plays," 17.

71. Sullivan, "Caffe Cino Plays," 17.

72. Leticia Kent, "Marching on MacDougal: Immovable Vs. Irresistible," *Village Voice,* April 13, 1967, 3.

73. Kent, "Marching," 8–9.

74. Leticia Kent, "Caffe Cino Summonsed in Crackdown by Police," *Village Voice,* April 2, 1967, 1, 29.

75. Robert Patrick, *Lights/Camera/Action, Robert Patrick's Cheep Theatricks* (New York: Samuel French, 1972), 113.

76. Gross, "Parallels in the Development," 181.

77. Robert Patrick, "Nudity on Stage in Greenwich Village," *Nude and Natural,* 46, clipping supplied by Robert Patrick.

78. Andy Milligan quoted in Patrick, "Nudity on Stage," 46.

79. Patrick, "Nudity on Stage," 47.

80. George Birimisa, interview by author, April 12, 2000.

81. Birimisa, interview.

82. George Birimisa, *"Daddy Violet,"* Prism International (Vancouver, BC), Spring 1968, 84.

83. Birimisa, *"Daddy Violet,"* 84.

84. Birimisa, interview.

85. Birimisa, interview.

86. Birimisa, *"Daddy Violet,"* 98–99.

87. Birimisa, *"Daddy Violet,"* 99.

88. "MacD. Group Hits Mayor with Writ," *Village Voice,* July 20, 1967, 3.

89. Magie Dominic, "Caffe Cino Part VIII," *Other Stages,* July 12, 1979, 5.

90. Charles Kerbs, interview by author, September 11, 2000.

91. Kerbs, interview.

92. Kerbs, interview.

93. Michael Smith, Theatre Journal, review of *Vinyl,* by Ronald Tavel, Caffe Cino, New York, *Village Voice,* November 9, 1967, 28.

94. Dan Sullivan, "*Gorilla Queen* Man Offers a New Play," review of *Vinyl,* by Ronald Tavel, Caffe Cino, New York, *New York Times,* November 4, 1967, n. pag., clipping *T-NBL + (Coll) 1967/68 T-Z, Billy Rose Theatre Collection, New York Public Library.

95. Smith, Theatre Journal, review of *Vinyl,* 28.

96. Robert Pasolli, "Theatre: *Empire State,*" review of *Empire State* by Tom La Bar, Caffe Cino, New York, *Village Voice,* February 1, 1968, 39.

97. M[ichael] S[mith], "Theatre: *The Brown Crown,*" review of *The Brown Crown,* by Haal Borske, Caffe Cino, New York, *Village Voice,* December 14, 1967, 44.

98. Michael Smith, Theatre Journal, review of *The Marriage Proposal,* by Anton Chekhov, Caffe Cino, New York, *Village Voice,* December 7, 1967, 35.

99. Michael Smith to author, March 27, 2004.

100. Robert E. Tomasson, "City Cleanup of 'Village' Is Ordered by a Justice," *New York Times,* December 27, 1967, 1, 74.

101. Pasolli, "Theatre: *Empire State,*" 26, 39.

102. Pasolli, "Theatre: *Empire State,*" 26.

103. Pasolli, "Theatre: *Empire State,*" 39.

104. Pasolli, "Theatre: *Empire State,*" 39.

105. Pasolli, "Theatre: *Empire State,*" 39.

106. "Scrapbook," 136.

107. "Scrapbook," 137.

108. Feingold, "Caffe Cino, 20 Years," 117.

109. Michael Smith to author, March 27, 2004.

110. Diane di Prima, interview by author, October 13, 2000.

111. Ross Wetzsteon, "Theatre: *Monuments,*" review of *Monuments,* by Diane di Prima, Caffe Cino, New York, *Village Voice,* March 14, 1968, 45.

112. di Prima, interview.

113. Michael Smith, Theatre Journal, on the closing of Caffe Cino, *Village Voice,* March 14, 1968, 41.

114. Wolfgang Zuckermann, letter to the editor, *Village Voice,* March 28, 1968, 4.

115. "Scrapbook," 124.

116. Edward I. Koch, letter to the editor, *Village Voice,* March 21, 1968, 4.

117. Gross, "Parallels in the Development," 176.

118. Patrick, "Other Brick Road," 10.

119. Patrick, "Other Brick Road," 10.

120. Josh Greenfeld, "Their Hearts Belong to La Mama," *New York Times Magazine,* July 9, 1967, 11.

121. Certificate of incorporation (unsigned), 8-MWEZ+n.c. 27646 #18; Caffe Cino [NYC] Miscellaneous 1965–?, Billy Rose Theatre Collection, New York Public Library.

122. Gordy, "Joseph Cino," 304.

123. Bob Metz, "Crackdown Is 'Major Strike' Against Mob," *Buffalo News,* August 24, 1989, http://www.newslibrary.com/deliverccdoc.asp?SMH=510220 (accessed April 20, 2000).

124. Ed Koch, "Blitzstein Murder Case Figure Cino Kept from His Brother's Funeral," *Las Vegas Sun,* September 8, 1999, and February 7, 2000.

125. State Gaming Control Board, Nevada Gaming Commission, *List of Excluded Persons,* 3.

126. Gordy, "Joseph Cino," 306.

127 Patrick, "Other Brick Road," 3.

128. Paul Foster, "A Nurse in a Madhouse," *Other Stages,* March 22, 1979, 7.

129. "State Reports New Evidence of Coffeehouse Graft to Police," *New York Times,* June 14, 1961, 21.

130. Smith, Theatre Journal, on the closing of Caffe Cino, 42.

131. "Scrapbook," 127.

132. John Gruen, "Underground: Catnip Overground," *Vogue,* January 15, 1968, 31.

133. Sam Shepard quoted in Leo Lerman, "The Third Stream of Off Off Broadway," *Mademoiselle,* March 1966, 146.

134. Douglas M. Davis, "The Expanding Arts: Success for 'Off-Off Broadway,'" *National Observer,* April 10, 1967, 20.

6. The Magic Lives On

1. Clayton Delery, "Caffe Cino: The Drama and Its History" (master's thesis, University of Lafayette [formerly University of Southwestern Louisiana], 1981), 101.

2. Doric Wilson, *Now She Dances!*, http://www.doricwilson.com, (accessed March 25, 2004).

3. Tillie Gross, "Parallels in the Development of London's Royal Court, New York's Caffe Cino, and Cafe La Mama" (PhD diss., New York University, 1994), 357.

4. Susan Sontag, "One Culture and the New Sensibility," in *Against Interpretation and Other Essays* (New York: Noonday, 1966), 300.

5. Sontag, "One Culture," 302.

6. Perry Anderson, *The Origins of Postmodernity* (New York: Verso, 1998), 13.

7. Albert Poland and Bruce Mailman, *The Off-Off-Broadway Book: The Plays, People, Theatre* (New York: Bobbs-Merrill, 1972), xvii.

8. Robert Patrick, interview by author, December 11, 1999.

9. Robert Patrick, "The Other Brick Road," *Other Stages,* February 8, 1979, 3.

10. Theodore Roszak, *The Making of a Counter Culture: Reflections on the Technocratic Society and Its Youthful Opposition* (Garden City, NY: Anchor Books, 1969), 205.

11. H. M. Koutoukas, *Tidy Passions, or Kill, Kaleidoscope, Kill, More Plays from Off-Off Broadway,* ed. Michael Smith (Indianapolis: Bobbs-Merrill, 1972), 3.

12. H. M. Koutoukas, *With Creatures Make My Way,* typescript, Billy Rose Theatre Collection, New York Public Library.

13. H. M. Koutoukas, *Only a Countess May Dance When She's Crazy, When Lightning Strikes Twice* (New York: Samuel French, 1991), 35–36.

14. Gross, "Parallels in the Development," 165.

15. William M. Hoffman, "Foreword," in *Untold Decades: Seven Comedies of Gay Romance,* by Robert Patrick (New York: St. Martin's, 1988), x.

16. "William M. Hoffman," *Christopher Street,* June 1978, 23.

17. Doric Wilson, interview by author, November 25, 1998.

18. Edward Rubin, "Review: *Temple Slave,*" *Greenwich Village Press,* April 1995, 11.

19. William M. Hoffman, "Introduction," in *Gay Plays: The First Collection,* ed. William H. Hoffman (New York: Avon, 1979), xix.

20. "David Starkweather," *Christopher Street,* June 1978, 23.

21. Michel Foucault, *The History of Sexuality. Volume I: An Introduction,* trans. Robert Hurley (New York: Vintage, 1978), 11.

22. Susan Sontag, "Notes on 'Camp,'" in *Camp: Queer Aesthetics and the Performing Subject*, ed. Fabio Cleto (Ann Arbor: University of Michigan Press, 1999), 62.

23. Sontag, "Notes on 'Camp,'" 56.

24. Hoffman, "Introduction," xxiv.

25. Robert Pasolli, "Theatre: *Empire State*," review of *Empire State* by Tom La Bar, Caffe Cino, New York, *Village Voice*, February 1, 1968, 26.

26. Bernard da Costa, "Les Jeunes Fous d''Off Off Broadway,'" *Réalités*, February 1967, 85.

27. Dan Sullivan, "Theatre: Actors Playhouse Presents One-Acters," review of *The Last Triangle* and *Only a Countess May Dance When She's Crazy*, Actors Playhouse, New York, *New York Times*, March 19, 1968, 41.

28. Tim Cresswell, *In Place, Out of Place: Geography, Ideology, and Transgression* (Minneapolis: University of Minnesota Press, 1996), 11.

29. Robert Heide and John Gilman, *Greenwich Village* (New York: St. Martin's, 1995), 2.

30. Heide and Gilman, *Greenwich Village*, 7.

31. Walter Michael Harris, "Cino Cuisino," typescript, supplied by Harris family.

32. Jerry Caruana, letter to the editor, *Village Voice*, April 13, 1967, 4.

33. Robert Dahdah, interview by author, November 24, 1998.

34. Randy Gener, "Back to the Cino: Remembering the Cafe Where Gay Theater Came Out," *Village Voice*, June 21, 1994, 5.

35. "Scrapbook of New York Public Library Exhibit of Caffe Cino Material," p. 114, file Caffe Cino (NYC) Scrapbook RE NYPL Exhibit, March 5–May 11, 1985, no. 20, 1985, box Caffe Cino 8-MWEZ+n.c. 27646, Billy Rose Theatre Collection, New York Public Library.

36. Charles Loubier quoted in Michael Feingold, "Caffe Cino, 20 Years after Magic Time," *Village Voice*, May 14, 1985, 51.

37. Leah D. Frank, "Robert Patrick," in *Contemporary Dramatists*, ed. D. L. Kirkpatrick, 4th ed. (Chicago: St. James, 1988), 420.

38. Phoebe Mooney, interview by author, November 17, 1998.

39. Merrill Harris quoted in Robert Patrick, "Caffe Cino: Memories by Those Who Worked There," *Los Angeles Theatres Magazine*, November 1994, 18.

40. Phillip Middleton Williams, *A Comfortable House: Lanford Wilson, Marshall W. Mason and the Circle Repertory Theatre* (Jefferson, NC: McFarland, 1993), 17.

41. George Harris III quoted in David Hirsh, "Remembering Hibiscus," *New York Native*, April 27, 1992, 20.

42. John Bell, "*Hibiscus* at La Mama," review of *Hibiscus,* by Michael Harris et al., La Mama, New York, *TheatreWeek,* May 18, 1992, 16.

43. L. C. Cole, review of *Hibiscus,* by Michael Harris et al., La Mama, New York, *New York Native,* May 11, 1992, 31.

44. Patrick, "Caffe Cino: Memories," 21.

45. Patrick, "Caffe Cino: Memories," 20.

46. Ingmar Bjorksten, "Report from Stockholm: Going Off Off Broadway the Swedish Way," *Village Voice,* August 24, 1967, 18.

47. Roland Rees, *Fringe First: Pioneers of Fringe Theatre on Record* (London: Oberon Books, 1992), 16.

48. Rees, *Fringe First,* 19.

49. Rees, *Fringe First,* 21.

50. Charles Marowitz quoted in Patrick, "Caffe Cino: Memories," 18.

51. Pierre Merle, *Le Cafe Theatre* (Paris: Presses Universitaires de France, 1985), 9 (all quotations are the author's translation of the French).

52. Merle, *Le Cafe Theatre,* 9.

53. Shirley Stoler quoted in Feingold, "Caffe Cino, 20 Years," 50.

54. Poland and Mailman, *Off-Off-Broadway Book,* xvii.

55. S. Isenberg, "Tale of Hoffman: *As Is* Completes a Circle," *Stages,* March 1985, 35.

56. Larry Loonin to Richard Buck, Billy Rose Theatre Collection, February 5, 1985, 8-MWEZ+n.c. 27646 #21, Billy Rose Theatre Collection, New York Public Library.

57. "Caffe Cino Closed in New Enigma," *New York Visitors Reporter,* April 11, 1968, 1+.

58. *Excerpts from the Opening Night Celebration of the 'Caffe Cino and Its Legacy Exhibition and Portions of the Formal Program,* VHS, 1985, Billy Rose Theatre Collection, New York Public Library.

59. Helen Hanft, panel participant, "Recovering the Past, Transforming the Future: The Story of the Caffe Cino from Those Who Lived It" (forum, Association for Theatre in Higher Education annual conference, New York, August 2, 2003).

60. *Excerpts from the Opening.*

61. Walter Michael Harris, interview by author, May 19, 2004.

Index

Wendell C. Stone is an instructor in the Department of Mass Communications and Theatre Arts at the State University of West Georgia. His essays have appeared in *Pioneering North America: Mediators of European Culture and Literature* and various other publications.

THEATER IN THE AMERICAS

The goal of the series is to publish a wide range of scholarship on theater and performance, defining theater in its broadest terms and including subjects that encompass all of the Americas.

The series focuses on the performance and production of theater and theater artists and practitioners but welcomes studies of dramatic literature as well. Meant to be inclusive, the series invites studies of traditional, experimental, and ethnic forms of theater; celebrations, festivals, and rituals that perform culture; and acts of civil disobedience that are performative in nature. We publish studies of theater and performance activities of all cultural groups within the Americas, including biographies of individuals, histories of theater companies, studies of cultural traditions, and collections of plays.